HARD LIKE WATER

YAN LIANKE

HARD LIKE WATER

Translated from the Chinese by
Carlos Rojas

Chatto & Windus
LONDON

1 3 5 7 9 10 8 6 4 2

Chatto & Windus, an imprint of Vintage, is part of the Penguin Random House group of
companies whose addresses can be found at global.penguinrandomhouse.com

Penguin
Random House
UK

First published in the United Kingdom by Chatto & Windus in 2021
First published in the United States by Grove Press in 2021
First published in China as *Jianying ru shui* by Changjiang Art and
Literature Press in 2001 and in Taiwan by Rye Field in 2009

Supported using public funding by
ARTS COUNCIL
ENGLAND

This book has been selected to receive financial assistance from English PEN's 'PEN
Translates!' programme, supported by Arts Council England. English PEN exists to
promote literature and our understanding of it, to uphold writers' freedoms around
the world, to campaign against the persecution and imprisonment of writers for stating
their views, and to promote the friendly co-operation of writers and the free exchange
of ideas. www.englishpen.org

penguin.co.uk/vintage

A CIP catalogue record for this book is available from the British Library

ISBN 9781784742904

The authorised representative in the EEA is Penguin Random House Ireland,
Morrison Chambers, 32 Nassau Street, Dublin D02 YH68.

Printed and bound in Great Britain by Clays Ltd, Elcograf S.p.A.

Penguin Random House is committed to a sustainable future
for our business, our readers and our planet. This book is
made from Forest Stewardship Council® certified paper.

MIX
Paper from
responsible sources
FSC® C018179

HARD LIKE WATER

Chapter 1

Encountering Revolution

1. Using the Reputation of the Revolution

After I die and things settle down, I'll reevaluate my life, and specifically the cracks between my speech, behavior, posture, and my chickenshit love. That "tender land" will be an excellent place to reflect on life, with beautiful drifting catkins and bright peach blossoms. Right now, however, they have taken the muzzle of a loaded gun and placed it against the back of my head, invoking the reputation of the revolution. With death lodged in my throat, I have no choice but to soon proceed to the execution ground and wait for the bullet. Laughing at the prospect of death, I'm prepared to cross the bridge that leads to the underworld. *Prior to the execution, I drank a bowl of wine, and did not feel a trace of resentment. Hatoyama prepared a banquet for me, with ten thousand cups.* Revolution must be like this. I'll lay down my life in battle, shattering my bones, scattering my blood, and destroying my body and my spirit. In three days or at most a week, Hongmei and I will both be standing on the execution ground, next to the river that runs past the base of the mountain. We'll both be wearing handcuffs as we kneel at the edge of the pit, after which we'll return to our tender land. Our remaining time is like the final drops of water in a Shangganling water kettle, each drop as precious as a jewel. My life's furnace is about to be extinguished, a furnace that ignited mountains and rivers, streams and gullies, and the entire land. It ignited the air and forests, water and women, animals and rocks, grass and footsteps, crops and men, the seasons and roads, as well as women's wombs, hair, lips, and clothing. *The spring river water flows west, as the east and west winds engage in fierce battle.* Mother, mother—after your son dies, please arrange for his grave to face east, so that he may view the town of Chenggang.

2. Painfully Recounting the Revolution's Genealogy

Let me painfully relate the story of a revolutionary family . . .

It was the first lunar month of 1942, and after a dog barked at night in the town of Chenggang in the Balou Mountains, the Japanese emerged from the village, having gleefully slaughtered the local men. The town therefore found itself with a dearth of men and a surfeit of widows. That was the night my father died, and I was born. On that night, there was a foul wind and a blood-colored rain that fell together with bone-white dragon scales. My father stepped out of his house to summon the midwife, but when he reached the town entrance a Japanese devil stabbed him with a bayonet. My father's intestines poured out of his abdomen, engulfing the bayonet, soaking the soil of our homeland, and igniting the vengeful anger of our People . . .

Comrades, dear comrades! We were once blood-red revolutionaries, and resistors in class warfare. Hey, could you please not interrupt me? I am invoking my identity as a member of the Chinese Communist Party to request that you not interrupt me and that you let me painfully recount my family history.

If you ask me to recount my story, I have no choice but to tell it like this. Only in this way will I be able to make my way out of the mess in which I currently find myself . . . Dragons beget dragons, phoenixes beget phoenixes, and my revolutionary energy has never flagged. I was born into the old society but grew up under the red flag, having been nursed on the sun's rays. In 1964, when I was twenty-two, I decided to continue the work of the revolutionary martyrs and joined the army. The army division I joined was devoted to capital construction projects—digging tunnels through mountains and valleys, building railroads under sun and rain. With lofty ambitions, we battled heaven and earth, and with great aspirations, we sought to make our vision of our motherland a reality. Over the next three years, I followed the army regiment through three provinces and nine counties, and was awarded four third-class merit badges, five company-level commendations, and six battalion-level commendations. My dossier became so full of these certificates that there wasn't room left for even a fart. The revolutionary army was a large school, and I was originally a cadre sprout supported by the company and the battalion. If I had continued to advance in status, I'm sure that by now I would already be a battalion commander or deputy commander, and I wouldn't need to ask you to post my court judgment and Hongmei's notice all over Chenggang. I know that throughout the town there will be flyers announcing my execution—in all of Chenggang's streets and alleys, on all of its walls and trees, and on all of its well platforms and mill houses. The announcements will appear everywhere there are people and will be as abundant as funereal spirit money, fluttering in the wind and blanketing the ground.

Heaven, oh heaven! Earth, oh earth! This joke is as vast as heaven and earth!

I hadn't ever expected that the sun could rush across the sky from west to east.

Had I known such a thing could happen, I definitely would have figured out a way to remain in the army. Regiment 80911 had wanted to enlist me. In the great year of 1967, our original regiment enlisted soldiers from all over the country, and everyone marched together, with a common goal and a shared objective. But as we attempted to implement communism and create a unified future, this unity fell apart, and part of our regiment was reconstituted into what became Regiment 80911. However, rather than enlisting in the new regiment, I instead asked to be demobilized. My commanding officer said, "Private Gao Aijun, if you transfer to Regiment 80911 and continue there, you'll eventually be promoted to the level of cadre." I replied, "I want to return home and pursue the revolution from there." I was done with the army. For the past four years, I'd been digging ditches, placing explosives, and building a railroad that would one day extend all the way to the next province. But every time we had a personnel shift, we always had to perform a quick march and depart. When we were building a great and glorious railroad to protect the nation, I spent twenty months digging a tunnel through the mountains—for those twenty months I didn't see anyone, couldn't return to my hometown, nor did I even go to the market. For those twenty months I didn't even once smell the scent of a woman. When our regiment finally emerged from that tunnel, we saw a marriage procession passing by, and immediately our entire regiment stood at attention, everyone's gaze giving a loud crackle. The new bride's beauty radiated outward for thousands of miles, illuminating the whole universe. The smell of her fragrance caused the regiment to collapse, as though it were deadly poison. After we reached our destination, the military supervisor and company leader told everyone to seize their spirit in order to search for flaws and to imprison their thought in order to pursue revolution. We then spent the next half month consolidating our spirit, purifying our hearts so they became like sheets of paper on which one could draw something beautiful. It was precisely as my own heart was being transformed into a sheet of paper that I decided to leave the army. I decided that I had already spent enough time in the regiment, and now wanted to return home to pursue revolution. What kind of person did I want to be? Did I want to be an honest person? To tell the truth, I missed my wife and even missed my mother-in-law. Needless to say, this was a tragicomedy created by the regiment's unique revolutionary conditions.

My wife's name was Cheng Guizhi, and although the name Guizhi, meaning "cassia twig," sounds very traditional and refined, my wife was actually all woman—with a woman's body and a woman's face. The rosy tint behind the blackness of her face and body was the same color as the cover of *Chairman Mao's Quotations*. She was of average height, with a pudgy physique, and when she walked her butt swayed back and forth as though her bloated flesh were attempting to liberate itself and reach the blue sky. Those of you who are familiar with the town of Chenggang will already have heard of her. Her father was the first Party secretary of New China following Liberation, and it was precisely because he was Party secretary that I married his daughter. Before I joined the army, Guizhi gave birth to our son, and the following year she returned to visit her relatives in the mountains along the Henan-Hubei border. At that time, our regiment was digging a tunnel under Peak No. 2 (excavating deeply, accumulating grain, never seeking hegemony) for potential war preparations. One day, I was pushing ballast inside the tunnel, when a new recruit rushed in waving a pickax and shouted, "Gao Aijun, a woman as large as a water barrel is outside looking for you—" I kicked the soldier and replied, "You must remain united and alert, solemn and lively." The soldier replied, *"If you have a friend afar who knows your heart, then even a vast distance can't keep you apart* . . . The woman waiting outside claims that you are her husband."

I stared in shock, then stumbled out of the tunnel.

It turned out that the woman in question was in fact my wife, Guizhi.

That night I slept with Guizhi in the regiment's reception room. That was a tent that was only half as large as this room. On all four sides there were walls made from bricks piled as high as a person, over which there was a tarp. Chairman Mao's poster was hanging on the wall, and there were several copies of his books on the shelves. The poster was positioned directly over the bed, such that Chairman Mao was able to keep watch over all the relatives and children who came to visit the regiment. Guizhi, however, didn't bring our son, Hongsheng, with her; instead she came alone. It was a few days before the decisive National Day construction battle, and I said, "We're very busy right now, why have you come?" She replied, "The wheat has been harvested, the autumn grain has been sowed, and currently there is nothing for me to do at home. If I didn't come now, when would I?" I said, "Preparations for the defensive battle have reached a critical juncture." She said, "Hongsheng is two years old and can already run around." I said, "Your coming here has made me lose face. Just look at you!" She glanced down at her new blue shirt, with its large collar and coarse fabric, and after a moment began to unfasten the buttons she had sewn herself. She asked, "Don't all peasants look like this?" Then she added, "Now that Hongsheng is already two, I've decided I want to get pregnant again, because I want a daughter. That's why I rushed over here by train and by car to see you." She explained that she had had an arduous journey, because she had accidentally taken the wrong train and ended up having to spend the night on the floor of a train station. Fortunately, she was equipped with a mouth and therefore in the end was able to successfully make her way here. She said that had it not been for her determination to have a daughter in addition to a son, she probably couldn't have found the regiment even if her life depended on it, and thus wouldn't have given me the opportunity to lose face. She asked if I resented her for being ugly, and if so, then why had I proposed to her in the first place? She asked why, if I found her so unattractive, did I impregnate her with Hongsheng?

As she was speaking, she proceeded to remove her clothes, then sat down on the side of the bed. The room was illuminated by a thirty-five-watt light bulb that produced a light with a golden tint, and when it shone on her it appeared to envelop her corpulent body in a dark red glow. The room was perfused with a feminine scent, like a pink mist. I longed to stare at her naked body. By that point I had already been in the army for two years, and before I knew it, my son was already two years old. I suddenly realized that my memory of Guizhi's naked figure had grown hazy, to the point that I had almost forgotten what she even looked like. I tore my gaze away from her, but she continued sitting on the edge of the bed for a while, then pulled back the sheets and crawled under them. As she did so, my blood begin to boil, and my throat became as dry as kindling left out in the sun for three years. To my surprise, I found that her breasts were as large and white as a pair of sheep heads, and as she was lifting up the sheets, they swayed back and forth, flashing a pair of hot red lights. As her breasts were covered by the sheets, I was reminded of how, when I was young and working as a shepherd, the sheep would often run through tall grass, and when they jumped up, their heads would briefly emerge before falling back into the grass. Guizhi's breasts surely hadn't always been this large, and I remembered how, when she failed to produce enough milk after giving birth to Hongsheng, I'd had to go down to the river to catch some fish for her to eat. What had her breasts been like at that time? It was like when you pick out the best flour, then use what is left over to make some steamed buns—although the latter is still white flour, beneath that whiteness there will inevitably be a layer of blackness. How was it that her breasts had become so large and so white? How was it that she now had two engorged sheep heads for breasts?

I asked, "Guizhi, is Hongsheng still nursing?"

She turned and said, "Of course. Even if I were to smear my nipples with chili sauce, he would still nurse."

I then felt I understood why her breasts were so engorged, as seductive as sheep heads. I said, "Do you want to get pregnant again?"

She replied, "If I didn't want to get pregnant again, why do you think I would have traveled thousands of li to come here?"

I began to remove my clothes. If I tugged at the bottom of my military coat, I could unfasten five buttons at once, as easily as unzipping a zipper. That was one of the first lessons that a new recruit had to learn, so that when defending against a sneak attack by American imperialists or Soviet revisionists, soldiers would be able to instantly go to sleep and instantly get up again. I stripped off my clothes, and as I was diving into bed, Guizhi suddenly sat up and turned off the light. Just as she was doing so, that pair of sheep heads poked up again through the grass, and my hands reached out as though I were trying to grab one. Afterward, however, I didn't immediately do it with her. After all, I was her husband, and she was my wife. Our bright red and resplendently luminous marriage certificate guaranteed our right to bear children and enjoy conjugal pleasures. However, I hadn't touched a woman for two years, to the point that I had virtually forgotten what a woman felt like, and therefore I first needed to caress her from head to toe. I caressed her hair, her face, and her shoulders—which were calloused from carrying a shoulder pail every day. I caressed her breasts, which seemed to have become even more engorged than before, and her belly, which was as soft as cotton. She lay there motionless, permitting me to touch and kiss her—but just as my lips and hands were about to reach her lower regions, she exploded. Screaming as though she had suddenly realized that the person lying on top of her was not her husband, she wriggled out from beneath me and turned on the light.

She left me sitting in the middle of the bed, with half the bed-sheets still on the bed and the other half on the floor.

She said, "Gao Aijun, you are a soldier in the People's Liberation Army, and the entire nation looks to you as a model. How is it that you leave home for two years and suddenly become a hooligan?!"

I stared at her in astonishment.

She exclaimed, "If you want to conceive a child, you should go ahead and do so. But why are you feeling me up? When you touched my head and my face, I could tolerate it, but then you began rubbing your hands all over my lower body. What are you, a soldier or a hooligan?!"

The lamp in the room was as bright as the sun. She stood at the foot of the bed, her complexion as green as fresh vegetables. The room was drowned in her humiliation. I stared at her for a moment, then developed an urge to get down from the bed and kick her. I wanted to kick her voluptuous breasts and her wide and soft belly. In the end, I didn't do so, and instead simply stared at her for what seemed like an eternity. I felt as though I were choking on something caught in my throat and was so desperate I wished I could spit out my own tongue. There was a chill in the air, and even though it was still the ninth lunar month, here in the mountains it got so cold at night that you would wake up freezing. My fellow soldiers from the construction regiment were sleeping in a building several dozen meters away, and the sound of the sentries' footsteps drifted over like the chopping of a boat's oars on the surface of a lake. I could hear the sentries changing shift. One said, "Password?" The other replied, "Defeat the American imperialists." The first one then exhaled and answered, "Protect the homeland." With this, they changed shift, and the night reverted back to deep silence.

As I was staring at my wife, it occurred to me that this would be an opportunity to kill her. At that point, this idea was still vague and inchoate, but it was then that the idea of killing her first began to germinate in my mind. In the end, however, I remembered I was a revolutionary humanist, and for a long time afterward I didn't return to this thought. That night, I grew tired of staring at her, as I waited until she, too, had seen enough of me. Only then did I pull up the sheets that had fallen off the bed and say, gently, "Go to sleep, Guizhi. Tomorrow I'll take you back to Chenggang."

I didn't even touch her feet that night, despite the fact that we hadn't seen each other for two years. But the next day, I didn't send her off after all, and instead the following night I acceded to her request. She wanted to get pregnant, so I did as she asked and got her pregnant.

She subsequently gave birth to a baby girl named Honghua. At this point, you must have noticed our family's revolutionary spirit? My given name is Aijun, meaning "love the army"; my son's name is Hongsheng, or "born red"; and my daughter's name is Honghua, or "red blossom." Ours is truly a revolutionary family! In fact, my family's political status was so resplendent that it could blind many onlookers. Our children's grandfather had been bayoneted by Japanese devils, and their father had served in the People's Liberation Army. Our children, meanwhile, were born under the red flag, grew up under the red flag, and should have become exemplary revolutionary successors. But fate had arranged for their father to meet Xia Hongmei.

It was love and revolution that would take their lives and the life of their mother, just as it was the Japanese who chopped off my father's head and hung it from Chenggang's outer gates.

3. Red Music

The Baiyun county train station consisted of a single two-story building, where a train would stop for just one minute each day. The railroad tracks, meanwhile, seemed to extend forever in both directions. In the fourth lunar month of that year, our army regiment dismissed and replaced its entire staff for political reasons, and I was demobilized. Chenggang was located seventy-nine *li* from the county seat, and I disembarked from the train just as the sun was about to set. In order to make it to the People's Armed Forces department the next day and complete the requisite demobilization paperwork, I had to stay overnight in the county seat. That night, just as the political situation was transforming in such an extraordinary manner, my love life reached a new vista. I was illuminated by a great sunbeam of love. You tell me: Was this not fate? Was this not an example of what is often described as revolution reaching a crucial turning point?

In the county seat, I stayed in a guesthouse at the People's Armed Forces department. For twenty cents, you could rent a room with a single bed, and fifty-five cents would get you a larger room with four beds. Generally speaking, prices tend to go through the roof at revolutionary moments. This is a historical rule. However, given that I had come to complete my demobilization paperwork, regulations stipulated that I be permitted to stay there for free. For forty-five cents, I was able to go to a state-owned canteen and purchase a bowl of my hometown's mutton stew, which I hadn't tasted for the longest time, as well as a bowl of beef soup and two baked biscuits. After I had successfully stuffed my belly, I saw that the sun hadn't fully set yet, and therefore—not having anything else to do—I proceeded to wander aimlessly through the streets. The county seat was no longer as vibrant and bustling as it had been before I joined the army. Light from the setting sun shone down on the shops' front doors, and both sides of the street were filled with a clattering sound. Previously there had been several factories in the area—including a rope factory, a cork factory, and a textile factory that made gloves for all the workers in the other state-run factories in the nearby city of Jiudu—but now barely anyone could be seen near these buildings. After the factories closed down, the empty buildings just sat there with their courtyards full of logs and rusting iron, like women who had died in childbirth. Yet the county seat was still the county seat, and the streets remained as wide as before. The roads were still paved in brick, and some old people could still be seen leisurely walking home with baskets of vegetables. The only difference was that the walls on both sides of the street were now plastered with big-character posters full of people's names with red Xs over them. This was not a new sight for me, and instead it simply signaled that the revolution had already begun to gather momentum here. Many young people wearing armbands brushed past me, as though rushing to attend a meeting. I was envious of the fact that they were from the city, and regretted that I wasn't one of them. If only *I* were the leader of their organization! If only they were all rushing to hear *me* lecture about the revolution! I watched as, one after another, they rushed past me—and as they did, I saw how their eyes would linger on me. I knew they were envious of my green army coat, and I was concerned that one of them might rip off my coat or grab my hat. I didn't stay in the street for very long and instead slowly headed out of town.

I followed the train tracks like the hero of a revolutionary epic. The scenery was quite beautiful, with a high sky and sparse clouds. There were no geese flying south, and in the twilight, cattle were feeding from their troughs. An old man was leading some sheep over from the railroad tracks, and as he came over from the vast wheat fields, the bleating of sheep resonated in my ears like a song. The county seat grew increasingly distant, even as the setting sun grew increasingly close. As the bright red sunrays shone down on the railroad tracks, they made a sound like water dripping onto sand. I walked along the tracks until, in my lonely and uncultivated heart, I heard that sound of loneliness growing louder and louder, and I abruptly came to a halt.

I saw that someone was sitting on the train tracks in front of me. Her face was as rosy as a morning sun, and her jet-black hair hung down over her pink blouse. In the distance were black trees and light green crops, and the smell of dirt, grass, and wheat drifted over from the field at the base of the hills. At first I saw only a figure sitting on the tracks; it was only after taking several steps forward that I was able to make out her long hair and women's clothing. When I realized it wasn't a man, I hesitated for a moment before approaching. Chairman Mao famously said that women hold up half the sky, but now I realized that it must have been precisely in order to wait for me that she had been sitting there holding up half the sky all day. She must have been waiting for me. I walked toward her, and she turned to me. I was startled by her expression, which resembled the expression girls have when they feel ignored. It was as though just a few days earlier she had been soft and delicate—like a vine-ripened fruit that accidentally got crushed when someone tried to pick it. Her face had an exhausted pallor. I could see that she was from either the city or the suburbs, given that she was wearing a pink blouse made from a synthetic fabric that you wouldn't find in rural areas at that time. I stood a meter or so in front of her and noticed she was staring intently at me.

She was staring at my new army coat.

I noticed she was wearing a pair of imitation army pants.

She said, "We should learn from our People's Liberation Army comrades."

I replied, "PLA soldiers must learn from all the nation's citizens. I've already been demobilized but haven't completed the paperwork yet."

She said, "If you haven't completed the paperwork, then you are still a PLA soldier."

I hadn't expected that she would gush with respect for me or that she would treat me as a model for the entire nation to emulate. I sat down on the tracks across from her—facing her the way I would face our political instructor when he came to address us soldiers in the army. I replied that we had already eliminated all the enemies we could see, but perhaps there still remained some we couldn't see? I asked her if she wasn't afraid, sitting here all alone? She replied that heaven is the People's heaven, and the earth is the People's earth, so what was there for her to be afraid of? As long as the American imperialists and Soviet revisionists don't invade, what is there to fear? I replied that even if American imperialists and Soviet revisionists were to invade, I still wouldn't be afraid—because when faced with our People's Liberation Army, the Americans and Soviets were but paper tigers. Then I waited for her to ask me my name, where I lived, and in which regiment I had been stationed, after which I would reciprocate by asking her name and where she worked. However, she just kept staring at me, then said something that made my heart leap and my clothes ache.

"Could you give me an article of clothing from your uniform? In exchange, I'm willing to give you five yuan and a ration coupon for a meter of fabric."

Embarrassed, I stammered, "My class compatriot, I'm truly sorry, but when I was demobilized I was given only two sets of clothing. Everyone who is demobilized gets only two sets. One is for me to wear, while the other I promised to give to my militia battalion commander."

She burst out laughing. "*Revolution is not a dinner party.* If you don't have any army clothing to spare, that's fine. After all, why would anyone give a perfect stranger such a valuable item?"

When she said this, I felt overwhelmed with guilt. It was as though I would be letting down Chairman Mao and the Central Committee of the Party if I didn't give her the clothing. I bowed my head and gazed down at the weeds growing through the gaps between the railroad ties. There were fairy bells and mugwort. A muddy, semiopaque mist lingered between us. After the sun set, we could hear the sound of the mist condensing and dripping down. The county seat was off to one side, and the village was also far away, at the base of the hill. It was as if this woman and I were the only people left in the entire world, together with the weeds and the wheat, the air and the solitude. As the time was rolling by between us, the large, round footprints of history appeared between the railroad ties. I saw that she was wearing a pair of foreign-looking black velveteen shoes with aluminum buckles, which sparkled in the sunlight like the Big Dipper.

> *Mountains—*
> *Great waves surging in a crashing sea,*
> *A thousand stallions,*
> *In full gallop in the heat of battle.*

Inside, a fierce battle was bubbling up, like boiling water for tea, while outside everything was as calm as still water. I stood there motionless, staring at her feet. She asked me, "What do you see?" She stuck out one foot and waved it back and forth, then wiggled her big toe such that the top of the shoe rose and fell. As she was doing this, her beautiful face began to blush, as though, at the touch of her partner's hand, she had fallen in love for the first time.

"I wasn't looking at your feet," I said. "I was noticing that not a single one of the stones in the bed of these rail tracks is round."

She said, "You *were* looking at my feet. I saw you staring at my toes."

I asked, "What's so attractive about your toes?"

At that moment, heaven and earth were startled, and the spirits wept. When you fight with heaven you mustn't fear the wind and rain, when you fight with the earth you mustn't fear deep gullies and ravines, and when you fight with other people you mustn't fear that they might use underhanded tactics.

She unbuckled and removed her shoes. In the blink of an eye, all ten of her toenails were revealed. Heaven, oh heaven! Earth, oh earth! Those toenails were painted in brilliant red, like miniature setting suns. They were all carefully trimmed—as round as crescent moons and as beautifully tender as the bright red tips of her fingers. I was startled. I knew that her nails had been painted with a polish made from crushed safflower. I saw the pink mist and could smell the rosy scent of a woman's fragrance. There was a semi-pungent odor of grass and earth too. People often say that no matter how great heaven might be, it cannot contain one's love, and regardless of how expansive the earth might be, it cannot contain one's affection. However, in this world, only revolutionary emotion is heavy, because the revolutionaries' bonds are taller than mountains and deeper than the ocean. Even the tallest mountain and the deepest ocean cannot compare with the breadth and the depth of a revolutionary's love at first sight. What kind of person should one try to be? One should strive to be honest. To be honest, at that point I felt as though an unspeakably beautiful flower was blooming inside my heart. But that flower was making a sound like a car driving through my chest. She pursed her lips and stared at me, as though she were about to give

15

me a test. In a single movement, she slid down off the tracks and extended her feet outward. Heaven, oh heaven! Earth, oh earth! She was using the radiance of those ten suns to bake my heart.

I felt an electric shock. Her beautiful feet were white with dark tan lines, and in some places the two skin tones mixed together to yield a purplish-red color. The parts of her feet that were normally inside the shoes were so white that they appeared bloodless. The red nails appeared thicker against that white background, and against their red thickness, her white feet appeared even thinner. If this is what her feet were like, then what might her calves, her thighs, and the rest of her body be like? Could the rest of her be even more tenderly white than her feet? I too slid down from the tracks, as though I had been seduced, and sat opposite her. I spread my legs so that her legs were between mine, pointing toward my chest. I don't know what my expression was like at that point; I just know that my heart was pounding and a river of blood was rushing through my veins. Even though there was no enemy secretly directing me, my hands trembled violently as I fumblingly reached out to touch her legs, as though I were exhausted from a long march. At that moment—at that great and divine moment—just as I was caressing her blood-red toenails, she pulled her feet away. The air between us suddenly grew chilly, though heaven and earth kept spinning. After a brief pause, however, the frozen gulf between us began to melt again, and small green shoots began to sprout. She held her legs back only for a moment and then, with a bashful smile, slowly extended them again. At that point, the railroad tracks' endless desolation warmed us up, just as the countryside's endless desolation boiled and burned us. The sun was blindingly bright, and it shone down on the fields like an enormous red-silk bedsheet draped over the land. A sparrow and a swallow had landed on the railroad track next to us and were chirping happily. I gently grasped her feet as though holding a flower in my mouth, placed them on my crossed legs, and with a trembling hand reached out to caress her red toenails. I began with her left foot and proceeded to her right, moving from her pinky all the way to her big toe. I could feel her toes trembling in my grasp and could feel the blood rushing through her veins. I stroked her toenails dozens—maybe hundreds—of times. I stroked them until the redness was as thin as a sheet of paper and until the floral fragrance of the nail polish was gently radiating from my fingertips. Following that gentle fragrance, there was a strong pink odor of woman's flesh, which pelted my head like raindrops. I was overcome by that red nail polish and that intoxicating scent and was so ecstatic that I felt I might pass out. My lips were trembling and my teeth were chattering. I began madly kissing her feet, proceeding from her pinky to her big toe and from her toes up to the top of her feet. But as I was kissing her, she once again pulled her feet out of my grasp.

We stared at each other, our gazes like blood-drenched swords.

It was at that moment that we heard a blast of opera music from the village's loudspeakers. First there was a bright red song, followed by countless cries and screams, as though from a mental asylum. From every direction, loudspeakers were broadcasting songs and slogans, and the loudspeakers from the village closest to us were broadcasting songs that were loud and bright, new and red, with sparkling lyrics, every word of which cascaded down like water flowing over a tall cliff onto the rocks down below. The musical notes shone and sparkled like silk, and each note was like a water droplet shattered by the lyrics. I saw her listening to a very familiar song, one I couldn't name at that moment. She appeared very excited, as though the melody were flowing like a wave over her face and directly into her veins. She remained frozen throughout the song and the announcement, staring intently in the direction of the village behind me. Her face resembled a wet red cloth that has frozen solid after being hung out to dry in the middle of winter. At some point she had put her hands over the shirt button directly below her neck—as though she wanted to unfasten it but was unable to do so because I was standing in front of her. Her fingertips were trembling as if she had touched a

17

red-hot piece of iron, and as she tapped that reddish-yellow button it produced a faint sound of flesh on metal. I wanted to figure out what that loud familiar song was, and therefore perked up my ears and listened. At that point, I realized that the easternmost loudspeaker was playing the black-iron and white-steel song "Carry Revolution to the End"; the westernmost loudspeaker was playing the clatteringly strong song "Overthrow the Reactionary American Imperialist and Soviet Revisionist Party"; the southernmost loudspeaker was playing the song "Dragons and Tigers Race to the Top"; while the northernmost loudspeaker was playing the red-filled-with-green-fragrance song "Please Drink a Cup of Buttermilk Tea" and the salty-sweat-and-tears song "Denouncing the Evil Old Society." Coming down from above was the earthy-smelling song "Not Even Heaven or Earth Are as Vast as the Kindness of the Party," while coming up from underground was the silken jumping-and-laughing sound of "The Sky of the Liberated Areas Is Bright." All these lyrics were so familiar that I could recite them word for word, and if I heard a single line I could sing the entire rest of the song. But for the life of me I couldn't figure out what that loudest, brightest, most moving, and passion-inducing song was, the one that was playing overhead, behind me, in front of me, and on all sides. Needless to say, she was similarly agitated by these songs, and she infected me with her agitation. I wanted to ask her what that oh-so-familiar song was, but just as I was about to do so, I noticed that her eyes—with which she was staring at my lips—had turned light purple. She had unfastened her top button, and now both of her hands were trembling over the second button.

This was how things stood.

The sky was high, and the clouds were sparse, and there were no geese flying south. The setting sun was the color of blood and cast red light in all directions. Her first two buttons had been unfastened by the opera songs she had heard, while the remaining three were unfastened by the ones I had heard. After all five of her buttons had been unfastened, her shiny pink blouse hung down on either side

18

of her chest like an open curtain, and between those two pink curtains, her pert breasts summoned me like a pair of lively, enormous, snowy-white rabbits.

The warm, beautiful sunlight began to congeal, as did the air around us. Heaven, oh heaven! Earth, oh earth! We stared at each other, neither of us saying a word. She removed her synthetic shirt and placed it on the railroad tracks beside her. As she did so, she remained seated on a patch of green grass between the tracks, her unclothed upper body held erect like a naked deity. *On a very fine day, the land, clad in white and adorned in red, grows even more enchanting! . . . All are past and gone, for truly great men, look to this age alone!* Shocked, I stared at her silently. The blood coursed through my body, and my qi blew like the wind. At that instant, my gaze landed on her body, as though I had already caressed her with my hands. Who could have expected that after she removed her clothes, her beauty would be so clearly visible? Initially I hadn't noticed that her hair was as black as a sheet of silk hanging down onto her shoulders. But once I was able to appreciate her white skin and the thin, beautiful body that previously had lain concealed under clothing, the blackness of her hair was revealed, standing in stark contrast to the whiteness of her skin. Her jet-black hair glimmered in the light of the setting sun as it draped down over her shoulders, and some strands fell into the crevice of her neck. Her neck was very beautiful—round and white with a hint of red, like a piece of jade that had been kneaded by the weather and by human hand. She seemed slightly embarrassed, while her increasingly animated face was held up, as though someone were using a jade column to support a full moon that was about to rise just as the sun was setting. However, as I moved my eyes down her body, I noticed that her hair, face, and jade-like neck could not compare to her snow-white breasts. I was instantly seized by the softness and stiffness of her pert breasts, and it was as if I had no desire to continue moving my gaze downward. Moreover, on those full and round breasts, her purple nipples resembled a pair of Chinese dates, each with a tiny

19

opening. I knew that this was where breast milk came out, something sweet and moist, capable of intoxicating a man. As I was looking at her breasts, I noticed that there was an array of indentations on her nipples, and that each was surrounded by an areola that went from dark red to light pink—and they were like a pair of tiny red umbrellas opened toward me. At the border of the areola and the breast skin, the juncture of red and white formed a peculiarly beautiful gear-shaped pattern. Beyond this was her cleavage, which was deep and narrow. I slid down from the railroad track and tried to place her feet on my legs, and to my surprise she didn't refuse. She let me hold her feet, caressing those red toenails as I stared at her snow-white chest. We were separated by only a leg's length. The distance between the two railroad tracks happened to be just wide enough for us to sit down and stretch out our legs. I'm not sure at what point a crow and an oriole landed next to us, nor do I know when some others joined, as well as several sparrows and swallows. From several meters away, the birds stared at her naked upper body. They didn't hop or jump, nor did they sing or eat. Instead, they carefully took a step or two toward her. The crows and the sparrows had black, white, and gray plumage, while the orioles had red and gold plumage that sparkled in the light of the setting sun. Apart from the oily green scent of wheat sprouts, the tender yellow scent of green grass, the hard black scent of the railroad tracks, and the soft red scent of the setting sun, there was only the faint scent of her body. Not every woman's body has this sort of delicate fragrance. I had never smelled such a scent on the body of my wife, Guizhi. Even in our nuptial chamber, even when my feelings for Guizhi were still as deep as the sea, I hadn't ever noticed that fragrance. But sitting on the railroad tracks under the setting sun, the woman before me smelled like a fresh peach or pear blossom. I stared at her, keeping my gaze fixed on her body. My eyeballs were painfully stiff, as though someone had stuffed marbles into my eye sockets. I felt light-headed, and my vision was blurred, but I could nonetheless see the peaks and crevices of her breasts and the snowy-white skin of her abdomen. Her grayish-white body hair was as soft as a baby's—short and as fine as the point of a needle—and as it swayed in the breeze it produced a tiny glow. The gentle feather-like rustling of her body hair seemed to quiet down, but then I heard another swaying sound. She appeared exhausted, and as she leaned toward me, two parallel creases appeared in her abdomen. I heard rapid footsteps next to us, time scurrying by. At that point the setting sun was about to dip below the mountains, and the mountaintops to the east of the county seat were glowing red, as if they were pools of water. The sky was high, and the clouds were sparse, and there were no geese flying south. The clouds shifted formation, leaving behind a beautiful scene . . . The pre-dusk coolness was already drifting over to us from the fields. Her shirt on the railroad tie was fluttering in the wind. She was surely soon going to get cold. By that point she had been sitting topless in front of me for what seemed like centuries. I should have felt her skin to see if she was chilly, should have used my clothing to cover her bun-like shoulders, and should have shared my body heat with her. Poetry came to me:

The sound of the wind, the cry of a crane, startled by the clanking of weaponry;
Ambushed from all sides, who wouldn't be frightened out of their senses?

Comrade, tell me, is it not somewhat inappropriate to use these two lines here? But how else could I express what I felt at that moment? I was about to take action, was about to cross over that barrier. Heaven, oh heaven! Earth, oh earth! The broadcast from the speakers around us suddenly paused, and the river of opera music suddenly dried up. It was as if a sky lit brightly by the sun became filled with clouds that quenched its heat.

Looking as though she were awakening from a dream, she grabbed my hands, which were touching her feet, and tossed them aside.

21

I felt as though I had stepped into a nuptial chamber and then been unceremoniously pushed out again.

I said, "Sunflower blossoms open toward the sun, and countless blooming flowers cannot be defeated."

She ignored me, and instead turned and began putting on her clothes.

I said, "If today we plant the seeds of friendship, revolutionary sentiment will continue to develop over the next millennium."

She kept ignoring me, finished putting on her clothes, and quickly walked away. As she followed the railroad tracks into the blood-red light of the setting sun, her body resembled a shadow, quickly disappearing from sight.

4. The Mighty Current of Revolution Is Exhausted

When I returned to the county seat, night had fallen and the streetlamps had just been lit. To my surprise, just as the sun was setting, I saw that an astonishing event had unfolded. The streets of the county seat were virtually empty, and there was barely anyone to be seen on the thoroughfare that I was walking down. The big-character posters with red Xs that had been placed along the street had all been torn down and were fluttering desolately in the wind. The brick-paved streets were covered in an array of crushed rocks and shattered tiles, looking as though the world had been turned upside down. The mighty current of revolution had been exhausted, as the river flowed eastward and dust blew in the wind. A shattered hoe or shovel handle had been tossed into the sewer opening, and a broken electrical pole was leaning against a courtyard wall, though somehow the nearby streetlamp was still lit. Very few of the other streetlamps that were still standing were illuminated, and some didn't even have bulbs. There were bright red drops on the side of the street, and I could smell the stench of blood. Realizing that the revolution had already been unleashed here, I felt a sense of terror, as though I were in a dream, one with many layers. I truly didn't understand what had unfolded. She—that beautiful twenty-something-year-old—what was her name? And how old was she, really? Was she from the city or from the suburbs? Where did she work? And why was she sitting on the railroad tracks outside of town? I found myself in a state of utter confusion. Shocked by how the county seat's streets now resembled a war zone, my memory of that woman became more indistinct. Who could say with certainty how black her hair was, how white her skin, how exquisite her face, and how beautiful her bare breasts? My memory of her was hazy and confused. The entire scene unfolded between the moment the sun first reached the western mountains and when it set, as red as blood. She and I barely said anything to each other during that span of time. Could it even be real? And who would ever believe it? But even as she and I were engaged in that degenerate and decadent anti-revolutionary encounter, a different revolutionary scene had been unfolding here, which left half of the county seat's streets destroyed.

Later, I heard that just as I had been caressing her red toenails, someone had seized control of the county's loudspeakers, such that the propaganda tools were once again returned to the hands of the revolutionaries.

Chapter 2

Preliminary Report
on Winds and Clouds

1. The Atmosphere of Chenggang

It was three days later that I returned to my hometown of Chenggang.

My return marked the explosive beginning of a drama of crazed love. Love and corruption, class difference and family ties, hatred and struggle, the Cheng Brothers and Neo-Confucianism, law and revolution, revolution and production, loyalty and foolishness, men and women, cocks and breasts, beauty and ugliness, food and hunger, fathers and sons, mothers and children, husbands and wives, branch secretaries and Party secretaries, handcuffs and ropes, straw and gold—all these things, in the end, are but insecticide. The four oceans were boiling in fury, and the five continents were buffeted by thunderstorms—I truly wanted to stomp on them so that they would never get up again and even wished I could piss on their heads.

If you permit me to leave this place alive, the first thing I'll do when I return to Chenggang will be to piss all over those things and shit all over the head of Chenggang's revolution.

But first I should say a word or two about our radiant town of Chenggang, in the Balou Mountains. The Balou Mountains are a range in the Funiu mountain system, stretching from the Cheng Clan Hillock in the east to Baiguo Mountain in the west. They are a winding eighty-*li*-long range, consisting mostly of hills and small mountains. In this range, peaks and valleys dissolve into one another, ridges abutting streams. The territory is located between 250 and 500 meters above sea level, and includes hills, fields, plateaus, and ravines, totaling 34,000 *mu*. This territory includes Luhun Ridge, which during the Spring and Autumn period was known as the Luhun Rong territory, and during the Han dynasty was known as Luhun county. All of this is recorded in the local gazetteers. Of course, the most celebrated site in the Balou Mountains is not Luhun Ridge but the town of Chenggang, which is located on an adjacent plateau. The town of Chenggang was originally called Cheng Village, though it was never an ordinary village. Similarly, now that it was recognized as a town, it was no ordinary market town but rather was celebrated as the former residence of the Song dynasty philosophers Cheng Hao and Cheng Yi. During the reign of the Yuan dynasty's Emperor Renzong, a temple was built in Cheng Village to commemorate these two ancestral sages. Later, beginning in the sixth year of the Ming dynasty's Jingtai reign, the temple was repeatedly repaired and expanded, with good feudal subjects adding bricks and tiles. The temple grew to a three-section courtyard. The front courtyard had the Lattice House Gate and the Bearing Respect Gate, the Spring Breeze Arbor and the Standing Snow Pavilion; the middle courtyard had the Taoist Hall and two wing rooms: the Gentle Wind and Sweet Rain Room and the Scorching Sun and Autumn Frost Room; and the rear courtyard had the Qixian Great Hall, on either side of which there were a pair of lecture halls. Each of the three sections of the courtyard was ten *mu* in size, with carved beams and painted rafters, dragon and phoenix carvings, steles and cypresses that touched the sky—making this a living incarnation of feudalism.

During the reign of the Ming dynasty's Emperor Tianshun, Cheng Village was designated a Cheng Brothers Historic Site. A stone memorial arch was built one *li* to the east of the village and was engraved with the words IMPERIAL EDICT, below which appeared the words CHENG BROTHERS HISTORIC SITE. Because this inscription had been fucking written by the emperor himself and was taking pride of place on that arch in the middle of the road, everyone had to see it on their way in and out of the village. When civil officials passed by, they were obliged to get down from their sedans, while military officials had to dismount their horses. As a result, Cheng Village became famous far and wide, becoming the Tiananmen Gate of western Henan's Balou Mountains. The loess hillock behind Cheng Village that marked the eastern end of the Balou mountain range came to be known as the Cheng Clan Hillock. Later, the population of Cheng Village expanded and became intermixed with the community living on the hillock. Eventually the two communities were formally combined, resulting in what was known as Cheng Hillock Town, which is to say, the town of Chenggang.

Eighty-nine percent of the residents of Chenggang were surnamed Cheng and were direct descendants of the Cheng Brothers. Ours was the only family surnamed Gao in the area, and therefore it was remarkable that I had managed to carve out a space for myself and enjoy such a brilliant career these past years. For all this I had the bright red revolution to thank. People who are exploited and oppressed can find escape only in revolution, and without revolution they have no choice but to live in darkness. *The strong pass of the enemy is like a wall of iron, yet with firm strides we are conquering its summit.* You mustn't interrupt me, because otherwise I won't be able to finish tracing my tale from the eastern to the western mountains.

Because the director of the county's military affairs office was attending a meeting in the military sub-command area, I had to wait three full days at the county seat for my demobilization papers to be processed. During those three days, I observed the fiery development of the revolution in the county seat and felt that throughout the nation an enormous wave of revolutionary fervor was surging forth with the strength of ten thousand horses.

In the county seat, I felt restless.

In Chenggang, both revolution and love had been waiting for me for a long time. After completing my demobilization, I returned home. I rode the bus for seventy-nine *li*, and as I was passing under the Cheng Brothers memorial arch, my blood began to boil, my palms grew sweaty, and I felt a sense of excitement that was just like the crazed infatuation I had felt three days earlier by the railroad tracks outside of town. I decided that the first thing I would do as soon as I returned home would be to tear down this memorial arch. The arch had been built under feudalism, but even now, several centuries later, when the residents of Chenggang have wedding or funeral processions, they always have to dismount and pause their music upon reaching the arch. Even long-distance buses must honk their horns when passing beneath it, in order to express their respect for the Cheng brothers. I was surprised to discover that although the revolution was spreading throughout the nation, even the driver of this bus from the city of Jiudu still stopped under the arch and honked his fucking horn. I didn't say anything to him. I knew that as soon as I could tear down that arch, everything would be over, and the curtains would be raised on the great revolution.

I disembarked at the Chenggang stop, and the first thing I smelled was the town's stench and dirt. The town's commune members were carrying night soil out to the wheat fields to serve as fertilizer. There was a large group of them, young and old, and their faces all had a relaxed expression. After they passed by, there was a sense of idleness in the town streets, as chickens pecked around for food and ducks wandered over waddling their fat butts. In the sunlight at the base of the gable wall of my classmate Cheng Qingdong's house, a sow was sleeping and a dog was lying next to it, its head resting on the sow's hind leg. What was even more extraordinary, there was a sparrow perched on the sow's belly, pecking for lice. This scene made you feel that you were as far from the revolution as Yan'an is from Hainan Island. I felt oddly disoriented, as though I had just stepped directly from a sweltering summer into a bitterly cold winter. Of course, I also felt warmly affectionate, since everything in the countryside was as familiar to me as the back of my hand.

I hoped I'd see something fresh and new, such as some big-character posters along my street or people with red armbands hurrying along.

But I didn't see any of these things. Instead, everything was just as I had left it. Flowing water doesn't become stagnant, and stagnant water doesn't flow. This was truly a pool of stagnant water.

I stepped into this stagnant pool; I returned to Chenggang. The town consisted of four streets: Front Cheng Street, Center Cheng Street, and Rear Cheng Street, together with a mixed-surname street behind Cheng Temple for other families, which is of course where we lived. On the west end of the street there were three tile-roofed houses, with a bare-ground courtyard and a gate opening to the south. This was the simple, ordinary Gao home. Just as I was about to reach the entranceway, a child from a neighboring house saw me and smiled, then suddenly shouted toward my house, announcing, "Auntie Guizhi, your husband has returned," before running off toward Center Cheng Street.

My wife, Guizhi, didn't come out to greet me. Instead, as I was pushing open the unlatched door, I saw that she was out in the courtyard rinsing wheat. Our son, Hongsheng, was standing next to her using a willow branch to shoo away the chickens and sparrows that had gathered around the wheat basket. Our daughter, Honghua, who was about a year and a half old, was lying on Guizhi's lap, apparently asleep. This scene was exactly like the one with the chickens, ducks, pigs, and dogs that I had seen in the road. The mountain sky and the rural land both appeared stagnant and lifeless.

Holding my bag, I stood in a corner of the courtyard.

When Guizhi and my son heard the door open, they both turned around. However, Guizhi didn't come and take my bag, nor did she realize that the person standing in front of her was a future revolutionary. Instead, she merely stared for a moment, then smiled and said, "You're back? Didn't you say you would be returning home a few days ago?"

Remembering the revolution unfolding in the city and the scene by the railroad tracks, I replied, "I was delayed in the city."

She said, "Come inside. Why are you still standing there?"

She added, "Hongsheng, greet your dad. Did you say it? Greet your dad."

Hongsheng, who was already five years old, didn't say anything, and instead he and Honghua, now awake, kept watching me timidly, as though this were not even my home. At that moment, I began to regret having proceeded with the demobilization process. I remembered what our commanding officer in the regiment had always said: "The revolution has not yet succeeded, so we must continue to struggle." As I was carrying my bags inside, I took the opportunity to move several benches next to the outer wall. I looked around the two inner rooms, then asked, "Where's my mother?" Continuing to rinse the grain without even turning around, Guizhi replied, "She wanted some peace and quiet, so she went to live on the Cheng Clan Hillock."

My heart skipped a beat; it was as though a bullet had exploded in my chest. But I didn't say a word and instead angrily ground my foot against the floor. I then went back outside and stood under the building's eaves. I looked toward the hillock behind the town, but all I could see was the Qixian Great Hall in Cheng Temple's rear courtyard and a corner of the Taoist Hall in the middle courtyard. The wind chimes hanging from the four corners of the hall were clanging noisily, and the sound cut through the courtyard. When I saw Cheng Temple, my heart sank, and I vowed that one day not only would I demolish the memorial arch, I would burn down the temple itself. Ever since I had moved to the town from the Cheng Clan Hillock, I had longed to destroy the memorial arch and burn down the temple. After having served in the army for four years, I was more determined than ever. At that moment, my son, Hongsheng, shouted, "Dad!" My heart melted at the sound of his voice, and I patted his head.

I said, "Call me 'Pa,' child. In the city, everyone says Pa."

Hongsheng shook his head.

I said, "OK, then call me Dad . . . Go, if you go inside and look in the yellow bag, you'll find some candy."

After eating the candy, the children kept shouting "Dad, Dad!" as though "Dad" were the only person in the world capable of giving them candy. At that time, all candy was wrapped in thin red oilpaper printed with sayings like *Fight Selfishness and Criticize Revisionism.* When the children threw their wrappers onto the pile of pig manure and chicken droppings in the courtyard, I quickly retrieved them. I told the children not to throw away their wrappers, because doing so would be reactionary. The children didn't understand what I was talking about, so Guizhi turned to me and observed, "This is the countryside, not your army regiment." I initially wanted to explain that the revolution unfolding in the city and the county seat had already enveloped heaven and earth, and that it was precisely for the sake of the revolution that I had been demobilized and returned home—but when I saw Guizhi's look of disdain, as thick as the courtyard wall, I had no choice but to bite my tongue. Moreover, her face appeared so dusty and dark, it was as though it had never been washed—which reminded me again of what had happened to me by the railroad tracks outside of town. This, too, made me swallow what I was about to say. All of a sudden, I didn't even want to look at my wife.

I once again stared up at the eaves of Cheng Temple.

At that moment, a child who had just run into the alley dashed into my home and shouted, "Uncle Aijun, the branch secretary wants you to report immediately."

Guizhi removed a soaking-wet bundle of wheat and placed it on the edge of the basin. It was as if the child who had run in had reminded her of something very important. With a lively expression, she shouted, "Go quickly! My father asked for you to go see him as soon as you returned, but while I was rinsing the grain I forgot to tell you." Then she asked, "What did you bring my father? He likes candy and canned goods from the city." She added, "Hongsheng and Honghua, go with your father to see your grandfather. Ask him if he wants any eggs and noodles, and if he does, I'll take him some this afternoon."

2. A History of Marriage outside the Revolution

I should explain that my father-in-law was also a Chenggang revolutionary. He served as a mail courier for the Eighth Route Army, and after Liberation was appointed to the position of village branch secretary. The dozen or so families living in the Cheng Clan Hillock were originally a production team belonging to the Zhaozhuang Brigade five *li* away. At the time, Cheng Village was only a small local market community where the township government office was located. The township's mayor, Cheng Tianmin, was a twentieth-generation descendant of the Cheng Brothers. In 1964, the government decided to elevate Cheng Village to the status of a town, but in order to do so they needed to find a way to increase the size of the community. Therefore, Mayor Cheng Tianmin and my future father-in-law, village chief Cheng Tianqing, held a meeting and decided to have Cheng Village absorb the dozen or so families currently living on the hillock, so that it could be promoted from a village into a town. The residents of Cheng Clan Hillock moved down and built a row of houses behind Cheng Temple, thereby becoming members of Cheng Village.

After joining Cheng Village, I became the son-in-law of Cheng Tianqing, who was now the town's Party branch secretary. On the day of our move, as my mother and I were cleaning up our new tile-roofed house, the branch secretary ambled over. He didn't sit in the seat I brought over to him nor did he drink from the glass of water my mother offered him. Instead, he simply stood in that new house with his hands behind his back and gazed at the walls, at the ground, and at the beams and rafters. Then he touched the two paulownia trees—each of which had a trunk as wide as a rice bowl—that were growing in what had now become the house's courtyard and said, "Technically, these trees should be public property, but now it appears that they belong to your Gao family."

Overjoyed, my mother gazed at the branch secretary. "Is that OK?"

The branch secretary said, "If I say it's OK, then it's OK. That's why I'm the branch secretary. What's more, I was close to your son's father, and now that he's gone, who's going to look after you and your son, if not me?"

My mother quickly poured away the cup of water that the branch secretary hadn't touched. Then she went back into the kitchen to poach an egg, even adding some brown sugar. After the branch secretary finished the egg, he turned and looked me over from head to toe. He said, "You're eighteen? You're in high school in the county seat? I hear that you're one of the top students in your class?" At that point I was still young and naïve, and I didn't realize that the branch secretary was hoping to make me his son-in-law. Blushing, I replied to him, never expecting that a matchmaker would come to our home that very night.

The matchmaker said to my mother, "Joyous news! The branch secretary has taken a liking to your son, Aijun."

I got married shortly after graduating from high school. Guizhi was the branch secretary's third daughter. She had a completely ordinary appearance, like a hill covered in yellow earth. She was actually a year younger than me but looked three to five years older. I'm not sure why she appeared so much older than me. Was it because she was so short or because her skin was so dark? Or was it because even when her uncombed hair cascaded down it couldn't conceal the countless moles that covered her face? The first time I saw Guizhi, the matchmaker had led me into her house like a mule. In Guizhi's room, the wall was covered in old newspapers, the sheets folded into long strips, as though a large dam were positioned against the wall. When I saw her appearance, I suddenly felt as though there was a clump of cotton in my throat that I needed to spit out. The branch secretary entered after his daughter and said, "The two of you can talk to each other. I am a Party member and a cadre, and when we hold general meetings for commune members, I always stress the importance of being able to marry whomever you want." He said, "Aijun, my child. I saw that your father died early, which makes you a descendant of the revolution. Your grades in the county high school weren't bad—and seeing that, I agreed to let my daughter Guizhi become engaged to you. After the two of you get married and have a child, I'll send you to join the army. In the army, you can join the Party, and after you return I'll help make you a village cadre."

Guizhi asked, "Why aren't you saying anything?"

I looked up at her.

Guizhi asked, "Do you resent the fact that I'm ugly? And if we're speaking freely, can I say that I resent the fact that your family is dirt-poor?"

I said, "Why aren't you in school?"

Guizhi said, "The black Chinese characters in the textbooks look like a cloud of gnats swarming in front of me, and when I try to read, my head feels like it's about to explode."

I said, "Can your father really help me become a village cadre?"

Guizhi said, "Didn't you hear what he just said? A year after we get married, and after we've had a child, he'll send you to join the army."

I said, "Why do we have to have a child before I join the army?"

Guizhi said, "If we don't have a child, how could I be assured of your love?"

33

I said, "When could we get married?"

Guizhi said, "If it were up to me, we'd get married in the first lunar month of this year."

I said, "Our family's pigs are not fully grown, which means I don't yet have enough money to get married."

Guizhi said, "My family has already prepared a dowry, and whatever your family needs, mine can provide. But there is one condition, which is that after we marry, you must do as I say. If your mother makes me angry, I'll smash a bowl in front of you, and if *you* make me angry, I'll hang myself in front of you."

In the first lunar month of that year, we got married.

3. Entering Cheng Temple for the First Time

I quickly led my son to my father-in-law's house. When we arrived, my father-in-law was sitting in a rocking chair in the sun, smoking and playing with his family's dog. (Is this what landowners in the old society were like?) He looked at the bags and cans of sweets I had brought him, and asked, "Are these from Jiudu, or are they our county's local products?"

I replied, "I bought them in a grocery store in Jiudu. They were produced in Zhengzhou, the provincial capital."

He took them from me and began sniffing them like a dog. He said, "Not bad. They smell very sweet." Then he added, "You should take these into the temple and go see your Uncle Tianmin, who recently stepped down from his position as mayor and now lives in the temple, enjoying peace and quiet and reading old books every day."

I emerged from my father-in-law's house. He hadn't mentioned wanting to prepare me to be a village cadre, nor had he mentioned the revolution or the village's nature, a pool of stagnant water. In fact, he hadn't even invited me to sit down, nor had he invited his grandson Hongsheng to eat something, let alone asked me about my

34

experience and deeds in the army. Instead, he simply told me to leave his house, and said that my children and I should go to Cheng Temple. *Revolution is not an invitation to a dinner party, nor is it a distribution of gifts; it is not an exchange of flattering and favors, nor is it painting and embroidery.* Nevertheless, I had no choice but to visit Cheng Tianmin. He was the former mayor and the most visible representative of the historical Cheng Hao. His ancestors included individuals who had passed the imperial examinations, and those of his grandfather's generation were *xiucai* scholars. As for Cheng Tianmin himself, before the revolution he had served as the principal of the county school, and in the first year after Liberation, the government recruited him as a prominent non-Party figure and appointed him to serve as the inaugural director of the county's education bureau. It was said that when the government tried to appoint him to be county head, he sensed the complex formidability of the revolution and therefore chose instead to serve in a lower position as town mayor. To this day, from the grasslands of Inner Mongolia to the fishing villages of Hainan Island, from the Gobi Desert in the northwest to the gulf of Bohai in the northeast and the region of rice and fish in the south, the revolution was raging, with red banners flying and trumpets blaring. It was precisely at this point that he proposed to step down from his position as mayor. Was he afraid of the revolutionary storm, or was he stepping down precisely in order to advance further, like a wily hare with three secret burrows? Once (when I was still as small as an ant), I saw him in the street while accompanying my mother to the Cheng Village market, but my mother quickly pulled me to the side of the road, and after waiting for him to pass, she pointed to him and said, "My child, that is the mayor. If only you could have even half of his education and become a village cadre when you grow up, I would feel that my widowhood had not been in vain." Why did she think I would be able to become only a village cadre? Why didn't she expect me to become the village chief or town mayor, or even the county head or district commissioner? In the courses I took while in the army, didn't the political instructor and the regimental commander keep telling us how Lin Biao was appointed division commander at the age of twenty? *The world is yours, and it is also ours.* If we are like the morning sun, then aren't you like the evening sun, meaning that you must soon set below the western horizon?

Cheng Temple was located at the end of Rear Cheng Street. With Hongsheng carrying those two boxes of sweets and me carrying the four cans, we proceeded from Center Cheng Street's second alley to Rear Cheng Street. When we encountered people along the way, they all repeated the same thing: "Aijun, did you leave the army?" I would simply smile and nod and then take a Golden Leaf cigarette out of my pocket and hand it to them. They would ask, "Where are you going?" to which I would reply, "I'm going to see the former mayor, who's waiting for me in the temple." They would say, "Aijun, if you become a village cadre, you should remember to look out for your fellow brothers," to which I would say, "Look at how lifeless the mayor is. How could I possibly become a village cadre?" At this point, if the person I encountered was literate and could see and think clearly, he might say, "If you can achieve the revolutionary 'three-in-one combination'—featuring a collaboration between cadres, technicians, and workers—that could make you a veritable youth cadre!"

I resolved that if I ever came to power, I would be sure to treat this person well. As long as his family didn't have any political problems, then when it was time to irrigate the fields, I could let his family get water first, and when it was time to buy fertilizer, I could let his family purchase several dozen *jin*. I would do this because this was what I had to do. Why? Because I, Gao Aijun, am a conscientious revolutionary.

This was before lunch. Most of the men who had gone into the fields hadn't yet returned, and the women were still at home cooking. As I was walking along Rear Cheng Street, I could see the sound of the bellows from each family's stove, scurrying out like a mouse through the cracks under the doors. Plumes upon plumes of smoke blanketed the blue sky with white clouds, making it resemble a grief-stricken face (but whose?). I grasped Hongsheng's hand. He kept glancing down at the two boxes of sweets he was holding, as the shiny paper glittered in the dark alley like flames. I knew he desperately wanted to eat one of those sweets, so when no one was looking, I opened the boxes and, after removing several sweets from each one, closed them again. As Hongsheng was eating the sweets, his face glowed with delight, and as he chewed happily, the glow from his face shone down on the ground of Rear Cheng Street. The courtyard walls, rear walls, and gable walls of the residences on either side of the street made Rear Cheng Street appear rather narrow, like a canal. Layers of plaster had peeled off, and I could hear the plaster and cement falling to the ground. As I watched Hongsheng devouring the sweets, imbued with a spirit that could conquer mountains and rivers, I asked, "Hongsheng, are those good?"

He replied, "They're delicious! They're even tastier than meat."

I said, "Your dad is going to join the revolution. After the revolution has succeeded, your dad will give you sweets every day."

He gazed up at me with a look of bewilderment.

I patted his head as though I were a great personage. It was at that point that Cheng Temple appeared before us. There was a tall brick and tile gatehouse, on which the characters spelling CHENG TEMPLE were inscribed in gold—each character as large as a basket. Below these characters were the large red gates. I didn't know whether some day in the future they would fall apart at my hand or whether they would stand unchanged, funneling cold air toward me as I faced them. At this point I didn't realize that my beloved was waiting for me inside the temple. As I approached, my clothing was a mess, and in opening the boxes of sweets I had gotten oil from the oilpaper all over my fingers. Everything occurred without any preparation—with the bricks and tiles arranged there as if by fate. As I walked past the wall of the temple courtyard, the perfectly straight line of heavy bricks fell behind me. I arrived at the temple's main gate, where two stone lions were squatting on either side and gazing up at me. I wiped my oily hands on one of the lion heads, as my son tugged at my hand and cautiously peered behind him.

I said, "Hongsheng, wipe your hands. Don't be afraid. Your dad is going to join the revolution."

The child shook his head and wiped his hands on his pants.

I said, "What are you afraid of? Your dad is going to join the revolution."

We stepped into the temple's outer courtyard. The ground of the outer courtyard was covered in twenty-centimeter-square bricks. The path from the Lattice House Gate to the Bearing Respect Gate was worn where generation after generation of Cheng descendants had previously walked, carrying incense and kowtowing to their ancestors. Tree roots were pushing up against the bricks and cracking them, and under the shade of the tree's canopy the bricks appeared moist and black. The bricks were covered in a layer of green moss, which also grew in the cracks between them, making the ground appear old but sturdy, and full of the color and smell of the feudal ruling class. This gave visitors a desolate and mysterious feeling of oppression and exploitation. Holding my son's hand, I walked along the brick path. He looked around, his small hand chilled by the temple's cold air. On the east and west side of the courtyard there were the eaves and columns of the Spring Breeze Arbor and the Standing Snow Pavilion. At that point, the temple's discolored dragons and ghosts, as well the painted lions and tigers, were all gazing fiercely at us, baring their fangs and brandishing their claws.

I said, "Hongsheng, are you afraid?"

He shook his head, even as his fingers grasped my hand even more tightly than before.

I said, "Don't be afraid. The day will come when your dad will destroy all of this."

He stared at me in disbelief.

I said, "Without destruction, there can be no creation. When you grow up, you'll understand."

The child stared at me in even greater confusion.

As I look back many years later, I feel that was the most mysterious and moving period of my life. For years afterward, no matter how earth-shattering the love and hate that I subsequently experienced, it was never as marvelous or unforgettable as the feelings I experienced at that time. I never again felt the same mysterious and moving warmth and beauty that I felt when I was with her—a warmth and beauty that was like divine water dripping onto my heart. I have never had an opportunity to see the Great Helmsman, Chairman Mao Zedong, in person, but I imagine that even if Chairman Mao were to pour me a glass of water with his own hands, or even if Comrade Jiang Qing were to cook me a bowl of poached eggs, the resulting feeling would not be as deep and moving as what I experienced at that instant. The water he would pour me would still be merely water, and the poached eggs she would cook for me would still be merely poached eggs, but what could possibly compare to what I felt at that beautiful, miraculous instant? Regardless of how vast heaven and earth might be, they are still not as vast as the Party's kindness; and regardless of how deep the oceans and seas might be, they are not as deep as the impact that instant had on me.

I heard footsteps that made me think of moss blowing through the courtyard—moist and heavy, the footsteps fluttered leisurely in midair. This was because that temple was so empty, even desolate; there was no one but the former mayor, who would periodically go there to find some peace and quiet. Other than national holidays and the birthdays of the Cheng Brothers, it was very rare for anyone to step into that courtyard or even to be given permission to go inside. The clattering of footsteps sounded as though they were coming from at least two people. I looked up in the direction of the Bearing Respect Gate and saw that the footsteps were pitch-black, and there was a moldy smell wedged within them. The steps proceeded unevenly, and it seemed as though there was the sound of a voice chanting or singing.

I looked up.

I noisily looked up, and with a bang, I saw her. She was holding a three-year-old child in one hand and a three-layer aluminum lunch box in the other. She was still wearing the same pink synthetic shirt, the same velveteen shoes with aluminum buckles, and the same imitation army pants that she had sewn herself. Everything was exactly as it had been when I first encountered her three days earlier by the train tracks outside of town. Her face had traces of worry and exhaustion, which gave her delicate skin a sickly pallor. The Bearing Respect Gate was not as large as Cheng Temple's main gate, but every brick surrounding the gate on three sides was emblazoned with a lotus pattern, and together they resembled a vine hanging down from the door frame. She was standing there, her mouth agape. One of her feet was positioned in the temple and the other was still outside. Between the lower edge of the doorway and her head, I could see that the grape lattice in the middle courtyard was not yet completely covered in leaves, but it was already shading the courtyard. Standing in the doorway, in that shadow, she looked like a painting. In those days, whenever you wanted to compliment someone's beauty, you would always say they resembled a painting, and she really did.

Needless to say, at the moment I saw her, she must have also seen me.

Our gazes cut through the emptiness of the front courtyard, where a cluster of sparks were shimmering like the halo from a welding torch. The air in the temple grew still, as the sunlight that was seeping down through the canopy of the old cypresses also stopped waving back and forth. The aluminum lunch box she was carrying bumped against the left side of the door frame, chipping off a piece of paint, as some dust drifted down from the door frame onto her head. Her complexion turned dark yellow, and her lips tightened into a thin red and white line. My heart seemed to stop, and my hands became so wet with sweat a ship could have sailed through them. As we stared at one another, the crows were building their nests in the cypress branches overhead, and from the sky above them fell their songs and twigs from their nests. The air's humid, musty smell assaulted my nose. The crows' sharp purple cries pounded my ears and chest like falling roof tiles. I didn't know then whether these cries were inauspicious or whether they were just ordinary crow calls.

I looked up into the tree, and when I lowered my gaze again she was in the process of trying to squeeze by me with her child (it turned out she already had a daughter, though five days earlier she hadn't looked at all like she could be a mother). Her footsteps were lighter than before, and her lunch box made a whispering sound as it swung back and forth. At this point I spun around to look at her, and my frozen blood began to thaw and surge into my head. I stared as she walked from the Bearing Respect Gate to the Lattice House Gate, then I quickly released Hongsheng's hand and rushed toward her.

I shouted, "Hey, hey!"

She turned around and said, "Three days ago I was possessed. From now on, it will be as though you never saw me and I never saw you that day. We have never seen each other before, and definitely don't know each other."

After saying this, she picked up her baby and stepped out of the temple and into Rear Cheng Street. She left like a thief sneaking away into the night. A sunflower faces the sun when it blooms, and its flowers bloom tirelessly. Tonight we'll sow the seeds of friendship, and friendly feelings of revolution will flourish for ten thousand generations. I continued standing outside of Cheng Temple's main gate until I saw her pass through the alley through which I had arrived, whereupon I turned and entered Center Cheng Street.

This was my revolutionary love, my fiery love. It didn't begin when I ran into her in front of Cheng Temple, but rather it had been born three days earlier. I knew our revolutionary love had not yet really begun. In front of Cheng Temple our love life had merely turned a new leaf. We had taken the first step in our Long March; the snowy mountaintops and grassy plains had not yet appeared. The revolution had not yet succeeded, and our comrades needed to continue to struggle. Hardship and adversity still awaited us.

My son was standing behind me, shouting, "Dad . . . Dad!"

4. A Revolutionary's Longing

Once you've eaten honey, you'll realize that sweet potatoes are not really all that sweet, and they'll never taste the same way again. After all, sweet potatoes are merely sweet potatoes, and they can never become honey.

I learned so much about the mysterious woman from visiting my mother's home. I found out that her name was Xia Hongmei and that she was the daughter-in-law of the former mayor, Cheng Tianmin. Her mother's family was from Dongguan, in the eastern portion of the county seat. Her husband's name was Cheng Qingdong, and he and I had been classmates in primary school, though after that I had gone to the county seat for high school, while he went to a local teacher's college. Later, I joined the army to help protect our homes and defend our country, while he returned to Chenggang after graduation to become a middle-school teacher. With this, our revolutionary and counterrevolutionary lives diverged.

After the dozen or so families who previously lived there moved down from the hillock, they left behind several dilapidated thatch-roofed houses and a handful of elders who, for some reason or other, were determined to continue living up away from everyone else. When I reached my family's home on the hillock, my gray-haired mother was shucking corn to feed the chickens. Seeing me, she immediately dropped the corn and took several steps in my

42

direction. Then, as she leaned against a tree and gazed at me, her eyes filled with tears.

I said, "Mother, I've come to get you and take you home."

My mother shook her head at me.

I said, "If Cheng Guizhi dares to treat you badly, I'll simply cast her off."

My mother stared at me.

I said, "I'm a Party member and want to join the revolution. In the future, the Party branch secretary Cheng Tianqing will have to do as I say."

My mother gazed at me with a look of terrified confusion, as if her son had gone stark raving mad. Before the revolution succeeds, one will necessarily encounter confusion. This is a lesson that history has already taught us. I didn't say anything else to my mother, because I knew she had a backward and ignorant side to her.

I sat with my mother in the entrance to the courtyard of our family's residence, and in the light of the setting sun I gazed down at the town of Chenggang. The canal that extended from Thirteen Li River was as straight as a chopstick. Water flowed through it year-round, and when it passed the base of the hillock behind the town, it resembled a sheet of silk hanging from the mountains. At that moment, I felt as though my eyes would be washed clean if I stared at the surface of the water, and if I looked at the temple's front courtyard I'd see that the red paint Hongmei's lunch box had chipped off the door frame was now still glimmering on the ground.

I asked my mother, "What is her name?"

My mother replied, "Her name is Xia Hongmei."

I said, "Where is she from?"

My mother said, "She's from the city. Her mother's family is from the area just outside the city gate."

I reflected for a moment. Then, almost as if talking to myself, I said, "How could she have married into Chenggang? Why would someone from the city want to marry into this remote town? Every-one wants to move up in society, just as water flows downhill. Based on her appearance, it would have been more appropriate for her to have married someone from Jiudu."

My mother looked at me, as though trying to determine what I was thinking. Then, as though solving a puzzle, she slowly asked, "What do you expect her to do? Chenggang is, after all, a town. The fifth day of every month is market day, and the number of people who pour in is definitely comparable to the number of people who go to the market in the city. Furthermore, Qingdong attended col-lege in the district, became a teacher, has a salary, and his father was mayor. And while Qingdong's father was serving as mayor, what was Hongmei's father doing? Her father was in town sweeping the courtyard, boiling water, and waiting on the mayor. So how could she not marry the mayor's son?"

This is how revolution is. Without tribute, there can be no foundation, and without sacrifice there can be no success. When Xia Hongmei married, she wasn't yet twenty. Her skin was white and tender, and everyone for miles around regarded her as a local flower. She was gracious in her speech and dexterous in her work. In a single day, she could knit one of those foreign-style sweaters that people in the city wear. If a group of women surrounded her in the village, asking her to say a few words, she would sing them one of those songs that only people from the city know and dance one of the foreign dances she had learned at school. As effortlessly as a bean begins to sprout once placed in water or a branch begins to bloom once spring arrives, her desire and pride not only shaped her life but also led to the splendor and the tragedy of her fate with me.

Mother remarked that it was too bad that Hongmei had become infected with this sort of revolutionary fever. Not only did Hongmei refuse to cook and wash clothes for the mayor, she even threw around the bowls and chopsticks he used. Mother claimed that the mayor had made Hongmei so angry that at one point she abandoned her husband and child and moved into the temple. Hongmei returned to her mother's home in the city, where she stayed for a few days. After she returned, however, she reported that she hadn't gone to her mother's home but instead had traveled to Beijing to see Chairman Mao, claiming that he had even shaken her hand. Mother asked me, "Where is Beijing?" Then she answered her own question, noting that Beijing is located thousands of *li* away to the north. Could Hongmei have made it there if she had tried to walk? Moreover, who is Chairman Mao? He is an emperor, so could she even have been able to see him? Could she have shaken his hand? Mother added that after she returned to the town, whenever she saw anyone she would always show them her hand—explaining that this was the very hand that Chairman Mao had shaken. She stopped using that hand to hold her chopsticks, and even stopped washing it—explaining that the warmth from Chairman Mao's hand still lingered on her own. Mother asked, "Wouldn't you agree that she is possessed?" She added, "Isn't it clear that she's gone mad?" Mother said that the mayor had told Cheng Tianqing to ask the Chinese medical doctor to come see her. Then three young men held Hongmei down, as the doctor inserted more than twenty acupuncture needles into her head and hands. Hongmei trembled for a long time, but when they removed the needles she was no longer possessed. Instead, she cooked when she was supposed to cook, fed the pigs when she was supposed to feed them, and when she was supposed to go to the temple to take food for her father-in-law, she did that too.

Perhaps I was also possessed? Perhaps the revolution had left me possessed? Perhaps Xia Hongmei had left me possessed? Perhaps I was possessed by both the revolution and by love? Beginning from the day when I saw Xia Hongmei in Cheng Temple, her voice and figure kept appearing in my mind. As soon as the loudspeakers in the streets began blaring, regardless of whether they were broadcasting songs or model operas, my body would become as agitated as though my shoes, my pant legs, the seat of my pants, and even my shirt

45

had caught on fire. Then that scene by the railroad tracks outside of town would once again replay in my mind, making it impossible for me to fall asleep. This onslaught left me listless, unable to sleep and uninterested in eating. The revolutionary ardor sliced me open as easily as a blade cutting through a knot. One night, as I was trying to extinguish the passion that consumed me, I pinched my leg. Then I pinched my penis so hard that it started to bleed, but I still couldn't get that memory of Hongmei out of my mind, nor could I extinguish the memory of what had happened by the railroad tracks.

The disease spread to my vital organs and proved impossible to cure. I knew that the world had no savior, that there was no immortal or emperor who could save me, and therefore I had no choice but to save myself. Saving myself was my only choice. During the day, I wandered around the village, and would loiter in front of Xia Hongmei's house on Front Cheng Street, hoping to catch sight of her. And if I couldn't see her, I would deliberately leave Chenggang. Therefore, I got up one morning and went to the countryside to visit my aunt's family and didn't return to Chenggang until after dark. When my uncle's family built a new house, I spent two days feverishly laying bricks. When I returned to town, I found myself unable to sleep, and in the middle of the night I couldn't help climbing onto Guizhi's body. I climbed on top of her because, to me, she was Xia Hongmei. I caressed her head, her face, her short and stubby toes, and her stinky toenails. At this point she turned on the light and, still half-asleep, looked at me and asked, "Gao Aijun, do you want me to get pregnant again?"

I replied, "I want another child."

She said, "Then stop pawing me and come here. Do you think you can get me pregnant just by stroking me?"

She didn't know that I immediately regretted this as soon as I said it, nor that as soon as I heard her reply, the fire in my loins immediately faded. It had been only a month since I had returned to Chenggang, and my desire for Guizhi had already completely faded.

But at that point I was merely a pig, a dog. I wasn't a determined revolutionary, and I couldn't help doing things for my wife. I gritted my teeth as I climbed on top of her, and she turned out the lights. Indeed, whenever we did it, she would always turn out the lights. Moonlight and an evening chill entered through the window. After the light in the room was extinguished, there was a yellowish burning smell. There was also a greenish spring scent, as well as a musty, mildewy smell of sheets that needed to be aired out. Hongsheng and Honghua were sleeping at one end of the bed, with Honghua's arm resting on Hongsheng's chest. Guizhi went over and covered them up again, then she turned out the light and sat on the edge of the bed and, like before, removed her underwear and placed it at the head of the bed. She pulled back the sheets, lay down, and said, "Come here. Do you want me to have another son or another daughter?" I replied that either would be fine. She said, "Come here. Why are you still standing there?" I replied that I felt a breeze, so I went and hung a piece of clothing in front of the window, blocking the moonlight, and another one behind the window screen. She said, "Come here. Don't you want another child? Honghua can already run around. I want another child." I had no choice but to slowly make my way toward the bed. If I didn't go over, it seemed like her gaze would cross hills and mountains to peer into my heart—allowing her to glimpse that unexpected encounter that I had had with Hongmei on the edge of town. But at that moment, my desire abruptly receded, leaving my body as cold as if a bucket of frigid well water had been dumped over my head. My member became as limp as a blade of grass covered in frost. I wanted to tell her to forget it, that we could do it another day. I wanted to tell her that I thought I was ill, and although I had just been erect, a cool breeze had made the tree topple over and the birds fly away. I celebrated my collapse, and the fact that I wouldn't have to climb atop her while thinking of Xia Hongmei—thinking of Hongmei's figure and complexion, imagining her breasts and cleavage, her fresh face and short hair, and her ten persimmon-like red toenails. After the tree fell, the monkey returned to its den, and that night I would be able to sleep peacefully. But at that moment, just as I had fallen asleep, a loud sound startled me.

The music blaring over the loudspeaker was the "Battle March Melody." I couldn't tell where the music was coming from, but the loudspeaker broadcasting the music sounded as though it had developed a rip. Perhaps it had been hanging from a tree branch for so long that wind and rain had worn away the surface of the speaker, such that the music playing over it developed some hoarse spots. It was as if the music were seeping out through the cracks in the bamboo. The resulting sound was harsh and yet very fluid. The rhythm and the notes were clear, forming a colorful cloud that entered my house through the cracks in the doorway, even pushing open the door. This colorful cloud surged in through the openings in the window, making the clothing I had hung there flutter back and forth. It blew in through the cracks in the rear wall, making the bedsheets tremble. As it blew in through the cracks in the tile roof, my entire body began shivering uncontrollably. I was energized by that music, and my body began to feel as though a swarm of ants were crawling through my veins. My blood began to boil, as my hands, feet, hair, neck, and all of my bodily crevices became covered in sweat. I knew I was about to become crazed again, and I felt as though countless surges of energy began pulsing from my outer limbs toward the area between my thighs. My member became erect, as stiff as a board. Eventually, when the song reached the lines, "I tripped one, captured another, and seized several American guns," in my mind's eye I saw a pair of railroad tracks extending toward me, next to which there was an endless field of wheat, where Hongmei was lying naked on the trampled stalks, beckoning to me. Meanwhile, next to me in the bed, Guizhi turned half over and said, "Are you going to do it or not? If not, then I'm going back to sleep." I nodded, then walked toward where Hongmei was lying. I saw her radiant body and smelled wheat as well as the fresh scent of her body. I reached the edge of the bed, whereupon I took off my shoes, unfastened my military-issued belt, and removed my pants.

However, the music playing over the loudspeakers suddenly stopped, and the world abruptly grew silent, like a musical instrument with broken string.

Guizhi slowly sat up in bed, put her underwear back on, and turned on the light.

"Gao Aijun, if you aren't ready to do it, then you shouldn't wake me up. I need to get up early tomorrow to cook. How can someone be like this every day? Is this useful to a household, like food or clothing? After you returned from the army, I asked you to do it several times, but you never finished. You are completely useless, yet you still want to do it? It's already been more than a month since you returned, so you should go find work somewhere. You're no longer in the army and are no longer under supervision. If you can't find a way to earn work points, then what do you expect our family to live on? Can we live on air alone?

5. A Revolutionary Melody Plays Once Again
Of course we couldn't live on air alone. Both farming and revolution can yield food to eat. Moreover, revolution often results from people not having enough to eat. Before I joined the army, Cheng Tianqing promised me that after I was demobilized and returned home, he would make me a village cadre, and it was only because he promised I could be a cadre that I agreed to marry his daughter. Permission to become a cadre was, therefore, the dowry he owed me. Now that I had already fathered two children with Guizhi and had been demobilized, it was time for him to make good on that promise. If I didn't become a village cadre, how would I be able to help foment revolution? And if I couldn't assume a local leadership position, how would I be able to help lead the revolution when the time came?

I resolved to go to my father-in-law and demand that he make good on his promise.

After breakfast, Guizhi asked me where I was going, adding that today the production team was heading to the area in front of the village to dig irrigation canals. I didn't answer and in fact didn't even glance at her. But when I left the house, she followed me out and handed me a shovel.

"If you miss a half day of work, you'll be docked four work points."

I threw down the shovel and walked away, leaving Guizhi standing there in confusion.

In the alley, the sunlight was as clear as glass and as bright as a revolutionary's heart. My father-in-law's neighbors had finished eating and were standing in their doorways holding their shovels and hoes, waiting for the production brigade bell to signal the beginning of the workday. As I passed in front of them, a revolutionary fervor seemed to lift me up. One villager asked, "Aijun, have you eaten yet?" I replied, "Yes, I have, and now I'm on my way to see the village branch secretary." The villager laughed and said, "Isn't the branch secretary your father-in-law?" I said, "At home he's my father-in-law, but in the village he is my work commander." The villagers stood behind me, smiling broadly. I thought to myself, *Go ahead and smile, because after the revolution there will come a day when if I tell you to smile, you'll smile, and if I tell you not to smile, then you'll have no choice but to cry.*

The sound of their laughter escorted me from Rear Cheng Street to Center Cheng Street.

As I was turning from a side alley into Center Cheng Street, I caught sight of Hongmei. She was walking shoulder-to-shoulder with Aiju, Guizhi's sister-in-law on her mother's side. Hongmei was still carrying her aluminum lunch pail. She must have been going to Cheng Temple to take her father-in-law some food. By this point, the bell releasing the second production brigade from work had

50

sounded, and many brigade members were carrying their tools and walking out of the village. Hongmei found herself wedged between several young female brigade members. My heart started pounding, and I remembered the hardness and softness I had experienced when the "Battle March Melody" had blared over the loudspeakers the night before. I didn't know how I could possibly proceed toward Hongmei and Aiju. My legs were trembling, but somehow I found that my stride had become stronger. I was truly grateful to those brigade members who had been joking with me, because if they hadn't helped suppress the fire in my loins, who knows what I might have done when confronted with Hongmei!

This was the second time I had seen her after returning to the village. She was now wearing a plain blue shirt. Her pants were made from the work fabric that had become popular in the city, and on her feet she was wearing a pair of similarly fashionable black rubber revolutionary shoes. I was still wearing my shiny green army uniform. As the women headed toward me, I stuffed my hands into my pockets and used my fists to pull the fabric tight around my hips. I'm sure you can't possibly understand, but at the time that kind of affect was perceived as fashionable and Western. Not all young people were able to walk along with both hands stuffed into their pockets, and they certainly weren't able to use their fists to elevate the region around their hips. In this way, I was showing that I had gone to school, served in the army, and seen the world. I demonstrated that I had ideals in my heart and power in my family. This was similar to what Hongmei was able to convey by wearing work-fabric pants and black rubber revolutionary shoes. These were class markers. I planted myself in the middle of the road and waited for Hongmei and Aiju to approach, my gaze hurtling toward them like a car. People moved aside to avoid me in the middle of the road, and Hongmei did the same. She looked away, as though she didn't even know me and was about to walk past me while talking to someone else.

I said, "Hey, I want to establish a revolutionary organization. Would you like to join?"

The group of women immediately came to a halt and stared at me as though I were speaking in tongues. I knew that when a revolution is just beginning, the biggest enemy is people's apathy and ignorance, and inspiration is your only path and your only weapon. I said, "Throughout the entire country, revolutions carried out by many different ethnic groups are erupting. The county seat has already been turned upside down, and only Chenggang is still but a pool of stagnant water." At that point, I saw that Hongmei's head, which had been facing the sky, was lowered. She squinted at me, as though seeing a stranger she wanted to get to know. Then, gesturing toward Hongmei, I asked Aiju, "Sister, who is this?" Aiju replied with surprise, "Don't you know each other? She's the daughter-in-law of the former mayor; her husband is a schoolteacher." I said, "Oh, your name is Hongmei. You are cultured and are from the city. But what I can't understand is, why don't you love revolution?"

Embarrassed, Hongmei stood on the side of the road, wearing a thick layer of blush and foundation. She said, "You're the son-in-law of the old branch secretary. I hear that you are also a Party member, so you must be very enlightened."

I said, "My enlightenment isn't worth mentioning, but if I pursue revolution, might I not be worthy of the organization?"

Aiju said, "Brother, if I join your organization, can I earn work points?"

I said, "How can the revolution calculate loss and gain? If you were to ask this question anywhere else, it would surely be grounds for a struggle session."

An older commune member remarked that without work points, everyone would starve. Someone else interjected something, and, laughing happily, they all departed.

Hongmei and I were the only ones left in the street. I initially thought she would leave with the rest of the group, turning into an alley and returning home. Instead, however, she continued standing there with me in the middle of the road. Her blush and foundation seemed to thicken, and a sheen of sweat appeared on her forehead. The corners of her mouth continued to quiver. I looked forward and backward, and saw that the street was now empty except for the two of us. The sun was exceptionally bright, and in the spring warmth there were early traces of summer heat. She and I stood there in a state of feverish anticipation. At first, I didn't know what to say and wasn't sure whether to talk about the revolution or to reminisce about the past. At that moment, the sound of people's shouts coming from Rear Cheng Street poured down on us like a sheet of water. One after another, the village's loudspeakers began loudly broadcasting an announcement by a village cadre: "Commune members charged with building the irrigation canal in front of the village should proceed quickly. Those who are late will be docked work points!" After this announcement was repeated three times, the song "The East Is Red" began blaring over the loudspeakers. Needless to say, this was a song that everyone knew by heart. However, as that muddy-yellow melody descended upon us, my body began to tremble and my hands became covered in a layer of sweat. A yellowish-white glow emerged from under the blush and foundation that covered Hongmei's face. I had no idea why we reacted in this way, and as the bright sound of "The East Is Red" resonated through Chenggang and made its way to the village street, I felt as though a locomotive were rushing through my veins. I saw the melody's notes falling through the air and rolling around at our feet like grapes and oranges. I smelled the orange-yellow music, which lingered around us like an intoxicating fragrance, and I saw how the scent of Hongmei's body emerged through the openings in her wrinkled clothing, as bursts of bright light shone in my direction. In that fragrance, I could smell her warm and delicate perspiration, which was like white velvet intermixed with the scent of her skin. Peering in through the wrinkles in her clothing, I again glimpsed her beautiful cleavage, which was like a mountain canyon. Sweat was pouring down that ravine toward her belly, before being absorbed by the fabric of her shirt. Synthetic fabric is not as absorbent as handwoven cloth, and her shirt had already developed countless sweat marks that appeared dark blue against the lighter fabric, as if ink had spilled over it. Seeing her like that—like me, unsettled by the music—I suddenly became very calm. It was as though I could see victory like a fire burning before me. It was as if the rosy light of the revolution were shining in through my window and onto my bed.

I wiped my sweaty hands on my pants and said, "Hongmei, let's pursue revolution together."

She stared at me for a while, then asked, "These past few days . . . you weren't waiting for me in the temple?"

I smiled. "It was you who said we had never seen each other before."

She said, "I didn't know you would raise this and drop it again." She dejectedly turned away, but then, just as she was in the process of turning back to me, the village's loudspeakers suddenly fell silent. Her face became totally composed, as though the memory that had left her so dejected had suddenly vanished.

"Do you really want to establish a revolutionary organization?"

"I've even come up with a name. We could call it the Red Flag Struggle Brigade."

"You should be careful. You don't want the branch secretary to order someone to poke acupuncture needles into your head and hands."

I laughed. "First I'll have to remove him from power, because if I don't, Chenggang will never be willing to pursue revolution."

At this point, the sound of footsteps resonated from the alleyway. Hongmei's face became deathly pale, and she immediately turned and walked away. I followed her and called out her name, asking her to let me see her hand. With a confused expression, she extended her hand, and I stroked her nails, shining with bright polish. Then

I said, "Someone is coming, so you should leave. Three days from now, I'll start a revolution in the Chenggang production brigade."

She walked away, her lunch pail swinging rhythmically by her side.

The person who emerged from that alleyway was none other than Hongmei's husband, Cheng Qingdong, carrying some books on his way to go teach his class. I hadn't seen him for several years and noticed that he was now wearing a pair of black-rimmed glasses. He appeared very cultured and intellectual and looked as though he were about to be swept away by the revolution.

Chapter 3

Hard and Soft

1. My Father-in-Law Cheng Tianqing and I

I said, "Father, there's something I want to discuss with you."

He replied, "Have a seat. Have you eaten yet?"

I said, "I don't want to sit. There is something I'd like to discuss with you."

He said, "Sit down. What do you want to discuss?"

I said, "There's something I want from you—something you said you would give me."

He said, "And what is that?"

I said, "To be appointed village cadre."

He said, "What kind of village cadre?"

I said, "When Guizhi and I got engaged, you said you would send me to serve in the army for a few years and that after I was discharged you would make me a Cheng Village cadre."

He stared at me in surprise.

I said, "Father, have you forgotten?"

He replied, "No, I haven't forgotten. But currently there are no empty seats on the village committee. We already have a deputy branch secretary, a production team leader, a militia battalion commander—we already have a turnip in every hole. We even have a production team accountant. Whom do you propose I dismiss so that you can step up?"

I said, "Father, you're the eldest member of the village committee and have already served as village branch secretary for several decades. You yourself could step down and let me serve as village branch secretary in your place. That way, you could enjoy more time at home with your children and grandchildren."

His eyes glinted. "*What* did you say?"

I said, "Even if you step down, the Yangtze will continue flowing downstream, one surge after another."

He said, "You bastard!"

I said, "Father, don't you fear the tide of revolution?"

He said, "You've been possessed."

He laughed coldly. "Damn! Where were you when *I* joined the revolution? Where were you when I was delivering letters for the Eighth Route Army? Don't forget that had it not been for me, you would never have been able to join the army in the first place, and your son and daughter would never even have been born. And now you want to make trouble? You have been possessed with revolutionary fever and want revolution. I'm telling you, it is precisely because I noticed you were possessed that I decided not to permit you to join the village committee. Had you not become so possessed, then the very day after you returned from the army I would have had you appointed village chief."

I said, "Father, you shouldn't rest on your laurels. You've already become a stumbling block for the revolution, and the revolutionary tide will soon sweep you away. If you're smart, you'll step aside like Cheng Tianmin and voluntarily hand over power. If you're not, you can simply wait for the revolution to sweep you away."

He shouted, "Get out!"

I left his house.

2. The Revolution Begins for Real

Everyone knows that the revolutionary wind cannot blow directly into one's sails, and that the road to revolution can never be completely straight. Conversely, when a peasant is trying to feed his ox, there will be periods of drought when the grass is dried up; and when trying to grow a tree he may encounter a thunderstorm that washes away the seeds he has planted. However, a lack of wind and rain is not frightening, nor is an excess of wind and rain. All counterrevolutionaries attempt to use mass murder as a means of extinguishing the revolution. They want to kill off the revolution while it is still in the cradle. They figure that the more people that are killed, the smaller the revolution will be, to the point that if everyone is killed, then the revolutionary flame will be completely extinguished. Yet, contrary to the subjective view of these counterrevolutionaries, in fact, the more people who are killed by anti-revolutionaries, the stronger the revolutionary tide becomes and the closer the anti-revolutionaries will come to being exterminated. This is an immutable law. Here in Chenggang, although for the moment murder is still out of the question, there is nevertheless an enormous clamor around attempts by the anti-revolutionaries to stifle and kill off revolutionaries. Who are our enemies? Who are our friends?

When a dog falls into a body of water it doesn't necessarily drown, and after it crawls back to shore it may bite people even more readily than before, and it may even spread its secret weapon—rabies. This is a revolutionary principle that must be noted. How should one deal with this sort of mad dog? The only way is to mobilize the masses such that they start shouting and fighting as though they just saw a mouse crossing the street, and that way they won't leave the mad dog any room to maneuver.

After a few days, I recruited several members of the Cheng clan's older "Qing" generation who had previously served in the army, including Cheng Qinglin, Cheng Qingsen, Cheng Qingshi, and Cheng Qingwang, together with several members of the clan's younger "Xian" generation, including Cheng Xianzhuang, Cheng Xianmin, and Cheng Xianfen. I also recruited several clan members who were still in high school or middle school, including Cheng Qing'an, Cheng Qinglian, Cheng Xianli, Cheng Xianqing, and Cheng Xiancui, as well as other residents of the mixed-surname street, such as Tian Zhuangzhuang, Ren Qizhu, Shi Dagou, Shi Ergou, Zhang Xiaoshu, and so forth. In the end, I recruited more than thirty people in all—men and women, young and old. The eldest was thirty-two years old but not yet married, while the youngest was only fourteen and had just started middle school. They all gathered in the courtyard of our house. Everyone was either sitting or standing—some were squatting down hugging their torsos, others were sitting on a bench, and still others were simply sitting on their own shoes. Those who smoked were enjoying cigarettes from the last couple of packs I had brought back from the army, while those who didn't smoke were eating candy I had bought at the town's department store. The moon was like water, brightly illuminating the courtyard. A light breeze was blowing, and everything looked very good. I told Guizhi to take Hongsheng and Honghua and go pay our neighbors a visit. Everyone was smoking and eating as they listened to my analysis of Chenggang's revolutionary situation, my assessment of the dire status of the world revolution, and my enthusiastic promotion of the Chinese nation. None of them had seen much of the world, but they were all full of hope for the revolution. These were all people whose ideals had not yet been realized. When I had summoned them to the meeting, I made sure to address them all as Brother and Sister, regardless of whether I had gone to their house or had simply run into them in the street. I had pulled each of them aside individually and told them to come to my house at seven o'clock that evening. I had said that I had something important to discuss, but specified that they mustn't tell anyone else about the meeting. In the countryside, people rarely made appointments for specific times and instead would give times of day like "before lunch" or "after lunch," "at sunset" or "at sunrise." Accordingly, everyone was startled when I asked that they meet me at precisely seven o'clock. They asked what the matter was, to which I replied that they would know when they came. Then I turned and walked away, leaving behind an aura of suspense. Half of the people I invited arrived at seven o'clock, while the others arrived closer to eight, and I didn't open my courtyard gate until the moon was already visible overhead.

Needless to say, I didn't fail to notify Xia Hongmei.

In fact, Xia Hongmei was the *first* person I notified. I waited for her at the temple gate until lunchtime, and when I saw her come out to get some food, I quietly told her that I wanted to convene a town revolutionary mobilization meeting that evening. After I explained in detail the relevant objectives, steps, and methods, she blushed with excitement and declared that she would attend even if it killed her. She said that this meeting might come to be seen as Chenggang's Zunyi Conference or its Gutian Conference, and that it might one day even be compared to China's first Communist Party conference, which had been held in 1921 on a boat in the Shanghai harbor—all of which had a deep and historical significance.

Unfortunately, although everyone else I invited showed up that evening, Hongmei did not. But how could the revolution proceed without her? How could she fail to attend such an important meeting? Was the long lecture I had meticulously prepared not written specifically for her ears? The banquet that I had made with her in mind was missing its most important guest. It was as if I had taken a gift basket to visit a relative but then, upon arriving, realized that the intended recipient was not home. So what could I do? The food was already cooked, and even though the guest of honor had not yet arrived, I still had to be a good host and feed my other guests—the same way that if the intended recipient of a gift is not home, I would still need to leave the gift for him of her. Furthermore, everything was done in order to promote the revolution and must be carried out in accordance with the revolution's requirements. Love must be contained within the revolution. Revolution is a foundation, and love is a house built upon that foundation. Revolution is a stem, and love is a flower that grows from that stem. Even without Hongmei, I would still pursue revolution. Without her, I would still ignite the fire of revolution in Chenggang. I had to close that room's door and temporarily let the flower wither! The wave had already arrived, and the ship of revolution had no choice but to weigh anchor and proceed forward. The eagle had already spread its wings, and could not fall again simply because it lacked a wave to ride . . .

At eight on the dot, I formally addressed the young people who were eating, smoking, and talking in my courtyard: "Everyone—silence, please. Students, friends, soldiers—silence, please!" When I addressed the young people in this way, they initially laughed at the novelty of it, but then, in accordance with my unusual request, they all fell silent.

I proceeded to analyze the global and national situation: "An immense thunderbolt has torn open a new world, and the interminable east wind is sweeping away the remaining clouds. Today's world is in the process of entering a new historical period that takes Mao Zedong Thought as its banner. Under the brilliant illumination of Mao Zedong Thought, hundreds of millions of revolutionary soldiers around the world are attempting to repair imperialism and to subject the entire old world to a process of violent advancement. The four seas are rising, and the clouds are raging; the five continents are trembling, and storms are roaring. Looking around the world, we see battle banners of Mao Zedong Thought flying everywhere, as the tide of revolution surges forward!

"Even under this unprecedentedly favorable state of affairs, there are still several flies buzzing around the room and bumping into walls. Led by the imperialism exemplified by the United States and the modern revisionism centered around the Soviet Union, assorted

61

reactionary countries are aggressively colluding with one another, forming a new holy alliance that is anti-Chinese, anti-communist, anti-socialist, and anti-revolutionary. It has advanced a crazed counterattack against revolutionary power, and promotes an anti-Chinese current.

"In China, even in the current socialist historical phase, we still have class division, class conflict, and class struggle. We still have a conflict between socialism and capitalism, and the danger that capitalism will be restored. It is important to recognize the longevity and complexity of these struggles. We must increase our alertness. We must promote socialist education, and correctly understand and resolve issues of class conflict and class struggle. We must correctly differentiate and resolve conflicts between the enemy and the self, as well as class conflicts among the people. Otherwise, our socialist nation will go to the other side. It will change form and undergo a process of capitalist restoration. If that were to happen, history would revert back to the old society, meaning that the people would suffer two rounds of hardship and endure two rounds of punishment.

"Currently, from the grasslands of Inner Mongolia to Yujia harbor on the Bohai peninsula, from the Gobi Desert in the northeast to the coral reef off Hainan Island in the south, in order to prevent revisionism from usurping the Party leadership and to stop a capitalist restoration, various villages and stockades have already thoroughly committed to class struggle, carried out the three great revolutionary movements, implemented socialist education movements, and are currently reordering the revolutionary class ranks in order to beat back capitalist and feudal counterinsurgencies. In the wind and waves of class struggle, from the cities to the countryside, they are training proletarian revolutionary successors, who will be able to fight external enemies and prevent internal problems. These revolutionary successors will further consolidate the proletarian camp and make it even stronger!

"Under the current circumstances, and given the current global and national situation, even if revolution has come somewhat late to our remote county, now it is unfolding here too. It has already pulled down a handful of anti-revolutionary agents in the county committee and county government. Political power has been returned to the hands of the proletariat. But here in Chenggang, and in the old Cheng Village, feudal forces are still powerful, and the light of the revolution's dawn has not yet appeared in the east. Here in Chenggang, the black wall has been built up to the point that it blocks, covers, and smothers all incoming light. Chenggang's revolution is like the dark night of Chi county, and although the wall of the capitalist class is high, the dawn's light is already there behind it, and although the mountain of the feudal class is vast, the proletariat has already begun to awaken, and there are already people who are raising their fists in revolution.

"Meanwhile, Comrade Xia Hongmei from our town of Chenggang—and it is unfortunate that for some reason she was unable to join us tonight—recently went to Beijing, and upon returning she reported that Chairman Mao had received hundreds of millions of young people and had shaken hands with many of them. Xia Hongmei was standing in the first row, and although she did not manage to shake Chairman Mao's hand, when Chairman Mao was shaking someone else's hand, his hand inadvertently bumped against hers. When his hand touched hers, it was as if at that very moment Mao Zedong Thought rained down on our western Henan mountain region and onto our town of Chenggang. In order to bring Mao Zedong Thought directly back to Chenggang and its people, Comrade Xia Hongmei was careful not to use the hand that had touched Chairman Mao's to hold chopsticks or wash her face. However, what response did her enthusiasm for Chairman Mao receive when she returned home? Party branch secretary Cheng Tianqing—who is also my father-in-law—dared bring in three militiamen and Chinese doctors, who claimed that Xia Hongmei had gone mad and needed to be forcibly confined to bed, where they applied twenty-seven acupuncture needles to her head and hands. What kind of behavior is this? This is the reality of a crazed counterattack on the part of the capitalist class and feudal forces against the revolution and the revolutionary proletariat. This is a despicable display of collusion between international anti-revolutionary forces and a small cohort of domestic anti-revolutionary reactionaries.

"In sailing across the ocean, we must rely on the helmsman, just as all living things must rely on the sun for sustenance. Rain provides essential nourishment for tender seedlings, and those engaged in revolution must similarly rely on Mao Zedong Thought. Comrades, fellow soldiers, let us sing this most beautiful song as we take action and welcome the dawn light. Let us trample Chenggang's darkness and welcome the first ray of sunlight on our road to revolution. Plum blossoms delight in a sky full of snow, and it's not surprising that flies have frozen to death. We have our great, invincible Mao Zedong Thought as our weapon, the strength and unity of our seven hundred million countrymen as our shield, and fraternal production brigades and revolutionary youth to serve as models. As we gaze out at the area around the Great Wall, we see furious fists rise up like a forest. As we look up and down the great river, we see the revolution surging forward like the ocean. Let us shout and surge forward, raise our fists, spread our steps, and open the new era and new road of Chenggang's revolution!

"Fellow soldiers, comrades, classmates! The first thing we must do, before the sun comes up tomorrow, is destroy the Cheng Brothers memorial arch, which represents the thought and power of Chenggang's anti-revolutionary faction. Today, the victorious light of the Cultural Revolution is shining down on the mountains and rivers of our great nation, but here in Chenggang the first place that the sun's rays touch in the morning is this feudal archway, which means that the first thing that motorists and pedestrians see is not the words LONG LIVE CHAIRMAN MAO but rather the phrase CHENG BROTHERS HISTORIC

SITE and the words IMPERIAL EDICT. Moreover, the latter characters are golden and resplendent and were written by hand by an emperor. What does this mean? It means that, even now, feudalism dares to defy socialism and dares to wage war against us. Fellow soldiers, comrades, *with power to spare we must pursue the fleeing enemy, and cannot simply seek fame like the hegemon-king Xiang Yu*. Let's come together and attack corruption, bind the black dragons, quell the tigers and leopards, and pursue the enemy. Let's destroy this stone archway, destroy the Party branch, and recover the Chenggang production team's political power!

"After retrieving our political power, we can select new village cadres based on everyone's revolutionary performance and ability. We can reconstitute a village committee, and whoever is able to serve as village chief can serve as village chief, whoever is able to serve as production team leader can serve as production team leader, and whoever is able to serve as militia battalion commander can serve as militia battalion commander. We need to replace everyone—from every production team's accountant to its leader, from the waterworks official charged with overseeing the irrigation canals to the scorekeepers charged with keeping track of the work points for each production team—we need to replace everyone! All political power must be handed to the revolutionaries. Even the watchman charged with guarding the fields and the forest ranger up in the mountains—even those positions must be taken by our revolutionaries or their relatives. After Chenggang's revolution succeeds and political power is restored, and after we manage to seize and accumulate revolutionary experience, our next step will be to use our victory to seize power in the Chenggang town government. The town government complex happens to be located here in Chenggang Village, but we definitely cannot permit revolutionary youth from other production teams to come and seize the government's great seal. We cannot permit youth from production teams in Liu Village, Zhuang Village, Datour, or Xiaotour to direct us. Instead, we must make every effort to cultivate ourselves into national cadres, into red revolutionary successors. We must administer and lead the members of Chenggang's seventeen communes, as well as their administration and general affairs.

"Comrades, fellow soldiers, classmates, the revolution requires that we endure hardship and sacrifice. It requires that we set aside our personal and family interests, and continually fight selfishness and repudiate revisionism. It asks that we support collectivism and fight individualism. However, the revolution is also capable of considering everyone's personal and family interests. As of tonight, everyone who takes part in an ordinary revolutionary activity will get credit for a full day's work after having worked for only half a day. For coming tonight we will give everyone ten work points. Everyone who takes part in some extraordinary revolutionary activity—such as destroying the memorial archway tomorrow morning—will receive twenty work points. Everyone who brings a steel tool like a shovel or hammer tomorrow will receive two work points, and everyone who brings an ordinary tool like a spade or a hoe will receive one work point. I, Gao Aijun, will record all of these work point allocations in my notebook, and after the production team is replaced in a few days, I will immediately notify the local production teams, so that your work points may be transferred to the correct team.

"Fellow soldiers, comrades, today's meeting of the Chenggang production team revolutionary mobilization is hereby concluded. Let us forge ourselves into red successors of the proletariat revolution. Let each of us temper ourselves into steel while standing in the storm of class struggle!

"After everyone leaves this meeting and returns home, you must all remain vigilant and mustn't reveal the intentions of our meeting to anyone. You mustn't oversleep tomorrow, and even while asleep you should keep the revolution in your heart. At six o'clock sharp, everyone should meet at the front of the village and wait for my directions.

"Please leave now, but tread lightly when walking along the village roads. You don't want to make a ruckus and risk having our class enemies notice our activities."

At this mobilization meeting, I felt as though I were at a mass study session. I spoke in a mix of local dialect and military-accented Mandarin. I enthusiastically lectured nonstop for an hour and half, sounding as though I were reciting everything from memory. Having prepared by reading the newspapers and studying for three days, I was able to speak fluently, gushing tirelessly for ninety minutes. Although I knew I spoke well, I hadn't realized that I was able to speak *that well*. While in the army, my commanding officer often said that I had what it takes to become an officer, and my instructor said that I had what it takes to become an instructor, though our regiment commissar didn't say that I had what it takes to become a commissar. That night, I lectured until the youths from the production team were stupefied, awed by my talent and ability. I wanted to make them feel as though I had gone to Anyuan with Mao Zedong, and that they were all revolutionaries who had been sent to Chenggang by exemplary higher-ups. In the past they had always heard my father-in-law ramble on in his heavy accent, but when they heard me speak that night, it was as if, while eating a meal of coarse grain, they suddenly took a bite of rice syrup.

Someone exclaimed, "Aijun, you speak so well! Where did you learn to speak like this?"

I said, "I'm constantly studying and reading newspapers, after which I go out and put what I've learned into practice."

Another person said, "Do you really dare to overthrow your own father-in-law?"

I said, "I'm not the one who wants to overthrow him; it's the revolution that wants to overthrow him."

The other person said, "Your father-in-law has not yet assigned our family a housing plot. If you assume power, will you sort out our housing-plot problem?"

I said, "Every plot of land should be controlled by a member of the proletariat. In assigning housing plots, we should first assign them to revolutionaries."

The other person said, "I'm a revolutionary, and you are welcome to send me to die for the revolution." Then he asked, "Would I really get work points for participating in the revolution?"

I replied, "Revolutionaries may endure hardship, but they won't have participated in the revolution in vain. Work points, grain rations, and housing bases—once we seize power, will these even be things we think about?"

He said, "Now, you must remember this."

I replied, "Don't worry. I have thirty men and won't lose any of them."

He said, "Aijun, you speak very well. In the future, you should organize us to read the paper and have study sessions, for which we should also get work points."

I said, "Of course I will. We'll read the newspapers, we'll study Chairman Mao's quotations, and we'll memorize Chairman Mao's texts. The revolution requires that you endure hardship, yet it also won't permit you to endure hardship. In the future, if any of you want to place work points ahead of the revolution, you should make sure that the revolution won't come raining down on your own head."

Everyone dispersed.

The moon emerged from behind Cheng Temple and silently slid up to the front of the town. The light was as clear as water, and the scenery was endless. The village streets were extraordinarily quiet, and the sound of everyone walking away was like a stone skipping over the surface of a pond. The footsteps ebbed farther and farther away, until there was the noise of doors opening and closing, followed by silence.

I escorted out the last few youths who were still asking questions and watched as they walked into an alley and disappeared into the shadows. Then I looked around at Chenggang's peaceful, moonlit scenery. Immersed in the delight that the revolution—which had not yet begun—would eventually succeed, my heart started pounding. I stood like the protagonist of a revolutionary movie standing on the deck of a boat in a raging storm and about to reach a wharf, and I wished my hair and clothing were being similarly buffeted by the wind, but unfortunately at that moment there was only a light evening breeze. If only there were wind and an ocean! If only I were standing there with long hair flying in the wind! It was not without regret that I placed my hand on my head, debating whether or not I should grow out my hair for the revolution. At that moment, just as I was about to head inside, someone emerged from the shadows behind our courtyard wall.

The storm had, in fact, arrived.

It arrived in a shocking fashion.

I asked, "Who is it?!"

She didn't answer and instead continued walking toward me.

I repeated, "Who is it?"

She walked up to me.

I said, "Why are you only arriving now? The meeting has already concluded."

She leaned against me, her entire body trembling. She placed her hands around my neck and pressed her icy-hot lips against mine. As though closing a door, she cut off my questions and complaints. I didn't know what had just happened. I didn't know why she would suddenly rush over, like a hero without enemies. Half embracing her and half pulling her away from the center of the street, I managed to move her to the shadowy area in front of my courtyard gate. Then I pushed her away and asked why she hadn't attended the meeting. She gazed at my face in the moonlight, then with both hands grasped the hand with which I had tried to push her away. "What makes you think I didn't come? Given that this was our first revolutionary mobilization meeting, how could I not attend?" She continued, "I was afraid someone might unexpectedly interrupt the meeting, so after lunch, I used the hot weather as an excuse to go up to the temple to take my father-in-law a fan. Seeing that he was sitting there quietly, I then went to your father-in-law's house to give him a medicine bottle he had left at my house. Upon finding your father-in-law at home listening to someone recounting an anecdote from Zhuge Liang's Three Kingdoms military campaign, I left. I passed in front of the houses of the Party branch secretary and the production team leader, then walked through the crowds in front of the village where people had gathered to enjoy the cool. Seeing that everything was normal, I came to wait outside this gate, listening to you mobilize the masses and enjoying the scenery."

She said, "Aren't you afraid that word of our activities will get out?"

I didn't reply and instead simply stared at her as if we were two revolutionaries in love, who had been separated but then happened to meet again on a small path under a moonlit sky. I wanted to hug her tight but found that I couldn't. I discovered with surprise that she was not only a warm, beautiful young woman from the city but furthermore a capable, enlightened, and experienced rural revolutionary. I placed one hand on her hip and ran the other through her hair. I stared at her for a while and finally began feverishly kissing her forehead, eyebrows, ears, eyes, nose, and mouth. But when I pressed my lips against hers a second time, she again asked me the same question: "Aren't you afraid that word of our activities might get out?"

I replied, "I'm not afraid, because whatever I might have overlooked, I know that you have already thought about it."

I spoke so well that my words were able to melt her heart!

She said, "Brother Aijun, you speak so well. You are clearly made of revolutionary material. If only you had returned a year earlier, our Chenggang production team's revolution would have already succeeded."

I said, "*The strong pass of the enemy is like a wall of iron, yet with firm strides we are conquering its summit.* If we apply the whip to the horses, we can definitely have Chenggang's revolutionary carriage drive nonstop night and day and press forward at high speed. In another two days and three nights, after Chenggang's revolution has already succeeded, and we have stabilized our position, we will revolutionize the Chenggang town government. When the time comes, I can become the town's Party committee secretary and you can become mayor."

She exclaimed, "My god . . . I'm not even a Party member yet!"

I replied, "You may not be in the Party, but your heart is already in the Party. After we overthrow my father-in-law, our first task will be to expand the Chenggang Party branch so that you can become a cadre."

She was very moved by what I said and was struck by the revolutionary gift I had brought her. Like a starving person who suddenly receives a snow-white steamed bun, she stared at that lovely gift, at a loss for words. The village was extraordinarily quiet, and the moonlight lingered over half of her body like water on a bed of sand. Her face was positioned in the shadow cast by the doorway, and at that moment I couldn't tell whether her face was faintly ruddy or fiery gold. I could only hear her heart pounding like a clock and her breathing as coarse as a roof beam. Needless to say, revolution had united our love canals and our affection was surging down them. She said, "Aijun, I feel faint." Then she placed my hand on her chest and collapsed into my embrace. I let my hand rest in hers like a fish swimming in water.

Perhaps I wasn't a very noble person. Perhaps, at that time, I wasn't yet a completely pure revolutionary. Perhaps I was simply confirming the dictum: *The revolution is where the revolutionaries are, because everything they do is necessarily for the revolution.* Like a snake, my hand extended toward her crotch, which was covered by a large wet spot, as though we had just had a heavy rain. My hand paused on the edge of that field. I remembered how I had missed the opportunity to fully watch and enjoy her when we met on the edge of town. I assumed that Hongmei must be completely different from Guizhi. Everything about her was attractive, and every part of her body exuded an intoxicating fragrance, including her hair, skin, the arch of her nose, the corners of her mouth, and her breasts. She even had a snakelike mark around her waist where she had been wearing her belt too tight. I wanted to examine her private parts, and after I was satisfied, I would finally do that thing. But I knew that that night I wouldn't be able to appreciate her as I had done that day outside of town. Instead, I could only extend my hand into that forest and grassland and savor her, as though wading barefoot in shallow water and picking flowers from among the water plants—not only in order to pick flowers but also to appreciate the water beneath the plants. I saw myself hunched over and walking through the water, and saw myself roll up my pants and carefully step through the stream, and saw my bare feet slowly slipping through the mud beneath the green water plants like a frightened fish about to burrow into the mud. Needless to say, wading slowly through that shallow water was much better than hurriedly diving in. When you abruptly enter, you are unable to enjoy the scenery, see the tiny fish swimming amidst the water plants or glimpse the sun peaking down through the gaps in the leaves. When the sunlight shines down on the water, it is as though a gold coin has fallen down onto the muddy bottom, and the golden light illuminates all the underwater roots of grasses, flowers, and trees, the nests of fish and shrimp.

I'll never forget the sight of her bare, sunlit upper body that day outside of town, and my hand seemed to pause in its exploration of the wet area between her legs. In the moonlight, I used my hand to sample the taste of those water plants, as if trying to count how many plants and flowers might be growing in that pool. After my index and middle fingers entered the water, they selected a plant stem and tugged at it. The moon shifted to the southeast, and as the shadow was passing over my body, it produced a faint whistling sound.

I said, "Hongmei, you won't call me a hooligan, will you?"

She said, "Aijun, I know you're only doing this because you love me."

Upon hearing this, my heart melted, like sugar dissolving in warm water, and I felt as though I were about to float away. But at that moment came the sound of footsteps from Center Cheng Street, together with the sound of someone talking. Hongmei and I both heard Guizhi leading the children back from her mother's house, and we both shuddered and froze.

Damn that Cheng Guizhi!

I said, "Let's go to the hillock behind the temple."

She replied, "Be patient. Tomorrow morning this stone archway will be destroyed, and after the revolution has succeeded, we can go to the bank of Thirteen Li River next to the village and live out the remainder of our days without having to see a single soul."

Upon saying this, she got up and walked away, departing in the opposite direction from that in which Guizhi and the children were approaching—like a backstage worker in a film ducking into an alleyway in order to avoid being seen. She left me all alone, as Guizhi's footsteps approached.

Damn that Guizhi!

3. The Battle of the Memorial Arch

I never expected what happened. Indeed, who could have? Our first Chenggang revolution ultimately ended in failure.

Having said that, we should have seen this coming.

At dawn, after the cock crowed three times, I quietly got out of bed without waking up anyone else, then grabbed an eight-pound hammer I had left outside the door. Finally, after checking again on Guizhi and the children, who were all still sound asleep, I went out.

Our meeting was held in the third production team's wheat field, and by the time I arrived, five or six hot-blooded youths had already gathered there. They were holding hammers and iron rods, together with shovels, hoes, and other tools. Someone asked, "Will they really give us work points for coming?" I replied, "Didn't I say so yesterday?" Reassured, the other person walked away. Next, Cheng Qinglin, Cheng Qingsen, Cheng Xianzhu, Cheng Xianfen, Cheng Qing'an, Tian Zhuangzhuang, Ren Qizhu, Zhang Xiaoshu, and Shi Ergou arrived one after the other. Naturally, Hongmei also came, arriving a little after I did. I asked her to take out the list of names we had prepared and, using a flashlight, record the names, weapons, and work points of everyone in attendance. Then I arranged for every-one to stand in formation like soldiers, with the tall ones in front and the shorter ones at the back, men in front and women behind. Then, leading them in marching and singing revolutionary songs, I eliminated the disorder from the regiment. By the time light began to appear in the eastern sky, I had already led the thirty-six-person regiment from Rear Cheng Street to the village's southern entrance on Front Cheng Street.

Although our steps were not perfectly coordinated, our voices nevertheless gradually became strong and synchronized. On the way from the marketplace to the area in front of the temple, the sound of our footsteps resembled popcorn popping on a summer day. But once I began chanting *one, two, one, two*, everyone's steps fell into a set rhythm. Then, everyone followed Hongmei's lead and started sing-ing the lyrics to "Sailing the Seas under the Helmsman's Command," their footsteps becoming completely synchronized. This wasn't sur-prising, given that the procession was made up of students, youth, and demobilized soldiers. The song dispelled everyone's drowsiness and silenced their idle banter.

Hongmei addressed the troops, saying, "I want everyone who refuses to sing and prefers to speak to step forward. Are you not afraid of being docked work points?"

Then, the entire regiment fell silent.

74

Hongmei shouted, "Everyone sing. Do you know that today is double work-points day? If you aren't going to sing, then you should at least shout."

Their voices resonated in front of the temple, as everyone sang until their throats were on fire. In the predawn haze, our troops proceeded east, heading in the direction of the eastern mountains, where the sun would rise. We marched from Rear Cheng Street to Center Cheng Street and then from Center Cheng Street to Front Cheng Street. We were careless and allowed ourselves to become blinded by the revolution and by the victory that surely awaited us. We noticed that people who had just woken up were opening their courtyard gates and staring at us. Rubbing his eyes, one of them saw us and asked, "What are you doing?" One of the troops proudly responded, "We're joining the revolution." The first person said, "But the sun isn't even up yet. What revolution are you joining?" The other person replied, "Before the sun rises, we are going to tear down the Cheng Brothers memorial arch." The first person stopped rubbing his eyes, and his face turned green upon realizing that Chenggang was going to be turned upside down. We noticed his surprise, and although we saw the people standing in their entranceways staring at us, we didn't notice that there were many more open doors than there had been before we left to greet the third production team in the marketplace, nor did we realize that many people had woken up even earlier than we had. In fact, we didn't even notice that the red double doors to the temple, which normally stayed closed until some time after the sun comes up, were already open.

As we proceeded west from Front Cheng Street, the eastern sky became completely illuminated. I don't know when the sun—which was the color of a pool of blood—reached the top of the mountain, but it was now illuminating the entire land. It lit up all the surrounding villages and towns, together with all the ravines and gullies. It left a bright layer of light over the memorial arch. We saw a group of people standing under the arch. There must have been more than a hundred of them, and they seemed to include representatives from every family. They were all carrying poles, pitchforks, cleavers, axes, scythes, and clubs, and looking at us as if we were the enemy. More importantly, in that crowd of a hundred-plus people, there were no youngsters, and instead most of the people were either adult laborers or old men, their white beards gleaming in the sunlight like fire. They were the fathers or grandfathers of the younger members of our own contingent. This crowd also included some women, who were the mothers of some of those who didn't have fathers. I was astounded by how many people were there, and was also surprised to find my own father-in-law standing on a stone hitching post beneath the archway. He had his hands on his hips and was staring furiously at our contingent, our footsteps, and our singing.

We came to a stop, as our steps and singing were wiped out by his gaze. In the ensuing silence, everyone crowded together, then everyone turned and looked at me. I saw that Hongmei appeared somewhat confused. There was a layer of perspiration on her forehead, and beads of sweat were glistening like pearls in the sun.

I solemnly walked over to the regiment and then, with my hands on my hips, I shouted to my father-in-law, "Comrade Mao instructed, 'We are faced with two types of social contradiction: namely, contradictions between the enemy and the self, and contradictions within the people themselves. These are two qualitatively different types of contradictions. Who is our enemy? Who is our friend? These are the key questions that revolution must answer.' Cheng Tianqing . . ."

I walked forward again and came to a halt about ten paces from my father-in-law. I addressed him in an even louder voice: "Cheng Tianqing, today the revolutionary youth of the Chenggang production team have come to destroy the stone memorial arch left behind by the feudal dynasty. You have brought a deluded crowd to stand in our way . . . I just want to ask you one question: Are you a member of the Communist Party, or are you an agent of the feudal-bourgeois class?"

I shouted as though I were fighting a battle, with a heroic spirit capable of conquering mountains and rivers. I saw that my questions were as strong as iron and steel and were hurtling toward Cheng Tianqing like bombs. He stood under the memorial arch's right-hand column, appearing as though he wanted to say something but was at a loss for words.

I hollered, "Cheng Tianqing, answer me! Are you an enemy, or are you a member of the Chinese Communist Party? Whom do you view as the enemy, revolutionaries or capitalists? Everything you are doing is already at odds with the Party's objectives, and if you don't pull back from the brink, you'll end up crushing your own foot with the stone you are trying to carry. As Chairman Mao said, 'If you treat your comrades as your enemies, you will place yourself in the position of the enemy. If you are determined to place yourself in the position of the enemy, you shouldn't be surprised that this son-in-law of yours won't recognize you as a relative!'"

His complexion went from green to yellow.

I hollered, "If you aren't prepared to answer my question, then you should tell your crowd to withdraw."

He didn't tell the crowd to withdraw. Instead, he turned to them while vigorously gesturing at us and issuing his distinctive command. I thought that crowd of commune members—carrying their poles, vegetable cleavers, and wooden clubs—was about to charge at us, but to my surprise, when he shook his head, everyone simply put down their cleavers, clubs, and poles, then moved to either side of the memorial arch. Next, six or seven men and women in their seventies and eighties emerged from the crowd, including Cheng Xianzhu's grandfather, Cheng Xianqing's grandfather, Cheng Qinglin's grandfather, and Tian Zhuangzhuang's grandmother. There was also Cheng Qing'an's maternal grandmother, who always dressed and ate like a young woman. They were all unarmed but maintained an impassive expression that left it impossible to determine whether they were frightened or whether they in fact shared their grandchildren's revolutionary fervor. Their wrinkles and gray hair flying in the morning sun became their most fearsome weapons. They walked over unsteadily from the memorial arch, tearfully calling out their grandchildren's names:

"Xianqing, quick, come home with your grandfather. This isn't a revolution. By being here, you are smashing your ancestors on the head with a hammer."

"Qinglin, your grandfather is begging you to go home. No matter how poor we might be, we can't try to earn work points by knocking down the memorial arch."

"Qingju, Qinghua, go home with your grandmother. If you want to knock down this memorial arch, you should first bury your grandmother beneath it . . ."

There followed a wave of tearful cries from these grandparents, after which the many mothers and fathers surged forward. Calling out their children's names, they repeated what the grandparents had said and, in the blink of an eye, shattered the revolutionary procession. They collected the hammers, shovels, and poles their children and grandchildren had been holding. With everyone shouting, there was complete chaos below the memorial arch at that moment. Shards of sunlight that had been shattered by the crowds drifted down, and the spittle from everyone's shouts was flying through the air. The road was piled high with the yellow footprints and red voices of comrades on their way home, and there were countless poles and ropes lying on the side of the road.

That was how our procession dissolved, like water absorbed by the soil. These first flowers of spring shriveled up when faced with an unexpected frost.

That was how Chenggang's first revolutionary movement died a premature death.

Hongmei was standing on the side of the road, and holding her hands up to her mouth like a bullhorn, she shouted, "Comrades, comrades-in-arms! We cannot leave. Everyone must stay behind! Our relatives are not the enemy, but we also cannot let ourselves be their captives. Wouldn't it be the ultimate humiliation if we were defeated not by true class enemies but by our own mothers, fathers, grandmothers, and grandfathers?!"

I ran over and stood on a stone hitching post in front of Cheng Tianqing. Shouting even louder than Hongmei, I proclaimed: "Comrades-in-arms, comrades! Increase your discipline, then the revolution's success will be inevitable. Everyone must increase their discipline! Everyone must stay here, and you mustn't rest until you have achieved our objective! Everyone should wipe their eyes, so you can all see what we are doing today. Our actions today have ramifications for the fate of the Party and the nation. Mao Zedong Thought and feudalism, capitalism, and revisionism are having their first encounter here in Chenggang and have entered into a raging battle. Accordingly, I ask that everyone not leave. If we can persevere, we can still achieve victory!"

Our shouts echoed back and forth beneath the memorial arch before radiating outward. Above the sky, below the earth, in the road, in the fields, in the villages, in the streets, and out toward the distant Balou Mountains—everywhere was filled with our bright red shouts, with our ardent enthusiasm and fervor. Some young people had freed themselves from their parents' grasp and were trying to stay behind to complete the mission, and it was at that point that Hongmei's husband, Cheng Qingdong, emerged from the crowd and rushed forward, grabbing her like a madman.

Hongmei struggled to free herself, and in doing so she accidentally knocked off her husband's glasses and ripped a piece of his clothing. I saw her hollering, partially out of desperation and partially to summon me. I jumped down from the hitching post, but just as I was about to go rescue her, a snowy-white, blood-red slap materialized on my left cheek.

My mother suddenly appeared before me.

"Get out!" she cursed, "If you dare make any more trouble, I swear I'll bash my brains out against this memorial arch!"

. . . .

That was how the Battle of the Memorial Arch ended in defeat.

Chapter 4

Overcast Skies

1. Revolutionary Thought

I didn't find Xia Hongmei on the banks of Thirteen Li River. We had originally agreed that after destroying the memorial arch, we would burn all the village's images of local deities and other idols and then meet up on the banks of Thirteen Li River after lunch, to celebrate our victory together.

But the Battle of the Memorial Arch ended in failure.

Before the revolution even had a chance to mature, it had been smothered in its cradle by feudalism. The wind sweeping through the tower heralds the storm in the mountains. As I headed toward the banks of Thirteen Li River, the other villagers gave me an odd look, as though I were possessed. I saw the young revolutionaries who had marched with me that morning. Now they were each holding a rice bowl while sitting on a stone in front of their house, and upon seeing me they either lowered their heads and started eating or else immediately turned away. I don't know if they didn't dare look at me because they felt embarrassed by their cowardly behavior or whether they—like their parents and grandparents—now thought I wasn't worth a second glance.

I assumed they must have felt embarrassed, because the blood rushing through their veins is revolutionary blood.

Thirteen Li River originates from deep in the Balou Mountains and goes from west to east. The river is thirteen *li* long, which is why it's called Thirteen Li River. It comes nearest to Chenggang three *li* south of the village, where it forms a shallow shoal on its way to Yi River. This shoal is what the people of Chenggang call "the riverbank." On that particular day, no one knew how depressed and discouraged I felt while standing on that riverbank. Unable to find any trace of Hongmei, I remembered a verse that all of you surely know by heart:

> You lost your husband Liu,
> I lost my wife Yang,
> Both souls have ascended to heaven.
>
> I ask the deity Wu Gang what he has brought,
> And with both hands he pours us
> A cup of osmanthus.

Then I wept, and pearl-like tears clattered noisily onto the stones beneath my feet.

There wasn't a soul to be seen on the riverbank, and as the river noisily rushed past, countless gold and silver scales of afternoon sun appeared on the water's surface. In the middle of the river there was a dam made of bowl- and fist-size stones, which raised the water to the level of my shins. The dam made some of the greenish-blue water flow northward along an irrigation canal located behind Cheng Temple. In this way that water was able to fulfill its destiny. As the rest of the water continued toward Yi River, it left behind a continuous white and bright sound that transformed the riverbank's stillness into a broad, deep expanse. Overhead, a couple of silver-white waterbirds were flying back and forth, and as their feathers fell through the air they spiraled and glittered in the sunlight, eventually landing on the water and flowing downstream. There were also countless tiny carp, some of which had already entered the birds' mouths but struggled out in midair and dove back into the water like knives, disappearing in the blink of an eye. Other than myself, there was no one to be seen along the entire riverbank. The first revolution had ended in failure, and it would have been excellent if Hongmei had shown up at that moment, as we had agreed. She was my only revolutionary comrade and my only reassurance. She was my only supporter and defender. She was my thought's sustenance and affection. She was my blood, my flesh, my spirit, my very essence.

I walked back and forth along the riverbank, repeatedly looking in the direction of Chenggang. When the revolution is advancing, we have boundless enthusiasm; but in moments of sorrow, there is only the endless sound of the river flowing. After I became fatigued and my eyelids grew heavy, I selected a stone from a high bank and sat down on it.

I don't know how long I sat there.

As I was sitting there, I proceeded—without actually realizing what I was doing—to engage in an activity that tainted the reputation of the revolution.

I masturbated.

It was only after I finished that I finally awakened from my stupor. I slapped my own face, then rinsed my hands, washed myself, and glanced over at the sun—which was now sinking below the horizon. At that point, I had no choice but to return to town.

The next day, after recruiting a child to take Hongmei a note that said, "Let's meet at the agreed-upon location," I went back down to the riverbank to wait for her. When I finally realized that she wasn't coming, I recklessly proceeded to her home, which was constructed in a courtyard arrangement found only in northern Chinese rural communities. The courtyard was paved with bricks that had been baked to a greenish-red color, and the corner posts and roof beams of the surrounding tile-roofed houses were all made from high-quality bricks. The borders of the doors and windows were tightly packed with brick inlays, and although the other walls were made of simple adobe, they were nevertheless covered in a mixture of clay and lime that gleamed in the sunlight. While this courtyard was not as imposing as that of Cheng Temple, the fact that Hongmei's family lived in a courtyard complex at all—at a time when most of the town's other houses were simple tile- or thatch-roofed buildings—revealed her family's position and status. The entire courtyard was filled with the smell of sulfur from freshly baked bricks and tiles. I was deeply envious of the former mayor, of Cheng Qingdong, and of this house. I thought that *I* should be the one who owned this house and courtyard. When I arrived, Cheng Qingdong was under the window of the tile-roofed house on the east side of the courtyard, brewing some Chinese medicine. He poured a large dose of medicine into an earthenware pot, added some water, then used his hand to gently push down the leaves floating on the surface. Next to the window was a bamboo basket half full of medicinal dregs. I walked into that courtyard of my dreams and let the odor of sulfur drift past my nose, then detected the faint medicinal scent that lay underneath it. Standing in the middle of the courtyard, I hungrily took a whiff.

"Cheng Qingdong, is Hongmei home?"

He turned around and gazed at me coldly.

"She returned to her mother's home."

I stared in surprise.

"When did she leave?"

He turned to put the medicine pot in the window.

"Yesterday, after lunch."

My heart lurched.

"When will she return?"

He placed a paper lid over the pot.

"I don't know."

I suddenly had an urge to go into the former mayor's house and sit there for a while. I wanted to enter Hongmei's room and sit on her bed. I wanted to gaze at the table and the chair in the mayor's house and at Hongmei's bedstead, the legs of her bed, the pattern and color of her sheets, the size of her pillow, the fabric of her pillowcase, together with any hair or sweat she might have left behind on the pillow—I wanted to devour all of this. But as I stood in the courtyard, it seemed as though Cheng Qingdong didn't even see me. After he had finished brewing his medicine, he pushed the dregs into a pile in the basket, then collected up the remainder that had fallen to the ground. I knew he was deliberately ignoring me because he was terrified of revolutionaries. Non-revolutionaries are always terrified of revolutionaries. I saw that there was a shovel leaning against the wall next to that window. The former mayor didn't employ any workers, and neither he nor his son were workers. Neither of them belonged to the proletariat, and yet, leaning against the wall was a shovel with a sharp, rounded blade. It occurred to me that I could use that shovel to chop Cheng Qingdong's head open like a watermelon. Instead, however, I simply stood there and said, "Qingdong, how many years has it been since we last saw each other?"

The hand with which he was cleaning up the dregs paused in midair.

"Aijun, you should have stayed in the army. Why did you have to return?"

I replied, "To pursue revolution, of course. I returned to pursue revolution."

He said, "How can Chenggang accommodate a revolutionary like yourself?"

I laughed and said, "If it can accommodate Hongmei, it can accommodate me."

He didn't understand what I meant by this. He stared at me for a moment, then looked down and continued cleaning up the dregs.

I asked, "Who's sick?"

He replied, "No one is sick."

I said, "Then who is this medicine for?"

He said, "For me."

I said, "What's wrong with you?"

He said, "There's nothing wrong with me. I'm perfectly fine."

I said, "If you're fine, then why do you need medicine?"

He said, "As a supplement."

I didn't ask anything else. At that point, I very much wanted to sit down. I wanted to go inside and sit down. I looked around, and my gaze came to rest on a bright red chair in the doorway of the main room.

I said, "Qingdong, we're former classmates who haven't seen each other for years. Why don't you invite me inside to sit down?"

He replied, "Gao Aijun, you should leave. My home cannot accommodate a revolutionary like yourself."

My face began to burn, and I said, "Are you really turning me away?"

He replied impassively, "I'm not turning you away. I'm simply asking you to leave."

I once again glanced over at the gleaming shovel, then walked out of that beautiful house that was filled with the smell of sulfur and Chinese medicine.

I emerged from Hongmei's home feeling dejected and even depressed. How could Qingdong have failed to invite me to sit with him? How could Hongmei have left without even saying goodbye? How could she, as soon as the revolution encountered a slight obstacle, have simply retreated to the shelter of her mother's house? How could she have forgotten about our scheduled rendezvous?

I spent the next three days in bed.

I fell into a deep funk and a dark depression. I felt that the revolution's future was bleak and my own life's prospects were uncertain. I felt like I was a skiff someone has abandoned in a vast ocean. But one day, at lunchtime, just as I was feeling most hopeless, Hongsheng began shouting outside, then ran up to my bed.

"Father, father! There's a letter! There's a letter for you . . ."

The letter was in a leather envelope, on the back of which was printed, in red characters, the phrase, LONG LIVE THE GREAT PROLETARIAN CULTURAL REVOLUTION! On the front was my name and address, and in the bottom right-hand corner was an empty space where the sender's name and address ordinarily would be. That was a letter from heaven, a letter from beyond heaven. It was a beacon of light brought by an angel to cheer up my dark spirits.

Aijun,

First of all, I salute your struggles on behalf of the revolution. Forgive me for having left without saying goodbye. I'll explain everything after I return. I'll return to Chenggang on the 26th. The dawn is before us, and the revolution will surely proceed from darkness into the light. I sincerely hope our revolutionary friendship will last forever!

Hongmei, 5/22

This was truly an angelic beacon illuminating my dark soul. Not only was Hongmei going to return to Chenggang and to my side, but more importantly, she wrote that she hoped our revolutionary friendship would last forever! And what is a revolutionary friendship? A revolutionary friendship is precisely the conjugal love that Hongmei and I shared. Like husband and wife, we would gaze at each other and caress each other when no one else was around. I would disrobe her one button at a time, as though ambling through one of the city's gardens. I would shift my attention from her hair, forehead, nose, mouth, and neck, to her breasts, stomach, and thighs. I would carefully inspect her most hidden areas and would slowly caress her body. She would accept my gaze and my caresses, and I would of course accept her attention, her touches, and her demands. From this friendship we drew the power to struggle, to discuss revolutionary countermeasures, and to plan revolutionary action.

I read the letter three times in a row.

When I noticed that Hongsheng was watching me, I gave him ten cents and told him to go to the store to buy some candy.

For lunch, I asked Guizhi to make me a bowl of noodles, and for dinner, I asked her to fry me some scallion pancakes.

Meanwhile, as the sun rose in the east and illuminated the four seas, my spirit welled up in my chest. I saw the dawn's rays lighting up the sky, the mountains and rivers full of love, and the road of socialism stretching ahead—as we proceed forward, hand in hand, onward and onward, onward and onward.

2. A Major Explosion (I)

The next morning, I got up and went to meet Hongmei.

My fighting spirit was soaring, and my passion was overflowing. I proceeded briskly down the road toward her, crushing the roadside forests and mountains beneath my feet.

Chenggang was a journey of about seventy-nine *li* from the county seat, of which sixty *li* was through the mountains. A long-distance bus typically needed about an hour and a half to traverse this distance, and if the bus was on the slow side it could take more than two hours. I assumed Hongmei would have breakfast and then take the bus, meaning that she would be on the first bus to reach town and would arrive not long after sunrise. I reached a peak eighteen *li* from Chenggang and waited there. This was a high peak from which you could see for more than ten *li* in all directions. At that time of year, the foliage of the pagoda trees on the side of the road was green and lush, and the ground was covered with a thin carpet of leaves that had withered prematurely. There were also some blossoms swaying forlornly on a branch, like stubborn clumps of snow. The hills on either side of the road were full of waist-high wheat stalks. Some of the stalks were green and gave off a damp odor, while others were yellow and weak. A layer of bare yellow earth was visible through the stalks and leaves, giving a strong earthy odor that spread in all directions. Ridges of peaks that nearly reached the sky extended in every direction, making this a truly wonderful setting. The road snaked out behind and in front of me like a gleaming silk thread. It ran through the Balou Mountains and disappeared into the Funiu Mountains. The air looked as though it had been washed clean, and the trees were a bright green. The sky appeared almost black, and the wheat fields dark blue. The rolling hills resembled a camel's back, each hill like a hump of clay. The endless mountains and rivers would wait patiently while revolutionary sentiment remained.

On that peak, I waited for Hongmei for what seemed like forever. I climbed up onto an aqueduct to see farther into the distance. From this perch, I felt as though I were hovering in midair, as though I could simply reach out and grab a handful of cloud. I suddenly thought of Chairman Mao standing on the gate over Tiananmen Square, serenely waving to the millions who had gathered before him. I impulsively stood up and, facing the hills before me, waved my right hand.

I waved and waved. *The Yangtze flows toward the east, with endless waves . . . For truly great men, look to this age alone.*

After I finished waving, I felt an unprecedented sense of vastness. I had never felt so satisfied. I felt like sand that has been parched for a long time and suddenly finds itself inundated by spring showers—as trees start to bud, weeds start to bloom, birds start to sing, and butterflies start to fly around. If this wasn't love's power, then what was it? If this wasn't great love, then what was that? Only revolutionary love could bring about revolutionary strength. Only proletarian love could permit revolutionaries to soar through the sky. I waved my right hand, then extended both arms as though I were about to fly away. I began to sing songs, like "Beijing Has a Golden Sun," "I Love Beijing's Tiananmen," "The Core Strength That Leads Our Industry Is the Communist Party," as well as "Unity Is Power" and "The Giant Blade Chops Off the Devil's Head." My hoarse singing was like a golden silk ribbon fluttering in the sunlight, filling the sky with color. And the lyrics sliced through the air like the whip of a flag in the wind, each word rushing through the air like a dagger or a bullet. I saw a middle-aged peasant plowing his field with an ox, and when he reached that irrigation canal he raised his hand to shield his eyes and inspected me carefully. After determining that I wasn't about to commit suicide by jumping into the canal, he directed his ox toward me. I was relieved he hadn't assumed I was possessed, and I resolved that after the revolution—and after I was appointed town mayor, county head, or provincial governor—I would definitely seek out this peasant the way an emperor looks for the man who gave him a steamed bun when he was once in need, and either build him a three-room tile-roofed house or else find a job for his son or daughter. I watched as the peasant drove his ox from the main road toward a gully and remembered clearly his head full of black hair with a patch of gray on the top. After the revolution, I would rely on this memory in order to find him.

As the peasant approached the gully, I faced him and, with my right fist raised high, I shouted, "The revolution will definitely succeed . . . If you say it will succeed, then it definitely will . . .

"I resolve that I won't fear sacrifice, and will pursue victory against all odds . . .

"I doesn't matter if I lose my head. As long as my ideology remains true, then you can kill me, Gao Aijun, for others will take my place . . ."

As I was shouting and shaking my fist, a bus appeared. It was following a coal truck that was slowly making its way down the mountain. I hopped down from the irrigation canal, and as the bus approached I stood in the middle of the road and blocked its path.

The bus stopped in front of me, and the driver poked his head out.

"You want a ride?"

I leaned against the door and peered in through the window.

"Is Xia Hongmei on board?"

The driver released his foot from the brake and drove away, saying, "You lunatic!"

I chased after the bus, shouting, "Xia Hongmei! . . . Xia Hongmei! . . . "

Then, after a short while, another bus arrived.

Once again, I stood in the middle of the road.

The driver brought the bus to a stop.

"What the fuck? Are you trying to kill yourself?"

I leaned up to the vehicle's window.

"Is Xia Hongmei on board?"

The driver drove away, exclaiming, "Who the fuck is Xia Hongmei?!"

I chased after the bus, shouting, "Damn it. Xia Hongmei is Xia Hongmei, that's who!"

A third bus stopped in front of me, and the driver said, "You do realize that this isn't a bus stop, don't you?"

I leaned up against the driver's-side door.

"Xia Hongmei isn't on your bus, is she?"

"Who the hell is Xia Hongmei?"

"She's my little sister."

"If you're looking for your sister, then you should look for her at home."

"She's returning from the county seat today, and I have something urgent to tell her."

The driver turned back toward the inside of the bus and called out, "Is there a Xia Hongmei on board? Please look around!"

No one said a word, whereupon the driver turned to me, shook his head, and then drove away. The vehicle left behind a plume of smoke.

In all, I stopped eight buses heading from the county seat toward Jiudu. When I first went out that morning, I saw many peasants going to work, and by midday I began seeing peasants returning home—but still there was no sign of Xia Hongmei. I read her letter again and confirmed that the appointment was indeed for the twenty-sixth day of this month. At that moment, I saw a ninth bus rushing toward me. As before, I stopped the vehicle and spoke to the driver, who in turn called me a lunatic and asked whether I was possessed. I told him that sooner or later the day would come when he would have to eat his own fruits and would crush his own foot with the stone he was trying to carry. He asked what in the world I was talking about, and I replied that if he cursed me, he would be cursing a revolutionary—and if he cursed a revolutionary, he would be cursing Chairman Mao's Great Proletarian Cultural Revolution. He replied, "If I say you're crazy, then you're crazy. Do you really think you're sane?" Then he drove on, sailing away in the wind.

Immediately after that ninth bus departed, Hongmei suddenly emerged out of the cloud of dust that the vehicle had left in its wake. It turned out that she had hitched a ride on a coal truck, and when she saw me on the side of the road arguing with the bus driver, she told the driver of the coal truck to pull over. Then she ran toward me, carrying a faded military satchel.

"Aijun, what are you doing here?"

I stared at her in astonishment.

"I came to meet you and have been waiting here since the very first bus this morning."

She stood in front of me, her face appearing as though shrouded in a mist of excitement. She had a burning light in her eyes, and after a pause, she stepped forward and grabbed my neck with both hands, positioning her face only a centimeter from mine. She was waiting for love to overtake her. Her warm breath enveloped my face as the corners of her mouth trembled. I could clearly see the bright light in her eyes, so fiery it seemed to melt my bones. I felt that if I didn't accept her embrace, I would surely collapse. With impudence, shame, and delight, I longed to strip off my clothes and immediately enter her body. However, another bus was approaching, and when the driver reached us, he stuck out his head and shouted, "It's broad daylight. What are you, a couple of corrupt elements?"

I reacted as though I'd just been hit over the head with a club. I felt chilled to the core, and my ardor immediately faded.

Hongmei continued to hang from my neck and said to the driver, "We just got married and are now husband and wife. I just went to Beijing's Tiananmen Square, where the Central Directorate received me. Today, I've returned home, and my husband came to meet me."

When the driver heard this, he replied, "Oh, OK." Then he put his foot on the accelerator and drove away.

After the bus departed, Hongmei released her grip, and I noticed that the bridge of her nose was covered in sweat. We both knew we had gotten a little carried away and had forgotten the revolutionary situation of this revolutionary age. In the distance, a couple more peasants were returning home after having spent the morning working in the fields.

Neither of us uttered a word, and instead we headed north. I walked in front, Hongmei several paces behind me, as though we didn't even know each other. Later, we would recall how we had pretended to be strangers that day. Eventually the morning warmth was replaced by a midday heat, which was tempered only by the shade of the pagoda trees along the side of the road. We walked quickly, burning with an unquenchable thirst. People on the other side of the street would occasionally look at us skeptically, glancing back at us even after they had walked past. At the same time, there was a steady stream of cars driving by. After we had proceeded forward for a while, we noticed a cluster of thornbushes halfway up the hill on the side of the road, through which there ran a small path. Without hesitation, I turned onto that path, and Hongmei followed me.

The path eased the nervousness and uneasiness we had felt before the storm, and we sighed with relief.

I said, "How is it that you went to your mother's house without telling me?"

She said, "After they dragged me home from the memorial arch, Guizhi's father asked someone to go find a Chinese medicine specialist to perform acupuncture on me. I escaped by scaling the bathroom wall and fleeing to the bus station."

I replied, "Damn it. If it hadn't been for the revolution, we would never have been able to be together."

She said, "The county seat has already been turned upside down."

I said, "If you look at history, every revolution has been initiated in response to the actions of those in power."

She said, "In the county seat, they have tied up the county committee secretary and are parading him through the streets."

I said, "It's like the Chen Sheng-Wu Guang uprising, Li Zecheng's insurrection, the Xinhai revolution, or the Shaoshan revolt . . ."

She said, "It's been reported that the new county committee secretary is only twenty-eight-and-a-half years old."

I paused. "What did you say?"

She walked over to me. "The current county committee secretary is only twenty-eight-and-a-half years old."

I was silent for a moment, then asked, "What happened to the former one?"

She said, "He was engaging in counterrevolutionary activities, which is why the masses paraded him through the streets. It was only upon seeing the revolutionary heat rising up to the sky that I decided to write you and return home today."

I gripped her hand—as though I had just lost something and needed to grasp onto something else. I noticed that her hand was not calloused like that of someone who was out working the fields every day. Although she of course performed housework like chopping

94

vegetables, cooking meals, and washing clothes, her hands remained smooth and supple, and her fingers felt like silk. She didn't realize what an impact her words had had on me—it was as if a bucket of ice water had been dumped over my head. I was twenty-six years old, but the new county committee secretary was only twenty-eight years old. I immediately felt a deep sense of urgency. I was determined to return home and eat Cheng Tianqing alive, shatter the protective sheet of glass covering the town Party secretary's desk, then bury alive Wang Zhenhai, who was now serving as both mayor and Party secretary. The revolution had not yet succeeded, so our comrades needed to continue to struggle. In the ravine to the east, someone was herding a couple of sheep to the river to drink, and I had no choice but to release Hongmei's hand and pass along the west side of the road.

On the west side of the road ran a long and narrow valley with wheat fields at the bottom. The peasants irrigating the fields stared at us. Behind us was a road, to our left was the valley, and although there weren't any wheat fields on the hills to our right, the weeds were waist-high. The hill faced a bend in the road, and as soon as the people coming up the road rounded that corner, they could see the entire hillside. We suddenly felt as though we had no place where we could hide. Neither of us dared to say openly where we wanted to go or what we wanted to do, but we both knew we desperately wanted to find somewhere we could do that thing. Hongmei's pink shirt was soaked in sweat and stuck to her body, making her breasts appear more pert than ever. Because of the sweat, her face became red and alluring and generated an aura of warmth that made her entire body emit an intoxicating fragrance that permeated the hillside. We had an unspoken understanding, like the one that exists between our shoes and the road beneath our feet. By that point we had already been walking through that hillside for quite some time. But Hongmei never suggested that we give up, and therefore neither could I. Indeed, I came out so early to wait for her precisely in order to find a quiet place for us to go—a quiet place where we could burn, explode, and revolt, shattering our iron chains and establishing a new love.

We headed south for a while and eventually stopped next to a knee-high clump of weeds. This was a gentle slope with a pile of soil at the top. The clump of weeds growing there was green and lush; it was almost as if that pile of soil had been placed there precisely in order to permit the weeds to thrive. Behind the weeds, there was an opening that attracted our attention.

We walked over to it.

A cold breeze emerged from inside and blew toward us.

This was an old tomb, and even after the bones had been dug up and reburied, the empty tomb remained at the base of the cliff. Hongmei and I both knew that in this mountainous region of western Henan, this sort of provisional tomb is often used for children who are too young to be buried in the family tomb, outsiders who die unexpectedly, old people who die when their spouse is in ill health and isn't expected to live much longer—in these sorts of cases the deceased may be buried in this sort of tomb, and after several years their remains may be dug up and reinterred in the family tomb.

Hongmei and I stood there motionless.

I said, "There are people everywhere. Where have they all come from?"

She looked around hopelessly, then gazed up at the sky.

I said, "If we return to town, we won't attract a single glance."

She said, "But I think I hear footsteps approaching."

I said, "This is actually the safest place for us to be. No one will come here."

She said, "Aijun, are we crazy?"

I said, "Hongmei, this is simply revolutionary love and affection. We aren't crazy in the least!"

I grabbed her hand and headed toward the other end of the tomb. It turned out that there was indeed someone coming toward us from the road. The footsteps drew closer, until we heard them directly over our heads. As we squatted down inside the tomb, I hugged Hongmei and grasped her hands. I waited until the footsteps receded into the distance, then turned and began crazily kissing her face.

I asked, "Are you scared?"

She replied, "What is there to be scared of?"

I looked around the old tomb.

She said, "I'm not afraid—what is there to be afraid of? That someone will eat us? Still, if we were to be caught it would certainly be the end of us. We would never be able to go back to Chenggang and rejoin the revolution."

I said, "But where could be safer than here?"

I told her to sit down while I went to the opening of the tomb to look out. The tomb was a meter and a half wide and two meters deep, meaning that it was as large as a small room, and it was tall enough to stand up in. The damp ground was perfectly flat and had a red tint. There were two wooden planks to support the coffin and a dozen or so bricks scattered around. In the areas that were shielded from the wind, the walls were covered in dust and cobwebs. In the deepest parts of the tomb, there was a thin layer of moss. Needless to say, after the corpse and the coffin had been removed, no one had gone back inside. It occurred to me that it would be ideal if this tomb were closer to Chenggang, because then Hongmei and I could use it as a secret rendezvous site.

Unfortunately, we were eighteen *li* of mountain road away from Chenggang.

Unfortunately, Hongmei and I lived in Chenggang, where finding somewhere to meet was more difficult than ascending to heaven.

I kicked aside the boards and bricks on the ground, then went out to collect some grass and weeds from the entranceway and carried them back inside. When I went out to collect another bundle, I saw that Hongmei had also collected a large pile. I said, "That's enough, that's enough." She replied, "Let's pile up more and make it thicker." We placed a layer of grass on the ground inside the tomb, and on the elevated area where the coffin ordinarily would have been, we put down a pile of dog's-tail grass to serve as a pillow. Then we should have immediately taken off our clothes and done that thing, the thing that we longed to do day and night, but for some reason neither of us made a move. Instead, we both sat down across from each other on the pile of grass, calmly gazing at one another. The hunger that originally consumed us had disappeared, and at that point we were both very calm.

She asked, "Don't you love me?"

I replied, "Of course I do."

She said, "Then why don't you do something?"

I took her hand and realized that her fingers were as cold as icicles in the middle of winter.

I said, "Your hands are freezing."

She laughed bitterly.

I said, "Are you scared? You seem really afraid."

She said, "Aijun, do you think we can really have a successful revolution in Chenggang? And what if the revolution doesn't succeed? I'm afraid that all of our dreams will come to nothing."

I said, "Hongmei, don't worry about the revolution not succeeding; all you need to be concerned about is the possibility that we might lose faith. Because if you have faith, you can forge a needle out of a rod."

Reassured, she nodded.

"Why don't you unfasten my buttons?"

Like a small child waiting for an adult to remove her clothes before going to bed, she let me unfasten all of her buttons. After I had removed her clothing, she continued sitting in the area near the entrance to the tomb, where there was more light, using her shirt to cover the area between her legs. She watched as I removed my own shirt and pants. I proceeded methodically, while continuing to admire her naked body. There was a cool, damp smell inside the tomb, which gave her face a faint pale hue, and on her snowy-white body there was a layer of goose bumps. I knew she was cold. Perhaps her heart was cold, and even the corners of her mouth were turning blue. But at that moment the midday sun began to shine into the tomb, enveloping her body like a scarf. I walked over, took the clothing I had just removed, and placed it in that sunny spot. I said, "Hongmei, please sit here."

She replied, "Aijun, just hold me. I feel faint."

I quickly picked her up and placed her in that spot of sunlight, as though she were an infant. Wearing only my underwear, I sat down in front of her, then placed her smooth, cool legs on my thighs. We sat there, as the sunlight flowed down from her shoulders, and from the tips of her nipples it splashed over my thighs. That sheet of sunlight made me feel warm and itchy, as though I were wearing wool clothing. At that point it was deathly silent inside the tomb, and the sound of air blowing in through the entrance resembled falling autumn leaves. As the air passed through the sunlight, it sounded like the pitter-patter of water droplets on a hot pan. Her hair was much longer than before and now almost covered her shoulders. A strand of hair was resting on her shoulder and breast, creating a bridge between them. In the sunlight, I saw dust particles hopping along that bridge, after which they were absorbed by the cool shadow next to her breast. There were also some particles that jumped out of that shaded area and returned to the sunlit portion of her shoulder, hopping along as though in search of the end of a ray of sunlight until they finally found her right nipple, which had just been roused from the cold. After her nipple was warmed by the sunlight, it shifted from purplish blue to purplish red.

I was agitated by that warmed nipple and began passionately caressing and sucking it. When the right-hand side of her body was already warmer but the left-hand side was still cool, I lifted her onto my lap, such that her legs extended past my waist. Then I pivoted my body halfway around, so that the sunlight could shine into the space between our chests—so that her chest could get warmed by the sun.

I said, "Are you warmer now?"

She nodded. "Can we get married?"

I pondered for a moment. "No, we can't."

She said, "Why not?"

I said, "Because you and I need to join the revolution. We both need to become revolutionaries."

She bit her lip and didn't respond.

By that point, her buttocks had been resting on my thighs for a long time, and I was beginning to feel somewhat uncomfortable. She tightened her grip on my neck and squeezed my thighs. Her breasts were rubbing against my chin, and every time she breathed they would brush against my lips. I didn't suck her nipples, because I knew she wasn't flirting with me or trying to seduce me. Instead, we were in the process of discussing a deep and momentous issue—we were thoughtfully assessing which was stronger: revolution or love. She looked at me in a state of semi-confusion. Her face, having been warmed up by the sun's rays, now looked as delicate as before, though it remained shadowed by a mist-like layer of confusion. In the innermost section of the tomb, a water droplet fell from the earthen walls and onto the old coffin stand, like a piece of jade striking a hollow pile of dirt. We turned in the direction of the droplet, then continued embracing each other.

I said, "Do you understand what I'm saying?"

She said, "Yes, I understand. Of course, revolution is more important. From the first year of high school I was a class cadre and a member of the propaganda team, so of course I understand that. I don't necessarily want for us to really get married, I just want for you to *be willing* to marry me."

I said, "I'm certainly willing to marry you. That would be my dream."

She said, "Really?"

I said, "Yes, Hongmei, really. But right now you've cut off the circulation to my thighs."

She changed her position, and said, "Aijun, when you came to meet me and led me to this tomb, was it merely in order to have me strip and sit here?"

I said, "I wanted to look at you. You have no idea how beautiful and seductive you are!"

She said, "Really?"

I said, "Really. Don't you know?"

She stood up. Although she was still using her shirt to cover the area between her thighs, her hazily visible long legs resembled a pair of jade columns, their milky-white color making me feel increasingly restless, even frantic and delirious. However, I restrained myself, because I hadn't yet seen enough of her. She stood in the entrance to the tomb, looking down at her chest and her legs. Then she looked up again, her face shrouded in a gorgeous glow, her smile like sunlight pouring in through an open window.

She asked, "What part of me do you want to look at?"

I replied, "I want to look at *all* of you."

At this point, she tossed aside the shirt she had been holding between her legs, and with a shout she proceeded to stand completely naked in front of me. She had a revolutionary's look of conviction and fearlessness, while in her eyes there was a flicker of pride, even arrogance. "Aijun, you can look at me wherever and however you want. You can look at me from now until sunset, and then from sunset until sunrise, or even until tomorrow or the next day." She said, "You can stand here and stare at me nonstop for three days and three nights. If we had enough to eat, then we wouldn't even need to leave this tomb for the rest of our lives. I, Xia Hongmei, will give every hair on my body—from my head to my toes—to a revolutionary, and that revolutionary is you, Gao Aijun!"

I was moved by her pride, and terrified by her nudity. I wanted to say something but found myself momentarily speechless. My words remained caught in my throat, though I myself wasn't even sure what those words might be. I looked up but saw that the patch of sunlight had shrunk and was retreating back to the opening of the tomb. Because of love and the flames of revolution, the chill had already faded from our bodies. A potent mixture of revolution and love now filled the tomb. At the same time, the tomb felt cooler than before, and I could see the dried grass outside the entrance swaying in the breeze. On the collar of the shirt Hongmei had tossed aside, I could see that there was a piece of thread glittering in the sunlight. There were many drops of water and specks of dust on the spiderweb in the corner of the tomb. I could see that on the innermost wall of the tomb there was a dappling of green moss, as well as several tiny plants that would never see the light of day. Each of the plants was only about as tall as a finger and had about three wilted leaves that looked as though they would fall off at the slightest touch. Hongmei stood near the tomb's entrance with her hands on her shoulders, lifting her breasts with her forearms. In this way, the sunlight shone directly onto her voluptuous breasts, making them glitter like gold. It was as though she were endowed with a pair of unimaginably bright silver suns, under which her upper body looked incredibly delicate and well proportioned. Her waist looked so thin that it seemed you could wrap your fingers all the way around it, and her hips exploded outward below it. How was it that when I ran into her that time on the outskirts of town, I hadn't noticed her thin waist and voluptuous hips? Was it because she was sitting down at the time? My lips were dry and my throat itched as though there were a chicken feather wedged inside it. I swallowed my saliva, bit my lower lip, and struggled to control my racing pulse. I wanted to keep staring at her—to devour her naked body with my eyes. I couldn't understand how she could have already had a child, because apart from some very faint stretch marks on her smooth belly, you would never have guessed she had given birth. She had supple thighs and long, slender legs, without a trace of extra fat. Her toenails were still red with nail polish, as though she had ten buttons fastened to the ends of her toes. Her toes made her legs appear bright, and her entire body look incandescent. With such an intoxicating body, how could she possibly be an ordinary woman? How could she be just a young woman from the countryside? If not a Buddha appearing in the form of a living woman, then what *was* she? If not a goddess that heaven had given mankind, then what *was* she? She had been standing as straight as a rod, but perhaps she had been standing for too long, for she proceeded to turn halfway around, allowing me to view every nook and cranny of her body.

She extended her left leg and leaned over, so her center of gravity was now positioned entirely over her right leg. In this way, that increasingly narrow patch of sunlight happened to shine directly on the triangular area below her belly, illuminating her dark and mysterious pubic region. Each of those soft pubic hairs revealed its persistence and strength of character. It was as if every strand of hair was struggling to stand up and straighten its back and—braving sun and rain—claim a piece of the world for itself. Golden yellow in the sunlight, that area was the size of half a fist, and the tip of every strand of hair glittered with a drop of reddish light. Because most of the sunlight was blocked from entering the tomb, and we had by then become accustomed to the half-light inside the tomb, I noticed that the tomb's earthen walls looked darker than before; they were now a watery-red color so dark it was nearly black. This blackish-red background made Hongmei appear even more beautifully white—as white as a marble statue of a goddess. I examined her so carefully and for such a long time that it was as though I were reading her like an essay. As I stared at her, I felt I should say something, but I wasn't sure exactly what. What could I possibly say that could live up to that scene of beauty on display before me?

I said, "Hongmei, believe it or not, it is for you that I am determined to bring the revolution to Chenggang."

103

She appeared to grow tired of standing, and shifted her weight to her other leg. The ray of sunlight now illuminated her from behind, as though a piece of glass were hanging over her buttocks. She looked at me and replied, "Gao Aijun, if you can initiate a revolution in Chenggang, I won't hesitate to die for you and for the revolution."

I made a fist, gripping so tightly that sweat poured out from between my fingers. I squeezed all of my hunger for revolution into my fist. I said, "Hongmei, I wasn't able to successfully lead the uprising, so how will I be worthy of the revolution, of this truth for which you have stripped naked and let me gaze at as much as I wish?"

A smile momentarily hovered over her face like a rosy cloud, then she looked down at her red toenails. She bent her knees and pushed out her chest as if she were about to turn around. She positioned her arms in a circle, with her fingers locked and palms facing upward. She didn't look at me and instead gazed at the wall to her right. She was relaxed, like spring catkins and poplar blossoms drifting in the wind. She resembled a dancer who had just finished a performance, with her pert breasts, trembling nipples, faint stretch marks, her raised posterior with the patch of sunlight visible on it, her tensed-up thigh muscles, together with that patch of hair that became even more mysterious and semi-concealed due to the way she was twisting her torso. She displayed her feminine mystique as though putting a vase of flowers on a table. Sweat poured out from between my fingers, making it necessary for me to continually wipe my hands on my army-issued pants. I felt I had to plug up my sweat-producing pores or else the blood in my veins might follow the sweat and gush out of my body. Outside the tomb, we heard people heading home after work, and it sounded as though they were directly over our heads. The effect of these timely footsteps was like a bucket of cold water being poured over my infatuated body. I noticed that when Hongmei heard the footsteps she turned pale, but as the sound receded into the distance she regained a flowery look of excitement. She gazed at me without saying a word, then suddenly broke the pose she had been holding and proceeded to stand on one leg. With one hand on her waist and the other above her head, she pointed to the ceiling. Because she was holding her breath, her abdomen was sucked in and her posterior was taut. This made her already-slender figure appear even more reedlike, as though a luscious peeled white shallot had been planted in the tomb's entrance. She proceeded to perform a series of Chinese opera dance routines, "Circling Crane," "Flying Goose," "Nesting Sparrow," "Phoenix Spreading Its Wings," and "Golden Chicken Changing Legs," as well as a series of bent-waist, hunched-back, half-turn, and full-turn poses. In quick succession, she performed more than a dozen of these moves. Soon three of her red toenails on her right foot were covered in mud from the ground, and because she kept lifting up her arms, several of her fingernails became dirty with red clay from the ceiling. Once, when she was straightening her back, several pieces of clay fell from the ceiling, sliding into her cleavage and then down her torso—leaving her abdomen looking as though it were covered in pink stars.

By this point the sunlight had receded to the entranceway to the tomb, and the weeds outside were no longer swaying back and forth. Hongmei proceeded to cycle through a series of dance moves and poses inside the tomb, looking completely engrossed. Regardless of how small the tomb was, she continued to cycle through her repertoire, displaying her feminine beauty. At that moment, the fire in my body was calmed by her beauty. She told me there was a culture palace in the county seat, and that she had been studying there ever since she was little. She said she had studied dance with a female instructor whom everyone had called an old hag and a corrupt and degenerate element. She said she also studied Yu opera with a male actor who specialized in singing female roles and who had transferred from the county's opera troupe to the culture palace. She claimed she was the most talented female opera performer in the entire region surrounding the city, and that she had once been selected by the school principal to perform opera songs and dances for the cadres who had been sent from the district and the provincial capitals to investigate the literacy efforts in the villages. Unfortunately, when it came time for her to go to high school, her father forced her to withdraw so that her elder brother could instead attend high school in the county seat. As a result, her dream of pursuing a career as an opera performer was destroyed by her father, who had spent his entire life working as a gatekeeper for the Party secretary and mayor, sweeping the courtyard and preparing tea. She said that if she hadn't had to withdraw from school, she might have been able to test into the district-level theater school, after which she might have been able to become a professional actor in a district-level or county-level opera troupe. By now, she would probably already have become the daughter-in-law of the county head or the county Party secretary. Had that been the case, she wouldn't have married into Chenggang and definitely wouldn't have had to lead this sort of dull life as the wife of a teacher and the daughter-in-law of the former mayor. If she had been able to become an actor in an opera troupe, then what would her life be like now? Would she still have met me that day on the outskirts of town? Would she still have been as passionately invested in political movements and revolution as she now was? Would she still have had silver acupuncture needles pushed into her head and hands? Would she have been willing to strip naked inside this tomb and perform her flying, standing, and leaping routines for me? Of course not. She would be enjoying a completely different fate.

It occurred to me that the reason she was able to approach me with this crazy energy in the tomb was because she had married into Chenggang and into Cheng Tianmin's family, and because her husband was that milquetoast teacher Cheng Qingdong. But why did she marry into Chenggang? Naturally, it wasn't to serve as Cheng Qingdong's wife, to bear and raise the Cheng clan's children. It wasn't to become a resident of this old and esteemed community. Instead, she had come to Chenggang to serve as a grave robber, a revolutionary activist and organizer, a successor of Chenggang's enterprise, a supplement for my unhappy marriage, a revolutionary with whom I could share a pillow, and someone who could serve as my right arm. I was grateful to her and overwhelmed by the remarkable favor she had granted me. At the same time, however, I felt bewildered by the extraordinary circumstances in which I found myself. I was surprised by her sudden appearance at my side and was awed by her loyalty to the revolution. I was embarrassed and delighted by her willingness to offer me her love and affection, and I was astounded by her refreshing ability to express her love at any time and even in unlikely locations. I gazed at her, not wanting to miss a single detail as I watched her shift from one pose to another. I saw how her expression and complexion shifted as her body changed positions. I saw how, when she adopted the flying pose, she looked upward and her face came to have an orange hue, as even her earlobes became as red as a pair of flower pistils. At that point, however, because her chest was relaxed and oriented downward, her breasts came to resemble a pair of red and white peony blossoms swaying back and forth, looking like they might fall onto the mud- and straw-filled floor of the tomb, and I couldn't help but reach out to grasp and support them. When she adopted the arched-back pose, her breasts nestled into her chest, pulling every wrinkle taut and making every blood vessel visible. But when she bowed her waist, such that her hands almost touched the floor, her lower abdomen and thighs were pulled taut, transforming that area into an endless flatland that seemed to be floating in midair in the middle of the tomb. Perhaps she didn't realize that she had opened a hidden door, a window to that room that had previously been in perpetual darkness—thereby sending her feminine beauty directly to my eyes. I saw water-soaked butterflies and fish in that secret room. I saw butterflies flying out the window and fish swimming under the door. My body once again became feverish, and my palms became covered in sweat, and my throat felt parched like a desert that hadn't seen a drop of rain for over three years. I couldn't control myself, but at the same time I didn't want to have to continue restraining my desire. I lunged forward and hugged her tight, then proceeded to lie down on the grass mat.

The tomb became so still, it was as though both of us had just died.

She stared up at the tomb's ceiling.

I stared at her.

I began making my way down her body. She was so tender and sensitive that, regardless of whether it was her calf, her thigh, her belly, her breasts, her shoulders, or her neck, no matter where I caressed her, her entire body would begin to tremble and shudder, filling the tomb with her hot breathing. Finally, after I slowly peeled the mud off her toes to reveal those ten toenails that resembled shattered sunrays, she pulled me close, grabbed my hand, and placed it on her breasts.

At this point, the throbbing of her breasts suddenly seemed to surge into my palms. I knew she was very restless and, like me, couldn't wait any longer. Her fire already burning hot, she was about to explode. Our revolutionary love had reached a critical point, and now everything was hanging by a thread. A pair of sparrows were chirping as they flew around their nest. One of them was bringing food, and the other was bringing straw to fortify the nest, and together they proceeded to work happily while singing a revolutionary song. Revolution is like climbing a tall mountain, at the top of which the sun appears large and round. With each step, we felt more enlightened, as though the sun were shining directly into our hearts. As our hearts warmed, we felt as though our happiness would surely last for millennia and millennia, millennia and millennia, millennia and millennia . . .

But . . . but, ah, but . . . Just as I spread her legs and was about to enter her, something sharp poked my knee. I felt around in the straw and pulled out an object—which turned out to be an old bone. Like a jujube or elm branch that had been buried underground for an eternity, the bone was black and gray. It was as thick as a finger, about four centimeters long, and its surface was riddled with worm holes. It was clear that this was a finger bone from the corpse that had been buried here. When I realized that this was a dead person's finger, I felt as though my entire body were enveloped in a frigid wind, and the blood that had been pounding through my veins had suddenly frozen solid.

I collapsed, and the dawn light disappeared.

I quickly threw the bone out of the tomb, but after doing so I discovered that I could no longer remain hard.

Hongmei sat up and gazed at me with a pitying look. I took her hand and used it to slap my own face several times. She struggled to retrieve her hand, after which she attempted to reach out to stroke my cheek.

I began to cry.

We leaned against one another and began to stare into that damp, dark red tomb as though looking at our own coffin. We were completely silent.

The sun retreated further from the opening of the tomb. The shadow in front of the tomb was light red, and there was a gleam of sunlight on every stem and leaf of the weeds growing on that pile of soil. The inside of the tomb remained as light as before, and even the silk-like legs of the spider in the corner were clearly visible. It was even possible to discern the vapor-thin layer of hairs on the spider's legs, which swayed back and forth when it walked. The straw beneath us had an indentation where Hongmei had been lying. The smell of death and decay mixed with the scent of damp straw to produce a greenish-red and milky-white mist that drifted through the tomb, and when it reached the tomb entrance and was struck by sunlight, it disappeared without a trace.

3. A Major Explosion (II)

It seemed that, in the dead of night when everyone was sleeping, a storm was rolling in.

None of you can possibly understand how this miracle occurred. Revolutionaries believe that miracles are created only by the revolution. For revolutionaries, the revolution is the source and the engine of all miracles. It is the sun and rain, the spring breeze and fertile soil. The revolution is the time and season of all miracles. So who could have anticipated what would subsequently unfold? Who could possibly have anticipated it?

First, as Hongmei and I were leaving the tomb, we became enveloped by a depression that was as deep as snow. Neither of us had anticipated that our fiery desire would be extinguished by the chill of that buried bone. We sat there waiting for our lust to be reignited, but the longer we waited, the more we became enveloped by that icy depression.

Eventually, however, we emerged hand in hand from the tomb and quietly proceeded forward, as though heading toward the tomb of our own love. As we walked along like a pair of corpses, neither of us uttered a word, but when we were about to reach the road to the mountain peak we heard the faint sound of a loudspeaker coming from a village. It was as though during the second lunar month's Waking of Insects solar term, the sound of thunder was transmitted from beyond the mountains. By this point the sun was already nearing the western horizon, and the fields along the mountain ridge were empty. In the distance, in the hills and fields along the ravine, several mountain goats were grazing, and it was unclear whether the goatherd was resting somewhere or if he had returned home to eat.

In the periodic silences between the loudspeaker announcements, you could hear the goats walking around.

We followed the path toward the road to the west of the tomb. The thistles had thorns that were half a finger long and would catch on our clothes. As we were walking along the road, our pant legs became completely covered in these shiny, black thorns, and our nostrils were assailed by a warm smell of vegetation.

I asked Hongmei to put her arm through mine, the way people do in the city, and she did. The sun was warm, and the fields were empty. Butterflies, moths, and locusts kept crossing the road, moving from one field to another. When we were halfway up the hill, we again heard the sound of a voice being broadcast over a loudspeaker. Because the loudspeaker was blocked by the trees, we couldn't hear clearly what was being said, but after the conclusion of the announcement, the loudspeaker broadcast the water-like sound of a flute and an *erhu* fiddle, followed by a revolutionary melody. We could see the notes of that melody hovering in the air like leaves and flower petals floating on the surface of a river. We picked up the pace, our hunger dispelled by the music. We listened as we walked, and when we got to a particularly exciting part of the song, we stopped in the middle of the road in order to hear the music and the lyrics. We stood there and impulsively kissed each other. She rolled up her tongue and inserted it into my mouth and had me suck it, and then blew cool air into my mouth through her curled-up tongue, accompanied by her sweet saliva. From her fresh breath and her mouth, I detected intoxicating hints of chrysanthemum, plum, peony, lotus root, pagoda blossom, apple, pear, orange, grape, as well the pungent smell of the wildflowers growing on the hill, including the light white fragrance of carriage-wheel blossoms, the heavy yellow smell of spring-greeting blossoms, the pungent and slightly sweet odor of dried branches and grass, the sticky and pungent smell of thatch grass and horsetail, and the black and sweet medicinal licorice smell of dragon creepers and climbing palm. As I held her tongue in my mouth, I once again heard the sound coming from the loudspeakers behind us. First there was some indistinct local dialect, then the bold and unrestrained sound of a revolutionary song. At this point, to our left and right, near and far, in villages and stockades—in short, wherever there were people and houses—it seemed as though everyone had received the order to turn on their loudspeakers and start broadcasting music and songs, so the entire mountain range became filled with bright rhythms and musical notes. The pagoda tree leaves by the side of the road trembled to the music, and the wheat stems in the fields swayed back and forth. The musical notes in the air bumped into each other, and the melodies on the ground surged forward. Hongmei and I were both aroused by this music. We surmised that the higher-ups must have had a new development they wanted to transmit into the hearts of the masses. We very much wanted to run up to the top of the mountain to hear this newest and highest command, but we were captivated by that music—it was as if we had been struck by a bullet of pure red passion. We couldn't restrain ourselves, extricate ourselves, or heal ourselves. Hongmei's cheeks had a deep red glow; her eyes possessed an insatiable hunger, and her mouth and nostrils trembled uncontrollably. I pushed her tongue out of my mouth, then forced my own tongue into hers as though it were a dagger. With the tip of my tongue, I searched for the roof of her mouth and the base of her tongue, in order to suck out her tongue's sweetness and crispness. We sweated, gasped, and struggled to breathe. Perhaps a village fifty li away was also making a broadcast. Maybe the loudspeakers in all the villages within two hundred or even five hundred li of us had begun broadcasting. From the city to the countryside, from the red pines on Daxing'an Peak to the coconut trees on Hainan Island, throughout the nine continents and the nine oceans, throughout heaven and earth, throughout the universe and beyond—there were loudspeakers everywhere, and they were all broadcasting songs and music. My ardor, which had subsided inside the tomb, once again began to course through my veins, from my head, my feet, and my hands, flowing directly to my member. I couldn't understand why those passionate songs and bright red melodies were able to ignite the fire in my veins and awaken my member as though rousing a sleeping lion, leaving it as erect as a piece of iron or steel. Hongmei didn't know whether she was aroused by the music or by my own fiery ardor, but in any event her entire body went limp, her face became flushed, and she once again grasped my neck with both hands—as though she would have fallen to the ground had she loosened her grip. I stuck my tongue deep into her mouth, caressed the roof of her mouth with the tip of my tongue as though my tongue were a live fish being roasted over an open flame. She reacted as though she had been assaulted, pulling away from my hard embrace. But then she lunged toward me again, pressing against my hardness like a soft cloth pushing toward a sharp blade, like a moth drawn toward a flame.

She moaned, "Aijun . . . Aijun . . ."

I picked her up and rushed toward an area to the east of the road. I knew this great moment would finally arrive, and if we didn't seize it we would regret it forever—and I would be so ashamed that there would be nowhere I could hide my face. I was afraid that the loudspeakers would suddenly stop broadcasting and that my member, which had been aroused by the music, would wilt again. For that reason, I didn't go back to that area on the other side of the grove and instead made for the ravine below the road to the north, where the road formed a natural cliff. There was a dense cluster of pagoda trees over the cliff, and it was there that we proceeed to do what we hadn't been able to do inside the tomb. As I was entering her body, I heard her cry out with a joy that resembled a golden-red sun at dawn on a spring morning. This cry rose up from our interlocked bodies and surged toward the dense canopy overhead, staining the leaves of the pagoda trees dark red. I saw her gaze up at the stars, at the moon, and at the cry that emerged from her soul like the sun rising over the mountains, and as this cry's blazing-white and fiery-red rays pierced through the gaps in the canopy overhead, they seared the edges and tips of the leaves, making them curl up and fall off. The leaves fell onto my shoulders and back and onto her flushed and radiant face and chest. Wave after wave of music continued to resound from the loudspeakers. The song lyrics glittered like pearls as they tumbled down from the roadside cliff, and the musical notes shone like silver and gold as they slipped into our ears like moonlight through the gaps in the pagoda leaves. The song coming from the east was the black-iron and white-steel "Carry Revolution to the End"; the one coming from the west was the uplifting and fiery-red "Beijing Has a Golden Sun"; the one coming from the south was the sonorous and forceful "Overthrow the Reactionary American Imperialist and Soviet Revisionist Party"; and the ones coming from the north were the clear and fragrant "Please Drink a Cup of Buttermilk Tea" and the warm-sweat and salty-teared "Denouncing the Evil Old Society." The song coming down from overhead was the profound and earthy-smelling "Not Even Heaven or Earth Are as Vast as the Kindness of the Party," while the one emerging up out of the earth was the hopping and fluttering "The Sky of the Liberated Areas Is Bright." We were surrounded by songs. We were lying on songs, breathing songs, and covered in songs. Songs gave me strength and passion, determination and tenacity. Whenever I found a tune with a rhythm like one of the marching songs we sang in the army, I would grab it and place it between her body and mine, so that we could thrust to it—fast or slow, light or heavy, we would match it until the song reached its climax, as her gasps rang out interminably. As soon as we heard that "Ah . . ." over the loudspeakers, Hongmei and I would also shout out "Ah!" until our cries drowned out the ones being broadcast over the loudspeaker, at which point they would shake down the green and yellow pagoda tree leaves overhead. Only then would we stop, victorious, as the sun shone brightly onto the earth.

Hongmei and I grabbed a tree branch and clambered out of the ravine and back to the main road. We followed the road to the top of the mountain, and only then did we hear—following the song and music—the Xinhua News Agency broadcast an important news release, which was that Chairman Mao was announcing another high directive.

Chapter 5

Policy and Strategy

1. A Turning Point (I)

Summer passed.

I spent that entire summer pondering a single question: How could I extract the strength of Chenggang's masses from their flesh and bones?

We had to rely on the masses. The masses are the true heroes—this is a truth universally acknowledged. When Hongmei and I bid each other farewell in the village entrance, she said, "We definitely must carry out the revolution to the end." I replied, "Don't worry, Hongmei. As long as we rely on the masses, we'll be able to reclaim the village's political power in no time at all." Then we bid each other farewell, and I watched as she walked next to the well platform on Front Cheng Street, after which she turned into Rear Cheng Street and hurried home.

I spent the entire summer sitting at home contemplating the great and profound phrase, *We must rely on the masses*. This phrase made me realize why the leaders of Chenggang's production team were unable to advance and instead found themselves all bottled up. Apart from the fact that local leaders all wore the decadent mantle of the Cheng clan, more important was the fact that we ourselves hadn't yet mobilized or succeeded in relying on the masses.

We hadn't yet written an essay around the verb *to dare*, nor had we mastered the corresponding policies and strategies. What are strategies? Strategies are the methods by which policies are implemented. And what are methods? Methods are the processes by which you assess and evaluate revolutionary insight. The verb *to dare* is a yardstick against which you may measure and check your revolutionary genius. This verb gives you both courage and a strategy, so how can there be masses who cannot be mobilized? There are no low-consciousness people, only low-quality cadres. Similarly, there are no weak masses, only impotent intellectuals. These are some very deep insights.

In order to mobilize the masses, I had to come up with a plan. I recorded four objectives in my leather notebook:

1. *Establish a three-person leadership committee, consisting of myself, Hongmei, and either Cheng Qinglin or Cheng Qingxian, an activist whom we recently cultivated.*
2. *Search newspapers and broadcasts—as well as accounts from Jiudu, the county seat, and various towns and villages—for examples of people who tried to obstruct the revolution and came to a bad end.*
3. *Print up flyers containing these examples and distribute them to every household and every commune director, thereby generating a sense of tension and uncertainty within Chenggang's political atmosphere.*
4. *In the resulting tense and uncertain atmosphere, mobilize the masses and seek an opening for revolutionary intervention.*

To achieve the first objective, Hongmei and I went to see Cheng Qinglin as soon as autumn arrived. I said, "Qinglin, we have something to propose. Do you want to join the cohort of revolutionary leaders? After we overthrow the Chenggang production team's Party branch secretary, you will become the production team's deputy village chief." Cheng Qinglin replied, "As long as I can become a village cadre, I'll do whatever you ask." With this, our three-person leadership committee was established, and there was no longer any need for us to consider Cheng Qingxian.

For the second objective, we spent half a month engaged in secret activities. We collected seventy-eight incidents, from which we selected fifteen representative examples and printed two hundred leaflets. To maintain absolute secrecy, I went to visit a fellow soldier in a neighboring county 180 li away and printed the leaflets there (the soldier in question worked in the county Party committee's printing press). These fifteen examples included the following:

1. *In Jiudu's Dongqu district, several revolutionary youths hanged the district committee secretary from the city gate tower and burned him alive because he didn't support their rebellious activities and furthermore was openly cavorting with a young woman.*

2. *In Hongmei's former school in an area outside the city, an elderly teacher was caught peeping into the women's bathroom, so students seized him while he was teaching and tied him to the blackboard, then proceeded to pluck out his eyes and feed them to the dogs.*

3. *In the East Datour production team, which was located only six li from Chenggang, the masses discovered that the Party branch secretary had dropped a copy of Chairman Mao's Quotations into an outhouse cesspool, and that he not only did not immediately fish it out, but he even took half of an adobe brick and used it to force the book, which had been floating on the surface, down to the bottom of the cesspool. However, no evil deed can ever slip through heaven's net, and eventually the brick disintegrated, and as a result, one day the revolutionary masses were excavating the cesspool and found that copy of Chairman Mao's Quotations, inscribed with the village branch secretary's name. Not only did*

the revolutionary masses remove the village branch secretary from office, they even broke one of his legs.

4. *Deep in the Balou Mountains, there is a village called Little Stream, where everyone who crossed the bridge was asked to take a box containing copies of Chairman Mao's Quotations. One female commune member wasn't willing to do so, so the young person guarding the bridge asked her, "Do you know who Chairman Mao is?" The women thought for a long time, then shook her head, whereupon the young man pushed her into the water and drowned her.*

. . . .

13. *A twenty-one-year-old revolutionary in the county seat is already a member of the provincial standing committee and the minister of propaganda. He is the youngest provincial-level cadre in the country to have been promoted because of the revolution.*

14. *Zhao Xiaqiu, female, twenty-six years old, is a worker in a factory in the district. After having been received by the political leader, she has already been appointed to the position of factory head, with the support of the factory's seventy-eight hundred workers.*

15. *In the Majia Encampment commune, which is located twenty-two li from Chenggang, there is an eighteen-year-old student who returned to the countryside to pursue revolution, and after overthrowing the village Party branch secretary, he established a new village branch. Because the revolution has benefits, he has recently become the commune Party secretary, and furthermore may also be appointed county committee member.*

These anecdotes were truly astounding, even terrifying, but also wonderful and joyful. Imagine that there was indeed a twenty-one-year-old who was appointed to serve as director of the county committee propaganda bureau, and a twenty-six-year-old who was appointed to serve as director of a factory with seventy-eight hundred workers. There was an eighteen-year-old who was appointed village branch secretary and member of the commune. *Poverty generates a desire for change—a desire to do something, and a desire for revolution.* This is how society is—it advances on a daily basis, as people's thought is continually transformed. *At the height of the revolution, you resemble the morning sun, the world is yours; it is also ours, but in the final analysis it is yours.* We have no choice but to take action. We can't be softhearted. When faced with gun-wielding enemies, we will nevertheless find victory. When faced with unarmed enemies, we definitely find victory.

We distributed those inky-smelling flyers everywhere, then stood at the head of the village, like people possessed. Whenever we saw anyone, we would stuff a flyer into their hand. One person asked, "What's this?" We responded, "A flyer." He asked, "What's it say?" We responded, "If you read it, you'll know." He said, "I don't know a single Chinese character. How am I supposed to read this?" We said, "Ask someone to read it to you, then you'll know." Everyone took a flyer and either read it or had it read to them—including the villagers returning from working the fields, those who had spent the morning herding goats and cattle, and the backpack-wearing students returning home for lunch. Some students read the flyers out loud as they walked down the street, as though they were still in their classrooms. An illiterate man went up to someone who was reading a flyer out loud, but just as the man was getting the gist of it, the reader suddenly stopped and turned pale. The illiterate man said, "Quick, finish reading." The reader, however, put away the flyer and said, "I'm afraid something might happen—something monumental." Then he hurried home, escaping into his house as though trying to escape disaster.

Something unexpected and miraculous did indeed come to pass. After the three of us on the leadership committee distributed more than thirty of the original two hundred flyers, the youngsters who had been dragged home by their parents and grandparents during the Battle of the Memorial Arch somehow returned to our side—reentering the revolutionary ranks. Cheng Qingsen, Cheng Qingshi, Cheng Qingwang, Cheng Xianzhuang, Cheng Xianmin, Cheng Xianfen, Cheng Qing'an, Cheng Xiancui, Tian Zhuangzhuang, Ren Qizhu, Shi Dagou, Shi Ergou, and Zhang Xiaoshu looked at the flyers, and although they initially appeared alarmed, after reading the flyers they immediately came over and helped us distribute the remaining ones. Each of them took about a dozen flyers, then proceeded to Front Cheng Street, Rear Cheng Street, the village entrance, the canteen, and the school entrance. They tossed out flyers like snowflakes in a blizzard—posting them on everyone's door and on the nearby date and persimmon trees.

Chenggang instantly fell into a frenzy, with every family discussing the district Party committee secretary who had been burned alive, the teacher whose eyes had been plucked out, and the Party branch secretary whose leg had been broken. In the streets on that autumn day, along with the sweet scent of ripe wheat, there was a half-black, half-white stench of terror. Someone asked, "Did people really push that person into the water and drown her?" Someone else said, "I know the Party branch secretary of East Datour. Did people really break his leg?" Someone who had a relative in East Datour anxiously ran over and asked what had happened and confirmed that it was all true. Furthermore, when the Party branch secretary's son heard that his father had used a brick to push his copy of *Chairman Mao's Quotations* to the bottom of the cesspool, he asked his father, "Is that true?" His father bowed his head and didn't answer. The son then slapped his father's face and kicked him in the rear.

A deep ideological struggle began to develop in Chenggang's houses and homes, and clear-eyed villagers noticed the irrepressible force with which the revolutionary flood was sweeping into

Chenggang. I knew I needed to borrow the strength of this easterly wind and quickly find an entry point into true revolution. I needed to find the enemy's throat and heart.

To put it simply, I needed to find—either from the village branch secretary or from the village head—the words or actions they were using to carry out the revolution, and in this way I would be able to overthrow the Chenggang Party branch.

Of course, in overthrowing Cheng Tianqing, I would have to destroy the Party branch. Of course, if I wanted to kill Cheng Tianqing and get away with it, I would need firm evidence that he was either a counterrevolutionary or had previously engaged in counterrevolutionary activities. Of course, it wasn't a problem if I couldn't find this evidence, because as long as I could dig up some dirt on his immediate relatives, that would be sufficient. After all, on the eve of the revolution, all roads lead to Rome.

By this point the Cold Dew solar term had concluded, and the hot autumn season had arrived. The sweet red smell of ripe corn began to drift over to the village from the fields, moving from west to east. The northerly wind would sometimes bring an almost tactile brownish autumn scent, like catkins and poplar blossoms drifting in the street in the early spring. This was the season that was least suited to pursuing revolution. During the revolution's development in the countryside, its progress was inevitably hampered by the harvest season. The revolution always needed to open a path for the labor required for the autumn harvest, and in the process inevitably paid a significant price. It occurred to me that I should find an entry point into the revolution before the harvest season began, so we would be prepared to strike while the iron was hot and overthrow Cheng Tianqing from his position as emperor of Chenggang.

I resolved to convene a meeting to address those who made up the backbone of the revolution.

Cheng Qinglin sent seventeen people the initial announcement of the meeting, and for the location we selected an unpopulated riverbank of Thirteen Li River (the same location where Hongmei and I had planned our original rendezvous). In order to mobilize everyone to critique Cheng Tianqing's errors and mistakes, I bought seventeen notebooks, seventeen ballpoint pen cartridges, and a box of red stamp-pad ink. I hoped that after I mobilized everyone, they would record all of Cheng Tianqing's errors and mistakes, and then affix their red-ink handprints to these testimonies. I hoped to use this secret meeting to find a incident of Cheng Tianqing dropping his copy of *Chairman Mao's Quotations* into the cesspool, a time when he miswrote the characters for "Chairman Mao" or carelessly said something that at first hearing was completely unremarkable but which, after further analysis, left everyone astounded and shocked. This sort of evidence would be an entry point into the revolution. Chenggang would feel the glow of dawn, and Cheng Tianqing would meet his doom. By that point it was noon and already very hot, and all the villagers were napping. In order to transform those seventeen pen cartridges into functioning pens, I went to my courtyard and broke apart a bamboo broom handle and used a cleaver to carefully cut it into seventeen pen tubes. Then I used string from my shoe soles to fashion them into working pens. Guizhi returned home. She was carrying some machine-made noodles and half a basket of chicken and duck eggs.

She asked, "What are you doing? That was a brand-new broom!"

I said, "Listen, you and I are not traveling down the same road. From now on, don't ever ask me what I'm doing."

She stared at me in astonishment. Her face had a green tint, as though she were about to explode, but somehow she managed to control herself. I knew she had something to ask of me. Every time she wanted to ask me to do something, she always made a point of trying to contain her anger.

She said, "Do you know what month this is?"

I didn't look up but instead continued stuffing the empty pen tubes with cartridges.

She said, "Today is my father's sixtieth birthday. Did you realize that?"

I glanced at her.

"He's sixty years old? National cadres have to retire when they turn sixty, so how is it that he still retains his position of village branch secretary?"

Guizhi's complexion turned a darker shade of green.

"Are you going to go celebrate his birthday or not?"

I said, "Revolution is not a dinner party. I don't have that sort of free time."

Tears appeared in Guizhi's eyes.

"Gao Aijun, I'm begging you, OK?"

I stopped what I was doing.

"Cheng Guizhi, I asked you to prepare a bowl of egg noodles for my mother's birthday a couple of weeks ago. Why didn't you do as I requested? But now *you* are begging *me*? OK, in that case, I'll also ask you to have your father make good on the promise he made four years ago, and let me succeed him as village branch secretary. OK?"

Guizhi fell silent. She stood in the doorway, looking rather pathetic. Perhaps she regretted her lack of filiality toward my mother, or perhaps she felt that her father should make good on his promise to let me serve as village branch secretary. Or perhaps, when faced with conflicts between family and politics, she felt unable to use her position and power as the daughter of a branch secretary. She only knew she was Cheng Tianqing's daughter, and when she walked along Center Cheng Street, townspeople in their sixties and seventies—or even in their eighties and nineties—would all come forward and greet her. However, she didn't realize that during the revolutionary period, politics would suppress everything else, and just a drop of political power would be capable of rendering a family's unequal influence meaningless. Guizhi had only received a few years of education and never read any books. She

124

was a typical rural housewife, who had never heard of newspapers like the *People's Daily* or the *Liberation Army Daily*, nor the journal the *Red Flag*. When faced with family conflict, she would always come out ahead, but it was inevitable that when her family conflicts became intertwined with sociopolitical movements, she would find herself at a loss. For her, politics was a sacrifice her family offered, the same way that, twenty years earlier in Zhao Shuli's novel *Little Erhei's Marriage*, San Xiangu became a sacrifice in China's marital revolution, even as Little Erhei and Little Qin were beneficiaries of that same revolution.

I continued working on those homemade pens that would permit me to lash out in both speech and writing.

Guizhi stood in front of me for a while, then took the noodles and the chicken and duck eggs into the kitchen. She brought over a stool and sat down in a shadowy area between the main room and the kitchen. I didn't know what she was thinking—and had no idea whether she was struggling internally or whether her mind was a complete blank. She sat behind me and, without blinking, watched as I fashioned those homemade pens. The sunlight passed over her face and the shadow passed behind her, until finally the blazing sunlight shone down on her. She, however, didn't appear to register the fact that her face was drenched in sweat because of the sun shining directly on it.

After I finished making those seventeen pens, I stood up and stretched. When I saw her sitting there in the sunlight, I felt a rush of kindness (sometimes kindness is a revolutionary's mortal enemy).

"The sun is shining directly on you," I said. "Tell your father to leave well enough alone. Once I become branch secretary, I definitely won't let him suffer."

She retreated back into the shade. Her face was blackish red from the sun.

She said, "My father is ill and has been for several days now. When he saw those leaflets you printed, he immediately collapsed."

She added, "Gao Aijun, my father is turning sixty, and I want to arrange two banquets for him. You should take this opportunity to go apologize to him. If you do, I promise that from now on I'll treat you well, and your mother too. I'll bring your mother down from the hillock to live with us. As long as you treat my father well, I'll be sure to look after your mother. OK?"

I stared at her in astonishment. With the humiliation of having to beg me, her face had developed a deep purplish hue I had never seen before. I suddenly viewed her with an unprecedented sense of revulsion, condescension, and pity. I found myself wondering how I could have married such a stupid, ugly woman? How could I have had a son and a daughter with her? How could she presume to use the favorable treatment of my mother as a bargaining chip? How could she claim a sense of filiality that had already been lost and use it to discuss important revolutionary matters? Can these sorts of household methods be used to address revolutionary problems? Can class struggle be resolved with a pair of chopsticks normally used for stirring up noodles? Can the proletariat accept a handful of rice and some beans from the capitalist class as charity? I stared at Cheng Guizhi's face, then looked down at the Seagull-brand watch on my wrist. Finally, I picked up the pens, notebooks, and ink-stamp box, and walked out the door.

"Gao Aijun!" Guizhi suddenly stood up and called out to me.

I stood in the entranceway without turning around.

"So you don't plan to attend my father's sixtieth birthday?"

I grunted in assent, then added, "Cheng Guizhi, tell your father that everyone is currently saving up for the revolution. Factories are conserving every piece of coal, and cities are conserving every drop of water. Throughout the country, everyone is adopting an attitude of *greater, faster, better, more efficient*, in working and promoting production, in order to establish socialism and bring it to a higher level. Chairman Mao said, *Diligently build factories, diligently set up stores, diligently develop all state-run enterprises and cooperative industries, diligently establish all other industries—everything must be established in accordance with the principles of diligence.* Increasing production, promoting frugality—these have already become the fundamental principles of socialism. As a Party cadre, your father is responsible for several thousand people, yet for his sixtieth birthday he wants to host a big, wasteful celebration? What is the meaning of this? Is this really for his birthday, or is there an ulterior motive?"

I walked out of the house, but as I was leaving I heard Cheng Guizhi shout, "Gao Aijun, I'll make you regret this!" At that point I didn't realize the significance of her threat. Instead, I closed the door behind me and shouted back, "The person who'll regret this won't be me but your father." Then I strode away.

The noonday alley was a hot sack. The cicadas' cries seemed to fall from the trees like fried grains of sand, jumping out of the empty sack and rolling around. Someone's dog stuck out its tongue, and when it saw me it lazily lifted its head, then fell back asleep beneath the tree. It was in this sort of peaceful moment, when nothing out the ordinary was taking place, that Chenggang's revolution underwent a fundamental transformation and began developing in a productive direction. This was fortuitous, but it was also necessary (necessity is the mother of fortuity).

After I shut the door, the Gao household fell silent.

The town of Chenggang that I left behind also fell silent.

As I was leaving, the jeep belonging to the town government drove over, and inside I saw the middle-aged mayor, Mayor Wang Zhenhai, who always kept his hair closely cropped. The jeep followed the road that looped around Chenggang, heading in the direction of the town government complex. I hoped the mayor would stop and exchange a few words with me, but instead the jeep disappeared in a cloud of smoke. Actually, I had known he wouldn't stop and speak with me. This is because he didn't even know me—he didn't know Chenggang's secret weapon, its so-called crouching tiger and hidden dragon. He didn't know that Chenggang contained a hidden

127

revolutionary genius, nor that that revolutionary would be his grave digger. After watching the jeep drive away, I picked up a rock and hurled it at the vehicle. I saw the rock hit a paulownia tree, knocking off the bark and causing sap to ooze out, and only then did I head back to Thirteen Li River.

Hongmei had already arrived at the riverbank. She had also brought her daughter, Tao'er, who was sitting barefoot by the riverbank with her feet dangling in the water. When Hongmei saw me, she looked as though she had let me down. Glancing at Tao'er, she said, "When I told her she couldn't come, she started hollering and crying, so in the end I had no choice."

I looked at Tao'er and said to Hongmei, "Come here. It's OK. We'll have a chance later."

We both knew what we would have a chance for later. We sat facing one another in the shade of a row of willow trees. Hongmei was wearing the sort of shorter dress that at that time people in town rarely dared to wear (such dresses were already very popular in the city, but the damned countryside was much more backward), revealing her jade-like legs, which were so entrancing they seemed almost fake. I could see on her legs the tiny hairs, which glimmered in the dappled golden sunlight that shone through the trees' canopy. She knew I was watching her. It had been a long time since we had had a chance to be alone together, and what we wanted more than anything else was to be alone together again. As if she knew what I was thinking, she turned and scooted closer to me. Then she removed her square-toed velveteen shoes, revealing her bright red toenails. She pulled up her dress, revealing her tender thighs.

My mouth went dry, and I swallowed my saliva.

Apart from the sound of flowing water, the riverbank was very peaceful. A flock of white waterbirds had gathered below the dam, where they were bobbing up and down. Tao'er started to shout, "Ma . . . Ma . . . Are those fish?" (In Chenggang, children generally called their mothers "Mom," and only Tao'er called hers "Ma.")

Hongmei turned and shouted, "Tao'er, go play. Your mother and uncle want to talk." Tao'er rolled up her pant legs and waded out into the water to catch some fish. Hongmei gazed at me, then looked over my shoulder at the road leading back to the village.

I asked, "Is anyone coming?"

She said, "No." Then she asked, "What if . . . we go to that grove of trees over there?"

No one knew better than Hongmei what I needed at that moment. I loved her. After asking me that question, she appeared ready to go. I knew that all I needed to do was to give my encouragement, and she would immediately strip for me. But I shook my head, and said, "No, now is not the time. Let's focus on the overall situation."

She nodded, then placed her feet on my thighs, such that her bright red toenails sparkled in the sunlight. At that point, Cheng Qinglin arrived, and Hongmei stood up as though nothing was amiss and handed him a pen and a notebook.

As more people arrived, Hongmei handed each a pen and a notebook. As she was doing so, she said something to them, bringing them into a mysterious revolutionary state. I sat on a basket-like stone on an elevated section of the riverbank and watched as everyone took the pen and notebook and then looked back at me. I asked, "Who hasn't arrived yet?" Hongmei and Cheng Qinglin replied, "Everyone is here." Accordingly, the meeting could now begin, and I could say what I had prepared.

However, instead I announced, "First, I want to tell everyone that within three days after we distributed those flyers, deputy branch secretary Cheng Tianshui, which is to say, Qingxian's uncle"—I glanced over at Qingxian, who was sitting on one of his shoes—"came to see me last night and told me that *Chairman Mao's Quotations* once slipped out of his pocket and he accidentally sat down on it. He said he knew he had committed a serious transgression, and that he was not worthy of serving as deputy branch secretary. He said he was willing to hand over his position to one of us, and added that he was willing to be educated as one of the masses and become an ordinary citizen under someone else's authority."

At this point, I paused to take a breath. I glanced around and saw that everyone's eyes were flickering like flames. I continued, "There is also a village electrician who came to see me and told me that he once wanted to see whether or not the cover of *Chairman Mao's Quotations* was insulated. To his surprise, however, the electrical wire short-circuited and scorched the book's cover, including Mao's portrait. He said he wasn't worthy of being an electrician and was willing to hand over his authority as an electrician to someone else. A production team accountant reported that he once dropped a Chairman Mao badge into a cesspool; a female director reported that once she mistook a sentence in her child's homework for a phrase by Chairman Mao . . . and so on. What does it all mean?" I raised my voice and waved my pen.

"It means we have won our first battle, and those people who committed serious mistakes are now cowering before me and before the great tide of the revolution. And what does this mean? It means that all comrades will be examined and, if necessary, cast aside by the movement. Everyone will be assessed and judged. We're not concerned that they'll commit mistakes. A comrade who makes a mistake and corrects it is a good comrade. But what should we do about those comrades who make mistakes and are unwilling to confess or correct them, and attempt to escape unpunished? There is only one option, which is to mobilize the masses, mobilize them again, and then mobilize them yet again. Once the masses have been truly mobilized, the truth will be revealed about those who have committed mistakes and attempted to slip away unscathed. Their real intentions will be revealed for all to see.

"Right now, you could say that the residents of Chenggang are mostly awakened and will soon be completely mobilized. Every Communist Party member, every Communist Youth League member, and every revolutionary youth must shoulder the responsibility of leading a fighting force. They must all lead the charge, be positioned in the vanguard, and stand atop the revolutionary tide—braving wind and rain, battling the stormy seas, and struggling with heaven, earth, and Chenggang's class enemies. They must overcome selfishness and foster public spirit, and above everything else, they must dare. They must fully reveal the mistakes committed by Party branch members, starting with Cheng Tianqing—putting these mistakes on full display for the masses, like rats crossing a road. They must make the masses realize that the person who can lead them to grasp the revolution and increase production is not Cheng Tianqing but the new agencies, teams, and branches that we have collectively established.

"At the moment, Cheng Tianqing has fallen ill, which means that the residents of Chenggang will be terrified. This is a sign that the success of the revolution is at hand. In order to avoid internal conflicts and the inappropriate pursuit of status and profit before the revolution succeeds, I want to make clear to everyone that although the objective of the revolution is to seize political power, this does not simply involve reallocation of old power. Instead, after seizing power, everyone will be assigned new positions. Whose position will be the highest, and whose will be the lowest? Who will have the most power, and who will have the least? This will all be based on everyone's effort and performance, on the level of their revolutionary consciousness, and on their ability to organize and mobilize the masses. We don't discuss rewards and punishments, but we have no choice but to consider people's performance. This is a point that I have to make clear to everyone—good things will not be given to those people who simply sit by and watch the movement or to those who fail to take an interest in the revolution and the mass struggle."

I added, "Now that each of you has a pen and notebook, I want you to spend several minutes quietly reflecting on party branch secretary Cheng Tianqing, as well as the deputy branch secretary, the village chief, the deputy village chief, and all the production team's cadres and their immediate relatives. Then I want you to write your reflections down in your notebooks and affix your handprint."

I had finished speaking but had no way of knowing what effect my words might have had on those who were the backbone of Chenggang's revolution. However, there was one thing I could see clearly, which was that no one dared to stand up to Cheng Tianqing and record anything in their notebooks. Instead, everyone stared at me, and I stared back. We inspected one another, and it seemed as though as soon as one person took the initiative to record something in his or her notebook, everyone else would immediately follow.

I said, "There is one point on which I would like to reassure everyone, which is that we won't publicly announce the name of the first person to reveal something unless it is absolutely necessary."

The situation at this point was not ideal. One person placed his pen on the ground, then sighed and said, "I really want to expose someone, but I'll be damned if I have anything to expose!" This was the deputy branch secretary's nephew, Cheng Qingxian. His remark seemed to be infectious, and soon several others also placed their pens on the ground and said something similar. From experience, I knew that at this point it was necessary to stop this countervailing wind that was dampening the enthusiasm of the newly awakened revolutionaries. I looked at them, then turned back to Hongmei.

Hongmei immediately understood what I was thinking. She walked to the front of the crowd and said, "I want to report on Cheng Tianqing and my father-in-law, Cheng Tianmin. The two of them often sit in the temple's middle courtyard and discuss national matters, sighing over the revolutionary situation. Once, the county's revolutionary youths sent an old Red Army soldier to parade through the streets, and Cheng Tianqing said that if he encountered the youths who sent this soldier to parade through the streets, he would chop off their heads."

(I truly loved Hongmei!) I said, "Write this down, and it will serve as evidence of guilt."

In front of everyone, Hongmei proceeded to write in the notebook.

Everything was resolved very simply. Either the East Wind prevails over the West, or the West Wind prevails over the East . . . Thankfully, it is usually still the East Wind that prevails over the West. Seeing Hongmei say and write these things, Cheng Qinglin said, "I want to report three crimes committed by Cheng Tianqing. I will write everything in this notebook, and if one day the revolution needs me to openly report these crimes, then even if I were threatened with decapitation, I, Cheng Qinglin, would still be willing to stand up and serve witness." Upon saying this, Cheng Qinglin stepped forward and squatted down next to Hongmei, then placed a notebook on his knee and began to write.

(*The morning sun rises in the east, and grain sprouts grow straight and strong;*
Sweet dew falls to the ground, and fresh flowers strive to bloom;
The great river surges forward, and carp leap o'er the waves;
Class conflicts do arise, but the wind and waves stand firm.)

Following Hongmei's and Qinglin's public denunciations, everyone else started writing in their notebooks as well. Some of them placed the notebooks on their knees, others positioned them on flat stones, while still others simply placed them at their feet and then sat on the ground to write. It was an incredibly moving scene. In the distance, the autumn crops had already ripened, and the dark red scent of maize drifted everywhere. Closer by, on the bright water of Thirteen Li River, there was the sound of Tao'er playing and the shadows of ospreys flying through the clouds. In the willow grove next to the river, there was a cool and gentle breeze. In the irrigation canal that ran behind Chenggang, there was the incessant sound of frogs croaking and jumping into the water. The sun was already high in the sky, and the sunlight was beating down on everyone as they wrote. I saw that the people who could write quickly had already completed a page, and some had even divided their narrative into sections labeled ①, ②, and ③. Even those who wrote slowly had completed more than half a page, piling the page with uneven script like piles of shit. I walked back and forth through this crowd of people writing denunciations and decided that after they handed in their notebooks, I would spend the entire night writing big-character posters, so that when the villagers woke up the next morning it would be as if a blizzard had passed through our town—with the walls of every street and alley covered with the filth, crimes, and excrement of Cheng Tianqing and Cheng Tianmin. I decided that after the revolution succeeded, if the people who had filled their notebooks with excrement couldn't be appointed to serve as cadres or production team leaders, then I'd make them forest rangers, production team clerks, or mill workers in the production team's electric-powered mill. In short, the question of who is friend and who is foe was a crucial concern both before and after the revolution. The revolution cannot be concerned with questions of rewards, but it definitely cannot permit those martyrs who shed blood for the revolution to endure hardship beforehand and eat bitter herbs afterward. This is not merely a question of what benefits the revolution—it is a particular issue of consideration when mobilizing the rural masses. When I began planning to write big-character posters during the mass denunciations, I not only had to consider where I would obtain the requisite pens, paper, and glue, I also had to consider what would happen once the revolution descended on Chenggang like a storm landing on a pool of stagnant water: How could a tiny ripple become a mighty wave flowing east, and how could a bowl of cold water manage to overturn rivers and oceans? I knew that this meeting on the riverbank would go down in Chenggang's revolutionary history books, because the denunciations that came forth from it would help Chenggang's revolution enter a crucial turning point. I knew that some of the methods we were using to mobilize the masses here in Chenggang weren't as refined those used by revolutionaries in the county seat, in Jiudu, or in the provincial capital. Others might mock our approach as rustic and childish, the same way that some people at the beginning of the Communist Revolution disparaged the peasant revolution that Mao Zedong initiated in Shaoshan as merely a rural insurgence. This kind of reaction was a result of people's inadequate understanding of the peasantry and their lack of familiarity with the countryside. It resulted from their inability to appreciate the unique feudal culture of Chenggang and the Cheng Brothers Historic Site. Engels once said, "The liberation of the proletariat will also be reflected in the military, where the proletariat will create its own new and unique fighting technique." The Chinese people's revolutionary struggle as organized by the Chinese Communist Party's leadership has now realized Engels's great prediction and established Mao Zedong's great military concept. When there are significant disparities between us and a stronger enemy, we mustn't confront the enemy directly—because if we do we will surely suffer severe losses, resulting in a significant setback for the revolution. Instead, it is only by pursuing guerilla warfare techniques that we'll be able to succeed in protecting ourselves and eliminating the enemy. *If the enemy advances, we'll retreat; if the enemy halts, we'll approach; if the enemy tires, we'll attack; and if the enemy retreats, we'll pursue.* This is the secret strategy of guerilla warfare. Mobile warfare, sparrow warfare, landmine warfare, sabotage warfare, maritime warfare, individual-based warfare, and village-based warfare—these are the techniques of our war. It was precisely these techniques, which initially weren't recognized as true military stratagems, that changed the fate of the Chinese people. Is there anyone today who would still look down on the techniques of mobile warfare or sparrow warfare? Tomorrow, after my revolution in Chenggang and the Chenggang production team succeeds, and later—after my revolution in the county seat, the district, and the provincial capital succeeds—who could possibly fail to make note of this secret riverside meeting in the historical records? When future generations write my biography, who could possibly fail to emphasize this unusual denunciation practice? When future generations study my personal history and the history of revolutionary struggle, who could possibly fail to acknowledge that this marked a crucial turning point in my revolutionary career?

As everyone was writing their denunciations, I strolled back and forth. I knew that these seventeen homemade pens and cheap notebooks would become historical souvenirs, but I didn't realize that an even more astounding development was about to unfold. I didn't realize that an even more immediate significance of this meeting that I had convened on the riverbank—in a mobile-warfare- and sparrow-warfare-like fashion—had already been revealed. That is to say, it turns out that one unforeseen result of this meeting was that it demonstrated the profound significance of this meeting, together with the depth and complexity of this turning point in Chenggang's revolutionary development.

Once Cheng Qinglin had inked his handprint to the three pages he had written, and as he was handing them to me, we suddenly heard blood-red cries and black-white shouts coming from the other end of the irrigation canal:

"Gao Aijun . . . Is Gao Aijun here on the riverbank? . . . Gao Aijun, where have you run off to?"

I turned in the direction from which the voice was coming and saw that the person calling out to me had his mouth open like an empty well.

"Hey . . . Are you all just a pile of corpses? . . . Is Gao Aijun there or not? Quick, tell him to run home! His wife, Guizhi, has hanged herself . . ."

I froze in shock.

Everyone froze in shock.

"Gao Aijun . . . Your wife has hanged herself. She's dead! Where have you disappeared to?"

Hongmei, Cheng Qinglin, and I immediately turned as white as sheets. As Hongmei gazed at me, a yellow sheen appeared on her pale face, and a layer of sweat formed on her forehead.

"Hongmei," I said calmly, "please collect the denunciations everyone has written. We mustn't lose a single one." (I was so great, I had the demeanor of a general.) I then turned in the direction of the shouts and ran back to the village. The villager who had been hollering looked in my direction, then shouted at me as though hurling bricks at my head.

"Aijun, quick! Your wife has turned pale, and her tongue is sticking out! If you delay, you won't have a chance to say a last word to her!"

2. A Turning Point (II)

Guizhi died.

In a clatter, Guizhi died.

As I was running back, the phrase *Guizhi has hanged herself* clattered through my brain like a chunk of ice, and once I got home the chunk exploded, leaving my body feeling simultaneously hot and cold, such that I could barely stand up straight. Guizhi hanged herself not long after I had come to the riverbank and was discovered when a neighbor came to borrow a bucket of water. By the time people rushed over and lowered her down from the roof beam, she had already stopped breathing, and her body was cold. The villagers then carried her into the entranceway and positioned her so her head was facing the courtyard, in the hope that the wind might bring her back from the dead. This hope, however, was quickly extinguished. She had already turned white, and when I separated myself from the crowd, I saw that her eyes were staring blankly ahead, her pupils covered by a cloudy film. I thought, what could have led her to do this, if not my failure to agree to pay homage to her father? But is a birthday really that important? Is it more important than your life? I bent over and placed my hand under her nostrils, attempting to grasp a thread with which I might pull her back to life. Her nose was so cold that it felt as though I were placing my hand under a block of ice. I realized she couldn't be saved. I felt as though the revolution and I now faced a much more complicated predicament.

I slowly stood up. The neighbors who had come to cut Guizhi down from the beam were all staring at me. Our children, Hongsheng and Honghua, were standing next to the body. They seemed to understand that something significant had occurred, though they weren't sure exactly what. They stared at me with a look of terror and incomprehension, and after a while they came over to my side, and each of them took one of my hands. Needless to say, this was a moment of great potential danger. I recognized that this danger applied not only to me but also to Chenggang's revolution and future, its direction and its route.

All the people who had gathered on the riverbank ran up and fixed their gazes on my face. Inside and outside, everything became so quiet that you could hear the whirring sound of air circulating.

I felt alarmed and frozen, as though countless icy insects were crawling over my body and into my heart.

Hongmei walked over, deathly pale. She proceeded to pull Hongsheng and Honghua to her chest—like a mother hugging her own children.

(Great Hongmei, I'll love you even after I die!) As Hongmei was taking the children, I saw that beyond the crowd gathered in the entranceway, there was an object someone had smashed under a table nearby. I left Guizhi's side and walked over, and the neighbors opened a path for me to walk through.

Everyone watched as I headed into the room, whereupon I suddenly saw that the object under the table was a plaster bust of Chairman Mao. Someone had smashed it open. A Chairman Mao poster that had been hanging on the wall had also been taken down and ripped up, and the shreds had been crumpled into balls and tossed into the corner, under the table, around the grain jar, and behind the door. As for the four-volume set of *Chairman Mao's Collected Works* that had been sitting on the table, two volumes were still in their original position, the third was open and balanced precariously on the edge of the table, and the rice-yellow cover of the fourth had been ripped into strips and tossed under the cabinet. I went into the east-side room, opened the door curtain, and saw that Mao's poster that had been hanging on the wall above the table had also been ripped up. I rushed over to the west-side room, opened the door curtain, and saw that the Mao badges that had been sitting on the windowsill had been reduced to dust and starlight.

(As Guizhi was ripping up and destroying these sacred artifacts, she must have been cursing me, saying, "Gao Aijun, try joining the revolution now! Gao Aijun, try joining the revolution now!" *Guizhi, how could you have done this? This is an extraordinarily serious crime!* . . . It occurred to me that after distributing two hundred leaflets throughout Chenggang, I hadn't distributed one to Guizhi. It is certainly true that it is always darkest directly beneath the lamp!)

I emerged from the west-side room.

Glancing at the crowd of people watching me, I announced, "No one move; I want to protect the crime scene."

I located Cheng Qinglin in the crowd and said, "Quick, go notify the town police. Tell them to come immediately and to bring a camera."

Cheng Qinglin stared at me in confusion.

I shouted, "Why are you still standing there?"

Cheng Qinglin said, "Brother Aijun . . ."

I stared at him angrily.

Hongmei walked over and said, "I'll go."

(Ah, the great, lovable Hongmei!)

Cheng Qinglin didn't say anything else and instead simply gazed at Hongmei. Then he seemed to realize something and promptly turned around and began to run out the door.

I located Ren Qizhu and Tian Zhuangzhuang in the crowd, and said, "I want you to stand guard and make sure that no one enters the courtyard."

The two of them immediately headed to the entranceway. (Later, one of them was appointed to serve as the production team's commander, and the other was appointed to serve as deputy commander.)

Finally, I looked around at everyone in the room and said, "I want everyone to go out to the courtyard. This crime scene must be preserved intact."

Everyone retreated to the courtyard, leaving the room empty—that is, except for the crumpled and ripped-up sacred artifacts that were lying around, together with Guizhi's lifeless body. Instantly, my family's skepticism disappeared. It had been swallowed by a nervous atmosphere resembling a forest of weaponry and a shower of bullets. It had been squashed by the weight of political struggle. As I waited in the middle of the courtyard, I felt my face become as hard as iron. Hongmei quietly walked up to me, as though wanting to say something to comfort me. In the end, however, she simply stood there silently. I said, "I want you to take Hongsheng and Honghua away. We don't want to frighten them." On hearing this, her eyes teared up, and she led the children to a corner of the courtyard.

Officer Wang, who had recently been appointed chief of police, hurried over with two uniformed cops, each of whom carried a fifty-seven-caliber pistol and had a Seagull-brand camera around his neck.

Guizhi's death scene was recognized officially as an anti-revolutionary suicide.

3. A Turning Point (III)

Cheng Tianqing went insane.

Guizhi's sudden death made him feel as though the world were collapsing, as though volcanoes were erupting, as though the Yellow River had flooded, as though the levees of the Yangtze had been breached, and as though the water of Bohai Bay had turned into gasoline and begun burning the coast of the mainland.

There is an aphorism that articulates a fundamental truth, and offers a revolutionary perspective that philosophy will never be able to achieve: *No event can ever owe its transformation to individual will alone.* That day, Cheng Tianqing had taken a nap, then got up, washed his face, and strolled around the courtyard. He had been watching his son and daughter-in-law and his daughter and son-in-law in the courtyard preparing meat and vegetables, and enjoying the sight of his grandsons and granddaughters in a corner of the main room jumping rope and playing house. It was at that moment that his own happy days came to an end. Someone barged in and shouted, "Branch Secretary, I have terrible news! Guizhi has hanged herself!"

Everyone in the Cheng courtyard froze in shock.

Cheng Tianqing stared at the person who had just arrived, and asked, "What did you say?"

The other person replied, "Guizhi has hanged herself. She hanged herself from a roof beam."

Before the founding of New China, Cheng Tianqing had been running around on the edges of the war zone, and therefore after hearing this news he was able to quickly collect himself and walk out of the house. From Center Cheng Street, he passed through an alley to reach Rear Cheng Street. By the time he got to my house, however, his pace had slowed dramatically. Ren Qizhu and Tian Zhuangzhuang, who were standing in the entranceway, didn't dare stop him. Instead, they shouted, "Party Branch Secretary!" and "Uncle Tianqing!" When the people in the courtyard heard them, they opened a path for him to enter the house. But when Cheng Tianqing reached the doorway, he saw Guizhi's pale face and glazed eyes and her tongue hanging out. He saw the pair of armed police standing in the entranceway. He saw the tall police chief taking photos of the ripped-up and destroyed Mao artifacts. Cheng Tianqing placed his hand beneath Guizhi's nostrils (exactly as I had done) and then turned pale, his forehead and the bridge of his nose becoming covered in sweat. I assumed that at this point he would stand up heroically, cast his gaze over the crowd, looking for me, then grab my collar and ask, *Why did Guizhi hang herself?* Instead his gaze came to rest on those ripped-up and shattered sacred objects, as though he already knew, even before entering the house, what Guizhi had been doing before she hanged herself. (Wasn't it the case that her family was always discussing me? Weren't they always saying that I had been infected with a revolutionary illness, which is why Guizhi had vowed that one day she wanted to destroy our household's revolutionary and divine objects?) Cheng Tianqing's eyes came to rest on the police chief's camera, then he called out, "Chief Wang." Without removing his eye from the camera, straightening his back, or even turning his head, Chief Wang calmly replied, "Secretary Cheng, this is simply extraordinary! Out of Chenggang's dozen or so production teams and its tens of thousands of residents, this is our first anti-revolutionary suicide!"

Cheng Tianqing suddenly stood up from his daughter's side, then replied coldly, "Chief Wang, it is too early to make a determination. It is up to your town mayor to determine whether or not this is an anti-revolutionary suicide."

The hand with which Chief Wang was taking pictures paused, and he looked at Cheng Tianqing in bewilderment. Then he asked, "What is your relation to the deceased?"

Cheng Tianqing replied, "She's my daughter."

Chief Wang said, "Oh," then added, "Go ask all the local mayors to come here. Let them observe this scene, and see whether any of them dare to claim that this is not a case of an anti-revolutionary suicide." As he was saying this, he resumed taking pictures, as though he didn't think Cheng Tianqing was worth a second glance. (Chief Wang was truly a committed revolutionary! Thank you, Chief Wang, I salute you, you committed revolutionary!)

Everyone present saw Cheng Tianqing's face turn as green as fresh vegetables. He stared at Chief Wang, then at the policemen stationed in the entranceway. Finally he turned and walked away, heading in the direction of the town government complex. Everyone knew he was going to look for the mayor, but after he left that day, Cheng Tianqing never again returned to my home.

Even after they buried Guizhi on the hillock, he didn't reappear in the village.

For seven days, there was no trace of him.

For half a month, there was no trace of him.

In fact, it was only after the harvest season, after the wheat had been planted, after the wheat seedlings had grown as tall as a finger, after there was a layer of green covering the brown soil—only then did he reappear. In less than two months, his hair had turned completely white. It was now long and disheveled, and there always seemed to be some feathers and straw stuck in it. The army coat he used to wear as soon as winter arrived was now nowhere to be seen, and whenever we saw him in front of the village, under the memorial arch, or in the rice paddies, he would always be wearing a filthy padded jacket that had a layer of dirt and grime on the collar even thicker than the collar itself. When the sun shone down on that collar, it produced a truly nauseating sight.

He had gone mad. He had truly gone insane. (History really is able to make a joke!)

After losing his mind, Cheng Tianqing could frequently be seen walking down the village streets, and whenever he encountered another villager he would either burst out laughing or else glare sullenly. If anyone raised their fist at him, he would immediately cower abjectly and cover his head with his arms. Sometimes he would even kneel down and start kowtowing, pleading abjectly, "My daughter has already died, so you mustn't beat me . . . I've acknowledged my crimes; isn't that enough? Given my status as a long-standing member of the Communist Party, and someone who joined the revolution before Liberation, please have mercy on me . . ."

(He was truly a disgrace to the Party and to the older generation of revolutionaries!)

He went mad protesting the injustice his daughter Guizhi had suffered. He filed a complaint at the county-level police station and the courthouse, but the people there simply said, "This is clearly a case of anti-revolutionary activity, so what are you complaining about?" He complained to the district-level courthouse, but the people there said, "Go home. Someone once was showing a movie and accidentally loaded the film in the camera the wrong way, such that all the political leaders appeared upside down. For this mistake, the culprit was sentenced to twenty years' imprisonment. It is fortunate your daughter hanged herself—because if she hadn't, who knows how many times she would have been executed."

Eventually, Cheng Tianqing invoked his status as an Eighth Route Army veteran and filed a complaint at the provincial-level courthouse, saying that if his daughter was guilty, then it was right that she had died, but why should Gao Aijun—who had forced his daughter to take that step in the first place—get off scot-free? An indictment was delivered from Chenggang to the county Party secretary, who in turn passed it on to Chief Wang, who by that point had been reassigned to the county police station as a result of his success in cracking the anti-revolutionary case. That indictment listed twenty-six crimes committed by Cheng Tianqing, accompanied by the red handprints of seventeen witnesses. Chief Wang sent someone to retrieve Cheng Tianqing from the road to the provincial capital, where he had gone to file another complaint. When Cheng Tianqing saw those twenty-six indictments, he was left speechless.

Of course, this doesn't mean that his indictment was the immediate cause of his mental breakdown. The fundamental reason for his collapse was his new status as an enemy of the revolution. He was now a class enemy who was horrified by the revolution. We all knew that after the revolution swept in like a thunderstorm, the enemies would all experience severe mental breakdowns that would highlight everyone's differences with respect to their relative significance, power, justice, solemnity, and class correctness.

However, we couldn't—and, indeed, we absolutely shouldn't—forget the principle that breaking ten fingers is not as good as chopping off just one. We can't—and shouldn't—forget that although all enemies are but paper tigers, the nauseating infection in their bodies has nevertheless already begun to fester, producing a corpse-like stench that is corrupting our own bodies and society. Nor can we forget that we have merely taken the first step in our Long March, and that the road to revolution remains very long.

In this way, the first step of the revolution succeeded.

Heedless of hardship, we proceeded toward the lighthouse.

4. A Diagram

Chenggang's revolution succeeded in a way that simultaneously accorded with and challenged our initial expectations. We followed the instructions of the higher-ups and transformed the local Party branch into a revolutionary committee and then established a new group of revolutionary leaders. For the convenience of those who arrive later, I'll draw a diagram. You shouldn't view this as a power distribution table for Chenggang's social structure after the revolution but rather as a liaison diagram for Chenggang's revolutionary work.

A work list of the Chenggang production team's newly developed Party branch:

Name	Occupation	Responsibilities	Remarks
Gao Aijun	Director of the Chenggang production team revolutionary committee	Responsible for revolution, production, and complete work	
Xia Hongmei	Deputy director of the Chenggang production team revolutionary committee	Under my direction, she oversees the complete work and is in charge of the revolution	No. 2, which is equivalent to what was formerly the village Party secretary
Cheng Qinglin	Production team director	Under the direction of Hongmei and myself, he is in charge of production	No. 3
Cheng Qingsen	Production team deputy director	In charge of waterworks production in the revolution	This comrade is illiterate. No. 4
Ren Xianzhu	Militia camp leader	In charge of revolutionary armed forces	Reassigned soldier. No. 5
Tian Zhuangzhuang	Deputy militia camp leader	Same as above	Reassigned soldier. No. 6
Cheng Xianfen	Production team female cadre	In charge of women's work	Exemplary female youth. No. 7
Cheng Qingzi	Production team accountant		High school student. No. 8
Cheng Xianzhu	Production team leader of first production team	Responsible for production and revolution for the first production team	Backbone of the revolution
Cheng Xianzhuang	Deputy production team leader of first production team	Same as above	Activist

Name	Occupation	Responsibilitiues	Remarks
Cheng Xianmin	Clerk		Backbone of the revolution
Cheng Xianqi	Contractor		Someone who can be relied on
Cheng Qing'an	Forest ranger		Backbone of the revolution
Cheng Qinglian	Mill keeper		Backbone of the revolution
Cheng Xianzhi	Production team electrician	In charge of electrical circuits for the entire village	Activist
Cheng Xianqing	Production team nursery school teacher	Because in reality there is no nursery school, this is merely in order to receive daily work points	Someone who renders meritorious service
Cheng Xiancui	In charge of the old people's home	There is no old people's home, and this is merely in order to receive work points	Someone who renders meritorious service
Shi Dagou	Director of second production team	Managing the revolution and promoting production	Revolutionary force
Shi Ergou	Deputy director of second production team	Managing the revolution and promoting production	Revolutionary force
Zhang Xiaoshu	Production team accountant	Keeping accounts	Middle school student
Deleted	Deleted	Deleted	Deleted

This diagram doesn't explain anything, but it clearly demonstrates my achievements with respect to Chenggang's revolution. It proves that the revolutionary blood inside me and Hongmei drove us to successful results, just as naturally as a sunflower faces the sun. This is how things stood: without revolution there is no power—because power is the object of revolution, and revolution is the means to achieve power. All of the revolution's power is itself the product of power. At the same time, the revolution's initial success demonstrates the need for struggle and self-sacrifice. It is common for people to lose their lives, and while some deaths are as weighty as Mount Tai, others are as light as a feather. If one dies for the sake of revolution, then one's death is as weighty as Mount Tai; but if one dies for oneself, one's death is lighter than a feather.

Chapter 6

Revolutionary Romanticism

1. A Red Sea

Being in charge of pursuing revolution and promoting production—this should have been my primary responsibility after I assumed my new position. However, Guizhi's suicide impacted me very directly, and after her death my daughter, Honghua, would often wake up in the middle of the night crying for her mother: "Where's my mom? I want my mom . . ." Her cries were as sharp and piercing as the great Lu Xun's dagger, cutting through the endless night and making it impossible for me to fall back asleep. This, in turn, inevitably sapped my energy for the following day.

Of course, after Guizhi's death, my mother finally moved down from the hillock and returned to her son's and grandchildren's side. The town government convened a mass meeting of the Chenggang production brigade, and after the names of new members of the revolutionary committee had been announced, my mother brought me a bowl of rice and hesitantly asked, "Aijun, tell me the truth, was it on your account that your father-in-law stepped down?"

I replied, "Mother, he was the one who committed grave mistakes. First, when he found himself in the grip of a nicotine craving, he had the gall to rip a page out of *Chairman Mao's Quotations* and use it to roll a cigarette. Second, when his grandson took a shit, my father-in-law couldn't find any paper, so he ripped another page out of *Chairman Mao's Quotations* and used it to wipe his grandson's butt . . . What is *Chairman Mao's Quotations*? It is equivalent to an imperial decree, and can you imagine anyone in the past ever daring to disrespect an imperial decree? Who would have dared refuse to kneel down in front of such a decree? Anyone who didn't do so would be beheaded. Meanwhile, although it's true that contemporary society is now democratic, and there is no need for us to actually kowtow to Chairman Mao's words the way one would have done to an imperial decree in the past, does that mean that you're free to rip out pages from *Chairman Mao's Quotations* and smoke them or use them to wipe your grandson's butt?"

I added, "Coincidentally, the page he ripped out merely contained Mao's saying *Revolution is not a dinner party*—because otherwise he would surely have gone insane, and it's not outside the realm of possibility that he could have been executed."

Unconvinced, my mother shuffled her tiny feet forward and took two bowls of rice to her grandson and granddaughter. From that point on, my mother resolved to shoulder all the duties and responsibilities involved in looking after a revolutionary family. Whenever Honghua woke up crying in the middle of the night, my mother would cradle her to her chest and rock her back and forth, and when she saw me emerge bleary-eyed from the side room (by that point I had started sleeping alone there) and proceed toward the east-wing room, she would say, "You should go back to sleep, because tomorrow you have work to do on behalf of the village. If you're going to be a cadre, then you must be a good one."

In this sham world, my mother was the greatest and holiest individual I knew. I have no idea how she managed to get Honghua to stop crying in the middle of the night, or how she managed to get Hongsheng to stop grinding his teeth and talking in his sleep. Following her arrival the house was always spick-and-span, and the table, adorned by its portrait of Mao and copies of *Chairman Mao's*

Quotations—together with the scroll of Mao's quotations hanging on the wall—was always gleaming. The tatami mats were always rolled up and placed neatly behind the door, and when no one was using the stools, they would always be put away in a corner of the room. When Hongsheng—who at that point was in first grade—got home from school, he would throw his book bag down on the floor of the courtyard or his room, but in no time at all it would magically be hanging from its wall hook where it belonged.

In this way, my mother permitted me to devote myself to the great work of pursuing revolution and promoting production. During the slow winter months, I used cement to rebuild the Cheng Brothers memorial arch, then painted it red and colored the edges. In large, Song-style characters, I wrote, LONG LIVE THE GREAT LEADER CHAIRMAN MAO! on the left-hand side; LONG LIVE THE GREAT CHINESE COMMUNIST PARTY! on the right-hand side; and NEW DIVINE LAND horizontally across the top. On the wall of each house in Chenggang I mounted a white board I had made using white lime mixed with fine hair, and then painted one side of each board red and used yellow paint to write, THE CORE FORCE LEADING OUR CAUSE IS THE CHINESE COMMUNIST PARTY, AND THE THEORETICAL BASIS GUIDING OUR THOUGHT IS MARXISM-LENINISM. I sent someone to chop down several willow trees from the banks of Thirteen Li River and sold the wood to raise money for some large Chairman Mao posters and accompanying banners with LONG LIVE THE GREAT LEADER CHAIRMAN MAO! on the left side and LONG LIVE THE GREAT CHINESE COMMUNIST PARTY! on the right. We hung these posters and couplets in everyone's homes, always on the wall across from the main room. At the front of every production team's work field, we erected a wooden sign that was one square meter in size, and on the side facing the direction where the sun came up in the east, we wrote the popular Three Loyalties slogan: LOYALTY TO CHAIRMAN MAO, LOYALTY TO MAO ZEDONG THOUGHT, AND LOYALTY TO THE GREAT CHINESE COMMUNIST PARTY. I deployed Party members, Communist Youth League members, youth, and demobilized soldiers, and then paired those who were more advanced with those who were more backward—such that the literate could help the illiterate, the young could help those who were middle-aged and elderly, and children could help their parents. Those who were over seventy years old were asked to try to memorize thirty quotations from *Chairman Mao's Quotations*; those who were between fifty and seventy years old were asked to memorize fifty; those who were between thirty and fifty years old were asked to memorize eighty; and those who were between sixteen and thirty years old were asked to memorize at least a hundred. In the name of the revolutionary committee, I notified Chenggang's schools that when elementary school students were being evaluated, it didn't matter if their test scores were low, since everyone could be promoted to the next grade as long as they could recite at least fifty of Chairman Mao's quotations. When elementary school students were being considered for promotion to middle school, in addition to being able to recite fifty of Chairman Mao's quotations, they also had to be able to recite his Three Classic Essays (namely, "Serve the People," "In Memory of Norman Bethune," and "The Foolish Old Man Who Moved Mountains").

I spent the entire winter racking my brain in an attempt to establish a fiery-red Three Unifications in Chenggang (which is to say, unifying the entranceway, unifying the household, and unifying the fields) and a process of "using a pairing method, so the entire village, young and old, could learn to recite Mao's selected works." I selected the villagers who had memorized more than their requisite number of Mao quotations, and awarded them work points based on how many quotations they could recite (offering them ten points for each extra quote). As for those who couldn't recite the requisite number of quotations, I made them forfeit work points (deducting twenty points for every quotation by which they missed their assigned target). If anyone was inclined to resist my orders, I would put them in a dunce cap and parade them through the streets (a total of thirty-nine villagers received this punishment). This system of awards and punishments made it such that all the villagers—men and women, young and old, excluding only those who were ill or insane—found themselves in a red-hot environment. As a result, everyone began frantically jumping around like fish in a pot of boiling water, though in the end no one was able to escape. At that point I came to deeply appreciate a certain truth, which is that one's environment determines everything. Or, as the saying goes, he who stays near the inkwell will inevitably get stained black. You may be a revolutionary in Yan'an, but who can prove that you weren't a counterrevolutionary agent when you were in enemy-controlled territories? I hoped to create a Red Revolutionary Base—which would be the first in the entire county. I hoped Chenggang could become a new revolutionary experimental plot. As soon as winter arrived, my efforts would yield results, and the revolution would burn in Chenggang's bitter cold. The walls of the streets and alleyways were covered in revolutionary slogans, and all the elm trees, pagoda trees, locust trees, paulownia trees, chinaberry trees, and toon trees throughout the village were full of revolutionary apples and revolutionary pears (which is to say, thin plastic sheets had been hung from the tree branches and painted with images of pears, apples, persimmons, peaches, apricots, and other fruit, and adorned with Chairman Mao's quotations).

The sky was full of red banners, the streets were filled with red scent, and the ground was covered with red blossoms. There were red seas and red lakes, red mountains and red fields, red thoughts and red hearts, red mouths and red words. When one person met another, he would first declare, "*Fight selfishness and criticize revisionism*—Have you eaten yet?" The other person would respond, "*Economize in carrying out the revolution*—Yes, I've eaten." The first person would say, "*We must overcome selfishness and foster public spirit*—What did you have?" The second person would answer, "*There can be no construction without destruction*—I had the same as always, sweet-potato soup." When someone wanted to go into someone else's home to borrow something, he would enter and say something like, "*Serve the People*—Auntie, let me borrow your family's basket." The other person would respond, "*We need to promote the spirit of Norman Bethune*—Go ahead. However, it's brand new, so be sure to take good care of it." The first person would say, "*Quickly and economically establish socialism*—I know. Thank you!"

If you had had a chance to go to the Chenggang production team during that period, you would understand what the "new era's red revolutionary base" was and who had a "sharp-eyed and clear-headed fighting spirit." On the day that it was announced that I would serve as the head of the village's revolutionary committee, forty-five-year-old Mayor Wang called me over to a corner of the conference room after the meeting and asked, "How old are you? Twenty-something?" I replied, "I was demobilized last year, and am now twenty-seven." Mayor Wang said, "Aijun, you are very awakened and are truly revolutionary material, but let me tell you two things. First, the revolution mustn't destroy Cheng Temple. After all, following Liberation, Beijing didn't crush even a single blade of twitch-grass on the wall of the Imperial Palace, and if you destroy Cheng Temple, you will shatter the hearts of all of the Cheng Brothers' descendants. If you lose the People's hearts, you won't receive any help from them. Second, you mustn't forget that in order to pursue revolution, you must promote production, because the peasants place the highest value on basic sustenance."

I said, "Don't worry, Mayor Wang, I understand that we must strive to preserve all facets of our revolutionary cultural heritage. I know that it is only through managing the revolution that we can promote production. Revolution is the premise, and production is the result. Revolution is the condition, and production is the objective." As I was saying this, Mayor Wang stared at me in surprise, then he patted my shoulder and said, "In that case, you should pursue revolution. The committee has faith in you." (I didn't realize that, in saying this, he inadvertently revealed his secret plot to overthrow socialism. Later, however, it was my wisdom that forced him to reveal himself.)

I knew that Mayor Wang didn't necessarily trust me (after all, he was closely associated with the former mayor, Cheng Tianmin), but he would be left helpless after I defeated him. Hongmei and I wrote a report titled, "An Experiential Document Detailing Chenggang's Efforts to Learn from Chairman Mao," discussing the Three Unifications and One Helping One movements that I had created in Chenggang. I mailed copies of the report to the county committee and the county government, as well as to the *Jiudu Daily* and the *Henan Daily*. To my surprise, before the county had a chance to respond, the *Jiudu Daily* and the *Henan Daily* both published the report on the same warm spring day, and moreover they both added an editor's note that said, "Chenggang's experience is a model of the Great Proletarian Cultural Revolution, from which the entire district and the entire province can learn." In this way, Chenggang became a revolutionary experimental plot from which the entire county could learn.

In the third month of that year, the county government designated the Chenggang production team as a "Red Light Pagoda Brigade" (taking inspiration from the Yan'an pagoda), while I was given the title "vanguard of the peasant revolution." A red silk banner with these titles inscribed in yellow characters was mounted in front of the production team's meeting hall. This was proof of our revolution's first great success.

2. Under Bales of Straw

My revolutionary spirit was in unresolvable conflict with my desire for Hongmei's body. Every day, Hongmei would appear before me, and because she was beaming with feminine enthusiasm and enjoyed a public role, she was appointed to serve as the production team's deputy branch secretary. Delighted by her new role, she became even more beautiful and enchanting, appearing as heroic as a magnificent spear made from cherry-tree wood. She certainly wasn't lacking in feminine beauty or revolutionary experience. On many occasions, we had an unspoken understanding, and we coordinated well. Before every meeting we attended, we would first go to the conference room and, in the time it takes to finish a bowl of rice, we would silently kiss and caress each other. As soon as we heard footsteps approaching, I would immediately return to the dilapidated speaker's podium (which was positioned on a chair in front of a desk made of willow wood), and Hongmei would begin straightening up the benches. Once the meeting concluded, we needed to wait until there was no one else around to resume that sort of soul-lifting activity, but the production team leader Cheng Qinglin and the militia camp leader Ren Xianzhu always insisted on speaking to us as they accompanied me all the way back to my house. (Class sentiment, marital love.) They kindly and warmly urged Hongmei, "You should feel free to return home, since Tao'er is waiting for you." Hongmei looked at me helplessly, and I told her, "You should go, and be careful on your way home." She therefore had no choice but to leave. These fellow revolutionaries were like an unshakable shadow, and they instantly intruded on the love between me and Hongmei. Once, at the conclusion of a meeting, I said, "Hongmei, after everyone else leaves, I want you to stay behind so that we can discuss an important matter." But after everyone had left, when Hongmei and I had just unbuttoned our clothes, and I had just laid her down on the top of three benches we had placed together, we once again heard footsteps in the courtyard and immediately found ourselves covered in cold sweat.

I walked out of the conference room and asked, "Who is it?"

"It's me, Branch Secretary. It's me," a core militiaman named Little Min announced, as he patrolled back and forth in front of the conference-room window.

I said, "What are you doing?"

The militiaman replied, "Our battalion commander told me to stand guard here. He said that the situation was complicated, and that last month a cadre from the Xiaotour production team was stabbed on his way home from a meeting. The battalion commander told me that I should wait for you and Deputy Branch Secretary Xia to finish your examination, and then escort you home."

Militia battalion commander, fellow soldier, my brother—I wish I could kick you in the groin and slap you in the face! When I returned to the conference room, Hongmei was still buttoning up her clothing and straightening her hair, and her face was covered in cold sweat. That night, we stood in the conference room against a wall positioned between the door and the window and—amidst the sound of the militiaman's footsteps—silently held our breath as we did that thing. After we finished, however, neither of us felt as though our soul was taking flight or our heart was melting. Instead, we both felt like someone who has no choice but to bathe in a pool of mud, and who afterward feels even dirtier than before and longs to find a clear spring in order to wash off the mud. We sat face-to-face on a pair of stools, holding hands and listening to the rhythmic, dusty footsteps of the core militiaman waiting outside.

Hongmei said, "If we continue like this, eventually we'll be discovered, which would definitely bury our revolutionary future."

I said, "Then what do you recommend?"

She said, "Let's resolve not to see each other like this anymore."

I said, "That won't do. That won't do at all! If we did that, you'd drive me as crazy as Cheng Tianqing." I added, "Tomorrow, I'll take you on my bike to that tomb eighteen *li* away."

The next day, I took the production team's only bicycle and arrived half an hour early to wait for Hongmei at our special place outside the village. When we arrived at the tomb, however, we found that it already had a new coffin, and the entrance had been blocked off with bricks and stones. Instead, we went to an isolated field to do that thing. We were not only a pair of great revolutionaries but also a pair of abject adulterers. We were not only a pair of enlightened individuals but also a pair of unwitting decadents. If you calculate carefully, in the days following the success of the Chenggang revolution—as marked by Guizhi's death and Cheng Tianqing's insanity—countless nearby sites were marked by our joy and our grief, by our nobility and our despicability, by our excitement and our shame, including places as varied as riverbanks, forests, fields, the road to the meeting hall, and the gully for inspecting production. Our revolutionary brilliance shone down on Chenggang's fields like a giant gaze, and our abject semen flowed through Chenggang's brooks and streams. Finally, the day arrived when the county's third-level grassroots cadre convened a revolutionary meeting of our production team to discuss the Three Unifications and the One Helping One campaigns. The county committee's organizational bureau director came to speak with me, and I was recruited to serve on the town's Party committee (though without being released from my own production responsibilities). I was delighted. I went to see Mayor Wang and all the cadres and Party leaders who had come to observe us, and escorted them back to the five trucks parked at the front of the village. After the leaders had departed, I found myself unable to contain my excitement over my new success—and my hot magma couldn't help but erupt. I found myself unable to contain the revolutionary ardor that was searing my flesh.

I summoned Hongmei to the wheat field belonging to the village's ninth production team. This field was located a half *li* from the village, and it was surrounded on three sides by other wheat fields and on the fourth side by a hill that was part of the Balou mountain range. We pretended we were going to inspect the Three Loyalties signs at the front of each production team's field and note the wheat's growth and the irrigation conditions, but instead we went to the side of the field. Except for someone's lamb grazing in the distance, no one was around. When we arrived, I stopped and stared at Hongmei.

She was wearing a blouse she had selected for the purpose of receiving the cadres who had come to observe the village, and I hungrily undressed her with my gaze.

She looked around and said, "Aijun, this is simply too dangerous. It won't work at all. Tomorrow, the second team of investigators will arrive, and if we are observed, all that we have achieved will be lost."

I said, "Hongmei, I was appointed committee member of the town's Party committee, and Bureau Director Li of the county committee bureau personally told me that after this next meeting there will be an announcement, after which a formal document will be issued."

Hongmei looked as though she couldn't believe her ears, but after seeing my red face and my crazed expression, she didn't say a word. Instead, she retreated to the edge of the wheat field and looked around, and when she returned she pulled me between two haystacks. She pulled down some straw and created a mat on the ground, then quickly stripped off her clothing.

The snow-white straw she pulled down emitted a warm smell of grass and earth mixed with a musty scent of rain and snow that came in bursts as she dug into the straw. It was as though she had opened the window for the odors to be released after they had been enclosed all winter. These warm, musty odors surged out from the wheat stalks, filling the space between the two haystacks. It felt like we were covered by a blanket of this hot white scent, and the late winter and early spring chill was banished. It had been a long time since I had had a chance to inspect her naked body, because each time we caressed each other like thieves, we were always so rushed and frantic, so timid and scared. But on this day, on the eve of my appointment as a member of the town's Party committee, the joy we felt upon seeing our revolution's continued success made me feel light-headed. It dispelled our caution and displaced our timidity. We were only a half *li* from the village, and only two hundred meters from Cheng Temple. All we needed to do was take a few steps around that hill, cross the stone bridge over the irrigation canal, and we would arrive in the village and at Cheng Temple. We were oblivious to everything. Hongmei threw down her clothing and then stood between the two haystacks, just like the time she stripped and stood in the opening of the tomb. A soft white glow and fragrance emanated from her body, as her feet—and her ten bright red toenails—were buried under the straw and her gaze lingered over my body.

"Congratulations on your promotion, Aijun," she said. "Good things come to those who wait."

I began unbuttoning my shirt, and said, "One day I'll become a real national cadre, released from production duties, and you can follow me as Party branch secretary. If I'm appointed mayor, you can be the deputy mayor."

She said, "Don't remove your clothes right now. Instead, look at me and see if I look any different."

I paused, then inspected her again. Suddenly, I noticed that she had a beautiful heart-shaped badge hanging from a red string around her neck. The badge was the size of a button, and was positioned between her breasts—like the sun rising from behind the Balou Mountains on a winter morning. I asked, "Is it good to have that souvenir badge hanging from there?" She replied, "This is my revolutionary amulet." Then she asked, "What else do you notice?" I shifted my gaze down and was startled to discover that her abdomen had grown significantly larger, and the stretch marks below her belt had become shallower.

"Are you pregnant?"

She shook her head, and her smile seemed to gain an added layer of color.

I said, "You're fatter."

She asked, "Do you prefer me fat or thin?"

I said, "I like you both ways."

She said, "If you like me dainty like a city woman, then I'll simply eat less."

"It's good if you're a bit plump." While saying this, I gently caressed her abdomen, and as I did so I felt her belly tremble under my finger. I caressed her abdomen a couple more times, whereupon she began to turn pale, and her gaze became fiery. I knew that before we did that thing, she always wanted me to appreciate her naked body, to caress her and say the sorts of things she loved to hear. I said, "Hongmei, you are even more entrancing than ever, and it's as though your entire body were made of jade." Smiling, she leaned against me, and as she did so I removed my shirt and fell back onto the haystack.

"I also haven't done that thing for a long time," she murmured, as she gazed up at the sky through the gaps in the straw. "You probably won't believe me, but Qingdong is ill and is only half a man anyway, and ever since that day in the tomb, I haven't let him touch me. No matter how much Chinese medicine he takes and how many times he kneels down before me, I still won't let him touch me."

I experienced a brief moment of shock and remembered the time I saw Cheng Qingdong brewing his medicine under the window.

She asked, "What are you staring at? Aren't you cold?"

I responded, "Is Qingdong really impotent?"

She said, "He drinks Chinese medicine every day."

I said, "That's good, then. Guizhi is dead, and Qingdong is ill." As I said this, I finished removing my clothes. I knew that I should thank her—to express my appreciation for her not having permitted Qingdong to touch her. By this point I had already stripped naked and didn't want to say anything else. The volcano's magma had already melted the quartz and had reached the earth's crust. I found myself unable to say a word. There was no time to say anything. My scorchingly hot gaze shifted from her abdomen down to her private parts. That gold-red-black-yellow triangle completely absorbed my gaze. I knelt down before her, with one of my legs between hers. When my knee touched the straw, it made a popping sound as though it were on fire, and when it touched her legs, which were even whiter than the straw, her entire body began to tremble.

She exclaimed, "Aijun . . . branch secretary . . . town mayor, I'm going to die, I'm going to die . . ."

Her voice made me feel as though my blood were going to surge out of my veins, overflow the dam, and fly out of my body. I already felt as though the blood and salt in my fingers, toes, and palms might spurt out. Flustered and frantic, I opened her legs and placed my knee between them. Needless to say, another intoxicating and heart-breaking moment was about to arrive, when her pliable, vermilion screams would cover the sky like a rainbow, shining down on the earth and the mountains and stimulating my crazed revolutionary spirit and will. But just at that moment (Heaven, oh heaven! Earth, oh earth!), we heard footsteps, which came to a stop right behind us.

(Roaring clouds, wind howling through the pines, the masses rush forward;
The sound of gunfire, and the military situation becomes perilous,
Everyone is shouldering an enormously heavy burden.
A mountain-like storm darkens heaven and earth,
a fire burns in my heart . . .)

I spun around.

Cheng Tianqing appeared on the side of the field.

Although it was already spring, he was still wearing the black padded jacket that had been part of his uniform. His face wasn't too dirty, and he looked at me and Hongmei with a gaze that was more white than black, with a green look of surprise on his face. I saw that things were not going well for him, and it was as if on the road to revolution we had been ambushed by the enemy. Just as I was turning my head, Hongmei sat up and grabbed her clothes.

At that instant—an instant that felt as long as a ten-*li* mountain range—Cheng Tianqing stared at me, and I stared back at him. My mind was a complete blank. I didn't know how to respond to this new development, nor did I have any inkling of what sort of earth-shattering events might follow. Cold vapor rose up from underneath my feet and swirled around my fingers and head, even as hot sweat dripped down from the tip of my nose. I thought I was about to collapse, and my bones felt as though they were made of rubber. At that moment, Cheng Tianqing suddenly lunged forward and knelt down before me and Hongmei and proceeded to kowtow as though he were pounding garlic with his forehead.

He said, "Have mercy on me . . . Please have mercy on me. My daughter is dead, and you mustn't kill me as well . . . I confess, I confess, OK? Given that I'm an old Party member who participated in the revolution before Liberation, please have mercy on me just this once . . ."

(This was truly a loss of face for the Party and for the older generation of revolutionaries!)

I sighed and slowly began getting dressed. I told Hongmei, "Don't be afraid." Then I finished putting on my clothes, fastened my buttons, and calmly walked out from the space between the haystacks. I proceeded up to where Cheng Tianqing was kneeling, then stood over him like Mount Tai. I asked, "What did you see just now?"

He said, "I'm at fault. I've let down Chairman Mao, and I've let down the Party Central Committee. I really didn't mean to use paper from Chairman Mao's book to wipe my grandson's butt . . ."

I raised my voice. "Father of Guizhi, I asked you what you saw."

He still didn't look up, and instead pounded his forehead on the ground and said, "Spare me, please. Please spare me in light of my service as a mail courier for the Eighth Route Army before

163

Liberation . . . I deserve to die a thousand times. I should die a thousand times . . ."

As he said this, he eventually stopped kowtowing, and instead he knelt there and repeatedly slapped his own face.

I said, "OK, I'll spare you this time. Regardless of whether or not you and Guizhi may have been counterrevolutionaries, one day of matrimony nevertheless means endless devotion, and you are, for better or worse, Hongsheng's and Honghua's grandfather. So, I say you should simply return home."

He stopped slapping himself and instead looked up at me.

I said, "Go! Go shoo away that sheep in the wheat field."

He kowtowed to me, then unsteadily got to his feet and walked away, heading toward the sheep in that distant field.

After he left, I turned around to look at Hongmei, who had been standing behind me, and saw that her face was covered with a look of yellow terror like a window curtain.

"If he utters a word about this, you and I are doomed."

I reflected for a moment, then turned to Cheng Tianqing, who was walking down a footpath through the field, and shouted, "Cheng Tianqing, if you didn't see anything, we'll let you live. If, however, you saw something and were to say anything about it, you would become an irredeemable counterrevolutionary, and I'm afraid that the revolution would not permit you to continue living on this earth."

I had assumed that he wouldn't hear me, but he did. He came to a stop, turned around, and from a distance bowed and kowtowed toward me and Hongmei. Then he got to his feet and walked away.

There were still some traces of winter chill in the early spring sunlight, and a breeze blew over from the hill and the irrigation canal. Cheng Tianqing had departed, but the lingering fear he left in his wake made us uninterested in continuing to do that thing. Instead, we sat on a millstone next to the wheat field, gazing out at the footpath, at the sheep that Cheng Tianqing had tried to shoo away, and at each field's eastward-facing slogan-filled signs. Hongmei and I tightly held hands, and she said, "Aijun, we have to think of a solution—one that won't affect our future or our revolutionary image and one that allows us to be together when we want. That way, if we want to do that thing, we can simply strip off our clothes like a married couple and do it."

I didn't say anything. Instead, I turned away from that distant footpath and happened to glance at the area between the haystacks where Hongmei and I had been hiding. As I did so, a magnificent plan began to take shape in my mind.

The clouds parted and the sun began to shine through, as the thousand-year sago palm burst into bloom. In my mind, there was a loud bang, followed by a deafening boom. In that instant, my enormous plan began to take shape and form, and to begin.

3. Reflections on a Paulownia Tree

I resolved to dig a secret tunnel from my house to Hongmei's, so that we could meet up whenever we wanted and do that thing just like a married couple, without even needing to leave our homes.

When this plan appeared to me like a ray of sunlight, my pulse began to race. However, I didn't immediately share my plan with Hongmei. This might well prove to be the most beautiful page of our love life, but I didn't want to say a word to her until I had completed my preparations. From the moment this plan first took shape in my mind, however, every time I thought of it I would become so excited that my blood would boil. I didn't immediately implement the plan, however, but instead first made sure the production team meeting site was completely set up, and then wrote three experiential documents. One was titled "'Three Unifications' Turns the Thought of the Masses Red"; the second was titled "'One Helping One' Yields a Red Line, and 'A Red Team' Yields a Sheet of Red"; and the third was titled "Reflections on Whether Cheng Temple Is a Residual Feudal Poison or a Cultural Legacy." All the attendees felt discomfited by Cheng Temple's intricate ornamentation and noted that many of the temple's tiles and bricks were engraved with imperial symbols of dragons and phoenixes. This quite clearly conflicted with the revolution's call for destroying the old and establishing the new. I very much wanted to demolish Cheng Temple and the memorial arch, thereby allowing the storm of revolution to sweep through Chenggang. However, if I were in fact to carry out this sort of mass cleansing, not only would it be at odds with the status awarded to the temple in the early 1960s by the provincial regulations on the preservation of cultural relics, but more importantly it would be like chopping off the heads of all of the Cheng descendants, who account for three-quarters of the Chenggang production team. On this point, that bastard Mayor Wang was correct when he observed that I couldn't afford to lose the support of the masses on account of Cheng Temple, since the People are the only force capable of creating history, and the masses are the only true heroes in the development of society. If we were to lose the support of the masses, we would lose the most basic condition for revolution. Was the Battle of the Cheng Brothers Memorial Arch not an instructive lesson? I hoped that before destroying Cheng Temple and the memorial arch, I would be able to receive an official document or an oral instruction from the higher-ups, which I could then use for support and protection as I proceeded to destroy the old. In "Reflections on Whether Cheng Temple Is a Residual Feudal Poison or a Cultural Legacy," I listed nine charges relating to Cheng Temple and the memorial arch:

1. *The existence of Cheng Temple and the memorial arch suggests that the black flag of Cheng-Zhu Neo-Confucianism is still fluttering amidst the red revolution, despite being in direct opposition to the revolutionary situation.*
2. *The temple and memorial arch attract many pilgrims and poison the thought of people for miles around.*

3. *The temple and memorial arch encourage superstitious activity (such as people secretly lighting incense before and after Lunar New Year, and an endless stream of people making offerings).*
4. *Every brick in the temple and the memorial arch reeks of the stench of feudal poison.*

. . . .

9. *The act of destroying the temple and memorial arch is equivalent to destroying the headquarters of Cheng-Zhu Neo-Confucianism, and doing so would therefore permit the great flag of Mao Zedong Thought to fly high over the Balou Mountains.*

I made several copies of this document and arranged for someone to take them to the county committee and send them to the district-level and provincial-level newspapers. In this way, the fields were fertilized and irrigated, and once the revolution reached the next stage, I would be able to begin implementing my glorious plan to destroy Cheng Temple.

One day when Hongsheng was at school and Honghua was out with my mother, I climbed a paulownia tree in our family's courtyard and, using the basic knowledge about tunnel-digging I had acquired while serving in the military, I peered through the tree leaves and surveyed the area. Using an elm tree behind Shi Dagou's house as my first benchmark, the toon tree behind Cheng Cuifen's house as my second benchmark, and the old pagoda tree in the entrance to Cheng Tianqing's house as my third benchmark, I estimated that it was approximately 550 meters from my house on Rear Cheng Street to Hongmei's house on Front Cheng Street. But between the two houses there was a corner of Cheng Temple courtyard and the houses belonging to Shi Ergou, deputy director of the second production team, and seven people surnamed Cheng, together with parts of Center Cheng Street and Rear Cheng Street. If the tunnel was a half meter wide and one meter high, it would generate 275 cubic meters of packed earth, and assuming that the ratio of packed earth to loose earth was at least 1 to 1.5, that would make 415 cubic meters of loose earth. Moreover, if halfway down the passageway, beneath Center Cheng Street, I were to excavate an area large enough to hold a bed—about 3 meters wide, 3 meters long, and 2 meters high—this underground room, which would serve as our nuptial chamber, would generate 18 cubic meters of packed earth, or 27 cubic meters of loose earth. Accordingly, if the tunnel were perfectly straight, it would generate some 300 cubic meters of packed earth, or 450 cubic meters of loose earth. If I were to pursue revolution during the day and engage in production (which is to say, digging the tunnel) at night, then, assuming I could dig 0.7 cubic meters of packed earth every night, it would take me 420 days to dig this tunnel of love. Four hundred and twenty days is nearly a year and a half. But what if I needed to leave home to attend a meeting? Or what if I needed to work overtime at night in Chenggang (whether during the peak agriculture season in midsummer, or to organize political study groups for Party members or production team members)? Or what if I were to fall ill with a fever? Or what if there was an error in my calculations, and the tunnel didn't reach its destination on my first try?

That is to say, even if I were to dig as quickly as possible—working every night without fail—it would in all likelihood take me nearly two years to complete the tunnel. (And during these two years, I would need to attain another objective, which was to become mayor). Two years might seem like a very long time—like an interminable night during which the sun never appears. But for a revolutionary head over heels in love, what does this amount to? Didn't the War of Resistance against Japanese Aggression last eight years? Didn't the War of Liberation last four years? Didn't I serve in the army for four years and spend a year and eight months digging a tunnel through the mountains? However, I never lost my will to succeed, and there was no obstacle I couldn't overcome. Who said this? Is this a slogan I wrote while serving on the production team, or is it some beautiful words I read in a report?

For us—as the bravest, wisest, most selfless people, armed with revolutionary thought—there is no obstacle we cannot overcome, there is no peak we cannot climb, and there is no miracle we cannot create. Accordingly, we arrive at the most difficult moment, rise to the most urgent juncture, travel to the most dangerous locations, and undertake the most dangerous assignments. Without blood and sweat, there can be no glory, and without sacrifice there can be no happiness. Without lofty aspirations there can be no great prospects, and without hard work there can be no possibility of success. Revolution starts from a storm, just as the spoils of harvest come after industriousness. Happiness is accumulated from blood and sweat, and bliss is derived from frustration. Hold your head up, walk forward, rain or shine; cross the ravine, embrace hardship, and swear never to lower your head. Advance, the future beckons! Work hard, the red flag lies ahead. Struggle, and the sun will shine forever!

But the problem still remains: Where will I dump those 450 cubic meters of loose soil that I'll dig up?

I walked around the paulownia tree and saw the irrigation canal that runs all year-round at the base of the Chenggang hill in the Balou Mountains. How many tens of thousands of cubic meters of soil could the canal hold? How much soil could the canal's water wash away?

Several days later, I made an opening in our family's courtyard wall and installed a door. Then I built a pigsty on the other side of the door and bought a couple of piglets. In this way, I created a back door and a path—both of which were hidden from view by the pigsty —by which I could access the irrigation canal behind the village.

I began digging one night in the latter half of the fourth month, on a night when the half-moon didn't appear until after midnight.

Needless to say, everyone else was still asleep, and the moonlight illuminated everything inside the village and outside the village with its milky light. I marked out the entrance to the tunnel in a sweet-potato cellar in my rear courtyard, then I collected a short-handled shovel, a pick, a hoe, a couple of rattan baskets, a lamp, a rope, and an iron hook, and took them into the sweet-potato cellar. Next, wearing the white shirt and green pants that I normally wore only when digging for the army, I crawled into the cellar and hung the lamp from the earthen wall. I spit on my palms and rubbed them together, knelt down with the pick, then lifted my arms and brought them down forcefully. When I lifted the pick again, the first bowl-size clump of yellow dirt fell to the ground. The smell of moist soil immediately overpowered the scent of sweet potatoes and decayed leaves that lingered in the cellar. Thanks to the revolution, it had been a long time since I had personally engaged in any heavy manual labor, because since I had become the highest-ranking official in the Chenggang production team, people would even bring fresh well water, grain, and vegetables directly to my house. After a new directive had come down from the town Party committee a half month earlier, even minor tasks like sweeping the courtyard and hanging things on the wall were handled by villagers who came to my house to discuss things. It was as if the villagers regarded it as an honor to work for my family. In the army, I had observed that the orderlies charged with bringing tea to military commanders and washing their clothes always had a proud smile on their faces, and now I noticed that the villagers working for my family always had an affectionate, warm, and even proud smile. I knew I merely needed to give the word, and countless commune members would immediately come to help me extend this passageway all the way to Hongmei's house. However, I couldn't do that. I definitely couldn't do that. Not only would the revolution not permit it, this kind of behavior would inevitably position me in opposition to the revolution and even make me an enemy of the revolution. So naturally I couldn't let anyone help me, nor could I share my secret with anyone. I was digging a dark passageway, a hiding place that Hongmei and I would treasure in our souls but would never be able to reveal to anyone else. It was a sublime proof of our great and divine love.

I filled two baskets with dirt, crawled out of the tunnel, then used the rope to haul the baskets up into the moonlight. Next, I went through the pigsty and out the back gate, following a path down to the irrigation canal at the base of the hillock. By this point the moon had already moved from over the hillock to a new position over the village, and in the moonlight the rafters and eaves of the rear courtyard of Cheng Temple appeared gentle and soothing, as if they were rocking back and forth. In the village streets, you could occasionally hear the sound of a dog or two barking, like a thin sheet of ice sliding down from the sky, whereupon the early summer moonlit sky would appear even more indescribably beautiful. The bright sound of flowing water in the irrigation canal circulated like drizzle under the moonlight. There was wet grass in the fields and under my feet. The frogs and cicadas grew quiet as I walked past, then resumed their light-hearted cries, drowning out my footsteps and the clattering sound of the baskets suspended from my carrying pole. The world became incomparably still, and in that stillness I could even hear the Balou Mountains breathing. It was as if I could hear the wheat stalks absorbing moisture and nourishment from the fields.

I carried the first load of dirt to the banks of the canal, wiped away my sweat, then dumped the dirt into the canal. When I stood up, I saw that the row of red-tile-roofed houses in the main courtyard of the town government complex in the northern end of Chenggang was illuminated in the moonlight, the houses all turned dark purple, as though covered in a layer of dried blood.

I resolved that, within two years, I would dig a 550-meter-long revolutionary tunnel of love, and furthermore I would rid Chenggang of all the obstacles that had been created by my political activities. I resolved that before I turned twenty-seven I would be appointed mayor and would become Chenggang's primary leader. That night, I dug 0.8 meters of tunnel and dumped nineteen loads of dirt into the irrigation canal. I looked over to the town government's tile-roofed buildings nineteen times, and nineteen times I repeated my vow. Finally, when the roosters crowed three times and the eastern sky began to be filled with milky white light, I pissed in the direction of the town government complex, then returned home and went to sleep.

Chapter 7

A New Battle

1. The Transformation of Cheng Temple

Three days before the beginning of the Full Grain solar term, I found myself faced with a formidable challenge. The previous day had been the anniversary of the birth of Cheng Yuxiang, the father of the Cheng Brothers. During the day, village life proceeded as usual, but when night fell the village suddenly became very peaceful. As usual, that night I hauled nearly twenty loads of dirt from the tunnel to the irrigation canal, but just as the sun was about to come up, Hongmei and Cheng Qinglin woke me up.

"This is a crisis, a fucking crisis! Last night, someone burned incense and spirit paper in the entranceway to Cheng Temple," Cheng Qinglin shouted as he lunged toward my bed.

"This is clearly an attempt to challenge our proletariat class with superstitious feudal activity," Hongmei said as she handed me the clothing I had removed when I returned home a little earlier. "If we don't immediately put a stop to this deviant activity, we'll be betraying the absolute authority of our revolutionary committee!"

I understood the seriousness of the situation. If we ignored this development, not only would it demonstrate the weakness of the new leadership—of which I was the center—but it could one day become powerful evidence that the "new red revolutionary base" was in fact a "superstitious tribe." In fact, it would affect not only Chenggang's revolutionary committee but the town's political livelihood and entire future. Without a word, I got dressed and, together with Hongmei and Qinglin, went directly to Cheng Temple. We saw that there were thirty piles of burnt incense sticks and spirit paper in the entranceway. I had heard that whenever Cheng Tianmin went to the county seat to attend a meeting, the main gate of Cheng Temple would always be locked, and therefore these people who had come to burn incense hadn't been able to enter the temple proper and instead had to burn their offerings in the entranceway. Upon seeing those rows of ashes and dew-covered incense sticks, I wondered how it was that I hadn't noticed them when coming back from digging the night before? Did that mean that these people burning the incense hadn't noticed me either?

Either way, I had to find the people who had burned the incense. After telling Qinglin to summon a member of the People's militia to come keep watch over the site, Hongmei and I went to the town government complex to see Mayor Wang, who had just woken up and was in the process of washing his face. We initially wanted to ask him to summon some comrades from the police station to help us solve the case, but after hearing our report he slowly wrung out his towel in the basin and said, "I see that those several *mu* of land at the front of your village need irrigation."

Hongmei and I were both unnerved by this response. It was as if we were not pursuing revolution but rather were idle and simply using the revolution to give us some kind of diversion.

"Today we will organize people to go irrigate the land," I said. "But Mayor Wang, the fact that there are people who still dare to burn incense and worship their ancestors is much more consequential than the need to irrigate the land and increase production on that plot."

Mayor Wang turned and looked at me and Xia Hongmei. His towel paused for a moment over the basin, then he said, "Gao Aijun, don't you know that I was a professional soldier? When I was in the army, I served as a battalion commander, and now I'm the town mayor. Xia Hongmei never served in the military, so she wouldn't understand, but you should know how subordinates should address their superiors."

I said, "Mayor Wang, the revolution doesn't distinguish between rich and poor. Subordinates should serve and respect their superiors, but it is even more important that their superiors serve and respect the truth."

Mayor Wang threw his towel into the basin, and the dirty water splattered all over me and Hongmei. "The truth is that if you don't irrigate your land, production will drop. If production drops, the people will go hungry, and if the people go hungry they won't follow the Party or pursue revolution." As he was hollering, blood rushed to his face and turned his cheeks deep purple. I wanted to tell him that the issue wasn't that if people were hungry they wouldn't follow the Party and wouldn't pursue revolution, but rather it was precisely because people were hungry that they would follow the Party and pursue revolution. This has been demonstrated by revolutionary history and is an irrefutable experience and truth. But before I had a chance to explain this, Mayor Wang opened a drawer and took out several pages of a document that had been copied by hand onto letter paper and tossed them at me. Hongmei and I took a look and saw that it was the text of the essay "Reflections on Whether Cheng Temple Is a Residual Feudal Poison or a Cultural Legacy," which Hongmei and I had sent to the county seat.

Hongmei and I both froze in alarm.

Mayor Wang said, "Go ahead and take it. If the two of you want to destroy Cheng Temple, you will simultaneously destroy the heart of the Chenggang production brigade. Let's see how you continue to work, be cadres, and pursue revolution after you lose community support."

Hongmei and I emerged from the town government building.

We decided to teach Mayor Wang a lesson.

Outside the town government's main gate, there was an area paved in bricks, around which were three paulownia trees. In the cracks between the bricks, there were a variety of weeds and insects. Hongmei took the copy of "Reflections on Whether Cheng Temple Is a Residual Feudal Poison or a Cultural Legacy" and asked me, "How could this have ended up in Mayor Wang's hands?" I replied, "This simply proves that there is a black thread running through the Party's internal organization, because otherwise how could this document have ended up in Mayor Wang's hands?" Hongmei's face turned slightly pale, as though a ruthless enemy were standing in front of us holding a gun. I asked, "What should we do?" She said, "We can't let Mayor Wang lead us around by the nose." Of course we couldn't let Mayor Wang lead us around by the nose. Just as China couldn't let Khrushchev lead it by the nose, how could we let a mayor lead us by the nose? When I looked through the leaves of the paulownia trees, I could see sunlight erupting like blood in the eastern sky, dyeing the eastern mountains and half the earth red while illuminating the world and the universe.

When the sun came up, I heard a dark pounding sound like blood vessels exploding. I saw a beehive fall from one of the pau-lownia trees and, with a snap, all the bees flew back into it. At that moment, I had a revolutionary inspiration. An earth-enveloping vigor emanated from the blood-red light of the rising sun and poured over me. From the fallen beehive I had the inspiration that revolution yields birth and victory, while a lack of revolution yields defeat and death. I gazed at Hongmei's face and saw traces of her earlier frustration and disappointment in her eyes. I said, "Motherfuckers. The mayor is a cock, and the battalion commander is a cock." She asked, "Do you dare challenge him?" I replied, "If I don't, what alternative do we have?" Then there was a period of silence, broken when I suddenly asked, "Hongmei, have you missed me? Do you miss doing that thing?" She looked away for a moment and saw a government cadre carrying a bamboo water bottle into the water closet to fetch some hot water. She watched as he lifted his foot to step over the twenty-centimeter-high threshold to the door of the town government's main building. She nodded to the cadre, then turned back to me and grunted in agreement. She said, "Aijun, Guizhi is no longer alive. But as long as you want me, I am always willing to give myself to you. As long as it's safe, we can do it anywhere."

I took her hand. Right there in front of the town government building's door, which was covered in red paint, under the slogan-filled scrolls that hung on either side of the door, and in the mottled sunlight that made its way through the paulownia trees' leafy canopy overhead, she threw caution to the wind and—like a dog or pig, a horse or ox—stuck her hand down my pants. When her soft fingers touched my brazen hardness, we both started to tremble from head to toe. We both stepped back as though we had received an electric shock, then nervously looked around.

An old man from the Cheng clan emerged from his house carrying a pail and proceeded to Rear Cheng Street well to fetch some water.

Hongmei and I looked at each other as the white heat on our faces fell clatteringly to our feet.

She said, "Aijun, I'll wait for you tonight on the bank of Thirteen Li River."

I stared at her half-white face, as though looking at a nude painting.

She said, "Don't you want to do that thing?"

I said, "Of course I do, I want it more than life itself!" Then I added, "But the current situation wouldn't permit it, so we should restrain ourselves. I've noticed that as long as I restrain myself and don't do that thing, I'm always left with an endless amount of energy and vigor—such that I can carry out any kind of revolution."

I continued, "Going forward, every time we successfully contribute to the revolution, we'll be able to go crazy doing that thing.

We should celebrate revolutionary acts by doing that thing—and that way doing that thing will be much more satisfying than if we did it ten or a hundred times a day."

She stared back at me the same way that I was staring at her. I didn't know whether she was looking at my mouth or at my nose (or perhaps she was gazing at me as though I were a nude painting?).

I said, "Today, we'll lead the masses into Cheng Temple. We won't worry about the building itself, but we will burn all the Cheng Brothers' writings stored inside. Then let's see what Mayor Wang proposes to do in response. Afterward, you and I can meet on the riverbank and celebrate by crazily doing that thing."

With this hungry longing to do that thing, we resolved to initiate an attack on Cheng Temple. We hoped that the failure of the attack on the memorial arch would become the mother of success and were confident that the subsequent attack on Cheng Temple would have to succeed—given that in the early summer period we had already seized Chenggang's leadership and gained many valuable revolutionary experiences and lessons. We therefore already understood that for the People (the masses), it is only the People (the masses) who are the true heroes, the true creators of history, and the true engine of historical development. I was already extremely clear that once one grasps class struggle, one's soul becomes deep and profound. I was already extremely clear that revolution is like war.

In fact, revolution is war. A production brigade's revolution is like a nation's war, or even a world war. War can bring the people destruction, but if we don't resist the armed interference and invasion from domestic counterrevolutionaries and international imperialists, and instead willingly permit ourselves to become oppressed or enslaved, then we will be fated to suffer even more destruction, sacrifice, and pain. That is to say, if we permit Khrushchev to lead us around by the nose and let ourselves be manipulated like marionettes by the revisionists—if we remain indifferent to this predicament and turn a deaf ear to it—then we will effectively push our nation to the brink of disaster and destruction. If that happens, our people will be transformed into new slaves, rendering our nation and our people into a different kind of colonial subject. In revolution and in war, the sacrifice of the minority can be exchanged for the security and happiness of the majority, or even of the entire nation. Lenin said, "War makes even the most civilized and cultured nations (or places, such as Chenggang) descend into a state of famine." However, as a powerful historical process, war is also capable of generating a spectacularly rapid social development. War is a wake-up call for the masses and arouses them by means of an unprecedented amount of pain and suffering. Revolution launches war and war promotes revolution, which is why history can hurtle forward like a locomotive.

Given that war can rely only on itself to be extinguished, just as revolution can rely only itself for success, why don't we use our experience and theory of revolutionary war to help direct today's revolution? Why don't we use a martial modality to promote revolution? We of course should use a revolutionary modality to launch war, and a martial modality to promote revolution. We naturally should rush into Cheng Temple and burn the Cheng Brothers' books, portraits, and all copies of the Four Books and the Five Classics, all the temple's manuscripts written on brittle yellow paper, the Cheng clan genealogies, Cheng Temple's property registry, and all the Cheng clan's other documents and canonical texts—all those leather-bound volumes, all those musty-smelling Buddhist scriptures stored in wooden boxes, those bearded ancestral portraits painted on enormous hanging scrolls, those ancestral spirits who were presented as scholars. Although it may be true that people only rarely look through this collection of documents, isn't it also the case that the Cheng clansmen in the Chenggang production brigade (and particularly those who are middle-aged or older) still view them with awe? Aren't all Cheng clansmen extremely proud of this collection of texts?

Don't they treat this collection as the soul of Cheng Temple? During the revolution, Cheng Temple received an unprecedented degree of protection from Mayor Wang, but what exactly is the relationship between Mayor Wang and Cheng Temple? Is Mayor Wang's relationship with the previous mayor, Cheng Tianmin, merely that of two generations of leaders? What kind of secrets do they share, such that Mayor Wang was willing to depart from the path of the Party and instead follow the direction of the feudal bourgeoisie, to the point that he now views promoting land irrigation as more important than crushing feudal superstition?

When Hongmei and I headed back to Cheng Temple, the morning sun that had emerged from behind the eastern mountains was bright gold—just like the expensive paint we had used when writing slogans on the walls. All the village's families had initially been shocked by the discovery that someone had been commemorating their ancestors by burning incense in Cheng Temple, but now they had come to their senses. Each family stood in the entranceway to the temple and watched for a while, then proceeded toward the temple while asking each other what was going on. At this point, Cheng Qinglin and several policemen holding red and white poles stopped me and Hongmei and announced, in a panting voice, as though taking credit for someone else's achievements, "Branch Secretary Gao, when the water recedes the riverbed will be revealed. The truth is now clear, and we have arrested several people who had been burning incense in the entranceway."

Hongmei and I abruptly came to a halt in front of a millstone in the middle of Rear Cheng Street. "Who did you arrest?"

"They are all Cheng clansmen from other regions," the militia commander replied. "This is probably because the revolution here in Chenggang has reached such a feverish pitch that there is no one who'd dare do this themselves. However, we searched several houses, and sure enough, we found several Cheng clansmen who had come here from far away. The locals had left, and the outsiders were living in the village. I arrested all of them and left them in the production brigade."

I asked, "Do the villagers know about this?"

Qinglin replied, "Most of them don't because they haven't woken up yet."

Hongmei added, "In order to sound the alarm, and to punish one person to serve as a warning to everyone else, we should parade these outsiders through the streets. That way, they will come to realize the greatness of our Chenggang production brigade's situation, and no one will dare spit or urinate in the face of Chenggang's revolution."

Qinglin said, "I agree. I'll go prepare the ropes and dunce hats."

With this, Cheng Qinglin prepared to lead the militia back to the brigade office on Center Cheng Street, but I stopped him.

"I hereby convene a branch secretary meeting right here and now." As I said, this, I placed one foot on the millstone and watched as everyone crowded around.

Qinglin, Hongmei, and several militia members looked at me.

"If we parade these people through the streets, we'll be wronging their relatives," I said. "The accused are all Cheng clansmen, and everyone who carries the Cheng surname will assume that we could round them up and subject them to struggle sessions. We should simply leave the Cheng clansmen from outside Chenggang for now and then apprehend them later. That way, we can perhaps receive the sympathy and support of the Cheng clansmen who were previously close to the old group. Moreover, after receiving their support, we'll be able to unite seventy or eighty percent of the masses. By that point, we won't even need to burn the texts in the manuscript depository, because if we destroy Cheng Temple, the Cheng clansmen won't try to stop us the way they did when we tried to destroy the memorial arch."

I said, "During the War of Resistance against Japanese Aggression and the War of Liberation, the People's Liberation Army used psychological warfare, and now we want to do the same. Our objective is to unite the masses and burn the manuscripts in the manuscript depository (which is the soul of Cheng Temple) in order to lay the groundwork for our next step, which will be to claim the political power of the town Party committee. However, if we lose the support of the masses, we'll also lose the possibility of claiming the political power of the town Party committee, and we will therefore become like a tree without roots, a boat without water, or a general without an army. This is the rule of revolution and the experience of people's warfare, and we definitely cannot go against these rules and experiences."

The militia battalion commander asked, "In that case, should we simply let the other Cheng clansmen go?"

I replied, "Yes, let them go. Let them all go."

Hongmei added, "I agree. Aijun stands above us and therefore is able to see further and think more deeply than we can. It's no wonder he is the leader of our group."

(Hongmei, you are indeed my heart and my flesh, my love and my soul!) Hongmei was always the first person to understand me, and our revolutionary love was now so strong that we were even more able than usual to read each other's thoughts.

2. The Battle of Cheng Temple

After releasing the Cheng clansmen who had been burning incense in front of Cheng Temple, we obtained the expected positive benefit with respect to the Chenggang production brigade.

When the sun was three pole lengths high in the sky, we released the suspects in front of Cheng Temple. Ray upon ray of sunlight shone down upon our ancestral nation's land, on our mountains and villages. The stones, walls, and empty fields in front of the temple were all full of people—commune members who had just woken up and hadn't even washed their faces yet. Everyone had just gotten out of bed when they heard that some people had been burning incense in front of Cheng Temple, whereupon they immediately turned pale, like dirty rags covered in frost. Needless to say, everyone knew something extraordinary was about to unfold.

At this point I noticed that my father-in-law, Cheng Tianqing, was still wearing that same jacket with cotton padding sticking out. He had straw in his hair and was standing hesitantly in the doorway. I was reminded of that time when he stumbled upon me and Hongmei behind the haystacks. So I glared at him, and he quickly retreated into the crowd. Cheng Temple's main gate was still tightly closed, but an ancient scent was emanating from the temple's front courtyard, as though a breeze were blowing through the crack in the door and into the crowd. I walked over to the main gate, the crowd immediately opening a path for me. The commune members all stared at me, waiting for me to announce the verdict in the incense-burning case. However, in the faces of the Cheng clansmen whose relatives had come to burn incense in front of the temple, there was a look of fiery desperation. They gazed at me, hoping I would save their relatives, as though waiting for my personal pardon.

I stood with one foot on the edge of the sitting area at the base of the stone lion and the other resting on the lion's rear leg, and with one hand on my waist and the other resting on the lion's head.

I suddenly remembered a documentary depicting Chairman Mao standing atop the Tiananmen gate tower on October 1, 1949, waving down to the people gathered below. I instinctively let my gaze sweep over the heads of the crowd assembled before me (it would have been better if the crowd had been somewhat larger). I was silent for a long time (having a long pause before speaking is a way we political leaders find dignity and enjoyment). I saw that the gazes directed at us were weak but steady, as though there were a slack string connecting us to the eyes of the members of the Chenggang production brigade. I knew I couldn't simply open my mouth and begin speaking. In the army, division commanders, regiment commanders, and county leaders all had to keep a moment of silence before speaking at any formal occasion—in order to gather their energy and generate a solemn atmosphere. So I stood on the seat at the base of the stone lion with a gaze that was simultaneously hot and cold—with coldness permeating the warmth, and warmth embedded in the coldness—and looked out at the crowd of townspeople that had gathered in front of the temple. I looked over those people under my authority, those commoners under my direction, and noticed how, during my silence, I could hear the commune members' hearts beating like rain pounding on the ground. I saw that the faces of the core revolutionaries in the front row had a greenish tint, and noticed the meter-long red and white poles the core militiamen were holding (these poles were specially made, and the militiamen always carried them around like rifles, as though they were their second lives), their layer of fresh paint glittering in the dawn sunlight. Meanwhile, the commune members standing behind the core revolutionaries and the militia all had a deathly pallor. They knew someone had committed a grievous crime in Cheng Temple, and although this didn't merit the death sentence, it certainly wouldn't be inappropriate to break the offenders' legs or cut off their fingers. In fact, the revolution might even require that. If I had been able to see which Cheng clansmen and their relatives had come last night to light incense, then irrespective of whether or not they were apprehended, and irrespective of whether after burning the incense they simply departed or returned to the Chenggang production brigade, any Chenggang residents who either burned incense or were direct relatives of those who had, would now be standing in the back of the crowd or a place where the collection of commune members was particularly dense. It was as if they were trying to hide, yet at the same time were sticking their heads out with a gaze that appeared far more traitorous and dozens of times brighter than in the past. Needless to say, those people who were half-hidden yet at the same time were watching me

184

with bright eyes—their families and relatives had definitely come to burn incense. I didn't know how cold my gaze was at that point nor how ambiguous it was. All I knew was that as soon as those people's eyes met mine, their eyelids would curl up like dry leaves, their eyes would drop, and their heads would bow like wilted grass under the hot sun. At this point, at this moment, at this instant, I suddenly understood that in this rural revolution, this rural war, sometimes you don't even need weapons or language, and instead you can subjugate the people with just your gaze. My father-in-law, Cheng Tianqing, served as Party branch secretary for half his life, but he always relied on his language, age, credentials, and gesticulations to direct the common people. I, however, didn't need any of this, only my gaze. I looked over their heads, faces, clothing, legs, and feet, and then, in the resulting silence, I coughed softly. Like a cold breeze that precedes a torrential downpour, I sent my hoarse, daggerlike cough directly into everyone's heart. Then I cleared my throat and announced to everyone in attendance:

"Today, members of our Chenggang production brigade witnessed how, in this new red Yan'an, there was an atrocious incident of burning incense to worship ancestors. If we analyze this incident more carefully, what does it mean? This is a paradigmatic example of a reactionary event that is simultaneously anti-Party, anti-revolution, anti-socialism, anti–Proletarian Cultural Revolution, anti–Great Leader Chairman Mao. After we seize the culprits, they should be either sent to prison or have their feet chopped off."

I said, "But I, Gao Aijun, definitely will not ignore my own relatives. Although I myself don't carry the Cheng surname, I'm still the village Party branch secretary of this village's sixteen hundred Cheng residents. Not only am I the Party secretary of the Chenggang production team, I am also a steadfast revolutionary; and not only am I a revolutionary, I am also the leader of the Cheng clan. According to the principles of revolution, I should seize everyone who participated in the incense-burning incident—men and women, young and old—and send them to jail. Or, at the very least, I should make them wear dunce hats and parade them through the streets. However, I won't do any of this—even though I know that if I don't, others may one day use this to attack me. However, for the sake of those of us who are surnamed Cheng, I will take the risk of committing a political mistake. While I do not condone last night's incense-burning and ancestor-worshiping incident, not only will I not parade the offenders through the streets, I am even opposed to handing them over to the police. Moreover, I will release everyone who has already been arrested, effective immediately."

(Everyone's eyes widened with surprise. Hongmei's face had a mysterious pink glow, and Qinglin had a discouraged expression, but the faces of the commune members and the masses—including all the local Cheng clansmen—were bright and warm. I knew I should go straight to the point.)

I said, "Fellow commune members and fellow countrymen, the incense-burning and sacrificing to the ancestors was an anti-revolutionary action, but more specifically it was, at the very least, a feudal, superstitious action, marking a return of a decadent class spirit. It is true that the Cheng Brothers are the ancestors of the current residents of Chenggang, but every age has different values. Now is the time of the new society, the Cultural Revolution, the dawning of an unparalleled new era. How could you come to burn incense and kowtow to the ancestors? You are confused! You are *all* confused! . . . What can I say about this? All I can say is that I don't blame you in the least. I don't blame my fellow countrymen, I don't blame my aunt and sister-in-law, I don't blame my grandmother and grandfather, I don't blame any commune members, and I don't blame this temple that our ancestors handed down to us, or the manuscript depository full of volumes and scrolls reeking of feudal bourgeois decay. I, Gao Aijun, have thought over all this, and the Party branch committee has also looked into this question. How will we turn over to the authorities those who burned the incense and sacrificed to the ancestors? Of course, the best thing would be to simply release the suspects and destroy the temple. But if we destroy the temple it won't be you who will be upset by it but rather I, Gao Aijun. This is a building that was built in the Ming dynasty, and it is not only the public face of our Cheng clan, it is also a symbol of the Chenggang production brigade. So, what should we do? I eventually decided that the only solution would be to burn the volumes, scrolls, and other artifacts stored in the manuscript depository. That way, not only could we protect both the temple and the people who burned incense and sacrificed to the ancestors, we could also show the higher-ups that we have burned the temple's soul. We have pursued revolution from the heart, and what is left of Cheng Temple is merely its dead husk."

I glanced at the Cheng clansmen, and they silently stared back at me, Hongmei, and Qinglin.

Hongmei announced loudly, "If you don't burn these volumes, you should at least send the suspects to the county police office."

An animated chatter ran through the crowd.

Cheng Qinglin took a step forward, then turned back to his fellow clansmen and said, "It's Secretary Gao's decision whether or not we burn the volumes. Secretary Gao's request for your opinion was merely his way of expressing respect, but who offers a toast without being able to accept a possible penalty? In the end, Secretary Gao will have no choice but to send several dozen people to the police station, and neither the temple nor the volumes it contains will be able to be preserved. By that point the chickens will have flown the coop, and the eggs will have been broken, but we won't have any regrets."

I shouted, "Is it that you don't actually want to burn those volumes?"

Someone standing in the center of the crowd shouted back, in a voice that was like a grenade being detonated, "Yes! . . . Burn them! Why would you want to keep those useless things?"

After this response, the crowd began chanting: "Burn them! Burn them now!"

"Only the People should be protected, while those old things should be incinerated . . ."

In this way, in response to my calls, people began to side with me. In the crowd, the shouts rose to a tempest, and the people lifted their fists to the sky. Following those shouts, the Cheng clansmen who had been hiding in the back of the crowd jostled their way to the front. They made their way toward me, like Red Guards trying to reach Chairman Mao's side. Of course, I couldn't let them idolize me the way Red Guards idolized Chairman Mao, because that would have made me a veritable anti-revolutionary. By the same token, how could I have them revere me the way they revered Cheng Tianmin? Was not the fervor with which they revered me comparable to that with which they had revered him?

Indeed, the esteem in which the Cheng clansmen held me surely now far exceeded the support and respect they had had for Cheng Tianqing and or Cheng Tianmin. This constituted success. It was the necessary result and need of revolution and marked the greatness of our achievement. By this point light from the rising sun had already reached the front of the village, and Cheng Temple was bathed in sunlight. I watched everything that was developing in the temple's entranceway. The temple itself didn't realize that its heart was about to be ripped out and burned to ashes by the Cheng descendants of the Cheng clan in whose honor it had been built. I hopped down from the stone lion, and the crowds surged toward me, shouting, and droplets of saliva rained down on me. Cheng Qinglin took a militia group and moved toward the temple entrance. I heard one of the militiamen ask, "Does anyone have any gunpowder?" Another responded, "Yes, we have enough to destroy not only the temple's volumes but also the entire temple."

Hongmei leaned against me and gripped my hand. She was secretly congratulating me for having mobilized the crowd, for my success, and for my great ability to obtain the support of the people. She was suggesting that success lay just ahead. By the terms of our secret agreement, we would be able to take advantage of the post-success revolutionary passion and crazily do that thing. We could find a secluded location and, forgetting everything, let our passionate enjoyment, or "livening," reach a heavenly site. (It would be truly great once the tunnel was completed and the underground room was ready, because that would be such a perfectly secluded location. Unfortunately, at that point I had dug only thirty meters, reaching only Rear Cheng Street, and had not even reached the edge of the temple.) Hongmei's hand felt warm and soft, and a soft smell of sweat and a mysterious feminine scent emanated from her tender fingertips to her palms. My body began to tremble, and I was afraid I wouldn't be able to resist doing something inappropriate. I coughed, and she immediately loosened her grip. The crowd had already gathered around the entrance to the temple, and the screams of children being trampled hovered over the temple entrance. My father-in-law was originally the temple's most powerful protector, but when he heard we were going to burn the temple's books, he began laughing darkly. With a smirk, he rubbed his hands together and projected an attitude of extreme impatience.

He had completely lost his mind.

The militia had arrived at the entrance to the temple.

Cheng Temple's main gate was still tightly locked, but someone was pounding on it, trying to force his way in. I made my way to the front of the crowd and shouted for that person to stop. Upon hearing me, the crowd immediately quieted down. I had never expected that a few words from me would be enough to make the entire village burst into tumult, and then a few more others would make them quiet down like magpies. I suspected that if I were to give the order, the villagers would immediately destroy the temple's three-room courtyard and dismantle the temple brick by brick. If that had indeed come to pass, Hongmei and I would have had a very different fate. This story would have flown down the middle of the road like a carriage, and perhaps our fate would not have been the execution grounds but rather a meeting hall or stage with bouquets of flowers, vast crowds of people, and thunderous applause. But I was too fond of the feeling of being like an emperor appearing before the people or a general directing his troops—I was simply too attached to that power of being able to rally multitudes with a single call. I initially assumed I was already a mature rural revolutionary and politician, but I didn't realize that, in pursuing revolution, I was still committing many infantile mistakes. In the end, I didn't let the crowd destroy the temple, nor did I let them pound on the temple's mahogany door.

Instead, I tore down the door myself.

This was just before the hottest part of the summer, and the sun had already begun sending down its searing rays. But after the temple door opened and the fresh air from the courtyard rushed out, the crowd followed me into the outer courtyard. Needless to say, some of them hadn't had an opportunity to enter the courtyard and see the manuscript depository for ten or twenty years, if at all. Now the moment had finally arrived, and it was the revolution that had granted the People this opportunity. Everyone rushed in, stumbling over each over as they crowded into this mysterious temple, joining the effort to destroy these feudal remnants.

I was the first person to enter the middle courtyard.

On either side there was a pair of wing rooms shaded by grape trellises, the Gentle Wind and Sweet Rain room and the Scorching Sun and Autumn Frost room. In the tenth month of the twenty-seventh year of the Guangxu reign (which is to say, 1901), when Emperor Dezong and Empress Dowager Cixi were returning to Beijing from Yan'an, they passed through the town of Longmen in Luoyang, where they each inscribed a plaque with the phrases SOURCES AND ORIGINS OF THE YI AND LUO RIVERS and ADMIRING AND FOLLOWING YAN HUI AND MENCIUS. These plaques were hung above the doors to the Gentle

Wind and Sweet Rain room and the Scorching Sun and Autumn Frost room, but now were covered by grape leaves. Four grapevines that had been planted in the courtyard dozens of years earlier, each with a trunk as wide as a rice bowl, were now full of tiny unripe grapes that would brush people's heads when they walked past. The plants' roots pushed up the bricks in the middle courtyard, reflecting the temple's simplicity and peacefulness. (The commune members had never been allowed to enjoy the grapes that these vines produced every year; instead the grapes were always consumed by Cheng Tianqing's village cadres, who would also give some to the town cadres and members of the county committee and the county government; because of this behavior alone, the cadres should have been removed from their positions.) As everyone surged from the front courtyard to the middle one, I thought they would cry out as they had done when they saw the front courtyard, but instead they were silenced by the solemnity of the middle one. They had surged in like a swarm of bees, but when they reached the middle courtyard, the gloomy chill and the sight of the grape trellises immediately silenced them. (This certainly helped explain why Cheng Tianmin had wanted to move into the temple and live in this celestial location!) I saw someone pick some grapes and put them in his mouth but then immediately spit them into his hand. At that point I resolved that I would definitely give everyone a bunch of grapes after they were ripe in order to demonstrate the principles and advantages of socialism, collectivism, and egalitarianism. This very small and practical act could permit everyone to appreciate how different Gao Aijun's relation with the People was from Cheng Tianqing's. Lost in thought, I had already traversed the eight-*zhang*-long courtyard and reached the manuscript depository. This was a two-story brick and wood structure with three rooms on the first floor; the middle of these rooms contained a passageway to the rear courtyard, while the two rooms on either side were piled high with furniture, artifacts, and dusty reed mats. In this middle passageway, leading to the adjoining room

191

on the second floor, there was a golden plaque with the words MANU-SCRIPT DEPOSITORY, allegedly written by the Cheng Brothers' disciple Zhu Xi himself. This plaque granted the building its presence and eminence in the center courtyard.

Hongmei and I stood on the first floor.

The commune members also stood on the first floor.

The villagers also stood on the first floor.

I told several militia members to stand in the doorway to the building, and told several production brigade cadres to follow me to the second floor. The staircase was to the left of the front door, and after it creakily carried us up to the second floor, we were confronted with an astonishing scene.

Back when I was still in school, I would often go to the manuscript depository, and I continued doing so even after marrying into Cheng Tianqing's family. I'm therefore a hundred percent certain that the walls of the five rooms on the second floor had originally been painted with white lime, to prevent fires, though over the years they had become caked in a thick layer of dust and grime. I remember that, under the north-facing wall, there had been a row of old-style red pine shelves, and above the middle door was a locked shelf filled with the Cheng Brothers' writings, including their *Posthumous Works*, *Additional Works*, and *Collected Works*, their commentaries on the *Book of Changes*, their *Explanation of the Classics*, as well as their *Miscellaneous Writings*. At that time, the Cheng Brothers had been the pride of the entire Balou mountain region. Teachers would often discuss them in class, and in the spring and fall they would take their students to visit this site. They would lead groups of students to the second floor of the manuscript depository building and stand in front of those bookshelves, where their students would listen as the teachers showed off their devotion to and knowledge of the Cheng Brothers. I remember how before I went to the county high school, there was a hunchbacked, lackey-like teacher. (He really was a fucking good language teacher, and my current ability to write is mostly thanks to him, so if one day people try to criticize him, I'll definitely defend him, though I can't let this influence my political life or future.) This teacher selected several students to stand in front of those bookshelves and listen as he introduced each of the Cheng Brothers' works. He explained how Cheng Yi, the younger brother, published more essays, including his "Memorial to the Renzong Emperor," "A Letter of Resignation Submitted to the Faculty of the Xijing Imperial College," "Treatise on How Yanzi Is Able to Learn So Well," "A Letter to the Prime Minister on Behalf of My Father," and so forth. As for Cheng Hao, the elder brother, there was only "Memorial to the Palace Master," "In Response to a Letter from Zhang Hengqu," "Inscription for Yan Leting," and so forth. Our language teacher asked us to write down and memorize everything he told us. He said that the examination questions provided by the district always included some supplementary questions about the Cheng Brothers, and if we answered them correctly we could receive ten or fifteen extra points. (That year there were indeed some supplementary questions of this nature on the exam, for this hunchbacked teacher, who by this point had already retired, was one of the people proposing exam questions.) Standing in front of this bookshelf, he also introduced Cheng Yi's and Cheng Hao's calligraphy and painting, telling us their birth and death dates, as well as the obstacles they encountered in their careers. Once, as I was looking through the second volume of *The Cheng Brothers' Complete Works*, I accidentally dropped it and knocked off the brittle cover. The hunchbacked teacher glared at me, and said, "This is the only extant copy of this book, and it's a scripture for governing the nation. How could you be so careless? Go write three self-criticisms and post them for everyone to see." I had no choice but to write the self-criticisms. I posted two of them in the schoolyard and the third in the classroom. It is for this reason that I longed to burn the documents and scrolls in the manuscript depository. I wanted to scorch the Cheng Brothers' hearts. Needless to say, this was also a revolutionary imperative. It was an excavation and attack to deepen the revolution and a display of power and resistance toward Mayor Wang.

Now, however, there wasn't a single volume, or even single page, of the Cheng Brothers' works on those bookshelves, nor was there a single example of their calligraphy. The rolled-up portraits of the Cheng Brothers' disciples Zhu Xi and Yang Shi that had previously been stored in a cabinet were also missing, and even the faded portrait of the Cheng Brothers' teacher, Zhouzi—which had previously been in the center of the bookshelf—was nowhere to be seen. Instead, the bookshelves were now full of the same four-volume set of *Chairman Mao's Collected Works* that can be found in any of the city's Xinhua bookstores. There were also many different editions of *Chairman Mao's Quotations* and *Chairman Mao's Selected Poetry*. There was a large-format edition of Marx and Engels's *Kapital*, together with copies of Lenin's and Stalin's works, more than a hundred volumes in all. From Karl Marx to Chairman Mao, the works of these five masters were arranged neatly on bookshelves that had been covered in red paper. The remaining shelves were either empty or else neatly decorated with the leaders' colorful portraits, and on the middle table, in place of the portrait of Zhouzi with its large mirrored frame, there was instead a copy of that vivid and vigorous full-body portrait of Chairman Mao holding an umbrella en route to carry out revolution in Anyuan.

I couldn't believe it. The manuscript depository was now full of works by Marx, Engels, Lenin, Stalin, and Mao Zedong.

That is to say, this most feudal location had already become Chenggang's vault of treasured revolutionary thought and proletarian theory.

That is to say, our revolutionary march had been slowed a notch, as enemies wearing revolutionary hats obstructed the real revolutionary activity.

That is to say, some people had already taken into consideration our plan to extend the revolution to Cheng Temple, just as Cheng Tianmin had already anticipated my decision to burn the works by the Cheng Brothers, those Neo-Confucian classics.

The village cadres were standing in front of the bookshelves in the manuscript depository, staring blankly into space with their pale, naïve faces. The light shining down through grape trellises and the intricately carved wooden windows landed gently on our faces and bodies, illuminating our embarrassment to them.

I heard that those manuscripts and documents had been removed from the manuscript depository two years earlier. Some people claimed representatives from the county's culture center had come to take them away, and others reported that they saw a jeep come, while others said that those representatives from the cultural center took only some tables and chairs but didn't seize a single manuscript. So, where did all the old manuscripts and documents go? Everyone stared at each other, with dark clouds over their faces. They began to suspect that the mayor must have transferred the books to the rear courtyard, and therefore they began clamoring to open the door leading from the manuscript depository building to the rear courtyard, so that they could search Cheng Tianmin's residence. However, I said to myself, in the event that it was in fact Cheng Tianmin who, two years earlier, had moved the manuscripts and scrolls, do you really think he would have left them here in the courtyard, where you could find them? But if we can't find the manuscripts, how can we deal with Cheng Tianmin? (Fuck his ancestors! Everyone knows that Cheng Tianmin is a member of the county-level Chinese People's Political Consultative Conference, and often fraternizes with the current county Party committee secretary. Although he's no longer mayor, his position is even better than that of the mayor). Can we force our way into the three-section courtyard that is his home? Do we dare break in and search the premises when he's not there? The revolution must advance under a process of reflection, and it is only by being farsighted that we can have high aspirations. In war, the most dreaded thing is when the enemy's position is unknown, and one must therefore attack while blind. In war, it is only by knowing oneself and one's opponent that one can be guaranteed success. Revolution and revolutionary war require offense but also defense and retreat—this is absolutely true. You defend in order to attack, you retreat in order to advance, you turn in order to go straight—this is an unavoidable phenomenon that we often observe in the course of development, and it is especially true of revolution and specifically of revolution's military action.

(Motherfucker, if only my relationship with the county head were like Cheng Tianmin's!)

Gazing out at the village cadres and commoners, I finally announced, "Our current task is to overthrow the capitalist raiders who are now in power, not to seize those who are already out of power. We cannot shift the direction of the struggle. Given that Cheng Tianmin had the foresight to hide the texts, he certainly wouldn't have placed them where we could easily find them."

I said, "Right now, the main contradiction involves our need to seize power from the town government, and after we resolve this contradiction, the secondary contradictions will easily resolve themselves. Cheng Tianmin and Cheng Temple are both secondary contradictions that will be resolved after the main contradiction. What do we mean when we say that once the headrope of a fishnet is pulled, its mesh will open? This means that we must first overthrow the town government, and then we can clean up the temple and those other messes."

That day, after we had eaten breakfast as usual, we went to the middle courtyard to retrieve Emperor Dezong's SOURCES AND ORIGINS OF THE YI AND LUO RIVERS plaque, Empress Dowager Cixi's ADMIRING AND FOLLOWING YAN HUI AND MENCIUS plaque, the MANUSCRIPT DEPOSITORY inscription that had been written by either Zhu Xi or Yang Shi, and seven other plaques from the front courtyard that had been inscribed during different historical periods in honor of Cheng Yi, Cheng Hao, and the temple. Then we took all these plaques to the location in front of Cheng Temple where people had burned incense and sacrificed to the ancestors, and proceeded to burn them. At the same time, we also destroyed the two steles that had been erected in front of the temple during the Song and Ming dynasties as well as the two stone lions that some high official had given the temple in the late Qing. In this way, we were able to declare a symbolic end to our revolutionary offensive—for now.

3. Victory

After we succeeded in burning a set of Cheng Temple's imperial plaques and destroying its two imperial steles, I heard that Mayor Wang was so furious that he smashed his rice bowls in the town government's canteen. This permitted us (permitted me) to achieve our (my) original goal. I had already recorded in my notebook the time, place, and witnesses of Mayor Wang's cursing and bowl-breaking. We had eradicated superstition, abolished feudal activities, reformed people's thought, and elevated people's awareness, so why was Mayor Wang so angry that he had to smash his rice bowls? How did he dare curse those bastards who would starve to death if they didn't irrigate their land? And who are these bastards? Is it us revolutionaries? If we are all bastards, wouldn't that make Mayor Wang a feudal lord? If it is said that revolutionary youth are bastards, then we will happily be bastards and show him to be a feudal lord! Let him carry the most outstanding, most powerful protective umbrella, in order to protect the Chenggang feudal class epitomized by this "Cheng Brothers' Neo-Confucianism." Lu Xun once said that silence is also a form of resistance, and perhaps it is in fact the *best* form of resistance. As for Mayor Wang and other issues, it is not that we wouldn't deal with them, but rather that the time wasn't right. But when the time was right, we would of course deal with them. If we didn't deal with them when the time was right, then we ourselves would need to be dealt with.

Given that by this point I was already officially the village branch secretary and a Party committee member, I could attend the Chenggang Party committee meetings, meaning that I could record in my leather notebook everything Mayor Wang said and did in these meetings. By early winter, when it was time to plant the wheat, I had already recorded in my notebook seventy-two reactionary things that he said.

He said, "Pursue revolution and protect production, because if production is insufficient, how can you pursue revolution!" (Revolution is primary and production is secondary, so in saying this, is he not inverting the relationship between revolution and production? And if not, then what is the theory of productivity?) He also said, "Woman is a jewel, revolution is a cock." (This is a classic example of anti-revolutionary rhetoric, but unfortunately this is something Director Li from the town's department of propaganda related to me, though that asshole would not be willing to write a testimonial or serve as a witness. Furthermore, he apparently subsequently regretted having told me. When I'm appointed mayor, I'll be sure to teach him a lesson and make him regret his recalcitrance.)

At a mobilization meeting during the busy summer season, as Mayor Wang was talking to the branch secretaries of each of the production brigades, he took Chairman Mao's saying, *If the People don't have an army, then they don't have anything*, and changed it to, *If the People don't have enough grain to survive, then they don't have anything*. At that meeting, Mayor Wang had several drinks and then went up to a Party branch secretary named Zhao Xiuyu (who was in her forties and very frumpy, and who definitely could not be mentioned in the same breath as Hongmei), took her hand, and said,

"Secretary Zhao, you look just like the wife of our second company commander from when I was serving as battalion commander. Like her, you are decisive in action yet as silent as a sealed bottle. Out of all of the production brigade's cadres, you are the one I trust the most." (Did they have an inappropriate sexual relationship? If they did, that would be fantastic!)

According to the village's revolutionary rules, after planting the wheat, we would enter the period of winter rest, at which point revolution and love would both reach a new level. That year, I continued working silently and patiently under Mayor Wang. The reason I was able to maintain my silence is because that year the vast engineering project I undertook for the sake of my love for Hongmei was not proceeding as smoothly as I had hoped. In the process of digging the tunnel, I kept encountering tree roots and other obstacles. After I had dug about a hundred meters, I reached a layer of red clay. Fortunately, that layer of clay, which had a consistency halfway between earth and stone, was only two meters thick, and it took me only three nights to get through it. But what would I have done if it had been ten or twenty meters thick? Would I still have been able to complete our tunnel of love? Even more unfortunately, when I was planning the project, I didn't make plans for ventilation, but after I had dug several dozen meters I found that the air had become so thin it was difficult to breathe. I considered many possible solutions, such as buying a small fan—but that would have required electricity, and the village frequently had blackouts. I also considered digging an airway in the tunnel, but although it would have been possible to do so, it wouldn't be very safe. Eventually, I decided that every ten meters or so I would take a semicircular shovel and, from inside the tunnel, punch an air hole as wide as a man's arm through the ceiling—making sure that the opening of these air holes was located under the foundation of some family's house or courtyard wall. As you know, house and courtyard walls in western Henan are made of stone and rise ten to thirty centimeters above the ground. If I dug the air holes beneath these foundations, no one would have the slightest idea that they were even there, though the air from above ground would still be able to pass through the openings in the masonry and enter the tunnel. This brilliant design made me realize that I was not only a revolutionary genius but also an engineering genius. I used all the mathematics and physics I had learned, together with all the knowledge and experience gained while serving in the army corps of engineers, and dug seventeen four- to five-meter-deep air holes up through the ceiling of the tunnel. One of the air holes opened under a millstone in the street, another opened into the hollow trunk of an old cypress in front of Cheng Temple, and the remaining fifteen opened under the foundations of walls. Fourteen of the latter holes proceeded very smoothly, and there was only one where I encountered a minor deviation—it ended up opening just outside of the courtyard wall around Cheng Guifen's house, but fortunately, there was a woodpile over the spot. I used a stone to hide that final air hole and felt sure that by the time the wood in that woodpile was used up, and the owner discovered the opening, he would assume that it had been made by a squirrel, fox, or some other wild animal. Moreover, it was even possible that the branches and leaves from the woodpile would cover it up.

In sum, although our path twisted back and forth, the future nevertheless remained bright. By that point my tunnel was already 250 meters long, and in another dozen meters or so it would reach the empty rear courtyard in back of Cheng Tianqing's house. Then I would excavate the underground room that would serve as our nuptial chamber. That way, when our desire became unendurable, Hongmei and I could meet in that underground chamber and strip naked. Unencumbered by even a single piece of clothing, we could laugh happily while discussing matters of work and revolution.

I hadn't yet told Hongmei about the monumental project I had undertaken for the sake of her love. Several times when we were out

200

in the fields happily doing that thing, she would caress my callouses and ask with surprise, "Aijun, what's wrong with your hands?" At one point I almost revealed my secret to her, but instead I simply said, "I was born to be a laborer and develop callouses after doing even just a little bit of physical work." I wanted to wait until I had extended the tunnel all the way to her house before telling her about my project. I wanted her to stare at me in surprise. Some day, after the revolution had achieved an enormous victory, such as when I'd been appointed town mayor or county committee member, she would be able to follow me and step into the tunnel, touch the mud walls, and sigh about my great love for her. I wanted her to remove her clothes as she walked into that tunnel for the first time, tossing an article of clothing to the ground every five steps, like heavenly maids scattering flower blossoms. In so doing, upon reaching the underground nuptial chamber, she wouldn't have any clothing left and would simply stand there completely naked. Then, while in that nuptial chamber, we would eat when we were hungry, drink when we were thirsty, and when we were neither hungry nor thirsty we would crazily do that thing. We would do that thing eight times a day, each time for up to three hours straight. The first time she entered that underground nuptial chamber, in the middle of the night, I would want to immediately satisfy my lifetime of hunger and thirst for her, and I would embrace her for three days and three nights, seventy-two hours in all. When we woke up, we would be completely revitalized, and she and I would reemerge from the tunnel and throw ourselves into the fiery struggle, fiery revolution, and fiery life. (Perhaps, on our way out of the tunnel for the first time, we would once again crazily do that thing, as though we were afraid of losing something, and in the light of the entrance to the tunnel, she and I would have simultaneous orgasms.)

However, all these plans were predicated on my ability to finish digging the tunnel and excavating the nuptial chamber. I had already redesigned the nuptial chamber, located four meters directly beneath Cheng Tianqing's house, such that I would set aside several cubic meters of soil, out of which I would fashion a bed. I would then drill two or three air holes in the ceiling, one of which would lead to the base of Cheng Tianqing's courtyard wall, while another would lead to the base of the rear wall of his bedroom or the base of his bed. Perhaps through the air hole leading to his rear wall or his bed, I would be able to hear whether or not Cheng Tianqing and his wife did it in bed, and I would be able to hear Cheng Tianqing reveal some secrets relating to the town or the production brigade. However, just as I was about to start digging the nuptial chamber, something intolerable occurred.

After the wheat was planted, I attended a town-level meeting for grassroots cadres, where I ran into Secretary Tian, who was charged with managing documents and keeping records for the town Party committee. Secretary Tian pulled me aside and asked, "Branch Secretary Gao, what did you do to offend Mayor Wang?" I knew perfectly well what I had done, but instead I said, "How would I dare offend Mayor Wang? I'm a staunch supporter!" Secretary Tian said, "If you didn't offend him, then how do you explain the fact that when the county Party committee organizational bureau was selecting a secretary of the county youth league committee last month, and you were the first of the three people nominated, when the organizational bureau sent someone to town to investigate, Mayor Wang told him that you were flashy but lacking in substance and that you loved to show off but were in fact the epitome of a fake revolutionary."

I stared in astonishment and immediately dragged Tian to the men's room outside the meeting hall.

"What else did Mayor Wang say?"

Secretary Tian looked out of the bathroom and replied, "He said you and Hongmei are a pair of revolutionary clowns, and if the two of you ever manage to achieve your ambitions, that will be an occasion for the common people to wail in despair and for the revolution to fall into darkness."

I asked, "What did the comrade from the organizational bureau say?"

Secretary Tian said, "The comrade from the organizational bureau was the deputy bureau director, and he seemed very disappointed to hear this."

I asked, "Who is currently serving as secretary of the youth league committee?"

Secretary Tian said, "I hear that they ultimately selected their second choice, who was previously the deputy factory director of a silk factory."

Facts will prove that the revolution would not be kind to Mayor Wang. He had already impeded historical progress and development, and now he had become a stumbling block for the revolution. If someone doesn't attack me, I won't attack them; but if someone *does* attack me, I most certainly will attack them. This is the international principle of China's revolution, and this is the fundamental principle for me, Gao Aijun, to enter the revolution.

Accordingly, I locked myself up at home and proceeded to spend three days and three nights preparing a document titled "Ripping Off the Ugly Face of Chenggang's Mayor, Wang Zhenhai." It was seventeen pages long and totaled thirteen thousand characters, and its subtitle was "A Ten-Thousand-Word Denunciation of Wang Zhenhai." The document was divided into the following sections:

1. *The problem of Wang Zhenhai's reactionary remarks*
2. *The problem of Wang Zhenhai's sexual relations*
3. *The problem of Wang Zhenhai's feudal activities*
4. *The problem of Wang Zhenhai's excess consumption*
5. *The problem of Wang Zhenhai's "theory of productivity"*

This document contained material that would capture the attention of Chenggang's revolutionary masses. In composing it, I deliberately miswrote many characters, then recopied the text in triplicate using my left hand. I sent one copy to the county committee, another to the county government, and the third to the county committee organizational bureau. In the following days, I didn't even check to see whether there was any response and instead initiated manure-collecting activities for the Chenggang production brigade. I asked that during the winter rest period, every family collect three to five cubic meters of manure and store it behind their houses, and then mix the manure with mud and use it to construct an irrigation canal. Then, every ten days or two weeks, they should bring several buckets of water to fill the trough, so that the vegetation would decompose and ferment, providing nutrients for the wheat that would sprout the following spring.

I've said that I'm a revolutionary, political, and military genius, and this denunciation of Mayor Wang certainly proved all that. On the sixteenth day after that ten-thousand-word document shot like a cannonball from the town's mailbox to the county seat, I asked Hongmei to copy it over again and send three more copies to various different county-level departments, with the author listed simply as "A Chenggang Revolutionary Cadre." Another ten days later, I asked Hongmei to make more copies, now using her left hand, and once again send it out in triplicate. That winter, under a variety of names, I sent out that document in triplicate nine times, twenty-seven copies in all (sometimes the document was slightly altered, using different subtitles), such that in the end, every county office and important official in the area had received a copy of this ten-thousand-word denunciation.

In the end, around the Lunar New Year, the county sent over a revolutionary investigation group, and the group leader turned out to be a former regiment commander who had stayed on to work in the county after the army implemented local military control (or what was known as the Three Supports and Two Militaries policy). This regiment commander worked in the town hall for three days and three nights and spoke with every cadre (this was an old tradition of military cadres). The investigative group that he brought from the town hall circulated through Chenggang's streets, seeing that the piles of manure were all arranged into neat rows. He kicked off the dried mud that was covering one of these piles, and immediately a warm, moist, and savory odor of decay surged out, sending the smell of grassy manure that had been fermenting all winter into his nostrils and those of every member of the investigation group.

On that day, the former regiment commander walked into the Chenggang production brigade.

He asked, "Is your name Gao Aijun?"

"Yes."

"Have you served in the military?"

"Was the officer able to determine this from my name?"

"I never judge people based on their appearance, nor do I make assumptions based on their name. However, I noticed that your production brigade's piles of manure are arranged into neat rows, and someone who has not served in the military wouldn't ask people to do this."

I laughed.

He asked, "You were given the county's label of 'revolutionary vanguard,' were you not?"

I laughed again, acting very bashful.

"How do you understand the relationship between revolution and production?"

I said, "If you want to conscientiously implement revolution, it is necessary to stimulate production. If production does not proceed, people will likely view revolution as merely empty words. If production proceeds, however, the revolutionary flag will wave in the wind wherever it is planted."

The former regiment commander's eyes lit up, and he stared at me without blinking.

"Gao Aijun, tell me the truth—was it not you who wrote that ten-thousand-word denunciation of Wang Zhenhai?"

My eyes opened wide.

"What ten-thousand-word denunciation?"

He continued staring at me and asked again, "Was it really not you who wrote it?"

I said, "Commander, have you completed your investigation? What did I write? Mayor Wang committed some mistakes, and it is true that I have critical opinions about him. For instance, his theoretical ability is not very advanced, he often curses, and he's too tolerant of the feudal, superstitious activites in our Chenggang production brigade. I have previously shared these opinions with people in the county government, but you cannot, on account of this, arrive at conclusions without having completed the requisite investigations. As Chairman Mao once said, 'Without investigation, there can be no freedom of speech'—"

The commander interrupted me. "During the three days I've been in Chenggang, I've spoken with more than twenty people. Everyone who sees me immediately becomes very nervous, and you are the only one who appears bold and straightforward and doesn't hesitate when you respond." The commander suddenly paused and then changed the subject and asked me, "How old are you?"

I said, "My age under the lunar calendar is twenty-eight."

He said, "Oh . . . that's not very old."

I said, "A revolutionary warrior is a brick who can go wherever he is needed."

With this, we ended our conversation. We had walked only half a *li*, but in that short span of time, my demeanor had managed to win over a county head and Party secretary with more than twenty years of experience, as well as a company or battalion commander. I was calm and collected, thoughtful and rational, and able to answer his questions easily and fluently. In this way, I was able to give the county head—who had just been demobilized from the army and assigned to work in civil service—a deep and very positive impression.

How could he not make use of the sort of talent that I embodied? How could Wang Zhenhai possibly impede my promotion and stop the wheels of history? As it turns out, I would soon be appointed Chenggang's first deputy mayor. Needless to say, this would be the most important move of my revolutionary career.

Chapter 8

Defeat and Celebration

1. The Foolish Old Man Who Moved Mountains

In old China there was a parable known as "The Foolish Old Man Who Moved Mountains," the story of an old man who lived on a mountain in the north. In front of his house's front door, which faced south, there were two mountains blocking his way—one of which was called Taixing Mountain, the other Wangwu Mountain. The old man decided to direct his sons to dig up these mountains with hoes, but a wise man who observed this simply smiled and said, "This is truly foolish, for it is impossible to dig up these mountains." The foolish old man replied, "After I die, my sons will carry on the project, and after they die, there will still be my grandsons, great-grandsons, and so forth. Although these two mountains are indeed very big, they aren't getting any bigger. Every time we dig up a bit, there will be that much less of the mountains left, so why can't we eventually level them completely?" God was deeply moved by this response, so he sent down two immortals to carry the two mountains away.

2. The Celebration Finally Arrives

The event unfolded as slowly as an old ox pulling a broken-down cart, and even more slowly than my progress on the tunnel of love. I had thought that the county head would take his soldiers back to the county seat and promptly appoint me as a national cadre—this being a key step in my advancement to town mayor, county head, district commissioner, and finally, provincial governor. But after the county head left, three days and then a week passed, but there was no news of my promotion. Half a month passed, but still there was no news of my promotion.

I was somewhat disappointed. After writing several self-criticisms, Wang Zhenhai remained town mayor, while I was still patiently serving as village branch secretary, which—together with being a town Party committee member not released from production requirements—is truly China's lowest level of rural cadre. Needless to say, as an experienced revolutionary, I couldn't appear overly anxious every time I encountered a setback, nor could I be easily infected by irritability. Instead, I acted as though nothing were amiss and that winter continued attending meetings, participating in struggle sessions, reading Chairman Mao's proclamations, and pursuing the manure-collecting campaign. In this way, I continued to act like the foolish old man who moved mountains, working every night without fail to slowly dig my tunnel.

That spring, I finally finished digging the underground nuptial chamber and even finished making the three air holes and the earthen bed. On that day, the sky was high, and clouds were sparse. It was a beautiful spring day, and the dawn light was bright and clear. I dumped my final load of soil into the irrigation canal and was about to sleep all day, whereupon Secretary Tian from the county government suddenly woke me up.

"Secretary Gao, you have a guest."

I rubbed my eyes and sat up.

"Revolution is not a dinner party, nor is it painting and embroidery."

Secretary Tian laughed.

"That is true, that is true. I know that serving as deputy mayor is merely the first step in your ten-thousand-*li* Long March. Snowy mountains and grassy fields still lie behind you."

As I rolled out of bed, my drowsiness immediately faded. Facing the mysterious-looking Secretary Tian, I asked, "What did you say?" He replied, "You are now Chenggang's deputy mayor, and your document has already reached the town government." I almost couldn't believe it. At that point I wanted to turn somersaults and scream. However, my mother was out in the courtyard feeding the pigs, and my children were about to leave for school. I assumed that it was just after breakfast time, so I suppressed my excitement and told Secretary Tian, "I'll treat you to lunch. If you want to have pig's head or ox entrails, we can go buy them."

Secretary Tian said, "Lunch? Everyone has already eaten lunch. What were you doing last night? You slept so long that now you're confused."

When I walked out of my room, I saw that the sun was indeed directly overhead, and the courtyard was full of yellow warmth and the fresh green smell of budding grass. As my mother put feed in the pig trough, she said, "Aijun, there is rice in the pot. Go have some."

I looked at my mother, with her headful of gray hair, and said, "Mother, my letter of appointment to serve as deputy mayor has arrived. As of today, your son is a national cadre!"

My mother stood there for a long time examining me—as though she no longer recognized her own son.

I spent the remainder of the day summoning all the members of the Chenggang production brigade and having them gather inside Cheng Qinglin's house (because Cheng Qinglin's father could cook well). From a state-owned restaurant, we bought some cooked beef, cooked pork, pork offal, winter turnip, cabbage, and yam-jelly sheets and noodles, as well as several *jin* of melon wine. In all, we prepared nine dishes and three soups. With Secretary Tian, we drank from the afternoon into the evening, and from evening we drank until dawn. Holding up a glass of wine, I announced to everyone, "I've been appointed deputy mayor. (Given that I haven't been released from my regular responsibilities, for the moment

I still have a rural residency permit.) This is a result not of my maturation and advancement but rather thanks to the collective struggle of the Chenggang production brigade. It is a triumphant symbol of everyone's collective effort. I urge everyone that from now on you must be even more unified and—in the shortest possible amount of time—find a way to remove Wang Zhenhai from his position as mayor. After I become mayor, I'll appoint Secretary Tian to serve as the deputy secretary of the town's Party committee, I'll appoint Hongmei to serve as deputy mayor and director of the town's women's federation, and I'll appoint Cheng Qinglin to serve as both town Party committee member and as the Party branch secretary of the Chenggang production brigade. As for the other Party branch members, they'll all be similarly promoted by one or two ranks. At that point, if any family encounters any difficulties—such as their younger brother or sister needing a job or their wanting to transfer their rural residency permit into a non-rural one—we can easily address them."

Everyone toasted me to celebrate my new appointment and eagerly awaited my promotion to either town mayor or Party secretary. Of course, the best thing would be to be appointed both mayor *and* Party secretary, since that way I would hold both political and administrative power. Everyone was excited and in high spirits, and after finishing five *jin* of 112-proof melon wine, we were all completely drunk. In fact, Secretary Tian was so inebriated he fell under the table, then grasped my hand and said, "Deputy Mayor Gao, after you are promoted to mayor or Party secretary, I don't dare hope to become deputy mayor, but you must at least help me transfer my residency permit. I don't want to have to spend five years working as a secretary, with my household residency permit still assigned to my family's original mountain district." I pounded my chest and replied, "Relax! If I, Gao Aijun, were not true to my word, could I be a true Party member? Could I be a true Party leader? If I were not true to my word, then how could I pursue true revolution?"

With tears streaming down his face, Secretary Tian drank another bowl of wine.

Then he collapsed.

I don't know whether Hongmei and I were actually drunk, but at the very least we were certainly a bit tipsy. From the moment I heard that I had been appointed deputy mayor to when the alcohol-soaked moon rose, my blood had been surging through my body like the Yangtze or the Yellow River flowing through the Chinese country-side. Succulent seedings sprouted in the spring rain, and sunflower blossoms opened toward the sun. In the north there was endless ice and snow, but around the Great Wall there was soft rain. Above and below the Yangtze River, a torrent flowed through the mountains like silver snakes! What else has the Jade Emperor provided? Look at that landscape with the red sun and white snow and the extraordinarily beautiful mountains and rivers. A bit of literary talent is passed down from the first emperor of the Qin to Emperor Wu of the Han, and a tad of literary excellence is passed down from the Tang and the Song dynasties. Genghis Khan, the son of heaven, only knew how to shoot his bow. All that is now in the past, and to see great men you must look to our contemporary era. Every drop of blood and every ocean spray is flowing and burning. Whenever Hongmei and I see each other, we can't resist peeking at each other over the dining table, and our gazes produce sparks when they collide in midair, so the white-colored scent of wine becomes filled with our peach-red yearning, and the many smells of the table become covered with our pink desire. Beneath the table at which everyone was toasting and congratulating me, my and Hongmei's feet were restless, and when she wasn't gently stepping on my foot, I was gently nudging her with mine. When she wasn't removing her shoe and placing her bare foot inside my pant leg, I was sticking my own foot inside her pant leg and pinching her calf with my toes.

After the wine was finished, we would stop at nothing.

I asked Qinglin's parents to look after those fellow revolutionaries who had followed me into battle. I said, "You should relax. After I'm appointed mayor, Qinglin will be appointed deputy mayor; after I'm appointed county head, Qinglin will be appointed deputy county head; and after I'm appointed provincial governor, Qinglin will be appointed either district commissioner, county head, or county Party committee secretary." Qinglin's mother and father couldn't believe their ears, and they remarked that if only their son could one day become deputy mayor and Party branch secretary like me, they would be content and would know the assistance they had granted me would not have been in vain. I told them that their aspirations were entirely too modest, the same way that a tiny sparrow cannot possibly understand the ambitions of a great roc. Then, before their dumbfounded eyes, I took Hongmei's hand and led her out of Qinglin's house. At that moment, the moonlight was shining down on us, and we were unimaginably content. As soon as we walked out the front door, Hongmei immediately fell into my embrace and stuck her tongue in my mouth. (My soul, my flesh—she always knows when I need her most!) Her tongue danced around for a while, then retreated again, leaving my mouth and my heart bereft.

"Tonight we need to be together, even if it kills us," she said. "But later, when half of this town government is yours, we won't have to sneak around like thieves anymore."

At that moment, I heard footsteps coming from Center Cheng Street. (How can you not pay attention to such things? Does the revolution let you not pay attention to everything? You give yourself over to blind emotion and are incredibly immature!) Without a word, I led Hongmei toward Rear Cheng Street. She said, "Where are you going?" I replied, "Don't ask any questions. Just follow me." I wanted to show her my great tunnel of love. I wanted to treat that great construction as a token of my love and give it to her (my soul and my body!). I had already been appointed deputy mayor, and although I hadn't been released from work requirements, I was nevertheless a national leader and a Party leader. My tunnel of love was now almost complete, and what better time than tonight was there to present it, celebrating my promotion, our success, and my inseparable revolutionary comrade?

We proceeded through the quiet night back to my home.

I heard my mother's voice through the window saying, "Aijun, are you hungry? If you want to eat, I'll cook you something."

I replied, "Go back to sleep, mother. If I want to eat, I'll cook something myself."

She said, "You've been running around all day. If you're tired, don't dig anymore. Just go to sleep."

I said, "Don't worry about me. Just take Hongsheng and Honghua, and go to sleep."

(Ah, mother! My great mother! One night when I had recently begun my project and had dug only about twenty meters, I emerged from the tunnel and found her standing in the opening, holding a lamp. She said, "Aijun, tell me the truth about what you are doing. I've already gone down and looked several times." Startled, I said, "Although we aren't in a state of war, the current situation is actually even more complicated. Does a month ever go by that you don't hear about someone being killed? That you don't hear about some anti-revolutionary being executed? Your son is a revolutionary leader, and how many people are watching me? . . . Even Chairman Mao called upon us to dig escape tunnels, so how could our family not do the same?" I added, "Mother, you don't understand revolution. Once you get on this ship, you can't get off, because if you do, that would make you a counterrevolutionary. We have to dig this tunnel, because with it we'll be able to boldly pursue revolution—and I'll be able to strive to become town mayor, county head, district official, and provincial committee Party secretary . . . Yes, your son has a chance to achieve all of this." My mother stood there silently. That night, after I went to sleep, she sat in the entrance to the tunnel for a long time. At dawn

I found several more bundles of cornstalks in the pigsty, such that the path to the tunnel entrance was hidden even more effectively.)

Now, someone new was finally entering my tunnel, and she would become the tunnel's matron and its raison d'être. I lit a lamp and led Hongmei toward the entrance.

The moonlight was flowing like water. The courtyard was cold and damp, and Hongmei's hot hand rested in mine like a cooked fish. As we were heading toward the pigsty, Hongmei poked my palm, and I squeezed her finger. I told her that the great, divine moment had finally arrived, and that all of our attention had been for the sake of this moment of irreverence and transgression. When we opened the pigsty's wooden gate, the two white pigs looked up as usual, but when they saw me they lay down again. When we reached the southwest corner of the pigsty, I put the lamp on the ground, moved the cornstalks out of the way, and the path to the tunnel opening popped into view in the moonlight.

The clouds over Hongmei's face fluttered like window curtains. In the deathly silence of the village, you could hear the breathing of each family's dogs and chickens, like a spring emerging in the middle of a desert. Hongmei stared at the tunnel opening—noting the wooden frame, the pulley, and the rope extending into the tunnel, as well as the soil baskets and assorted tools scattered around the entrance. She fixed her gaze on my face.

I said, "Go down with me."

I took the lamp and stepped into the tunnel, then led her inside. Once we were standing inside the tunnel, I kissed her face and said, "Hongmei, if you are able to find someone else who loves you as much as I do, I'll die right before your eyes." As I said this, I extended the lamp deeper into the tunnel, and in the lamplight the straight, warm tunnel resembled an enormous cloth bag fluttering in the wind.

The cloud that had previously hung over Hongmei's face had now gone, to be replaced by a reddish-purple look of astonishment, visible in her forehead, eyes, eyebrows, nose, and puckered chin. Her mouth was half-open, as though she wanted to close it but was unable to, and on her lips was a smell of steel and catkins. She appeared to have been struck by some kind of magic, captured by a mysterious force. She stared in astonishment. She forgot whether it was daytime or nighttime and didn't even know whether she was in heaven, hell, or the mortal world.

I said, "Follow me inside."

She continued standing there, her face frozen.

I stepped further into the tunnel and said, "When it is completed, the tunnel will be 550 meters long." I added, "After several dozen more meters, it will reach your house. Then, whenever we want to do that thing, we won't need to go anywhere, we won't need to worry that someone might see us, nor that the revolution doesn't permit this kind of love. Instead, I'll enter the tunnel from my house, and you can enter from yours. In the middle, there is a room with a bed. That way, we'll be able to enjoy a conjugal relationship without fearing a thing."

She continued staring in shock.

She simply couldn't believe that anything could happen to our love—that our love could undergo a process of change, becoming even more beautiful. She couldn't believe that the person standing in front of her was not only a great revolutionary figure but also an exceedingly rare kind of romantic. The lamp I was holding flickered, and the mud-like light shone onto her startled face. Appearing in relief against the tunnel's mud walls, her white face began to flush. Her half-open mouth made it seem as if she wanted to say something but wasn't able to get it out. She simply stood in the entrance, staring at me and gazing down the arrow-straight tunnel. It felt like she remained motionless for a year and stayed silent for a lifetime.

I once again bowed down and began to lead her forward. Although autumn had just ended, and the earth's warmth had already begun to recede, the tunnel was filled with the warm and fragrant smell of earth, like the scent that people along the riverbank enjoy just before the wheat ripens. Hongmei followed me, stroking the tunnel walls and ceiling with her hand. Every ten steps or so, I would have her stop and stand up straight below one of the air holes. I told her where each air hole opened up: under whose courtyard walls, which hollow tree, or which millstone. I told her about the air hole that opened under the wall where Cheng Tianqing's bed was located. I explained why the tunnel needed air holes, and why the air holes had to open into the cracks between the stones of the foundations of other people's houses. I explained how I had been digging this tunnel for two years and a few days, how many baskets and shovels I had destroyed in the process, and how many loads of dirt I had dumped in the irrigation canal behind the village. I told her that if anyone were to come and inspect the canal, they would notice that many of the water plants had been covered in dirt. Fortunately, no one ever looked that closely, and the water plants grew quickly, soon emerging from under the soil that I dumped on them. I said, "Hongmei, listen! Every air hole is like a flute, and through them sometimes you can hear someone moving a bed or a table around, chopping wood or crushing stones, or the boisterous sound of family life." I placed my head beneath the seventh air hole and said, "Hongmei, put your ear here and listen. We are now directly below Cheng Qinglin's house." However, Hongmei did not place her ear next to the air hole. Instead, standing in that space that was just barely big enough for two, but where it was possible to lift one's head and straighten one's back, she just stared at me in confusion. Her eyes tearing up like mountain springs, she said, "Aijun, let me see your hand."

I extended my right hand, which was the one that wasn't holding the lamp.

Hongmei used her fingertips to caress my callouses, as tears dripped from her eyes. (So beautiful and deep was my love, that even if it had just been for the sake of these tears, I would have felt that my tunnel had been worthwhile.) Her tears fell onto my wrists, like bugs crawling through my heart, making me feel as though my heart had been soaked in warm water. At this point, I found it difficult to control myself, and my veins were pounding as though they were about to explode. I wanted to proceed immediately to that eight- or nine-square-meter nuptial chamber with its earthen bed. However, when I tried to lead Hongmei further down the tunnel, I bumped my head against the ceiling, and pain washed over my feverish brain like a bucket of ice water.

She said, "Are you hurt?"

I said, "I'm fine."

She said, "Is it that you can't wait to do that thing?"

I laughed.

She said, "What were you saying when we arrived at the entrance to the tunnel?"

I said, "I wasn't saying anything."

She said, "You were in the middle of telling me something."

I said, "Oh, maybe I was telling you to take off your clothes. Inside the tunnel, it's warm in the winter and cool in the summer."

She proceeded to remove her clothes as she walked, and each time she removed an article of clothing, she would toss it to the ground. That way, her discarded clothing resembled a row of flower blossoms. I began retreating into the innermost part of the tunnel, and as I did so, I watched her unfasten her buttons and remove her clothes. I watched as, under the clay walls that were as muddy as the lamplight, her naked upper body appeared as white as silk—as though she were a nude portrait moving in the yellow light. I began to remove my own clothes. Given that I was stripping as I walked backward into the tunnel, I had to place my lamp on the ground. By the time I had removed my shirt, she was already standing under a different air hole, where she proceeded to stretch out her sore back, such that her voluptuous breasts, like a pair of sheep on a mountain top, stood erect under the tunnel ceiling, while the dark area between her legs resembled a black chrysanthemum blooming in the tunnel. My gaze froze. I stared at her naked body as though I were seeing a book or a newspaper for the first time in a long while. I saw that there were particles of dirt stuck to her breast and her belly, resembling flower pistils against her white skin. I noticed that in the triangular region below her abdomen, the skin was as smooth as silk, without any discernible stretch marks. I smelled a strong odor of dirt, and there was a reddish-white feminine scent mixed with the smell of peach and plum blossoms. I knelt down below those scents and completely forgot that I was about to be promoted to deputy mayor and that I was a revolutionary and a political and military genius. Instead, I knelt down and began crazily kissing that black chrysanthemum blossom, to celebrate our love and my promotion and to toast another victory in the revolution and a new stage in Chenggang's history. I kissed her belly and her abdomen, the triangular region below her abdomen, and that black chrysanthemum that was shedding petals in all directions. I kissed the fresh, soft white dirt on that black chrysanthemum, and the smooth flesh of her thighs, which was pulled taut when she stood up. I kissed her fingertips and fingernails, which were eager to ruffle through my hair. I also wanted to kiss her toenails, which resembled ripe red grapes, but when I bowed my head, I saw that her feet were buried in a pile of loose earth that I hadn't yet cleared away, and therefore I had no choice but to lift my head and place her grapelike nipple in my mouth, sucking it into the back of my throat. She was excited by my frantic kisses, and in the cool tunnel her entire body began to burn, as though a clump of clay had become heated and fallen down, leaving her paralyzed under the air hole below the wall separating the courtyards of the Cheng and Hong households, as my throat produced a bright and peach-colored gurgling sound. I knew she had now lost control, and I couldn't wait until we reached the nuptial chamber's earthen bed. She proceeded to lie down in front of me, as though she had just casually unrolled a brand-new mat, whereupon I immediately lunged at her, like someone wanting to throw his body down onto a cool mat in the middle of summer. The ground was cool and damp, but her body was dry and hot. As I lunged at her, her stifled, parched voice flowed out into the lamplight, like spring water flowing out from between cracks in rocks. I said, "Hongmei, don't be afraid. If you want to scream, go right ahead. This tunnel is our home, and even if you shout your lungs out, no one will hear you." As I said this, I moved her leg until she was in the position I wanted, then I abruptly inserted my hardness into her. At that moment—at that crazy, divine, miraculous moment—her cry of pleasure burst out louder than ever before, erupting from her wet mouth together with her coarse panting. Her scream was sharp and bright, fluttering in the tunnel like a strip of red silk. The dirt in the tunnel's ground and ceiling began to tremble, and the lamp next to us began to sway back and forth. That sound flowed through the tunnel, but was quickly absorbed by its muddy walls. When she cried out, I enjoyed a rare feeling of hardness and greatness and felt a rare sense of strength and connectedness. I initially thought I could make her cry of pleasure last forever, or at least until her body ran out of energy and her throat became hoarse. For some reason, however, I suddenly experienced a complete collapse, as my body became drained of energy.

I fell onto her.

Her third cry had only half erupted before it started to fade out.

We gazed at each other with a yawning look of regret.

The swaying lamp made a sound like a millipede scurrying around.

I asked, "Am I sick?"

She said, "What sort of illness could this be?"

I said, "Perhaps the same one that your husband has?"

She said, "Aijun, let's not mention Qingdong at a time like this, OK?"

I said, "But do you think I have the same illness as he does?"

She said, "How could you be suffering from that? The problem is that we've been forced to contain ourselves for too long, and now that we finally have a space like this where we can let it all out, we run into trouble. After a while, everything will be fine. I'm sure it will all be fine."

We sat there quietly for a while. We held hands, consoling one another as we felt the chill from the tunnel's ground and walls drenching our bodies like rain, until our skin was covered in goose bumps. I handed her a piece of clothing, saying, "Put this on. If we proceed a little farther, we'll reach the underground nuptial chamber." She threw the clothing to the ground and said, "I won't wear this. For years, we haven't had a chance to stroll around naked like a married couple."

(I truly love her—my soul and my flesh!)

Naked, we proceeded toward the nuptial chamber. Because of our earlier excitement and my subsequent collapse, we were both very quiet. As we headed into the innermost portion of the tunnel, I no longer hung back to admire her nakedness, and instead I took the lead, holding the lamp in front of me with one hand and leading her forward with the other. The mud underfoot absorbed our feet's urgency. We passed beneath Rear Cheng Street, under a corner wall of Cheng Temple's rear hall and a tree in Cheng Temple's front courtyard, under the foundations of Cheng Qing'an's and Cheng Qinglian's houses, as well as Tian Zhuangzhuang's house. Finally, we arrived at that underground nuptial chamber. I had made the room's walls completely smooth and the ground perfectly flat and had dumped a thick layer of white lime on the earthen bed, so that when the lime mixed with the dirt, the humidity would be reduced. One air hole in the room led to an opening at the base of Cheng Tianqing's rear courtyard wall, another led to an opening next to the bed in Cheng Tianqing's bedroom, while the third led to the base of the kitchen wall of Cheng Tianqing's neighbor, Cheng Xianqi. I placed the lamp over the bed, and in the nuptial chamber the lamplight became even more dim than it had been in the tunnel. The opening to the tunnel leading to Hongmei's house was located above the chamber's northern wall.

Hongmei stood in the nuptial chamber, using her hands to cover the area between her legs. She shifted her gaze from the ceiling to the wall, and from the wall to the earthen bed, until finally her gaze came to rest on the opening of the tunnel that would lead to her house.

"Aijun, when will this be finished?"

"If I work quickly, I'll need another half year, and if I'm slower, I may need seven or eight months."

Hongmei looked at me, then squatted down, hugging her shoulders, her legs pressed tightly together. In this way, she resembled a round ball perched on the earthen ground.

I said, "You're cold, aren't you?"

She replied, "Aren't you? Come hug me."

I squatted down and hugged her. Her smooth skin had a layer of rice-like goose bumps that pressed against my body, giving me an unprecedented sense of comfort and pleasure. Normally, whenever we were naked together, her excited body became so hot that it seemed as though it could boil water. This was the first time that the chill of her body penetrated my skin and poured into my veins, and it was the first time she rolled into my embrace like a ball. Her head rested on my face and shoulder, and her breath blew onto my neck. Her hands grasped my throat, and her breasts pressed against my chest. Her nipples, like a pair of ice balls, pressed against my ribs. We were stuck together on the floor of the nuptial chamber, united as one. Under the flickering light, we warmed each other up and stared at each other. She said she could pick a fight with Qingdong, to give her an excuse to move into a room in the corridor area of the house, and I replied that I could dig the tunnel so that the opening would be located directly under her bureau. That way, whenever I wanted her, I could take the tunnel to her house and knock on the base of the bureau, whereupon she could come down and join me. Conversely, if she wanted me, she could take the tunnel to my house, then climb up to my family's courtyard and either cough softly or knock on the window, whereupon I would go down into the tunnel to meet her. I added that if our enemies started plotting against us, or if World War III really did break out, we could use this tunnel to escape. She said she couldn't see that far ahead, and added that if she could come down into this tunnel and have me embrace her whenever she missed me, she wouldn't feel that she had lived or joined the revolution in vain.

I said, "Hongmei, do you think that I'll some day be able to revolutionize my way into the position of town mayor or district commissioner?"

She said, "If you become mayor or commissioner, you won't stop liking me, will you?"

I said, "We are revolutionary companions, a couple made in heaven. If I leave you, it would be as though the revolution had lost its engine. And why would I have spent two years digging this tunnel if I were thinking about leaving you?"

She said, "Aijun, you must believe that you are a revolutionary genius. Your genius is in no way inferior to that of Lin Biao. In fact, compared to Lin Biao—"

I immediately covered her mouth, and said, "I just want you to tell me whether, if I continue pursuing the revolution, I'll eventually be able to become mayor or district commissioner."

She said, "All you need to do is keep directing the revolution and maintain a correct political standing. As long as you retain this same revolutionary passion when you are in your forties or fifties, you should be able to become provincial governor."

Infatuated, I stared into her eyes.

She asked, "Don't you believe me?"

I said, "I do believe you."

She asked, "And if I continue pursuing the revolution with you, what position will I be able to attain?"

I said, "A position at the county, district, or even the province level—all these are possible."

With a smile she kissed me and said, "Without Chairman Mao, there wouldn't have been the great Jiang Qing; without Lin Biao, there wouldn't have been the great Ye Qun; and without Gao Aijun's skyrocketing success, I, Xia Hongmei, could not even consider the possibility of having a county-level, district-level, or province-level position. I understand this principle. If I didn't, how could our love be as deep as it is, and how could you have accepted me as your revolutionary companion?"

I didn't say anything else (my soul and my flesh!). As Hong-mei made these remarks, she stared into my eyes. By this point we had already been sitting together on the ground for a long time and had been liberated from the tunnel's chill. The topic of revolution had summoned our inner warmth, and I felt the blood begin to surge again. Strength returned to my body. The chill faded from her, and the goose bumps disappeared from her skin. Her body became white and shiny, warm and flexible. Her breasts once again started knocking against my chest like a pair of rabbits trying to break out of their underground burrow.

I said, "I'm currently only a deputy mayor and have taken only the first step in our Long March."

She said, "Now you've taken the first step, the second will be that much easier."

I said, "Now that I'm deputy mayor, I'll have more opportunities to attend meetings with that bastard Wang Zhenhai and therefore will have more opportunities to pull him down from his position as mayor."

She said, "The director of the women's federation has a mouth that is puckered like a persimmon, to the point that she must not be able to even eat anything. I'm sure that I could do that job better than her."

I said, "The revolution has given us this sort of opportunity, and if we can't seize it, then we are fools."

She said, "The revolution is certainly good, but it has forced us underground."

"I see some dirt on your body." I pointed to her left breast, which had a bean-like clump of soil on the nipple—as if her nipple had grown a new nipple of its own. She looked down at that clump of dirt and moved to wipe it off, but then her hand stopped in midair.

She said, "Please wipe it off me."

I said, "Would you ask the mayor to wipe away that clump of dirt?"

She said, "Mayor Gao, please wipe away the dirt from my breast."

I said, "Heavens, could you call upon the district commissioner to do such a thing?"

She said, "Commissioner Gao, why don't you use your tongue to wipe away that piece of dirt?"

I said, "Good god, you dare to address Commissioner Gao as if you were speaking to your own child!"

She said, "Governor Gao, why don't you use your tongue to lick up the piece of dirt on my nipple?"

I said, "Could a governor do this sort of thing?"

She said, "A governor is still a man. Didn't Chairman Mao and Lin Biao have children with Jiang Qing and Ye Qun? Governor Gao, I'm begging you to lick up the piece of dirt on my nipple."

I said, "Call me a revolutionary."

She said, "Revolutionary genius, you are China's rising star, and the spring water of your tongue can moisten the nation's parched people and its parched land. Please use your spring water to wash away the piece of dirt on my nipple."

225

Her voice was both bright and dark, halting and continuous. This was a recitation and a eulogy, a supplication and a flirtation. Her eyes shone down on my face, and her hands continually caressed my body and my crotch. I was moved by her magnetic voice, and my throat and lips once again became parched. I was anxious to do that thing again, but I struggled to control my thirst, because I wanted to continue to bask in her revolutionary language. I pinched her ears and lips, resting my lips on her shoulders, as though holding the golden-red face of a bodhisattva. "I'm not only a revolutionary genius, I'm also a political genius," I said. "Is it possible that you don't recognize my political genius?"

She continued caressing my crotch with one hand and holding her breasts with the other. Each movement was very slow and careful, so that the piece of dirt would remain balanced on her nipple. "Esteemed revolutionary, politician, and comrade, given that you are a public servant of the masses and a civil servant of the People, I am asking you to lick up this piece of dirt."

I said, "Not only am I a revolutionary and a political genius, I am also a military genius. If I weren't a military strategist, do you think I would have been able to dig this tunnel?"

She brought her hands together and held them between her breasts and under her nose. With her head half-cocked and her eyes closed, she knelt down in front of me and said, "My most esteemed strategical genius, and peerless politician. My young and promising mayor; my talented county head; my district commissioner, devoted to public interests; my provincial governor, full of organizational ability and the art of leadership; my emperor, for whom I have the utmost love, loyalty, and reliance—Comrade Gao Aijun, your humble subject, your commoner, your plebeian, your revolutionary sweetheart and your lifelong companion, your future lover, spouse, and empress, is kneeling down before you with a speck of dirt on her nipple and is entreating you to use the tip of your tongue, which has revolutionary love as its base, to lick it clean. In order to celebrate yet another revolutionary victory in Chenggang; in order to celebrate how, in the revolution, you have begun your great ascent from village chief to mayor, I ask that you lower your noble and wise head that is full of revolutionary consciousness, and lick off the speck of dirt that has fallen onto the great nipple of this great woman during our great revolutionary storm!"

When she finished this declaration, which sounded as though she were reciting it from a prepared text, she bent down—to see whether or not that piece of dirt on her nipple would fall off on its own. Then she crawled over and grabbed my member with both hands and gently kissed it, then kissed it again. She kissed it three times in a row, then straightened her back, such that her nipple was now positioned in front of my face.

I thought I should swallow that piece of dirt.

Gazing down at her pert breast, at the nipple at its center, and at the piece of yellow earth stuck to the nipple, I said, "Albania's heroic populace, which has become Europe's great socialist torch, the Soviet revisionist leaders, the group of traitorous strikebreakers, and Yugoslavia's Tito faction—compared with you, they are all just mounds of earth, while you are a cloud-piercing mountain." I added, "Please don't call me a revolutionary, a politician, or a military officer. Please don't call me town mayor, county head, district commissioner, or provincial governor. We revolutionaries hail from all of the world and have united together for the sake of a shared revolutionary objective . . . All revolutionary groups must look after one another, cherish one another, and assist one another." I added, "We Party cadres and national cadres are merely ordinary workers, not elders riding on the heads of the People. All of us worker cadres, regardless of the status of our occupation, are merely orderlies for the People. Everything we do is in the service of the People, on behalf of the People, for the People's welfare, and for the People's well-being, which is also our own well-being. It is all done on behalf of the People's happiness, which is also our happiness. Only lackeys of the masses can be considered true cadres." At this point, I began to lick that piece of dirt with the tip of my tongue. I had to lick it three times before I managed to dislodge it from her nipple, whereupon a sweet, earthy taste warmed my mouth. Before my chapped lips had even left her nipple, I swallowed that piece of dirt as though I were swallowing a chunk of gold. Then I stuck out my tongue again and licked her nipple. Under the moisture of my tongue, her nipple became even more swollen than before, as though a purple grape had suddenly grown there. I took that grape—and even half of her breast—in my mouth and began sucking ravenously. As I sucked on her breast, she began to moan—hoarse and trembling, as though an intermittent stream of red water was spurting onto my face, my body, and my heart. I could no longer control myself, as blood flooded toward a certain part of my body. She couldn't restrain herself either, and she began moaning my name—calling me town mayor, county head, and district commissioner, calling me revolutionary, political, and military genius. She asked me to rescue her, saying, "I can't stand it anymore, Mayor Gao. Save me!" As she called out to me, she collapsed to the floor, where she proceeded to flop around like a fish on a riverbank.

I carried her to the earthen bed.

"Aijun, quick, enter me," she said. "I'm about to pass out, Mayor Gao. You must enter me. If you don't, I'll die!"

She cried out incoherently while gripping my thigh with both hands. "I'm about to die, Aijun. You must enter me . . . If you don't, I'll be tortured to death. You went to all this trouble to dig this tunnel, was it not so that we could be together like husband and wife?"

I knelt down in front of that black chrysanthemum between her legs.

"Enter me, Aijun. For my sake, and so that in the future we'll be able to focus on the revolution. Quick, enter me. What are you waiting for?"

I bit my lower lip.

She said, "Revolutionary, military strategist . . . quick, enter me!"

My god! . . . I finally released my lip, which I had nearly bitten in half. I once again collapsed spectacularly, like a mountain crumbling or a house falling into rubble.

She said several bright, pink things, then her voice gradually faded away. Eventually, she stopped speaking altogether. It was as if she had suddenly understood something. She rested on the bed for a while, then sighed, sat up, and looked at the wet spot I had left in the middle of the earthen bed. She looked at me without saying another word.

After my second collapse, it was as if our ardor had been doused with a bucket of water, and instantly a chill descended on the nuptial chamber. Even the lamp appeared less bright than before. Hongmei sat down in front of me, the look of disappointment on her face as gray as the bed beneath us, a pair of tears working their way down from the corners of her eyes. In order to express my regret and powerlessness, I slapped my own face twice. The sound of those slaps was bright and sharp, but in the tunnel they sounded low and dull, as though we were inside an urn. When she saw I was slapping my own face, she turned pale, and that pallor made me feel reassured— as though I had wronged someone, and then that other person had turned around and offered a self-criticism. In order to make her feel guiltier, I once again knelt down before her and began slapping my own face. By the time she had recovered from her initial shock, I had slapped myself five or six times.

Acting as though she had committed a monumental mistake, she knelt down and grabbed my hand. "Aijun, what are you doing? Did I criticize or blame you?"

Upon hearing this, I began to slap my face even harder, while also pounding my chest and pinching my thighs and my member. I exclaimed, "You've let me down! You've let me down! I painstakingly dug this tunnel, and this is how you repay me." The more I said and did this, the harder she tried to pull me away, as though in terrified self-reproach. But the more she tried to pull me away, the harder I beat myself. I felt a feverish combination of pleasure and pain in my face, body, thighs, and everywhere else, as the sound of her self-recriminatory tears washed over my heart.

As she was crying and I was beating myself, choosing her words carefully, she said, "Aijun, let's try to direct the loudspeakers into this tunnel. Earlier, when we were out in the fields, wasn't it the case that you were always raring to go whenever the loudspeakers were broadcasting music and revolutionary songs, but stymied when they stopped?"

I stopped hitting myself.

I hugged her tightly, as the lamp ran out of oil, the light flickered, and then the tunnel became as dark as a tomb.

3. Dialectical Contradiction

There are two levels to the question of the differences between the particular and universal levels of contradiction. The first level notes that contradiction can be found in the development of all things, while the second is that a contradictory movement can be found in the development of every particular thing.

Lenin explained the universality of contradiction as follows:

"In mathematics, there are positive and negative numbers, and differential and integral equations.

"In mechanics, there is force and reaction.

"In physics, there are positive and negative charges.

"In chemistry, there are processes of atomic combination and decomposition.

"And in social sciences, there is class struggle."

In life, there is birth and death.

In humanity, there are men and women.

In literature, there is truth and fiction.

Because of the extraordinarily vast scope of things and their endless development, some things are characterized by their universality in some situations and their particularity in others, and conversely other things are characterized by their particularity in some situations and their universality in others.

The question of the relationship between the universality and the particularity of contradiction is precisely that of the relationship between the generality and the specificity of contradiction.

This principle of the relationship between generality and specificity, between absoluteness and relativity, is precisely the quintessence of the question of contradiction—and if you don't understand this, then you have essentially abandoned all dialectics.

Chapter 9
Prosecuting the New Revolution

1. The Development of Contradictions, and
an Important New Contradiction

Things develop gradually, but the arrival of a total contradiction is abrupt. As soon as one contradiction has been resolved, another is created, the latter often coming unexpectedly. We may think that the latter contradiction is completely without basis, but in reality, even as we are resolving the first contradiction, we are already establishing the foundation for the second. That is to say, we are inadvertently interchanging the essential and nonessential aspects of contradiction. The nature of things follows from this elusive kind of development. At a certain stage in the development of these two types of contradiction, they may exchange places, the second replacing the first. Alternatively, the first contradiction may be resolved and disappear, while the second becomes the first. A third contradiction may appear and take the place of the second.

Perhaps the day will come when the third contradiction will rise to the position of the first. This is the law of the development of contradiction.

This was the state of things.

This is how things were.

Hongmei's husband, Cheng Qingdong, died. After I spent three years laboriously digging this tunnel, and after Hongmei and I happily used it for another two years, this same tunnel then became her husband's tomb. This was the state of things. After one fundamental contradiction is resolved, a new one is created.

The tunnel was finally completed in the twelfth lunar month, nine months after my appointment as deputy mayor. It was completed more than half a year behind schedule, and the primary reason for the delay was that after I was appointed deputy mayor, the number of meetings I had to attend increased exponentially. Given that I was a revolutionary youth, I not only had to organize and attend countless meetings in my hometown, I also had to attend additional meetings in the county seat and sometimes even in the district seat. Every time I left Chenggang, however, my horizons were broadened, my theoretical knowledge was expanded, my political awareness was increased, and I was able to meet more high-level political leaders. All this helped lay a solid foundation for the next step of my career, but the drawback was that it delayed the completion of my great, divine tunnel of love, which in turn further exacerbated my corporeal longing for Hongmei.

Fortunately, we were able to set up our underground nuptial chamber even before the remainder of the tunnel was completed. Using the goodwill I had gained as a result of having helped connect electrical and broacasting cables to several elderly households covered by the nation's Five Guarantees social safety net, I asked the production brigade's secretary to go into town and purchase some insulated wire and cable. Next, I drilled a couple of small holes below the window in the back of my house, and threaded the electrical wire and broadcasting cable through the holes into the tunnel. Inside the tunnel, I connected the wires to several lights and also installed a two-hundred-watt bulb in the underground nuptial chamber; then I took some old broadcasting equipment that the town's radio station had previously thrown out and moved it into the tunnel. (Although as deputy mayor I wasn't released from work requirements and still had a rural residency permit, by this point my revolutionary career had entered a crucial transitional phase, where I could look forward to being promoted to town mayor or county head. When I said I wanted to borrow the equipment in question, the broadcaster fixed it for me and sent it to my home that same night. Such is the strength of power!) I installed three loudspeakers in the ceiling of the nuptial chamber and inside the earthen bed. Next, I laid out some straw and reed mats on the bed, then constructed a two-layer wooden box with a crack in it, filling the crack with moisture-resistant lime. I used the box to store the radio microphone, a blanket, a mattress, and other items that were sensitive to moisture. Hongmei furnished the bed with blue bedsheets she had received when she first got married, together with a pillow and a pillowcase decorated with mandarin ducks. In that way, that underground room became a true nuptial chamber. After I finished excavating the tunnel, Hongmei used moisture-resistant oilpaper to cut out a "double happiness" character connoting matrimonial bliss and posted it over the bed. Meanwhile, on one of the room's other three walls she posted large portraits of Marx, Engels, Lenin, Stalin, and Mao Zedong; on the second she posted portraits of Li Yuhe, Li Tiemei, Yang Zirong, Ke Xiang, Wu Qinghua, and Yan Weicai, while on the third she posted classic quotations and slogans, such as: IT IS THE CHINESE COMMUNIST PARTY THAT IS LEADING OUR INDUSTRY'S PRODUCTIVE FORCE; FIGHT SELFISHNESS, REPUDIATE REVISIONISM; ALL THE NATION'S PEOPLE SHOULD UNITE AND CARRY OUT THE GREAT PROLETARIAN CULTURAL REVOLUTION; and so forth. Furthermore, she had carefully laminated the paper on which these portraits and slogans were printed, demonstrating the loyal meticulousness with which she approached revolution and love in this damp environment.

Our understanding of dialectical materialism had not yet been perfected, just as our study of the theories of contradiction and practice remained merely academic. We hadn't used these theories for revolution or production, or to help us understand the reality of life or the contradictions of love. We had assumed that once the tunnel and the underground nuptial chamber were completed, and after Hongmei had quarreled with Qingdong as usual, she would move into our new mansion and furthermore would bring with her the bureau, chest, and table that had come with her dowry. When Qingdong was teaching at school, I dug the last few loads of soil to extend the tunnel to the area immediately behind Hongmei's bureau. I then removed the bureau's baseboards and arranged Hongmei's clothing so that it covered up the special plank. Assuming that all this was completed perfectly, we would manage to resolve all the revolutionary contradictions pertaining to our love or lust for one another.

The day I finished digging the tunnel, we did that thing on the earthen bed. We wanted to do it more, but at that moment my member still wasn't working properly. I tried having her slap me several times, as a result of which my member did in fact become hard, and we happily proceeded to do that thing several more times. In the days that followed, after the radio microphone and the speakers were connected, whenever we wanted to do that thing, we would turn on the broadcasting equipment, adjust the needle to the Central People's Broadcasting Station or the provincial radio channel, where revolutionary songs would inevitably be playing. The speaker that was placed over the head of the bed was originally a low-frequency woofer, and combined with the naturally low acoustics of the tunnel, the result was that every time a piece of music or a song was played, every time a marching slogan was shouted, and every time an important revolutionary leader's speech and the newest, highest directives were broadcast—the tunnel would be filled with bright red music and an atmosphere of deep excitement. Hongmei and I would find that we couldn't restrain ourselves, and we would throw ourselves onto the bed, tear off our clothes, and luxuriate in the red music flowing over our sheets, as I caressed Hongmei's smooth, white skin. We listened as those portraits and slogans resonated to the music, as my blood coursed through my veins. In this atmosphere I would do that thing with Hongmei for what seemed like an eternity. This was how we were able to enjoy several times more happiness and beauty than a typical married couple. In fact, precisely because we weren't yet married, we were able to enjoy several hundred times more pleasure than an actual couple. Every time we did that thing, we would lie on the bed afterward and exclaim, "The revolution is certainly worth it, and even death itself would be worth it!" During that brief, beautiful period, we had countless opportunities to enjoy our status as great revolutionary lovers, which was wonderful and profound, terrifying and exciting. In winter, we could be completely naked in that tunnel and yet wouldn't feel cold at all. Instead, every time we did that thing, we would find ourselves covered in sweat. In the heat of the summer, all the villagers would go to the open area in the front of the village, where they would lie down on their reed mats, enjoying the breeze and shooing away mosquitoes with cattail fans. At the agreed-upon time, after waiting for everyone to leave their homes, Hongmei and I would enter the tunnel and lie together on the cool earthen bed. Once, when I was waiting for Hongmei in the underground nuptial chamber and she didn't show up, I proceeded to where the tunnel opened up under her house. I knocked lightly on the bottom of her bureau, whereupon I found a note that read:

Esteemed Mayor Gao, Great Revolutionary,

I am having my period and have gone down to the banks of Thirteen Li River to help my daughter wash her clothes. Therefore, there is no need to wait for me today. Please use your firm and indomitable revolutionary perseverance to think of me. Without perseverance, there can be no extraordinary pleasure—this is something that you have constantly taught me.

Your revolutionary lover, a Hongmei plum blossom.

A revolutionary salute!

Written at noon.

236

Dejectedly, I returned from her house, not realizing that by that point she had already finished washing the clothes and had entered the tunnel through the opening under my own house. Standing naked in the underground nuptial chamber, she had already prepared the bed and turned on the music, and had even washed several cucumbers and placed them at the head of the bed, so that we could eat them after doing that thing. In the winter of the previous year, I had been sleeping one night during a snowstorm, when I seemed to hear someone tapping on my window. I got up and went into the tunnel, but the nuptial chamber was empty. I initially assumed I must have been hearing things and was about to return to my bedroom, when Hongmei suddenly jumped out of the chest at the head of the earthen bed. Completely naked, she lunged at me like a white butterfly. During those two years (and what a short two years they were!), we would meet in the tunnel almost every day we were both in the village, and we would do that thing almost every time we met. Sometimes I would have to leave for three to five days, and when I returned I wished I could sneak into her house through the tunnel and crawl into her bed. Of course, in doing so, I would have been taking an enormous risk, and if I made a mistake I could easily end up burying our revolutionary futures—particularly since by that point Hongmei's daughter, Tao'er, was ten years old and would sleep at the foot of Hongmei's bed every night. Therefore, every time I returned from a meeting in the county or district seat, I would send someone to Hongmei's house to formally notify her: "Branch Secretary Xia, Mayor Gao requests that you go listen to his report on the spirit of the meeting." (The villagers called me simply "mayor," never adding the modifier "deputy"—which was good, because not only did it sound better, I regarded it as an anticipation and a premonition of my future status.) When I gave her my report, it would always be on that earthen bed, and we would do that thing while I told her about the spirit of the meeting and related anecdotes. Once, I returned from a meeting and found that I couldn't restrain my desire for her, and I yearned to see her like a starving man yearns for food. I therefore sent someone to tell her, "There's an extremely urgent matter that needs our attention. Come immediately!" If I wanted to see her on a particular night, I would tell her what time to show up in the production brigade meeting hall. Based on the time I specified in my message, she would always be waiting for me punctually in the tunnel (my soul, my flesh, my revolutionary lover and life!). Sometimes, before "come immediately," I would add "you must." If it happened to be a mealtime when I sent someone to tell her "you must come immediately," within minutes she would appear in the tunnel, her hands still covered in flour from kneading dough or mud from washing vegetables. During that period, every time we finished crazily doing that thing, the sheets, our bodies, and the loudspeakers would all be covered in her white or yellow fingerprints. Naturally, when she herself went to the county or district seat to attend some meeting (though this didn't occur very often), upon returning she would have someone ask me if I wanted her to report on the spirit of the meeting, whereupon I would proceed into the tunnel and wait for her. I always resented the fact that she didn't report to me on the spirit of the meeting more promptly and instead kept me waiting—to which she replied, "You should be thankful that I return home first to wash up and change my clothes. After a long-distance bus ride, I always return completely covered in dust."

I said, "Don't worry that the dust won't wash off; just be concerned that it can't be swept away."

She said, "I emphasize prevention and am concerned about hygiene and increasing the People's health."

I said, "You must be brave and be willing to go to battle. You mustn't be afraid of sacrifice and instead must be willing to fight and advance, to fill the breach left by our fallen comrades. Only in this way can the world be ours and all the demons be eliminated."

She said, "Qualitative transformation begins from quantitative change, and a great disaster begins from a small sprout. If contradictions are not resolved when they are still small sprouts, setbacks and failure will inevitably come in the future."

I said, "You won't develop painful abscesses just because you wash yourself later than usual or happen to take fewer baths than usual, and even if you do, such things will quickly be cured. Like the word 'private,' the abscesses will disappear after being criticized."

She said, "In the short term, dust is an invitation for illness, and in the long term it is an obstacle to happiness. Running water doesn't become stagnant, and stagnant water doesn't run. If you're dirty and don't clean yourself promptly, the dirt may develop into a disease that will eventually reach your soul, and you'll regret it as though you crushed your own foot with the stone you were carrying."

I said, "We must carry an iron broom in one hand and a heavy staff in the other, since what is the point of having tiny ants celebrate the nation or having tiny bugs try to shake a tree? When facing feudalism, we are invincible; when facing the Five Black Categories, we'll rise up with fervor; when facing American imperialists and Soviet revisionists, we must force them to return to their own countries."

Afterward, I didn't need to use a loudspeaker, and even less did I need to beat myself to make my member hard. Instead, in the warm environment that we created using revolutionary songs, not only could I successfully do that thing, I could further develop our memories, eloquence, knowledge of theory, and class consciousness.

Even without relying on broadcasts or self-beatings, I was able to make myself hard every day and do that thing. And although the happiness Hongmei and I were able to create was short-lived and was not nearly as crazed or lengthy as when we were listening to songs and music, it was nevertheless as warm and gentle as a drizzle falling on parched earth, as a cool breeze blowing on a sweat-soaked body, or as sucking on one of those sour plums they sell in the city when your throat is parched. We were very proud of this discovery. Sometimes we even felt that whether or not we actually did that thing was of secondary importance, and instead the primary thing was the excitement and pleasure we derived from our revolutionary verbal battle.

Afterward, whenever we met for a rendezvous in the tunnel, we dispensed with the loudspeakers and instead would casually mention something and then proceed to engage each other in a verbal battle. We engaged in battle over the old pickax that had been left in the tunnel, over the dust on the earthen bed, and over the tunnel's megaphones and loudspeakers. We engaged in battle over the straw, bedsheets, water droplets, and boxes, as well as over the hair, fingernails, breasts, pillows, air holes, and clothes. Other than the quotations and the portraits of political leaders hanging from the walls, everything in the tunnel that could be seen or thought of became a potential object of verbal battle. We even used semi-obscene and semi-divine language to pursue a revolutionary poetic battle of words revolving around male and female genitalia. As with a drinking game, the loser of the round would be the person who was unable to answer or who deviated from the specified topic. We agreed that whoever won a round would kiss the loser fifty or a hundred times (until their lips were numb), and whoever lost a round would have to caress the opponent's private parts or would have to place the opponent's member in their mouth. We were like pigs or dogs, naïve and innocent, as though we had returned to our youth. We were completely shameless. We were even beneath pigs and dogs. Yet we were also pure and chaste, sincere and genuine. I gestured at the shovel lying on the ground, and said, "*Pursue revolution, promote production; use a shovel to overturn the earth.*" Hongmei replied, "*By using a shovel to incite revolution, we can terrify the enemy.*" I said, "*A shovel can overturn not only the earth but also the heavens, and a billion people will burst into smiles.*" She said, "*A shovel can be used as a rifle, with a heroic fighting spirit.*" I said, "*I like to look at endless waves of grain, and in all directions there are heroes in the sunset mist.*" She said, "Gao Aijun, Mayor Gao, in that last statement you didn't refer to a shovel. My back itches, so your punishment is to scratch it." I said, "Xia Hongmei, Party Branch Secretary Xia—without a shovel, how would you harvest the endless waves of grain? The sole of my foot itches, and as punishment you must scratch it ten times."

She scratched the sole of my foot ten times, and we both laughed and proceeded to turn everything upside down in bed.

She pointed to her hair and said, "*My hair is long, and my experience is not short. Women hold up half the sky.*" I pointed at my own hair and said, "*My hair is short, but my experience is long. The nation's affairs are close to my heart.*" She then pointed at her eyes and said, "*My heart is clear and my eyes are bright, my eyes are bright and my heart is broad.*" I pointed to my eyes and said, "*With my piercing gaze, I stare at the American imperialists and Soviet revisionists. With my piercing gaze, I will burn up our country's own evil spirits.*" She then pointed to her left breast and said, "*I eat grass and produce milk. Watch as I, Hongmei, proceed into battle.*" I pointed to my right breast and said, "*I emphasize form for the sake of beauty, but in the end am nothing but a pool of stagnant water.*"

She said, "Gao Aijun, a breast is not a form, and milk is not water. My thigh itches, so I want you to lick it."

I therefore proceeded to repeatedly lick her thigh.

For three months, we almost completely lost our revolutionary spirit and our initiative as we became completely absorbed by these revolutionary word games. Apart from obligatory meetings and study sessions, we stopped going out—we stopped going to the fields to oversee production and even stopped going to the production brigade meeting hall to attend meetings relating to class struggle. We no longer paid attention to our neighbors' quarrels over property boundaries and didn't care that the irrigation canal collapsed during the final autumn rain and needed to be repaired. We didn't care that the wooden stand in front of the village with the phrase PROPAGANDA GARDEN OF MAO ZEDONG THOUGHT had been toppled by the wind. We didn't care that there had been a lawsuit after the son of a rich landlord urinated on the head of the son of a poor peasant. Instead, we handed all these matters over to Cheng Qinglin, hinting that he should consider them preliminary practice, since after Hongmei and I were promoted, he would need to know how to handle all the work related to the Chenggang production brigade. Each new game gave us a new experience, but after having used every object in the tunnel as a topic for our verbal sparring, we would sometimes run out of topics and instead sit naked on the edge of the bed staring silently into space—like someone at a banquet who is unable to come up with an appropriate response for a drinking game. Sometimes, when we were at home or out at a meeting, we would suddenly think of a new topic and experience a surge of delight. We would immediately write the idea down on a sheet of paper, and then we would fold it up and find someone to deliver it to our opponent—so that they could make the appropriate mental and material preparations for their response and the crazy bout that would inevitably follow.

By the twelfth lunar month (that dark, dark month), the earth and heavens were bitterly cold, and all the villagers were sitting idly at home. These villagers were particularly fond of getting together and warming themselves by the fire, and after discussing some revolutionary topics they would chat about everything under the sun, just to pass the time. During that period, the village's young men would gather in my house, while the young women with revolutionary passion would gather in Hongmei's house. During that period neither Hongmei nor I could come up with a good topic for which we would need to go underground, and therefore, more than half a month passed without our meeting up in the tunnel. I felt that that half month passed as slowly as though I were walking from the town to the county seat or were traversing the hundred *li* from the county seat to Jiudu. I very much wanted to find a topic for which I could invite Hongmei to meet me in the nuptial chamber, but I simply had no inspiration. One day just after lunch, however, Hongmei

242

asked her daughter, Tao'er, to bring me a note on her way to school. I opened the note, and saw that it said:

> *Quickly write the newest and most beautiful text.*
> *Quickly paint the newest and most beautiful images.*

I knew that Hongmei, too, must have felt that the preceding half month had passed very slowly, and that she had finally come up with a new topic. Without waiting for my guests to arrive at the usual time (and even forgetting to give Hongsheng his school money), I pushed aside my rice bowl and immediately proceeded into the tunnel.

When I reached the nuptial chamber, I found that Hongmei was already waiting for me. When she saw me, she broke into an excited smile, and under the lamplight she resembled a pink curtain hung in front of a window. Needless to say, we first embraced and kissed, and after settling our debts from the previous half month I noticed that the Shuangling-brand alarm clock on the cabinet was ringing. I asked her about the beautiful new text and images to which she referred in her note, whereupon she removed two pencils and two piles of paper from her pocket and handed me one of each. She explained that the county's department of education had appointed Qingdong to represent Jiudu at the "Learn from Zhang Tiesheng" meeting that had been convened by the district's education committee, and when Qingdong left for the meeting, his fountain pen had fallen to the floor—which had given her inspiration for a completely novel topic.

I said, "What is it?"

She said, "Guess! It has to do with pens."

I replied, "Guns."

"It is guns, but it's also *not* guns. It's not guns, but it also *is* guns." She looked at me mysteriously for a moment, then explained, "The phrase *Political power grows out of the barrel of a gun* includes five key words: 'gun,' 'barrel,' 'out,' 'politics,' and 'power.' So, I propose that we take each of these five words and use them as our topics.

For instance, first we'll take the word 'gun' as our topic, and each of us will have five minutes to write a 'seven rule' poem dedicated to Marx. Then, we'll take 'barrel,' and each of us will have five minutes to write a short essay of at least two hundred words dedicated to Engels. Then, we'll take 'out,' and in five minutes we'll each write five aphorisms dedicated to Lenin. Then, we'll each take 'politics,' and in five minutes will write five Neo-Confucian philosophical phrases dedicated to Stalin. Finally, we'll each take the word 'power,' and in five minutes we'll each write five heroic sayings dedicated to Chairman Mao."

Although I recognized that she must have already planned out her answers, giving her a distinct advantage, I nevertheless enthusiastically agreed to her proposal. I asked, "What will be the penalty for the person who loses?" She laughed and said, "You can pick the penalty." I said, "If I lose, I'll unfasten all of your buttons and take off your clothing using only my mouth. Similarly, if you lose, you'll have to remove all of my clothing using only your mouth."

Her eyes glittered with excitement, and she exclaimed, "OK!"

With that, we began our competition, which was creative and original, but which also contained, buried within it, the roots of a future disaster. After placing the clock on the bed and the paper on the mats, we squatted down next to the bed. Over the next twenty-five minutes, the only sound to be heard in the nuptial chamber, apart from the urgent ticking of the clock, was our excited breathing and the scratching sound of pencils on paper, together with the occasional rustling as we gazed up at the leaders' portraits and the whirring of the gears in our heads.

The atmosphere in the room was very tense, and the light was muddy, as our sweat poured down like rain and our wrists became numb. Under our sheets of paper the reed mats whispered; under our pencils the paper rustled; and in our hands the pencils were screaming. The clock's brassy sound was like a hammer pounding down on our heads. When we peeked at each other, our gazes were like a hawk's talons. The leaders' kindly smiles flowed down our backs like warm water. In reality, those twenty-five minutes were a hundred-meter sprint of ideological awareness, theoretical ability, and literary talent. We were attempting to conquer each other, to engage in a battle that would end with love's triumphant return. It was a time-limited, simultaneous performance after our corporeal and spiritual contradictions had been resolved. I knew that Hongmei had already prepared her responses prior to beginning the competition, and consequently, while I, revolutionary genius that I am, required twenty-four minutes to complete my five assignments, she needed only twenty-three to complete hers.

This event represented the culmination of our competition—a meeting of two heroes. After we finished, we took the poems, essays, aphorisms, phrases, and sayings that we dedicated to Marx, Engels, Lenin, Stalin, and Mao, and pinned them below the corresponding portraits. Then we began to read and assess our work.

The poem Hongmei dedicated to Marx read:

Gun (枪)
A "seven rule" poem
   —Dedicated to Marx

Your thought is a bullet
And my pen is the barrel of a gun
Class enemies light fires
Let them rot from oral and written attacks.
The American imperialists and Soviet revisionists are forced to the borders.
Angrily swinging my massive cudgel, I bring this to an end.
The people of the world are united
In their common hatred of the enemy.

The poem I dedicated to Marx read:

Gun
A "seven rule" poem
  —Dedicated to Marx

The morning sun rises over Laiyin River
Great theory releases a bright light
Like a blade slicing the old world
Or gunfire shattering the dawn stillness
There is a boundary between bright day and dark night
There are two camps of advanced reactionaries
The power of imperialism must perish
While communism spreads throughout the whole world

Note: The phrase *the whole world* refers in my poem to the global commonwealth, which is to say, the entire globe's implementation of communism.

(Her poem had a novel topic, combined with a great and momentous tone; while mine had a firm standpoint, combined with poetic charm and pictorial splendor—which was particularly evident in the line "The morning sun rises over Laiyin River." Verdict: tie.)

The essay I dedicated to Engels was as follows:

Barrel (杆)
  —For Engels

The word "barrel" refers to a rod, and the word "rod" refers to weaponry. Your great work Socialism: Utopian and Scientific *is indeed a theoretical weapon for the proletariat to use against the bourgeoisie, and a great cornerstone for socialism to affirm its scientific basis with respect to capitalism, and offers an explanation of a materialist conception of history and of the surplus theory of value. It permits socialism to develop from a utopian ideal into a science; it permits socialism to open the door to a scientific class struggle of the proletariat; it permits the working class to observe the process by which medieval society, which is to say individual small-scale production, undertakes its necessary development toward capitalism and ultimately to a proletarian revolution. It permits the exploited and oppressed proletariat to see the beacon of their own emancipation and progression toward the future.*

(Hongmei's assessment: "It's good but perhaps a bit hollow. Also, it doesn't resemble an essay as much as a piece of expository writing, and furthermore, it's rather pedantic." I agreed with this assessment.)

The essay Hongmei dedicated to Engels read as follows:

Barrel
    —For Engels

The word "barrel" refers to a flagpole.
    Marx is the most, most, most important person in the world, and therefore his love for Jenny also became the world's greatest, greatest, greatest love. However, had it not been for Engels's selfless and spectacularly communist assistance, would we ever have had Marx's Kapital? And without the great Kapital, would we have had Marx and Jenny's great love? If it can be said that Marx is the greatest component of Marxism, then we must acknowledge that it was Engels who served as the great bridge that helped launch Marx forward. If it can be said that Marx is Marxism's great flag whistling in the wind, then Engels is Marxism's flagpole. As the flag flutters in the wind, it relies on the flagpole's support, and if we celebrate the rumbling of machinery, then we should celebrate even more the spirit of the silent screws. If we revere the spiritual flag of Marxist theory, then we should revere even more the spiritual flagpole of Engels's support, which helped raise that flag to the sky.

(My assessment: "This essay features a series of imaginative connections, from barrel of a gun to flagpole and from flagpole to the relationship between Marx's success and Engels's status as a spiritual flagpole. Moreover, this brilliant essay has a hundred more characters than my own 'Barrel' essay. I therefore acknowledge defeat.")

Out (出): Aphorisms
     —For Lenin

Author: Xia Hongmei
△ *Invite the word "self" to walk out, and invite the word "collective" to enter.*
△ *If you walk out to connect with the masses, you'll encounter the enchanting sight of another village; but if you close the door and lock yourself off from the masses, you'll have no way of returning to the mountains and streams.*
△ *If you walk out and look up, you'll see the cloudless sky above, and the collective will appear, iridescent; but if you return home and face the wall, you'll see only darkness, and the individual will appear, tainted.*
△ *When there are a pair of mountains (山 + 山 = 出) overhead, you won't be able to see the sky; but if you move this pair of mountains away, a great avenue to the sky will open.*
△ *If you wish to find questions from the struggle along two roads, to find meaning in the depths of your soul, and find answers in Chairman Mao's works, then you must go out and carry out a test in practice for the struggle.*

(I thought that these five aphorisms were indeed quite good, but they would be more appropriate as dedications to Chairman Mao, and it seemed somewhat odd to dedicate them to Lenin. Hongmei, however, asked, "Didn't Lenin also advocate collectivity and selflessness? Wasn't the communist spirit advocated by Lenin grounded on the concept of the collective?" I had no response to this, and Hongmei laughed.)

The aphorisms I dedicated to Lenin were:

Out
　　　—For Lenin

△ *Your act of writing out* The State and Revolution *is a beacon light for the advancement of revolution.*
△ *Your act of writing out* Philosophical Notebooks *is a great synthesis of Marxism-Leninism.*
△ *Your act of writing out* Imperialism: The Highest Stage of Capitalism *is a great prophecy of society's advancement, predicting the inevitable victory of the proletarian revolution.*
△ *Your act of writing out* Critique of the Gotha Program *is like the Big Dipper in the night sky, illuminating the path for the future implementation of a socialist nation governed by a dictatorship of the proletariat.*
△ *Your act of writing out* Our Revolution *is like a dagger slicing off the clothes of international opportunism. It is like an ax cutting open the path for Russia's revolution.*

(Hongmei's assessment of these five aphorisms was: "Compared with mine, these aphorisms are indeed closer to Lenin, however in each case the word 'out' appears only in the phrase 'writing out.' Not only is this rather monotonous, it is rather opportunistic." I acknowledged Hongmei's critique, and more importantly, I knew that *Critique of the Gotha Program* is actually one of Marx's works—but given that at the time I couldn't remember the titles of any of Lenin's other works, I had no choice but to replace one of them with one of Marx's. Fortunately Hongmei didn't notice this. Verdict: another tie.)

The philosophical phrases dealing with "politics" (政) that I dedicated to Stalin were:

1. *Feudal government wants to be the grave digger of the proletariat, but at the end of the day it merely ends up burying itself. Even if the proletariat unwittingly exploits and oppresses others, it will still become the grave digger of the feudal class.* [Hongmei exclaimed, "Good!"]

2. *Revolt is the calling card of revolutionaries, while conservatism is the epitaph of anti-revolutionaries.* [Hongmei asked, "Did you come up with this yourself, or is it from someone else?" I replied, "Xia Hongmei, you don't give me enough credit!" Hongmei fell silent, but the look of respect she gave me was as if she had seen a true poet.]

3. *If you live to benefit the people, then even if you die, you will still live forever. But if you live to benefit yourself, then even if you are still alive, it will be as if you were already dead.* [Hongmei exclaimed, "Excellent!"]

4. *When revolutionaries use violence for the sake of revolution, this is a form of political humanism, but when anti-revolutionaries implement democracy for the benefit of the capitalist class, this is a form of the most anti-humanist fascism.* [I thought I remembered having read some essay that Stalin wrote about violence, and it seemed that there was some connection between Stalin and violence.]

5. *Stalin is not merely a military figure; more importantly, he is a political figure. He inadvertently became a global hero but during World War II erected a great monument to heroes. Although Hitler was also a military figure, he was no political figure, and though he dreamed of becoming a global leader by establishing a global hegemony, during World War II he ultimately fell apart and committed suicide, having been reduced to the status of a mere clown.*

[Hongmei said, "Aijun, your knowledge is truly impressive. For this round, I acknowledge defeat."]

The philosophical phrases dealing with "politics" that Hongmei dedicated to Stalin were:

1. *When you are standing, the Soviet Union stands on politics; but when you are toppled, the Soviet Union will be toppled by its politics.* [This is deep, but it is more an aphorism than a philosophical phrase.]
2. *You may die, but you will always live on in the hearts of the socialist people. Khrushchev may still be alive, but the socialist people will always regard him as a political demon.* [This was similar to what I wrote. I remarked, "You must have peeked at mine!" Hongmei replied, "Isn't it enough that I already acknowledged defeat?"]
3. *Originally, the world did not have political paths, but as people walked around, paths began to form.* [I said, "This was Lu Xun's point. You should change it to, 'Anywhere people walk, even if there were no political paths there to begin with, paths will form. Conversely, anywhere people do not walk, even if there are already political paths there, paths will disappear.'"]
4. *If one has a political lamp in one's heart, then there will be light even in the darkest night. But if one does not, then there will be darkness even in the middle of the day.* [That is certainly true.]
5. *If you live for the sake of revolution, then your life will be worth a thousand taels. But if you live only for yourself, then your life won't be worth even a single needle. Regardless of whether you are worth gold coins or a single needle, the solution is action.* [This one was merely average, and furthermore didn't even include the keyword "politics."]

The five heroic slogans featuring the keyword "power" (权) that Hongmei dedicated to Chairman Mao were:

△ *What is the highest thing in the world?*
The power that the People grant to Chairman Mao is the highest thing in the world.
What is the reddest thing in the world?
The sun over Tiananmen is the reddest thing in the world.
What is the most intimate thing in the world?
The great leader Chairman Mao is the most intimate thing in the world.
What is the happiest thing in the world?
Serving the People is the happiest thing in the world.
What is the most glorious thing in the world?
Initiating revolutionary struggle is the most glorious thing in the world.

△ *The sky is bright, the earth is dark, but our red hearts will never change. Streams will flow and rivers too, but we must keep the power we hold.*

△ *If you wield power on behalf of the People, then the People will be able to rest easy. If you wield power on behalf of the Party, then you will closely track the Party Central Committee. However, if you wield power on your own behalf, then prison will be the only thing that awaits you.*

△ *When you have power in hand, you should keep the People in your heart. When you have power in your heart, you should have Mao Zedong Thought in your soul. If you have power in your soul, then you should have loyalty to Chairman Mao flowing through your veins.*

△ *If you defend political power, you'll be able to make it through a critical juncture and brave the storm, and if you defend political power, you'll be able to traverse a path of struggle and face the world.*

The five heroic slogans featuring the keyword "power" that I dedicated to the great leader Chairman Mao were:

△ *We hold red power in our hands and hold Chairman Mao in our hearts.*

△ *The heavens may shift and the earth may shake, but my red heart's loyalty to Chairman Mao will never falter. Heads may roll and blood may flow, but we will never lose the power we have recaptured from the hands of class enemies.*

△ *Even if we launch a class struggle today, we'll still have the support of our class brothers. And even if World War III breaks out tomorrow, we'll still have our position, the political power of the proletariat, and Chairman Mao's smile.*

△ *Power is seized from the hands of class enemies; willpower is forged in the furnace of class struggle; a red heart is nurtured from Mao Zedong Thought; and class consciousness is developed through diligent study.*

△ *For the sake of revolution, not only will I work hard, I will work even harder for my comrades. I will not only do another good deed, I will do even more good deeds. For the sake of power, I will not only engage in another struggle, I will engage in another, even deeper, struggle. For the sake of revolutionary love, not only will I not hesitate to sweat and bleed, I won't hesitate to sweat and bleed my final drops of sweat and blood. So that Hongmei's plum blossom may bloom forever, not only will I struggle to a higher level of power, I will do everything I can to attain even greater power.*

After Hongmei finished reading the heroic slogans I dedicated to Chairman Mao, she stood silently under Mao's portrait for a long time. She was utterly astonished by my final lines: "For the sake of revolutionary love, not only will I not hesitate to sweat and bleed, I won't hesitate to sweat and bleed my final drops of sweat and blood. So that Hongmei's plum blossom may bloom forever, not only will I struggle to a higher level of power, I will do everything I can to attain even greater power." By this point, we had already been aroused by this new and most stimulating competition, and now we felt restless, excited, and also exhausted. This exercise, where we each spent twenty-five minutes displaying our linguistic talents, left us both trembling with excitement as we argued animatedly over the readings, all so that afterward we could enjoy either having our opponent remove our clothes with their mouth or else removing our opponent's clothes with our own mouth. Because each of us wanted to be the one to be undressed, we originally expected to engage in a long debate before reaching a final determination of who was the ultimate winner—each of us arguing that our own compositions reflected deep thought, lofty ideas, beautiful language, and abundant talent, while our opponent's compositions were shallow, far-fetched, and strained. However, after Hongmei finished reading my final two lines, she instead just stood there silently and reflected for a moment, then exclaimed, "Aijun, how would you like me to undress you with my mouth?"

I lay down on the bed.

I told her to first strip naked, then kneel down next to the bed. Next, I told her to begin with my neck and unfasten each of the buttons of my military uniform, and then unfasten each button of my sweater and my shirt. After each of these articles of clothing was removed, she could use her mouth to unfasten my belt, unfasten the buttons on the front of my pants, and then use her mouth to remove my pants and underwear. Her lips were smooth and moist, and her tongue was nimble and dexterous, and as she was unbuttoning my buttons and removing my clothes, I felt as though a beautiful bug were crawling up and down my body—such that each time it reached a new location, the bug's warm breath would blow on my skin like a cool breeze blowing on my overheated body. I was already aroused and could hardly wait to do that thing with her. Back when we had finished reading our compositions I had already been as hard as a rock but had controlled myself. I wanted to have her lips, teeth, and tongue wander up and down my body, and I enjoyed this sensation for at least forty, maybe sixty minutes. I watched as she panted over my body, and her sweat poured down and left behind a pool of perspiration resembling the world's largest pearl. Only then did I pounce like a thunderbolt and throw her beneath me, as though she were a sheep I had been chasing for hundreds of *li* through the mountains.

Finally, her limber, passionate, and sharp plum-colored screams once again echoed through the tunnel, refusing to dissipate. After excitedly doing that thing like a thunderbolt, we quietly lay in bed. She caressed my shoulder with one hand and rested her other hand on my chest—panting contentedly, as though she had been treading water and had finally made it to shore. Meanwhile, I was running one hand through her hair and using the other to caress her breasts. I looked past Hongmei's shiny forehead, at the opposite wall, where the products of our game were hanging.

I said, "Hongmei, you've improved!"

She blinked, "What?"

I said, "Your literary talent and knowledge of theory, your verbal talent and class consciousness—they've all improved."

She laughed. "You've trained me well."

I said, "You're too modest."

She said, "Really! You are a revolutionary teacher." She turned over and took my hand, and it was in fact like a student wanting a teacher to lead her forward.

I held her hand in mine and proudly replied, "I'm not only your teacher, I'm also your adviser."

She stared at the ceiling fastidiously and said sadly, "I don't want you to be my teacher or my adviser. All I want is for you to be my lifelong revolutionary lover."

I also stared at the ceiling, which was covered in drops of water, and said, "Aren't I already your revolutionary lover?"

She replied, "I said '*lifelong* revolutionary lover.'"

I said, "Our relationship will definitely be lifelong."

She said, "That's hard to say. You don't realize how much potential you have, and so far I'm the only person in the world who knows it. Right now you are only the deputy mayor, but who knows how things may change once you are promoted to county head, district commissioner, and provincial governor?"

I said, "Would the revolutionary structure permit me to constantly change my mind?"

She said, "That's true. Even if I permitted it, the revolution wouldn't."

I said, "Actually, Hongmei, I'm also afraid that you might have a change of heart."

She replied, "I won't. I definitely won't."

I said, "How do you know?"

She said, "Because if I did, you could fire me and strip me of my Party membership."

I said, "I could?"

She said, "You have the power. You must make sure that you will always be my leader."

I said, "Yes, that is true."

At this point, she looked away from the ceiling and suddenly sat up. Gazing at the portraits and slogans on the wall, she said, "Aijun, we should swear an oath."

"What sort of oath?"

"We should swear an oath of our love for each other, before these great figures."

"OK." I also sat up. "But as a gesture of respect, we should first put our clothes back on."

"No need." She added, "We are their children, and when children are naked in front of their parents, they are natural and unashamed."

I reflected for a moment and then said, "Yes, that's true."

We therefore stood naked in front of the portraits and our brilliant compositions and held our breath.

I first raised my right hand and said, "I swear that I, Gao Aijun, apart from maintaining a lifelong loyalty to you, our great leader Chairman Mao, will also remain loyal to your thought and to the socialist road, and apart from filially supporting my mother and enabling her to enjoy a comfortable old age, I will also maintain a lifelong loyalty to my love for Xia Hongmei and will let our love and affection endure and flourish."

Hongmei looked at me and said, "And what about after you become county head, district commissioner, and provincial governor?"

I faced the portraits of the four great men, and holding my right hand even higher, I swore, "My appointments may change, but my heart will not. I'll love you until the seas dry up and rocks crumble."

Hongmei turned and stared at me. "How about when I'm old, decrepit, and full of wrinkles. What then?"

I bit my lower lip. "Even after I turn one hundred, my heart will remain pure, and my gray hair will continue to reveal my true feelings."

Hongmei asked again, "What if you change?"

Her skepticism angered me, and I furiously swore, "Then you can tell the Party Central Committee and Chairman Mao that I'm corrupt and degenerate, that I'm a fake revolutionary and a false socialist. You can print our relationship on flyers, and after I become county head, you can distribute those flyers throughout the committee courtyard; after I'm appointed district commissioner, you can distribute the flyers throughout the provincial Party committee courtyard; and after I'm appointed provincial governor, you can distribute the flyers throughout the city of Beijing."

She didn't say anything else.

When I lowered my right hand, I saw her standing there, her skin as white as a jade column. There were, however, a pair of teardrops in her eyes.

I said, "Your turn. Swear!"

As I had done, she slowly raised her right hand and gazed up at the portraits. The veins in her right arm appeared dark green, like vines in the spring.

She said, "Apart from the Three Loyalties that Comrade Gao Aijun mentioned, I will also work hard to raise and educate my daughter, Cheng Tao'er. I want for her to study hard and make progress every day, so that she may become a most excellent revolutionary successor. I want to make sure that she won't have to endure any hardship in this lifetime and will have perpetual good fortune. I want for her to have a good job, good prospects, a good husband, and a good family."

(I suddenly realized that when I was swearing my oath, I had completely forgotten to mention my own children, Hongsheng and Honghua. After hearing Hongmei, I silently swore an oath to my children, repeating to them the same thing that Hongmei had said regarding her daughter.)

"With respect to my relationship with Comrade Gao Aijun" (I jumped with surprise and looked back at Hongmei, seeing that the skin between the joints of her pinky figure had turned red), "I know that I've let down my husband, Cheng Qingdong, but my relationship with Comrade Gao Aijun is of the purest sort of revolutionary love—like the relationship between Xiao Changchun and Jiao Shufeng, or between Pavel and Tonia. I swear to you, my elders, that I will be Comrade Gao Aijun's loyal revolutionary lover until death—and in the event that I should have the slightest change of heart, may I be blinded, struck by lightning, and have my corpse be left in the open after I die!"

I said, "And how about when Gao Aijun gets old?"

She said, "When Gao Aijun gets old, I'll remain his lifelong companion, as though I were his crutch."

I said, "And when he becomes county head, district commissioner, and provincial governor?"

She said, "Even if he were sent to prison, I, Xia Hongmei, would still take him baskets of food."

I said, "And what if, before he grows old, he falls ill and is no longer able to provide you with a woman's pleasure?"

She replied angrily, "I, Xia Hongmei, am your revolutionary comrade, your battle companion, and your sister. I'm not a parasite who merely looks to you for corporeal pleasure. If you fall ill and can no longer provide Xia Hongmei with physical pleasure, she won't have a change of heart, nor will she feel any resentment. Conversely, as long as you need her, and as long as she is able to bring you happiness and pleasure, she will make every effort to do so and will do anything you ask."

I asked, "And what if I ask her to do something, and she doesn't do it?"

She said, "Then you can draw that most private part of her body, including all of her moles and her veins, print the image on leaflets, and distribute them throughout the world."

I said, "You may put your hand down."

She said, "I want you to raise your hand again."

I once again held up my hand.

Holding her own right hand high in the air, she swore, "With the blue sky above and these great people serving as witnesses, I declare that my oath today is completely true and sincere. If, in the future, I go back on any of these words, you may have me decapitated and leave my lifeless body lying unburied in the open."

I was truly moved by Hongmei's oath. I thought that I should say a few things that would be even more moving, so I lifted my right hand higher, thought for a moment, and said, "With the blue sky above and these great people serving as witnesses, I, Gao Aijun, declare that if there are any insincerities or falsehoods in what I've said today, you must terminate my future prospects and destroy my reputation. In front of the assembled masses, you must shred my body into ten thousand pieces and have the countless masses, including my own children and grandchildren, stomp on the fragments of my body—such that for years to come, for generations to come, I'll have no hope of getting rehabilitation or redress."

As I expected, the love and affection that I expressed in my final oath left her profoundly moved and overcome with emotion. (I truly did have a very rare oratorical skill and was a speaker of eternal truths.) When I finally lowered my right hand, she gazed lovingly at me with eyes full of tears.

I gazed back her.

Both of us were moved to tears by each other's sincerity and hugged each other tightly. All we could do was hug each other, such that her smooth, naked skin pressed against mine, and my own rough skin pressed against hers. We rushed down the tunnel, rolling around together as though we were a single person. The tunnel's moisture entered our bodies through our pores that had been opened wide by our excitement, penetrating deep into our skin, our veins, and our bones. Water droplets fell from the ceiling, splattering mud onto our bodies. We rolled around in the mud like truck wheels, profoundly moved by each other's corporeal sincerity.

At this point, a quantitative change became a qualitative one, and a new contradiction arose.

A crisis was imminent.

The wheels of history changed course.

The revolution fell into a spiraling trap.

I have no idea how deeply we slept or for how long. At some point, however, there was the faint sound of footsteps approaching, though it was hard to tell if I was hearing them in my dream or in real life. Almost simultaneously, Hongmei and I both sat up, like two fish that had been caught and released again. We saw Hongmei's husband, Cheng Qingdong, holding a flashlight, his face as green as iron, suddenly appear in the underground nuptial chamber. He appeared thin and frail, and as he approached through the tunnel, he didn't know where he needed to duck, and consequently twice bumped his head against the ceiling, leaving him with clumps of mud in his hair and on his forehead. Needless to say, he had been astonished to discover this long tunnel leading to his home, but when he found me and Hongmei sleeping naked on the muddy ground, he immediately fell into shock. When we woke up, and I saw Cheng Qingdong's iron-like face, the first thing that came to mind was that I needed to grab the pants I had left at the head of the bed—as though the significance of Cheng Qingdong's sudden appearance was not that he was going to catch a pair of adulterers but rather that he was going to steal our clothes. Just as I was getting up to grab my pants, Hongmei asked calmly, as though she had just woken up in her own bed, "Qingdong, didn't you go to attend a meeting in Jiudu?"

Cheng Qingdong fixed his gaze on Hongmei's body, and from between his clenched teeth he squeezed out three greenish-purple words: "You . . . are . . . shameless!"

These three words instantly roused Hongmei, as she realized with a shock what had happened. Turning pale, she instinctively covered the area between her legs with her hands, and proceeded to kneel down before Qingdong, as though her entire body had cramped up. As this was happening, however, as I went to grab my clothes, I forgot myself for a moment and turned to see what she was doing. As a result, my intentions were revealed, and Qingdong was able to grab my and Hongmei's clothes before I could.

Just as this extraordinary event was unfolding, a subtle contradiction developed out of this special condition. While the old contradiction had been resolved, a new contradiction emerged, as the earlier secondary contradiction was transformed into a primary contradiction. That is to say, I had assumed that once Cheng Qingdong grabbed our clothing, he would attempt to negotiate with me and Hongmei and try to coerce us in some way. Instead, however, he simply grabbed our clothing and headed back toward his house (the pink knitted underwear I had given Hongmei fell to the ground, and he hurriedly picked them up). It was actually as if he wasn't trying to catch a pair of adulterers but instead simply wanted to steal our clothes. His pace was both urgent and flagging, and he left the tunnel as though trying to flee. He seemed to want to run, but since he was unfamiliar with the route he instead had to settle for walking quickly. In the blink of an eye, he and the shadow he cast on the walls of the tunnel disappeared from view, leaving behind only his earthy-yellow footsteps, which echoed through the tunnel and knocked up against my and Hongmei's naked bodies and our empty skulls.

The lamplight flickered.

Qingdong's footsteps became fainter and fainter.

Suddenly, Hongmei, who was still kneeling on the ground, sprang to her feet. However, as though scalded by the ground beneath her, she quickly fell down again. With both palms facing upward, she clenched her hands into fists and placed each next to her breast. Then—with her forehead covered in bead-size drops of sweat—she looked in the direction of the tunnel opening toward which Cheng Qingdong was headed and shouted, "Aijun, if Qingdong makes it out, you'll be ruined!"

This struck an alarm bell in my mind and gave me a divine inspiration. In showing this fatal contradiction, Hongmei had given me a key with which I might resolve it. I can't remember what precisely I was thinking about at that moment (perhaps about the basis of the theory that revolution is inseparable from violence?); or maybe I wasn't thinking anything at all; or perhaps the phrase *Revolution is inseparable from violence, and sometimes violence is still the most effective form of revolution* flashed through my brain. In any case, I grabbed the shovel sitting in the corner of the nuptial chamber and began advancing (with vigorous strides) toward Qingdong.

Just think, how could Cheng Qingdong have been as familiar with that tunnel as I? He was wearing padded winter clothing and was also carrying my and Hongmei's clothes, while I was completely naked, so how could he possibly outrun me? Just as Qingdong was about to reach the air hole located directly below his own house on Rear Cheng Street, he heard me pursuing him and panicked, tripped, and fell.

The shovel I was holding came down on his head like a blade, and I chopped off his head as though I were slicing a melon.

That was how he died. With a scream, and as his blood splattered over the tunnel's muddy walls, he died.

2. The Shovel's Revolutionary Song

Man: *Grasp revolution, promote production*
With a shovel, turn over the soil.
Woman: *With a shovel, undertake revolution*
Leave the enemy trembling with fear.
Man: *With a shovel, turn over heaven and earth,*
A billion people burst into smiles.
Woman: *A shovel can serve as a gun,*
As we maintain a fighting spirit.
Man: *I gaze happily at the endless waves of rice and beans,*
And see heroes, everyone under the setting sun.

3. Struggle Is the Only Medicine for Those Afflicted with Revolution

That was a very dark day.

We dragged Cheng Qingdong's corpse back to the nuptial chamber and buried it beneath the slogans we had posted on the northern-facing wall. After burying the corpse, we knew we would never be able to return to this tunnel, which had given us so much spiritual sustenance and corporeal pleasure over the preceding two years. With Cheng Qingdong buried there, even if we went back, we'd never again be able to enjoy the same sort of spiritual or corporeal climax.

When I took Hongmei home, the night was already three *zhang* deep. As we fumbled our way out of the tunnel through the opening behind her bedroom bureau, we both felt energized but also exhausted. However, as soon as Hongmei saw Tao'er, who had already fallen asleep in the moonlight while waiting for her to return, she immediately collapsed and hugged her daughter. Then, without crying or sobbing, Hongmei began trembling, as though she were freezing cold.

I said, "How can you act like this? At this time of night we should be particularly quiet."

She said, "You should leave, before Tao'er wakes up."

"You must remember what we said," I exhorted her as I left her house. Then I went sauntering through the streets as though I were simply returning home late from a meeting.

I didn't run into anyone on my way home.

I didn't even see a dog.

One day passed.

Two days passed.

Three days passed.

Chenggang's production brigade continued as before. The winter wind was still as cold as before, ripping to shreds the posters on the village propaganda notice board. The midday sun was still as warm as before, and the villagers who didn't have a stove to keep them warm all gathered outside in the sunlight, to chat and check themselves for lice. Every morning, I could hear the rumbling sound of the well pulley, as people went to fetch water. Over the course of those three days, I twice went into town to attend meetings, and as Mayor Wang was reading official documents, he would still proudly nod his head. At the end of the meeting, he asked me, neither warmly nor coldly, "Deputy Mayor Gao, do you have anything to report?" I replied, "No, nothing." He said, "OK, then the meeting is adjourned." Everything proceeded as before—as though absolutely nothing out of the ordinary had occurred. It was only when the school was supposed to offer Cheng Qingdong's language class and his podium remained empty—only then did the other teachers remark, "Has Teacher Cheng still not yet returned from his meeting? Then today we'll continue teaching mathematics."

On the fourth day, Hongmei went to Cheng Temple to see her father-in-law, the former town mayor Cheng Tianmin, and said, "Father, Qingdong went to attend a meeting in Jiudu, but why hasn't he returned yet? The meeting was originally only supposed to last one day, and even after taking travel time into account, his trip should have lasted only three days. Today is already the fourth day since his departure." On the fifth day, Hongmei once again went to Cheng Temple to see her father-in-law and anxiously said, "Now it has been five days, and he still hasn't returned!"

On the sixth day, Hongmei went to Jiudu to look for her husband. Cheng Qingmin held Tao'er by the hand while escorting Hongmei to the town's long-distance bus station. When Hongmei returned from Jiudu on the seventh day, however, she brought back a startling revelation—reporting that the "experience-exchange meeting to learn from Zhang Tiesheng," which Jiudu's department of education had originally planned to convene seven days earlier, had been canceled, and while some of the participants had received the notification and had aborted their trips, the participants who didn't receive the notification had turned around as soon as they reached Jiudu and returned home. At the same time, during those several days, there had been an enormous traffic accident in Jiudu, together with two factional struggles. In the latter struggles, both sides used guns and bullets, leaving three people dead and more than a dozen wounded. The corpses of two people who had been killed by accident lay in the square for two days without anyone coming to claim them. In the end, under the novel and magnificent orders of the relevant government department, the two corpses had been taken away to be cremated.

(The sky is blue, ah, the sky is blue! The land is vast, ah, the land is vast!)

That was how Hongmei returned from Jiudu carrying a burial urn. It was dusk when she disembarked from the long-distance bus, whereupon she immediately saw a crowd of pale teachers and students waiting for her. She saw the silent production brigade Party branch cadres and commune members, whom I had brought, and she saw Cheng Tianmin sitting in the middle of the crowd, with Tao'er in his lap. Her eyes filled with tears, her legs turned to rubber, and she almost collapsed into the embrace of Cheng Qinglin, who had come to receive the ash-filled urn.

I said, "Why are you crying?"

"I saw Tao'er and realized that from now on she'll be fatherless."

"You don't trust me to treat her well? I have a basic fatherly awareness and humanism."

"I do trust you. But all the same, she still will have lost her biological father."

"It seems you still miss Cheng Qingdong and don't value our revolutionary friendship as much as your relationship with Cheng Qingdong. You must emerge from the shadows, gaze into the future, concentrate on the light, and focus on the big picture. You must prioritize our future prospects and our revolutionary cause. You must forget the past and join the struggle at top speed and without any burdens, so that we can more quickly and effectively realize and implement our ideals."

"What was the spirit of the document you studied two days ago?"

"It described how we must focus on agriculture and learn from Dazhai."

This is how things unfolded. The storm passed. No one doubted that Cheng Qingdong had been killed by a stray bullet during the revolutionary struggle in Jiudu. We could now look back and analyze the series of events. It was clear that Cheng Qingdong must have suspected our relationship for some time but couldn't say anything because he had no evidence, and moreover didn't dare say anything because Hongmei and I were openly acting as revolutionaries, and moreover wasn't willing to say anything because he had the typical cowardice of a rural intellectual. Therefore, it was only after he went to Jiudu to attend a meeting that he had an opportunity to suddenly return to the village, whereupon he was able to enter Hongmei's bedroom and, finding her gone, discover the opening to the tunnel. But how could he have avoided running into anyone on his way home from the bus station? Did he deliberately avoid people so as to be able to make a surprise appearance at his own home? Or did the streets happen to be completely empty on the day and time he returned? Or, perhaps someone *did* see him, but it didn't make a big impression, and after Hongmei brought back the ash-filled urn from Jiudu, that person probably didn't trust their own memory. After all, people die all the time. From now on, whenever someone dies in our production brigade, regardless of who it is—whether it's a cook or a soldier—as long as they've performed some useful work, we'll make sure to organize a funeral procession and a memorial service in their honor. This will become a tradition, and this practice will be introduced to the common people. Whenever someone in the village dies, there will be a memorial service that will help relieve our grief and unite the people. We set about organizing such a memorial service for Cheng Qingdong.

After we buried Cheng Qingdong's ashes, Cheng Tianmin fell ill and spent half a month hospitalized in the town's health clinic. After Cheng Tianmin was released, it was evident that he had aged precipitously—just as Cheng Tianqing had done after Guizhi's death. Cheng Tianmin was now so decrepit that he swayed back and forth when he walked, and after returning to Cheng Temple, he almost never left again. People very rarely saw him in the village. This is how things were. Struggle is cruel; revolution is heartless and sometimes even seems barbaric. This is inevitable and even necessary. In the days that followed, and for that entire winter, Hongmei was listless and lacking in vigor. Regardless of how much I encouraged her to face reality, focus on the future, maintain her high ambitions, and attend to revolutionary principles for tomorrow's struggle, she remained distracted, as if she wasn't even listening to me. I told her that what needed to happen had already happened and what needed to pass would pass. She replied that whenever she fell asleep, she would see Qingdong's head being chopped off by my shovel as though it were a melon being sliced open, and would see Qingdong refusing to close his eyes, even as we tried to bury him. In order to help her emerge from the shadows as quickly as possible, I would affectionately embrace and caress her at every opportunity, as soon as no one was around, regardless of where we happened to be. She, however, offered no response. When I took her hand, it was as though I were picking up a stick, and when I kissed her lips, it was as if I were kissing lifeless pieces of rubber. I attempted to rouse her by unbuttoning her clothes and caressing her breasts, and although she didn't resist, she also didn't respond in any way, acting as though I were a famished person and she were but a cold bun.

That winter, Hongmei became a zombie in the revolution, a live clay figurine in our love, and a true sympathizer of the Chenggang villagers. That is to say, she contracted a case of revolutionary depression. As her leader, as her revolutionary guide who had vowed to die with her, as her comrade and lover who had endured hardship with her—I had a responsibility to rescue her from this depression. I knew that for sick revolutionaries, the best medicine was more revolution, and if she had stumbled in revolution, she would get back to her feet in revolution. During a non-wartime period, the primary mode of revolution is struggle, and the primary mode of struggle is attending meetings. Whether or not one is permitted to speak at meetings, whether one is permitted to criticize others or be criticized by others—this kind of struggle may help eradicate the revolutionary's symptoms.

To this end, I repeatedly encouraged Hongmei to attend meetings—arranging for her attend as many as possible in my stead, while also pushing her to the podium on all the occasions where she was permitted to speak on my behalf. During the second lunar month, at the end of winter, the county issued the town some cheap urea fertilizer. This was Japanese-produced urea, and it came in nylon sacks. In accordance with custom, the town distributed the urea to each production brigade, which in turn distributed it to each production team. After all the urea had been distributed, the town collected the empty sacks and distributed them to the relatives of soldiers, revolutionary martyrs, and elders covered by the five social guarantees. We had already drawn up a plan for distributing the urea and the empty sacks. Apart from the relatives of soldiers and revolutionary martyrs, and the Five Guarantees households, every family's urea sack was just large enough to make a pair of pants or a dyed shirt. The plan was to distribute the remaining sacks to Party cadres, those who were the backbone of the revolution, and to other active participants in class struggle. But just at that moment, the town convened a grassroots expansion meeting, which was enlarged to include every production team's leader. At this meeting, Mayor Wang, without waiting for Party committee investigation, decided on his own accord to announce the previous year's average summer and autumn grain-production figures, writing them on an enormous white sheet of paper that he then posted in the town's meeting hall. On this sheet, it was reported that, the previous year, the Chenggang production brigade had produced only 210 *jin* of wheat and 290 *jin* of corn per *mu* (we relaxed the manure-collection movement that year), which averaged out to an annual production of 190 *jin* per capita, making every daily work-point allotment (ten points) worth only seventeen cents. That is to say, if a laborer worked for a full day, he would earn only seventeen cents and would be issued only a total of six *liang* of coarse and refined grain. (Our Chenggang production brigade was the socialist collective that consumed the most returned grain—or grain resold by the state back to the site of production.)

Our bridgade had the lowest productivity of the entire town, while the brigade with the second-lowest reported that it had yielded an average of 320 *jin* of grain per *mu*, paying thirty-five cents per work point. The highest productivity could be found in the Wangjiayu Village production brigade deep in the Balou Mountains, which produced 427 *jin* per *mu* and paid fifty-one cents per work point. The Party branch secretary of the Wangjiayu production brigade was none other than the Zhao Xiuyu whom I mentioned previously, and Wangjiayu Village was also Mayor Wang's home. I let Hongmei represent the Chenggang production brigade at this meeting. The meeting was initially scheduled to run for a day and a half, with participants' room and board organized by the town government. During the first half-day, participants would study political documents; during the second half-day Mayor Wang would summarize recent revolutionary activities and production levels; and during the third half-day there would be a general discussion. In the afternoon of the first day, when it was Mayor Wang's turn to offer his summary, he posted the tally sheet in the meeting hall, whereupon the cadres of the other production brigades all exploded. When they saw that although the "New Yan'an" revolution was already in full swing in Chenggang, its average per capita grain allotment was only 190 *jin* and its average daily work-point allocations were worth only seventeen cents, everyone stared intently at Hongmei. More importantly, after Mayor Wang finished reading from the chart, he announced, "In order to realize Chairman Mao's directive to *pursue revolution and promote production*, this spring everyone should take half of their fertilizer and their relief grain and donate them to the production brigades and production teams whose grain productivity exceeds 350 *jin* per *mu*, while those production brigades whose productivity exceeds 400 *jin* per *mu* will be awarded at least sixty *jin* of relief grain and fifty bags of cheap urea."

The meeting hall erupted in excitement, as everyone gazed jealously at Wangjiayu's Secretary Zhao Xiuyu.

During the rest break, Hongmei left the meeting hall.

"Wang Zhenhai is openly insulting our Chenggang production brigade," she announced.

Hongmei had returned to the production brigade and found me (why did I go to the production brigade department that day?), and said, "Wang Zhenhai announced to all the other production brigades that we are a false model—like an inedible image of a fried pancake reflected in a mirror or a lusterless reflection of the moon in a pool of water."

Because of the fervor and subsequent decline of our love, we had already placed the struggle to displace Mayor Wang on the slow track, for we had never expected that, during the busy autumn period, he would give me and Hongmei an additional storm to contend with. This confirmed the saying that in revolutionary struggle, if you don't defeat your enemy, your enemy will defeat you, and if you give your enemy an opportunity to breathe and grow out his feathers, he will lunge at you like an eagle. If we are given less fertilizer, how will we ever be able to engage in production in the spring? If we are given less relief grain, how will our people eat? As Hongmei was giving me these updates, I was folding up a sheet of paper. While doing so, I told her coldly yet firmly, "Class conflict cannot be reconciled, and struggle definitely cannot be halted." Hongmei replied, "This is a case of 'Wang Zhenhai giving us a new road to follow.' We have already distributed urea sacks to all the commune members, and if now the higher-ups don't issue us more fertilizer, how will we be able to explain it to the poor and lower-middle peasants and to the class activists?!"

I can't recall exactly why I went to the production brigade that day, but in any event, I sat down at the table and began slowly folding up the papers that were sitting there, as though I couldn't hear a word Hongmei was saying.

Hongmei said, "Gao Aijun, why don't you say something? You used to go on and on every day about how you wanted to topple

Mayor Wang, and how you yourself wanted to be released from production, like him. However, the past two or three years I haven't heard you mention any of this. Mayor Wang dares to behave tyrannically toward you, pissing and shitting on your head, yet you don't dare respond with even a fart."

I continued staring at the papers in my hand, folding them even after they couldn't be folded any more (I was studiously attempting to present the appearance that everything was OK). I continued until I had folded a sheet of paper into a perfect cube.

Hongmei became anxious. She grabbed the papers I was holding and threw them down onto the table, and said, "Gao Aijun, don't you call yourself a revolutionary and political genius? Now you must go out and engage in revolution. You have to go out and give advice to the masses. You have to go out and declare war against Wang Zhenhai. So, why are you sitting here without saying a word? Is it because you don't dare to come forward? Are you afraid that you wouldn't be able to defeat him? Is it because you feel helpless?"

As Hongmei said this, her face began to regain its earlier brightness and agitation, and once again had the restless excitement it used to have whenever we discussed revolution. I could see how the revolutionary medicine was having an effect on her—and particularly on the depressive state into which she had sunk when the revolutionary struggle encountered a setback—or perhaps she, as a young and attractive female Party branch secretary, felt humiliated by Wang Zhenhai. I stood up and, grinding my foot in the ground, said, "Damn it, it turns out that different classes cannot be reconciled with one another. If you don't put him to death, he will eventually aim his gun at you."

I added, "Hongmei, it's not that those acts will go unanswered but rather that it's simply not time yet. When the time is right, we'll definitely take action. At the moment, Wang Zhenhai is once again shooting bullets at our Chenggang production brigade, precisely when you and I are upset. But you're right—we can't just sit here and act as if nothing is happening, turning a blind eye toward his callousness."

I added, "Hongmei, you should return to the meeting hall and carefully observe Wang Zhenhai and Zhao Xiuyu. I simply can't believe that there isn't something going on between them. Wang Zhenhai's wife is paralyzed and is unable to do it. I simply can't believe that, under those circumstances, that bastard Wang Zhenhai could be such a saint."

Hongmei stared at me without moving.

I said, "Go on. You should eat lunch at the meeting hall. The most important thing right now is to observe Wang Zhenhai, because if we can find any evidence that there is something going on between him and Zhao Xiuyu, we'll be able to bring him down for good."

Half-skeptical, yet energetic, Hongmei walked away.

The next time Hongmei returned from the meeting hall, it was in the afternoon. We once again met up in the production brigade, and sitting at the table with elm legs and a willow top, which on several occasions we had used as a bed, I asked, "How's it going?" She responded somewhat mysteriously, "There have been some unexpected developments. While we were eating lunch, Mayor Wang took several pieces of meat from his own bowl and placed them into Zhao Xiuyu's. Zhao Xiuyu said, 'I don't want any, I don't want any,' but Mayor Wang said, 'Don't worry. People like me who are able to leave the commune have more opportunity to eat meat than those of you who remain here in the mountains.'"

I asked, "Did Mayor Wang give anyone else any meat?"

Hongmei said, "I didn't see him do so."

I became rather excited, and asked, "Was there anything else?"

Hongmei said, "When the meeting concluded, Mayor Wang stood in the entrance to the government building and bid farewell to each production brigade's Party branch secretary. I feel that he shook Zhao Xiuyu's hand particularly firmly and held it for an unusually long time."

I asked, "When they were shaking hands, did Zhao Xiuyu blush?"

Hongmei replied somewhat regretfully, "At the time, I was standing behind her and couldn't see her face clearly, but I felt that Mayor Wang's eyes were particularly bright."

I said, "Fuck his ancestors! I'm two hundred percent certain that they're having an affair."

She replied, "They aren't necessarily having an actual affair, but it's clear that Mayor Wang is unusually affectionate with Secretary Zhao."

I said, "You don't understand men. They're definitely having an affair." Then I asked, "What did they say when they departed?"

Hongmei reflected and then said, "Wang Zhenhai held Zhao Xiuyu's hand and said, 'Xiuyu, you should still proceed with that matter as I instructed, and if you run into any problems, you can simply put the blame on me.' Zhao Xiuyu replied, 'Mayor Wang, where we live, the mountains are high and the emperor is far away, and if I run into any problems, I won't drag you in.'"

I pounded the table with my fist, knocking the only empty water bottle onto the floor. "And what is 'that matter'? If it isn't a sexual relationship, then what else could it be? This clearly reveals that Mayor Wang's relationship with Zhao Xiuyu is out of the ordinary." I added, "Hongmei, Chairman Mao put it well when he said that the only thing the Communist Party fears is conscientiousness. As long as we are conscientious, there is nothing that we can't accomplish. Chairman Mao also said that anti-revolutionaries appear in disguise, giving people a false appearance. However, given that they are anti-revolutionaries, they are unable to completely conceal their real appearance, and inevitably the day will come when they will reveal their fox tail. If we are conscientious, then as soon as Mayor Wang reveals his fox tail, we'll have no choice but to seize it and pull him off the political stage."

Hongmei said, "Aijun, in order to catch an adulterer, you have to catch the pair. At the very least, someone will need to write us a disclosure letter."

I smiled and grabbed Hongmei's hand.

"Fuck his grandmother! Tomorrow you should borrow ten yuan from the production brigade's accountant. As Yang Zirong said, 'If you aren't willing to enter the tiger's lair, how do you expect to capture the tiger?' The two of us should pay a visit to Mayor Wang's home in Wangjiayu Village, and there we'll be able to get the material for a disclosure letter."

The next day, we went to Wangjiayu Village, deep in the Balou Mountains, where we proceeded to carry out an even deeper and broader class struggle.

Chapter 10
The Great Victory

1. Going behind Enemy Lines (I)

To eliminate the devils, we went behind enemy lines.

In a class-based society, revolution and revolutionary war are unavoidable, because otherwise there would be no way to make the leap of societal development or to overthrow the reactionary ruling class and let the common people gain political power.

The revolution is the People's revolution, and only by mobilizing the masses will it be possible to carry out a revolution.

(Hongmei, did you bring enough money?

(I brought fifty yuan, which should be enough. If I want to build a house, I should be able to build a tile-roofed one.

(This time we've burned all our bridges. If we purchase anything, we should buy back several copies of Mayor Wang's certificate.

(This is such a long trip, and we don't even know whether or not the people of Wangjiayu Village will denounce Mayor Wang.

(Relax! I don't believe it's possible for someone to never commit a mistake and never betray anyone, but as long as you have money, you needn't worry about inciting the masses.)

What is the true iron bastion? It is the masses—the millions of masses who truly support the revolution. This is the true iron bastion, which no force can topple. Anti-revolutionaries cannot topple us, because we will topple them. Millions of people will gather around an enlightened revolutionary leader and help promote the great revolution, thereby allowing us to seize political power and claim victory.

China's revolution is, at its essence, a peasant revolution.

In using this foundation to pursue a long-term revolutionary struggle, we cannot ignore the perspective of the remote rural districts that are currently serving as revolutionary bases. The more remote a rural village is, the easier it will be to mobilize the peasants. This is the particular advantage of China's villages and villagers. However, it would be incorrect and unfortunate for us to ignore the perspective of the peasants who are actually doing the difficult work.

From 1927 to the present, our emphasis has been on the countryside, and we have used the countryside to surround the cities, such that we'll finally be able to seize the cities and their political power.

(Aijun, my legs are exhausted, and I'm dying of thirst.

(I'll get you some water. Just wait here.

(Why don't you carry me for a while? There's no one else around.

(Carry you?! Did Jiang Qing ever dare to have Chairman Mao carry her? Did Ye Qun ever dare to have Lin Biao carry her?

(Then just kiss me.

(It's been a long time since you asked me to kiss you. It seems your revolutionary depression has finally been cured.

(Mayor Gao, you should shave.

(If I grow a beard, then maybe when I see Zhao Xiuyu she won't recognize me, since we've only seen each other once or twice before.

(I don't believe your per-*mu* grain production could possibly reach five hundred *jin*. Are your fields piled high with fertilizer?

(If the soil is good, it's not impossible to have a good harvest.

(If only we could mobilize Zhao Xiuyu, we wouldn't worry about not being able to overthrow Mayor Wang.

(Last night I dreamed I was able to knock down a tree with a single punch, and with another punch I was able to knock a hole in Cheng Temple's rear courtyard wall. Today, we'll definitely achieve success at the Wangjiayu Village meeting. We'll definitely achieve great success.

(Did you dream of me?

(Did *you* dream of *me*?

(I dreamed that as we were doing that thing on the desk in the production brigade's office, one of the desk's legs snapped.

(My god! Hongmei, last night I *also* dreamed we were doing that thing on the desk. When I thrust, you cried out, and blood appeared between your legs. Then one of the desk's legs snapped, and we fell to the floor.

(Did you really see blood in your dream?

(I dreamed that blood was flowing like a river from between your legs.

(That's good, Aijun. If you dream of blood, that is a sign that you'll enjoy success.)

The law of revolution—this is something no political leader or anyone directing the revolution can avoid studying and resolving.

The law of mass revolution—this is something no political leader or anyone directing a mass revolution can avoid studying and resolving.

The law of China's mass revolution—this is something no political leader or anyone directing China's mass revolution can avoid studying and resolving.

The law of northern China's mass revolution—this is completely distinct from the law of mass revolution that arises out of a revolutionary base in southern China, for it is determined by the politics, culture, geography, and living conditions of northern China. No one leading a northern mass revolution can avoid considering and resolving this question.

The law of the Balou Mountains' mass revolution is completely different from that of the rest of northern China and even the rest of the northern Henan mountain region. This is because this law of mass revolution is determined by the specific history, politics, and culture, and the specific geographic conditions and living conditions of the Balou Mountains, and it is something that anyone who participates in, guides, directs, or leads a mass revolution in this region must consider, study, and resolve. All other questions and contradictions derive from this.

(Aijun, have we reached Wangjiayu Village yet?
(Oh, we're almost there. It may be that village up ahead.)

The revolution we are currently pursuing is historically unprecedented. Our revolution pertains to the specific geography of this Balou mountain region, and consequently we must study not only ordinary laws of revolution but also particular laws of revolution, as well as even more particular laws of mass revolution in northern China's western Henan, Balou mountain region.

I, Gao Aijun, was born and bred in the Balou Mountains. When I was in school I was a talented student, and when I was in the army I was an outstanding soldier, and when I was a squad leader I was the most outstanding squad leader in the entire military company. Some lines from poems and songs that I wrote while I was enlisted are still popular among soldiers, and it is possible that several decades after my death they will remain on everyone's lips—such as the line: *The bright moon in front of the bed is like a layer of frost on the ground.* One poem I wrote was:

A revolutionary warrior is a fired brick that can be taken to wherever
it is needed;
A revolutionary warrior is a piece of clay that can be carried to
wherever it is needed;
A revolutionary warrior is an adobe slab that can be placed wherever
it is needed.

Another slogan that was derived from my writings was: *View your military garrison as your hometown and view the People as your parents.* Some of my rousing words were published in the *Liberation Army Daily* and the *Engineering Corps Daily*, and during the years I spent pursuing revolution in the countryside after being demobilized, various provincial-level and district-level newspapers would periodically write me and ask for manuscripts. I was cultured, experienced, and had a good memory. I was eloquent, decisive, and not afraid of sacrifice. I was bold, crafty, and had the best understanding of all the people and things of the Balou Mountains, hills and streams, trees and shrubs, birds and animals, men and women, old and young, sand and dirt, worms and cicadas, pigs and dogs, sex and love, spring and fall, tree leaves and mountain paths, guiding principles and regional dialects, policies and oxen, poverty and affluence, marriage and burial customs, happiness and women, livestock and annals, air and houses, sluts and chastity, greatness and men, revolution and famine, well-being and crops, as well as the Cold Dew and Winter Solstice solar terms, success and power, worship and ravens, cow demon snake spirits and landlords rich peasants anti-revolutionaries bad elements rightists, the masses and poor and lower-middle peasants, the proletariat and farm tools. From the moon and stars above, down to dog farts below, there is nothing that I don't know and nothing that I don't understand. So, how could I not reach Wangjiayu Village and immediately achieve success? How could I not become the Balou Mountains' powerful and revolutionary new star and rise high in the sky?

I went behind enemy lines to eliminate the devils.

I was willing to risk dismemberment in order to topple the emperor from his throne.

2. Going behind Enemy Lines (II)

Now that I reflect and try to add up everything that happened to me, I discover a great law that I certainly would never have discovered on my own—which is that the most complex things in the world are always the simplest, and the simplest things are yet the most complex. This is because revolution has a beautifully exquisite variation, a profundity and simplicity that allows revolutionaries to derive pleasure and stimulation from revolution and to fearlessly throw themselves into the revolutionary torrent.

Would it be difficult to cure Hongmei's depression?

Would it be difficult to overthrow Mayor Wang?

Would it be a simple matter to prove my suspicion that Mayor Wang was carrying on an adulterous relationship with Secretary Zhao? And was there any difference between accomplishing these objectives and achieving my broader revolutionary goals?

In the end, I succeeded.

In the end, I accomplished my objectives easily. Not only did I bring down Mayor Wang, I had him designated as an active anti-revolutionary and sentenced to twenty years' imprisonment. The unexpected ease of this truly made me and Hongmei appreciate the magic and stimulation of the revolution. It allowed us to reemerge from under the cloud of Qingdong's death and return to the sunlit stage of revolutionary struggle. In this way, we came to understand why everyone—even the blind and the crippled, even stupid pigs and wild dogs—wanted to pursue revolution. They all wanted to become, and indeed *could* become, revolutionaries.

Hongmei and I arrived at the Wangjiayu production brigade just before sunset. This was our first trip into the depths of the Balou

Mountains, and to reach this location we had to travel sixty *li*. We walked half the distance, and for the remaining half we hitched rides on horse- and ox-drawn carriages. On our way there, we had many delightful discussions, and sometimes we even stopped on the side of the road in uninhabited areas, and twice we took off our clothes and did that thing (Hongmei had finally regained her earlier passion and screamed with pleasure). When we reached Wangjiayu Village, I was so exhausted that my eyesight was blurred, my legs were burning, and all I wanted to do was to go to someone's house, drink a bowl of cool water, and fall asleep in a bed. Located on a hillside, Wangjiayu Village was a natural village within the Wangjiayu production brigade. The village was where the production brigade department was located. Secretary Zhao, however, lived several *li* away, in Zhaojiawa. Wangjiayu Village was located only three *li* from the horse path leading up to the mountain peak, but that three-*li* path was as twisty as a sheep's intestines. Some of the wheat growing on the hillside had already broken out of the winter cold and was lush and green, while the rest looked as though it had recently been sowed. When that terrain was viewed from a distance or from high up, some parts appeared dark with vegetation, like thick clouds, while others were a patchwork of yellow and red, brown and purple—such that the entire hillside resembled an enormous carpet. There wasn't a soul to be seen along the ridge or on the path, only a couple of mountain goats grazing on the cliffs next to the road. The sweet, earthy smell that drifted up from the fields was warm and bright as it circled around beneath my nostrils. Under the light from the setting sun, the smoke that emerged from the village's chimneys came to assume a beautiful red hue, as though it was so many strands of silk fluttering in the breeze. On that day Hongmei was wearing a red sweater I had bought for her using production brigade funds, under which she had a four-button, small-collared shirt, and as she walked she used her shirt flap to fan her face, until eventually she stopped walking altogether.

As we were walking, a hare suddenly dashed out of the field next to us. It was yellow and white, and it stopped in the middle of the road and stared at us with its fiery eyes. When Hongmei waved at it, the hare took a couple of steps back toward the field, then turned around and looked at us again.

Hongmei shouted, "Aijun, quick, come look!"

Perhaps this hare was some sort of spirit? And guess what it was directing me to see! I saw that the field containing the burrow was square in shape and more than two *mu* in size. Half the wheat sprouts were jet black and about fifteen centimeters tall, while the other half were still greenish yellow and only about eight centimeters tall. If you looked toward the edges of the field, however, you would see an area full of sprouts that looked like they had just emerged from the soil but had not yet woken from their winter slumber, as though they had just been sown. (We must carefully analyze this occurrence, searching for its causal relations and grasping its principal contradictions or the clues to its principal contradictions, and only in this way will it be possible to resolve the contradiction and complete our work.) Was it possible that this wasn't even a field? Yet it clearly *was* a field, and the large ridge grouped these three different kinds of wheat sprouts together. But why does a single field have three different kinds of wheat sprouts?

Hongmei shouted, "Aijun, look at this hare!"

(Oh, that great hare!) I took another several steps forward, reaching another field, this one triangular. I noticed that in this new triangular field, there was again a combination of wheat sprouts that had just emerged from the earth and others that were already green and flourishing.

(Without discovery, there can be no creation, and without creation, society will keep walking in place and will never be able to advance.)

Hongmei shouted, "Aijun, where are you going?"

I said, "I'm going to take a piss."

"Do you have to walk that far to take a piss? Is it that you're afraid of me? If you're afraid of me, then tonight you shouldn't sleep with me."

I went to the front of that same field with the two or three different kinds of wheat sprouts and kicked some clods of earth in an area where different-colored sprouts were growing. As I was kicking the second clump of earth, I made a remarkable discovery. My foot struck something with a thud, and it was as if a tower suddenly emerged out of the ground. I noticed that there was a wooden stake buried several centimeters underground, and when I leaned over and pulled it out, I saw that it had a name written on it: *Wang Baomin*. I proceeded to another field with different-colored wheat sprouts and unearthed another stake, which also bore a name: *Wang Dashun*.

Altogether, I dug up six wooden stakes, each of which had a different name written on it. At this point, my brain exploded, as though a bright light were shining directly into my head. It was as though a red flag had just been planted in recently recovered enemy territory. It was as if a clarion call suddenly rang out from the top of a tall mountain, or a lighthouse suddenly appeared amid a vast ocean. Hongmei stood next to me and asked with surprise, "What are you doing?" I handed her one of the stakes, then proceeded to dig at a different location—to prove my astounding discovery. Hongmei stared at the stake for a moment, then dropped it and ran over to help me dig in that new location. Soon we succeeded in digging up yet another stake with a name on it.

Like mad dogs searching for food, we quickly dug up four more stakes.

Finally, we dug up a short and thin stake, and when we noticed the name written on it, the excitement on our faces immediately melted away. We both knelt down, our hands trembling, as though we were trying to hold a red-hot iron. Our bodies trembled, and we couldn't catch our breath.

Written on that final stake was the name of our mayor: *Wang Zhenhai*.

At this point, we heard the murky sound of ox hoofs and foot-steps coming from the mountain path. When we looked up, we saw an old man pulling a plow and driving an ox down from the mountain ridge. Neither Hongmei nor I said anything, and instead she merely looked at me. I hugged her tightly to my chest as I rolled under the earthen ridge next to us. As though we had just thrown a grenade and were taking cover, we rolled under a sixty-centimeter-tall earthen embankment, and then, still hugging each other tightly, we lay there without moving. The entire time, the tips of our tongues were fight-ing each other like a pair of snakes—sometimes mine would suc-ceed in entering her mouth, while at other times hers would make inroads into mine. I sucked her sweet saliva into my mouth and held it there, whereupon she acted as though she had been wronged and tried to suck it back, leaving me no choice but to use my tongue to push even more saliva back into her mouth. As the ox hoofs and footsteps approached, they seemed to press down on us like stones or clay slabs—suppressing our excitement, such that we didn't dare speak, move, or even breathe loudly. Instead, all we could do was use the tips of our tongues to celebrate our great discovery, the bril-liant success of our early battle, and the unparalleled greatness of our victory. The ox hoofs proceeded along the overgrown path, as soft and leisurely, peaceful and comforting as a hollow paulownia board striking a muddy surface, with the old man's footsteps sound-ing equally leisurely and amiable. As those sounds drifted by us, Hongmei and I continued to hold our breath and to remain perfectly still. I kept grappling with her dexterous tongue, trying to capture it like a slumbering snake. I lay on her supple body and waited for the old man and the ox to pass. Once they entered Wangjiayu Village, which was bathed in the light of the setting sun, I returned the tip of Hongmei's tongue to where it belonged. Hongmei and I both sighed, and, holding the wooden stake with Wang Zhenhai's name on it, we hugged each other under the earthen embankment.

She exclaimed, "So, the people here really *do* dare to distribute land to every family!"

I replied, "What Chairman Mao called 'capitalism' will return, but it really isn't that frightening."

She said, "This is much more significant than the idea that Wang Zhenhai and Zhao Xiuyu may be having an affair."

I said, "Let's collect these stakes, as well as some additional evidence that this was supported by Mayor Wang. If anyone refuses to remove him from office, they themselves should be removed from their own positions."

Then, with a clatter, the sun set behind the mountains. The only sound to be heard from the mountain ridge was this clattering sound of the sunset—a sound that only rural deities like mountain folk are able to hear.

3. Going behind Enemy Lines (III)

That night we stayed in a small courtyard with three adobe-tile-roofed houses. Because Hongmei was worried about lice and fleas, we picked a family in which the son had just gotten married, where the color of the twin characters above the door of the nuptial chamber hadn't yet faded. When we entered the village, the commune members all stared at us in surprise. We discovered that life in this village was really heavenly. Those families that had dinner early brought their rice bowls to the doorway, while also holding a fried or steamed bun in their hands. (Fuck his ancestors!—this is the kind of food that people in Chenggang can eat only on New Year's, but here people have it every day!)

Everyone stared at me and Hongmei (but mostly at Hongmei), as though we had just fallen from the sky. They stared at Hongmei's jade-white skin, jet-black hair, long neck, and red sweater, at the tender whiteness of her small-collared shirt, and the straight-leg pants that these people from the countryside had never had a chance to wear. (Most locals still wore pants with a wide waist and thin legs, and the men would fold the pants down at the waist and wear them with a belt, while the women's pants had an opening in the waist, which could be on either the left or right hip, since there was no difference between the front and back of the pants.) When the women and girls saw Hongmei, their eyes lit up even more brightly than when they saw me. Meanwhile, when the men and boys looked at her, they immediately turned away, shifting their gaze to me instead. Seeing her, they all stopped eating and instead sat there with their bowls, chopsticks, and steamed buns frozen in their hands.

We told them that we were county cadres who had come to conduct soc-ed (socialist education) sessions in the countryside, but now we needed to hurry back to attend a meeting in town. Given that dusk had already fallen, however, we hoped to stay over until morning. At that point, a middle-aged man (we later learned that this was the leader of the production brigade and his name was Li Lin) placed the rice bowl he was holding onto a stone and said, "You can stay in Jiao Degui's house. His son just got married last month, so the house has a new bed and bedding."

(What simple and sincere proletarian emotion!)

We were escorted to Jiao Degui's home, and as soon as we entered we saw that it was a large compound with a courtyard. There was a brown cow tied to a date tree and an old plow hanging from the eaves, and the person who greeted us was none other than the old man we had seen just before sunset. Hongmei stared at me for a moment, and I glared back—whereupon she immediately followed my example and acted as though nothing were wrong. Old Man Degui led us into his front room, then had his new daughter-in-law go to the kitchen to fry us some scallion pancakes and fix us some egg and noodle soup. Then he told his son to straighten up the nuptial chamber. In order to prevent the possibility that Brigade Leader Li Lin might send someone to notify Secretary Zhao that some county cadres had come to Wangjiayu Village to conduct soc-ed sessions, we kept chatting with him. After Li Lin finished eating with us, he had Degui's son take his rice bowl back to his home.

After dinner had concluded, and the moon was about to come up, we all felt rather awkward sitting in Degui's house. At that time, Hongmei was teaching the new bride how to knit a sweater out of coarse yarn. (My wise Hongmei—my heart, my flesh, my ideal revolutionary companion!) I took out two one-yuan bills and placed them in Old Man Degui's hand, explaining that this was to cover the food he had prepared for us, adding that it was room-and-board money that we soc-ed cadres were obligated to give to poor and lower-middle peasants when we went down to the countryside.

Old Man Degui angrily returned the money, saying, "In your lifetime, how many other chances will you have to come to the Balou Mountains?"

I handed the money back to him, saying, "Even if we only come once, we still have to pay. These are the Party organization's traditions and regulations."

Old Man Degui retorted, "What kind of rule is this? You are Party members, and therefore when you eat the food of poor and lower-middle peasants, you are eating your own family's food. Who ever heard of having to pay when eating your own family's food?"

Then Hongmei weighed in (my soul and my flesh, she plays such a good accompaniment!), saying, "Uncle Jiao, please just accept this. If you don't, then when we return to the county, we'll have to perform a self-criticism at the Party group meeting."

I quickly added (this resembled a well-rehearsed performance), "These are the 'Three Main Rules of Discipline and the Eight Points of Attention'—this is all specified, these are all rules sent down by Chairman Mao."

Finally, and with considerable embarrassment, Old Man Degui accepted the money.

Li Lin was having a post-meal smoke, and at that point he knocked the bowl of his pipe against his shoe and announced, "How about this? Each of you can contribute twenty cents. That way Degui receives forty cents, which will count as receiving the food allotment for two cadres, and we won't be breaking any rules. I hear from Zhenhai that when he goes down to the countryside, he too has to pay his hosts food money."

He mentioned Wang Zhenhai. He finally mentioned Wang Zhenhai! Hongmei stopped teaching the bride how to knit, and asked, "Who is this Zhenhai?"

Li Lin replied, "It is Mayor Wang—Chenggang's Mayor Wang."

Feigning surprise, I asked, "Is Mayor Wang from here?"

Li Lin and Degui proudly replied in unison, "His house is the third one behind ours."

Hongmei and I both acted as though we had unexpectedly encountered an old friend. We repeatedly emphasized how well we knew Mayor Wang and how much we admired and respected him. I explained how on this trip we were doing work on behalf of the county's organizational bureau, after which we would submit documentation to the county head and the county Party committee secretary and draft an announcement for a meeting. I went on to say that Hongmei was a correspondent in the county committee's propaganda bureau, who wrote reports directly for the district-level and provincial-level newspapers. She effectively worked as a journalist, as if she were a reporter for a provincial-level newspaper living in the county. I said that her article praising a commune Party secretary had been published in the *People's Daily* and that this commune Party secretary was already the youngest Party secretary in the entire county committee. At this point, the eyes of Brigade Leader Li Lin, Old Man Degui, and that pair of newlyweds all grew wide under the light of the oil lamp, as they stared in astonishment, as though a pair of deities had suddenly landed in Wangjiayu Village.

Brigade Leader Li Lin said, "Heavens, you mean that you're close to the county head? You should be sure to tell him more good things about our Zhenhai, because Zhenhai is constantly racking his brains on behalf of the common people."

(This all bore a distinct resemblance to dialogue in a play!)

Hongmei said, "I went to interview Mayor Wang—but this simply consisted of our sitting down to chat. Mayor Wang is not the kind of person who likes people to compliment him, and when you interview him, you feel like you should say good things only about others and not say a single good thing about him."

Brigade Leader Li Lin slapped his thigh and said, "That's right, I understand him all too well. From the time we were children, we grew up together in the same piss-soaked mud pile, but later he joined the army, became an important figure, and then he returned and was appointed mayor. I know that from the time he was young, whenever he happened to have some kind of advantage, he would always try to give it to others."

I said, "So, he is the kind of person who never acts on his own behalf but rather is always trying to help others? The county committee has long wanted to establish this sort of model for all the county's cadres to learn from, but they weren't able to find a good example."

Li Lin lit another pipe and said, "You can suggest to your county head that they might use Zhenhai for this purpose. Although he isn't very cultured, he is always thinking of the People."

Hongmei immediately stopped beating around the bush and took out a pen and notebook (my heart, my love, my flesh and soul!), and said, "What are his achievements? Please be specific."

Li Lin's pipe paused at the edge of his mouth, as though he wanted to say something, but then he swallowed his words. As he continued looking at Degui and his family, there was a long silence.

I said, "If there is something that isn't convenient for you to say, then you shouldn't mention it. The current situation is extremely complicated. However, if you are able to use Mayor Wang's good deeds to provide a model for the poor and lower-middle peasants, then as long as he was really acting on behalf of the common people, the masses, and the Party, even if he did something bad, we'll keep our silence. And as long as the county head and the Party secretary know about it, then not only will we not criticize him, we'll even praise him."

I looked at Brigade Leader Li Lin, then continued, in a somewhat mysterious tone, "Do you know the primary reason Zhao Qing was recently promoted to his current position as deputy secretary of the county Party committee? He was originally the Party secretary of the Damiao commune, and it's said that last year he gave land to every family in the commune, with the result being that the village's per-*mu* grain-production rate reached four hundred and fifty *jin*."

(In the movie *Tunnel Warfare*, when the secret agent disguised as the director of an armed working team entered Gaojia Village, he used the same method to try to entice the masses to work harder and produce more, but he ultimately failed and was arrested. He was an enemy, and he was unprincipled, while we are revolutionaries and represent principles and progress.)

Hongmei said, "What do you mean, four hundred and fifty *jin*? Actually it was four hundred seventeen and a half *jin*."

I said, "It was in fact four hundred and fifty *jin*. His village had the highest grain-production rate in the entire county."

Hongmei said, "It's not a question of a high rate of production but rather of his audacity in daring to secretly distribute land to everyone."

I said, "That is true."

Brigade Leader Li Lin's eyes flickered, and his lips trembled. Old Man Degui kept looking at him as though urging him to quickly say something.

Finally, Brigade Leader Li Lin asked, "Did they really distribute land to every family?"

Hongmei replied, "The county head and the county committee secretary both knew about it but helped keep it a secret."

Brigade Leader Li Lin said, "They didn't make the commune Party secretary go to jail? They didn't make him step down?"

I said, "He did it for the People, which is why they promoted him to county Party committee secretary."

Brigade Leader Li Lin was indignant on behalf of Wang Zhenhai, saying, "I see that the two of you are not the kind of people who are inclined to persecute others [*What a joke!*], nor are you revolutionaries [*Another joke!*]. I'll tell you the truth: our village's land was redistributed to the villagers five years ago, on Zhenhai's orders. Five years ago several people in the village starved to death, so when Zhenhai was appointed mayor, he told Secretary Zhao to distribute land to every family in the village, and now our average annual grain-production rate is several dozen *jin* more than that of the village you just mentioned."

Over the next several days, we enjoyed considerable success in exploring the enemy's position, and through this careful examination, we deliberated over our plans for war:

Those threatening Tiger Mountain rely on enemy bunkers
And it appears they want to use stratagem to get the upper hand
We pick experts to pose as bandits and infiltrate the enemy's heart and mind
And in this way we can collaborate with outsiders
From a position within the bandit's lair
But who will we send to carry out this extraordinarily important task?
Both Gao Aijun and Xia Hongmei have the ability to carry this out

They are both from poor peasant backgrounds
    and both are of good quality
And from the time they were young
    they endured endless suffering on behalf of their ideals
And with a bellyful of resentment they sought out proof of the enemy's crimes
And swore that they would eradicate the enemies
In the revolution they participated in countless battles
And though countless families were destroyed and countless lives were lost
They nevertheless achieved many successes
I believe that their hearts are as red as fire
Their will is as strong as steel
And they'll definitely be able to achieve victory over the bandit chief Zuo Shandiao.

This was another sincere family, and several ears of corn from the previous year's fall harvest were hanging under the eaves of their house. Brigade Leader Li Lin asked us to note the inexhaustible storehouse of grain under the house's eaves; then he led us to a small room to see the man's collection of cans of wheat and soybeans. As we entered the room, we were almost smothered by the smell of rotting grain.

I asked, "Do they have enough grain?"

The man replied, "Even if our life depended on it, we still wouldn't be able to consume all this grain."

Hongmei asked, "Do you think it is best to distribute land to each other, or to sow it collectively?"

The man looked at Li Lin.

Brigade Leader Li Lin said, "You can answer. They are all good people. You can say whatever you want to."

The man said, "We are grateful to Mayor Wang. Of course, it's better when the land is distributed to everyone."

I said, "For Mayor Wang, would you be willing to write up a description of the land-allocation arrangement that we could take back with us?"

The man replied, "I would, but I don't know how to write."

Brigade Leader Li Lin looked at Hongmei and said, "Why don't you write it for him, and then let him add his handprint?"

So Hongmei wrote out the man's testimony.

We visited several more families and obtained additional evidentiary documents. Finally, when we were returning to Old Man Degui's house, the night sky was already full of stars, and the ground looked as though it were covered in frost. We hadn't realized that the nights in the Balou Mountains could be so quiet that our footsteps would seem as loud as shattering bamboo stalks. I saw that on the mountain ridge across from Wangjiayu Village there was another village hovering over the hillside, and from there the light green sound of dogs barking traversed the intervening ridges and ravines and dissipated over our heads. Hongmei asked, "What village is that?" The brigade leader replied, "It is Zhaojiawa, which is the village of Secretary Zhao's family." We were suddenly reminded of the affair between Zhao Xiuyu and Mayor Wang. We had originally come to find evidence of their affair, but the revolutionary situation is ever-changing, and just as one can find simplicity within complexity, one can similarly find complexity within simplicity.

I said, "Brigade Leader Li Lin, if Zhao Xiuyu was the person who actually implemented the policy of redistributing land to local families, and if Mayor Wang was merely a supporter, wasn't Mayor Wang concerned that Zhao Xiuyu might one day sell him out?"

Li Lin said, "How could she possibly do that? Not only is Xiuyu a Party branch secretary, she is also the eldest daughter of Wang Zhenhai's aunt. How could she sell out her own cousin?"

The moon looked like a moist sheet of white paper stuck to the sky, and the shadows of the trees rustled as they swept back and forth in front of the entrance to the village. In this uncannily quiet mountain night, we could hear the wheat sprouts climbing out of the ground in the plots of land that had been distributed to the village's families, and in the brigade leader's breathing we could hear surprise at our lack of familiarity with the simplicity of this mountain community's social relations.

Li Lin said, "People in the mountains are very concerned with questions of character, and Zhenhai decided to distribute land to everyone in an attempt to guarantee that the several thousand people living in Wangjiayu Village would have food and clothing. Who would betray their conscience to report him?"

(So, that's the way things were! It was only after entering and then leaving the masses that we finally came to understand this. The masses are the true heroes and the force that creates history.)

We returned to Old Man Degui's home. No one in his family had yet gone to sleep; they were all waiting for us. As soon as we entered the courtyard, Old Man Degui, holding an oil lamp, came out to greet us. He said, "You and my son can sleep in the front western room, which also has a new set of bedding. Meanwhile, she and my daughter-in-law can sleep in the new house, because they are young."

Hongmei and I both stared at him in shock. We desperately needed to sleep together naked in the same bed, so that we could kiss and embrace each other, touch and caress each other, and crazily celebrate our victory! We desperately needed to hug each other and share the same dreams as we plotted our next revolutionary action! I looked at Hongmei and saw that her bright eyes were sparkling in the moonlight. At that moment, my eyes were illuminated by hers. We each glanced at the other and instantly reached a mutual under-standing, and as our pulses synchronized with one another (such was love—great revolutionary love!), I said to Old Man Degui, "Any arrangement is fine with us. After all, we aren't yet an old couple, though it's true that we've already been married for several years."

Both Li Lin and Old Man Degui stared at us with astonishment. "You are married?"

Hongmei blushed, "We haven't been married for all that long."

Li Lin said, "Then why didn't you say so sooner?" He turned to Degui and said, "Why don't you have your son and daughter-in-law sleep in the front room, and let these two cadres sleep in the nuptial chamber?"

Accordingly, everything was successfully arranged. Not only did our expedition—our excursion into enemy territory—allow us to master the enemy's inside information and gather evidence, Hongmei and I were also able, for the first time in our lives, to spend the night together in a real newlywed bed.

That was an extraordinary night.

4. Going behind Enemy Lines (IV)

We went behind enemy lines
And exterminated the devils
With our worker and peasant brothers
We are a single family.
We all came from the same roots
And have all experienced hardship
The house we built
The grain we sowed
Landlords, compradors, and blackhearts
Have completely exploited us.
We went behind enemy lines
And exterminated the devils
Following the Communist Party.
We now take up our knives and guns
The day for a war of resistance has come
In front of us is the light of the dawn
The blade falls down on the devil's head
We seek liberation
We killed one and took another captive,
Then we went to collect their American arms.

Chapter 11

The Winds Suddenly Shift

1. The Tragedy of *Pagoda Tree Village*

Sometimes, when the revolution arrives early, it can leave us with a kind of paralyzed consciousness—such that we may come to believe that all the twists and turns in the road to revolution are merely contingent, while success is as necessary and inevitable as the sun emerging from behind the clouds or dawn bringing new light. This is a flawed way of thinking and will bring us countless losses and bloody lessons as we struggle to establish a revolutionary foundation and a mass red base. We must remember that the reason revolutionary success may sometimes arrive early is because we correctly implement the Party's policies, directives, and paths, and because we mobilize, rely on, and immerse ourselves in the masses. If, on account of our success, we forget this point, it would be as though we had forgotten the enemy's existence and transformed our success into our own grave digger. Remember this—you absolutely must remember this. Otherwise an even greater failure may appear before you.

Unfortunately, in the end, I did indeed forget this point. Hongmei and I were left befuddled by our sudden and unexpected success, and we completely forgot that it is necessary to remain calm when enjoying victory. We forgot that, when faced with accolades and fresh flowers, you must be wary of complacency and guard against conceit and impetuosity, and as a result we guaranteed that failure would follow on the heels of success. Moreover, while our success ended up being several times greater than we had originally expected, the resulting failure ended up being several *thousand* times more momentous than we could possibly have anticipated.

The comedy made us laugh, but the resulting tragedy left us so grief-stricken that we wanted to die. The comedy of success spelled the end to my and Hongmei's young lives and set the stage for the ensuing tragedy while simultaneously giving us our own elegy. Just as we were personally collecting the oral testimonies (personal evidence) and the buried wooden stakes (material evidence) that proved that Wang Zhenhai had redistributed land to local families, I once again sent the prefectural Party committee another letter of disclosure, to earn more serious consideration from the higher-ups. In these letters, I called Mayor Wang's activities a covert attempt to overthrow socialism. (I was astonished by how much I resembled a great prophet.) As it turned out, the earth-shattering event I described ended up coming to pass.

That month, we had originally been waiting for the county to notify us that it was time to make additional disclosures regarding Wang Zhenhai's capitalist consciousness. Before the end of the month, however, we received a notification that both Wang Zhenhai and Zhao Qing—who had previously served as the Party secretary of Damiao commune and was currently serving as the county's Party committee deputy secretary—had both been seized one night and sentenced to twenty years' imprisonment (which once again proved the forceful and irreconcilable nature of class struggle). It turns out that Zhao Qing, like Wang Zhenhai, had taken land from a mountain district production brigade and redistributed it to the peasants. (Heavens, to think Wang was exposed by me! I'm not sure whether I'm a deity or a mere mortal, but I heard that Zhao Qing increased his production brigade's productivity from 220 *jin* per *mu* to 450 *jin*, as a result of which he was promoted to county committee deputy secretary, but I never expected that, like Wang Zhenhai, he had similarly advanced by sacrificing socialist collectivism.) More importantly, even in my wildest dreams, I had never expected that Zhao Xiuyu would also be detained—though in the end she was imprisoned for less than a month, whereupon, following an interrogation session, she proceeded to write a statement that read, "The land distribution had nothing to do with Wang Zhenhai, and instead it was entirely my (immature) decision"—after which she committed suicide. There was also Brigade Leader Li Lin, who I hear was beaten to death by several dozen local villagers in retaliation for his having introduced me and Hongmei to locals who could write us testimonial letters. The villagers believed that had it not been for Li Lin, Hongmei and I would never have learned about the land distribution scheme, and therefore Wang Zhenhai wouldn't have been seized by the government; Zhao Xiuyu wouldn't have committed suicide in prison; and their privately owned land wouldn't have been returned to the communal basket. Instead, Zhao Xiuyu ended up killing herself and Li Lin got beaten to death. What a tragedy—what a heartrending tragedy! This was entirely a product of the peasants' myopia and narrow-mindedness. It was a tragedy resulting from ignorance caused by isolation and from a lack of awareness of collectivism! However, every time the villagers remembered Zhao Xiuyu, Li Lin, and Old Man Degui and his well-behaved son and daughter-in-law, they inevitably felt heartbroken, as though they themselves were at fault rather than those who had been punished. I resolved that after Hongmei and I were promoted to county head and town mayor, we would definitely grant the Wangjiayu production brigade an extra several thousand *jin* of returned grain, and we would have people send plenty of fair-price fertilizer to their village. This was the least Hongmei and I could do for Wangjiayu. Although we were a revolutionary couple, we were nevertheless still a pair of humanists. As for Wang Zhenhai and Zhao Qing being sentenced to twenty years' imprisonment, and the possibility that Mayor Wang might be stripped of his Party membership and all his extra-Party affiliations—all this took everyone by surprise, but it fell within a certain revolutionary logic. After all, it is the shared ideal of the state, the nation, the Party, and the People to quickly and economically establish socialism and implement communism. In both the Party and the constitution, it is specified that China's national character is socialist, and the ultimate objective of the Communist Party is to implement communism. At the same time, the foundation of both socialism and communism is collectivism and the implementation of socialist collective ownership—this is a principle as simple as ants lining up to return to the nest or dogs peeing on the side of the road to remember their way home. However, Wang Zhenhai and Zhao Qing dared to give the state's land back to individual villagers—and if this isn't an example of capitalism reinserting itself back into socialism, what is?

In every district, the town mayors and the commune Party secretaries dared to oppose the state, the nation, and the Party—and if the proletariat isn't able to establish a dictatorship, then who will be? Is it possible that you haven't heard the story from the famous play *Pagoda Tree Village*? Have you not heard the dialogue between Guo Daniang and Cui Zhiguo?

> CUI ZHIGUO: (Laughing.) *I'm asking you, what kind of socialism would you call this? Do you have bulldozers? Do you have hydropower stations?*
>
> GUO DANIANG: *We have Party leaders and Chairman Mao! As long as our poor and lower-middle peasants are united in spirit, are able to organize together to form good cooperatives, and always follow Chairman Mao, we'll be able to achieve socialism and communism!*
>
> CUI ZHIGUO: *I see that the pursuit of full granaries is one direction we might take, for which we would need to pursue a policy of "three horses and one plow," doing things alone, and enriching one's own family. If eighty percent of the peasants in Pagoda*

> Tree Village can have three horses and a plow, they would all
> be able to live very well!
>
> GUO DANIANG: *Where do you get all of these from? If they really do*
> *as you describe, then the poor will become even poorer, the rich*
> *will become even richer, and the poor and lower-middle peas-*
> *ants will be exploited and need to beg for food. Would that not*
> *take us back to the old society? Is that what your father meant?*
>
> CUI ZHIGUO: *No, no, no! How could he be at such a high level? This*
> *is what a great personage might say, but my father nevertheless*
> *would very much agree with this sentiment . . .*
>
> GUO DANIANG: *Ah, so it turns out that this great personage does*
> *indeed wear the same pants as landlords and capitalists . . .*

The work concludes with the commune led by Guo Daniang being completely victorious, and the arrest of Party secretary Deng, who never appeared on stage but continued to maneuver from behind the scenes and insisted on following a capitalist path.

In the sixth month, heaven's soldiers punish the corrupt, and they use an endless rope to tie up the legendary roc.

It is said that when Wang Zhenhai and Zhao Qing redistributed land to the peasants, the county's county head knew about it and gave them his tacit support. Furthermore, it turned out that the county head, Wang Zhenhai, and Zhao Qing were all demobilized cadres who had fought together in the Korean War and the Sino-Indian War. They were war comrades who had fought in the same trenches. How could we prove that they weren't part of the same anti-revolutionary group? How could we prove that they weren't trying to overthrow socialist collectives and carry out a capitalist restoration? This surprising and heartening information flashed before us like a lightning bolt. I stared in amazement, absolutely dumbfounded. At that moment I was in the process of eating, and both my mouth and my eyes immediately opened as wide as a bowl. After commiserating with Zhao Xiuyu, Li Lin, Old Man Degui, and the other Wangjiayu villagers, I stood up, faced the sky, and shouted:

The red flag is lifted up by the west wind
Today we'll bind the black dragons
The path through the forest is slippery with moss
but finally the wind unfurls the red banners like paintings
The sun is shining brightly
The birds are singing loudly
Gray scholar trees and dark tung trees
Green elms and tender toon trees
There are orioles and swallows everywhere
As well as gurgling streams
The mountain road enters the clouds
May I ask where you are going?
The sparrow replies:
> *There is a jeweled palace in the fairy mountain.*
With my back to the blue sky, I look down,
And what I see is a human world full of city walls.

2. The Revolution's Unexpected Success.

Not long after we uncovered the land distribution scheme, Hongmei and I were picked up in a sedan and taken away. The person who had sent for us was not an ordinary cadre, but Party secretary Guan from the prefectural Party committee, someone who had participated in the Long March and was a political commissar of a military sub-command. He was thin, dark-skinned, and had gray hair, but his eyes sparkled brightly, and he still wore his old military fatigues. By that point, we already knew that something significant had occurred. Two county cadres whom I didn't know well suddenly burst into my home as I was eating breakfast and took my bowl. They looked at the corn soup in the bowl and asked, "Are you still drinking this? Let's go. From now on, you'll be eating special rations." I stared at them in bewilderment, whereupon they said, with great familiarity, "The district political leaders will want to speak to you and Xia Hongmei directly. Now that you and she succeeded in seizing an anti-Party and anti-socialist group, they will definitely want to promote you to mayor and to make Xia Hongmei town Party committee secretary."

However, we didn't want to serve only as town mayor and town Party committee secretary. Only when we saw the sedan parked in front of the Cheng Brothers memorial arch did we realize that Director Liu from the county committee's organizational bureau had come to pick us up. Director Liu was an experienced and steadfast man in his forties, but he was slightly hunchbacked, such that he resembled someone in his fifties. He enthusiastically shook my hand, softly addressing me as "County Head Gao." Shocked by this form of address, I felt as though I had been struck by a lightning bolt, but I immediately realized what he meant. Another county committee cadre escorted me and Hongmei out of the alley, whereupon Director Liu said very mysteriously, "Get in the car, County Head Gao. Don't ask any questions. When we reach the county seat, you'll understand."

In this way, we were taken away from Chenggang. We bid farewell to Cheng Temple, to the Cheng Brothers memorial arch, and to the thousands of members of the Chenggang production brigade. We bid farewell to revolution and struggle, war and friendship, enemies and friends, Cheng Qinglin and the masses, streets and alleys, paths and fields, mountains and forests, livestock and dishes, and so forth. I sat in the car's front seat, while the three others sat in the back. In the rearview mirror, I saw that Hongmei's face was covered in a sheen of excitement, as though wisps of dawn clouds were hanging over it. At that moment, what I wanted more than anything else was to be able to sit in the back seat, so that I could lean close to her and let our legs touch and our hands discreetly rub together—so as to transmit to each other our excitement and trembling joy. However, I had already been assigned to the front seat, as a result of having been designated a new revolutionary star by the director of the prefectural committee's organizational department. But was I being appointed full county head, or merely deputy county head? Perhaps only deputy county head, given that I wasn't even thirty years old, had previously only been a deputy mayor, and my residency permit was still assigned to the Chenggang production brigade. At the end of the day, I was still just a peasant. In normal conversation, people never add the prefix "deputy" when addressing individuals with a deputy appointment, and this fact now caused me considerable agony. The excitement and anxiety of not knowing whether I was a full county head or just a deputy county head—but at the same time not daring to ask anyone—left me so anxious I couldn't sit still. In order to demonstrate my nature as an extraordinary revolutionary, all I could do was sit there without moving, and it wasn't until the car passed the underground tomb located eighteen *li* outside Chenggang, the place where Hongmei and I had madly, crazily made love, that I finally turned toward the window and softly coughed.

Hongmei coughed twice, as though in response. This sedan— and that was the first time either of us had ridden in one—had indescribably soft seats, and during the ride I wondered countless times whether or not this jet-black sedan would belong to me once I was appointed county head. We drove past the Chenggang production brigade, Hongku commune, Daping commune, the county seat's old city district, quickly traversing the seventy-nine-*li* distance and soon arriving at a small courtyard behind the county committee building.

The courtyard was square, with tile-roofed houses on three sides and two half-open iron gates in the front. When we arrived, rifle-bearing sentries checked the car's license plate and opened the gates for us. We parked in this small courtyard, with its red-tiled buildings, red walls, and red-brick paving. (It was as if we had fallen into a pool of blood.) Director Liu was the first to get out of the car, and he initially went into one room, then led us into the reception area outside another set of rooms. He respectfully poured us some tea, then invited us to have a seat on a pair of couches. This was the first time either of us had ever sat on a couch, and we were surprised to discover that these seats were even softer than those in the sedan. While seated, we felt as though we were in prison, and wished we could press our butts against the edge of the couch and stand up. Fortunately, Director Liu was busy pouring us tea and didn't notice. Moreover, what did it mean that the director of the prefectural Party committee organizational bureau was personally pouring us tea? Director Liu placed two cups of tea on the stand in front of us (it was only later that I realized that sort of low, red table was called a tea stand), then said, rather mechanically, "This is the residence of the prefectural Party secretary, who has now relocated to the county seat, and in a little while he'll come out to speak to you. In the meantime, please have some tea." Upon saying this, he excused himself and left the room.

I knew that the Party secretary of the prefectural Party committee was called Guan Mingzheng, but couldn't believe that he would actually meet with us in person or that the revolution could have generated such an earth-shattering development. All I had done was to make a trip to the Balou Mountains and reveal Wang Zhenhai's covert act of redistributing land to local households. Our objective had been to remove Wang Zhenhai from office as quickly as possible and in the process lay claim to the power he held. How could we have ever anticipated we would end up exposing the nation's largest attempt to restore capitalism? How could we have anticipated that this case would end up bringing down the county head? The heat of success arrived prematurely and left us blinded and confused, boiling our innards such that we couldn't sit still. We were completely unprepared for this premature success, and just as the first time we returned to the Chenggang revolution and displayed infantile symptoms of revolution, this time the success of the revolution propelled us into a disaster.

After Director Liu left the room, Hongmei and I didn't dare speak out loud. We stared at each other thirstily, and we each felt that the other's gazes were like red-hot iron rods in a blacksmith's furnace that longed to be doused in cold water, just as we each needed to get calm and coolness from each other. We sat on the couches and watched as Director Liu turned around outside the window. Our hands (her left and my right) suddenly grasped each other. Her hand was hot and soft, and it throbbed. The blood flowing through the veins in her fingertips was pounding in my palm, as though a waterfall were pouring onto my hand.

She said, "Aijun, our revolution has succeeded!"

I replied, "Do you know what kind of positions we'll be assigned?"

She said, "Chenggang's power will definitely be given to you."

I laughed.

"At the very least, you and I will be promoted to a deputy county-level position!"

She abruptly pulled her hand back and stared at me coldly.

I lightened my tone and said, "You may even be promoted to a full county-level position. Our success will then skyrocket!"

She looked around inside and outside the room, then slowly shook her head, as though she couldn't believe her eyes.

I wanted to use Director Liu's words to prove to her the correctness of my guesses and hypotheses. However, a sound suddenly appeared out of nowhere, like a small piece of wood falling from the table or windowsill. That sound made us both freeze in our tracks. It was only then that we both noticed that there was a door in the wall directly across from us. It was only then that we noticed that, in addition to a pair of couches, a tea table, a desk, a rotary phone, and a face-basin stand with a basin filled with crystal-clear water, there was also a red door covered with a white curtain embroidered with the characters for "serve the people." The door behind the curtain was closed, and neither of us knew whether the sound we had just heard came from inside or outside the room. We were afraid that Secretary Guan might suddenly show up at the door. We were afraid he might have overheard our discussion and might have observed us surreptitiously holding hands.

We made an effort to separate our hands and then carefully place our butts back onto the edge of the couches where we had been sitting. Our throats felt dry, but we didn't dare to drink any of the tea from the cups in front of us. We had a strong urge to strip off our clothes and roll around naked, but at the same time couldn't bring ourselves to even move to sit closer to one another. We had been told that Secretary Guan was attending a meeting in a conference room, but were afraid he might suddenly walk in through that doorway with the white curtain. So we sat there without moving or saying a word, waiting for Secretary Guan's arrival as a hot summer day waits for a cool breeze, as China's endless dark night waits for a bright lamp, or as the dark old society waits for a red sun to rise in the east. Time resembled water accumulated behind a sluice, and our anxiety was like an ant running around on a hot skillet. It was oppressively hot inside the room, and there was the faint smell of red paint. Motes of dust were dancing in the sunlight that entered through the window and the doorway. We felt we could hear them knocking against one another and could see their shadows flitting across the floor like tiny black butterflies. We could detect a fragrance that Secretary Guan had scattered around, a crisp floral scent that wafted in all directions. Time became increasingly sluggish (I resolved that after I was appointed county head, I would live in this courtyard, in this apartment), and the air became increasingly warm and sultry (I wondered whether Hongmei and I should get married once the revolution achieved another enormous success). The specks of dust in my eyes multiplied, and the room's reddish-gold light became increasingly dim (I thought how nice it would be if, at this moment, Hongmei and I could hide out in an uninhabited ravine somewhere in the Balou Mountains). The room's fragrance increasingly came to resemble a mixture of morning grass, warm horse manure, and boiling meat (I thought that if I had been in

307

Chenggang at that moment, I definitely would have Hongmei strip and dance naked in front of me). We were simultaneously bored and cautious—we wanted to drink but didn't dare touch the cups in front of us; we wanted to cool off but didn't dare touch the buttons on our clothes; we wanted to do that thing, but we didn't dare hold hands. We desperately wanted to find something to do (such as read a newspaper or study a document) and to find an appropriate topic to discuss (such as recent international developments or the Party Central Committee's new directives). I let my gaze stray from the tea stand to the desk, where I noticed that there was a large copy of *Reference News* under the phone. When I stood up to get the volume, a ten-centimeter color photograph slipped out. I picked it up and looked at it, and saw that it was a picture of a middle-aged female soldier. She was wearing glasses and a brimless hat, and appeared both friendly and stern, as though she were peering down at something. At the bottom of that photograph, meanwhile, there was a note that read: "My beloved wife!"

I felt that the woman in the photograph looked very familiar, but I couldn't put my finger on who she was. I couldn't believe she might be someone famous. If she in fact was someone well-known, then who would be bold enough to write that line on the photograph? I stared at that photograph and at that "My beloved wife!" inscription, then excitedly handed the photograph to Hongmei.

Hongmei glanced at the photograph, whereupon that solemn, unforgettable moment we had both been waiting for suddenly came to pass. We heard some footsteps outside the doorway. These footsteps were neither urgent not leisurely but warm and rhythmical, resonating in an unforgettable manner outside the window. We knew this must be Secretary Guan returning from his meeting, which meant that the historical moment of decision—which would determine whether we would be appointed revolutionary successors in town or revolutionary helmsmen in the county seat—had finally arrived. The crucial conversation—which would determine whether we would rocket to prominence or need to laboriously climb the ladder step-by-step—had finally arrived. Hongmei and I looked at one another and then simultaneously stood up from our couches just as Secretary Guan appeared in the doorway. As I mentioned, he was thin, dark-skinned, gray-haired, and bright-eyed, and was wearing an old military uniform. In short, he looked just as we had expected (though we were curious about his relationship to the female soldier in the photograph). When he entered, he looked at us radiantly, then gestured and said, "Sit, please, sit! Have some tea!"

(He was so kind and affable! But what was his relationship with the female soldier in the photograph?)

As Secretary Guan was gesturing for us to have a seat and drink some tea, he pulled over a chair and proceeded to engage us in conversation for about three minutes:

"I have inspected your dossiers, which aren't bad at all. The revolution needs more people like you.

"Do you realize the significance of your discovery and revelations regarding Wang Zhenhai? The provincial-level officials have taken great interest in this matter, and even the central leadership has offered written comments. This was a terrifying time bomb hidden beneath socialism's collective body, and if you hadn't discovered it then, at some point it would have detonated, blowing a black hole in socialism's blue sky.

"Little Gao, my comrades in the prefectural Party committee organizational bureau want to assign you to a county-level position, and we can discuss whether this would be as county head or as county Party committee secretary. The heavier the burden, the more this would be a test put to you by the Party organization. But there is no need to worry, because as long as you work fearlessly, and as long as you master the relevant routes and Party guidelines, you'll definitely persevere."

Secretary Guan turned to Hongmei and continued:

"Little Xia, during the past four years that I've been working in the district, I've rarely encountered such an enlightened female revolutionary as yourself, particularly in the countryside. You and little Gao are very unusual youth cadres—young and with great promise and a boundless future. As for whether you'll be appointed director of the county-level women's association or deputy county head, let's decide that after further consideration. Of course, even if you are appointed director of the women's association, you'll still be a member of the county Party committee, a deputy county-level position."

Finally, upon receiving our delirious expressions of gratitude and our assurances that we would definitely make good on the education and cultivation we received from the upper-level organization, Secretary Guan stood up and, in a deep, hoarse, yet powerful voice, said, "My other meeting hasn't yet concluded. Why don't you first go to the guesthouse, and this afternoon we'll find time to discuss all this in more detail." He looked at us and added, with a smile, "I know your respective household situations. Each of you has experienced a family tragedy, but neither of you permitted your will to be crushed by those setbacks. You are truly a rare couple, and if you harbor comradely affection and revolutionary love for one another, then I, in my capacity as Party secretary of the prefectural Party committee, would be very happy to serve as your matchmaker. The only condition is that after the marriage, you wouldn't be able to remain in the same work unit, and instead one of you must be reassigned to work in either the county or district seat. This is a Party regulation. The Communist Party doesn't permit people engaged in revolutionary work to open mom-and-pop stores."

Finally, Secretary Guan affectionately shook our hands, walked us out of his office, and arranged for someone to escort us to the county committee guesthouse.

3. Shadows under the Sun

Like flower buds yearning for a spring breeze, like parched earth longing for water, like petrels waiting for a storm, and like floodwaters waiting for the sluice gates to open, we settled into our respective rooms in the guesthouse and waited for our worker escort to leave. But he seemed to understand that Hongmei and I were future county leaders and, therefore, kept solicitously showing me where the towels and soap were and reminding me that when I finished the drinking water in my thermos bottle, I should call to him and he would refill it. He explained which of the switches over the bed controlled the wall lamp, which controlled the ceiling lamp, and which controlled the radio. (There was even a radio in the room, meaning that we could pipe in revolutionary songs and music whenever we wanted!)

The worker was both thoughtful and garrulous, helpful and annoying. After he finally left, I immediately turned on the radio above the bed, and music from a revolutionary model opera was piped into the room. Then I headed over to Hongmei's room, but when I entered the hallway I ran into Hongmei, who at that moment was on her way to my room. When she saw me, she uttered the very same words that I had planned to say to her: "Aijun, above my bed there's a radio that is currently playing the revolutionary model opera *Taking Tiger Mountain by Strategy*."

I replied, "Come to my room. The cabinet above my bed also has a radio."

We returned to my room.

When we arrived, we locked the door, pulled the blinds, turned on the radio, and proceeded to strip naked. Neither of us said another word, nor did we make a single gesture to each other, and instead, silently and crazily, we proceeded to do that thing.

We did that thing to celebrate our success and our happiness. We did that thing to calm our excitement and enthusiasm. We did that thing to deepen our comradely affection and our revolutionary love for one another.

As I was doing that thing to the rhythm of the music playing over the radio, I had assumed that Hongmei would scream passionately, or perhaps would turn pale and faint, sweat streaming down her face. In the end, however, she didn't scream and she didn't faint. Instead, she stared affectionately at me and caressed my face with both hands, whereupon she suddenly began to cry, tears pouring like a waterfall down onto the pillow. I was startled by the sound of her crying. When I saw her tears, I was afraid I had injured her, so I slowed down and wiped away her tears.

I asked, "What's wrong?"

She caressed my face even more affectionately and replied, "Nothing."

I said, "You're crying, and now your pillow is completely soaked."

She said, "Aijun, we are worth it, the revolution is worth it, and even death itself is worth it."

I pushed a strand of tear-soaked hair behind her ear.

"So, that's why you're crying?"

She said, "I remembered what happened in the past, and my belated fear made me cry."

I said, "What are you afraid of? We have our ideals and our ambitions. We dare to struggle, and in an instant we transitioned from low-level figures to county-level officials. As long as we work, work, work, and as long as we pursue revolution, revolution, revolution, we'll surely be able to attain a full county-level, deputy district-level, full district-level, deputy provincial-level, or even a full provincial-level position. We'll be able to advance from the position of peasants to high-level cadres, and after we become high-level cadres, what will our past deeds amount to? For revolution there must be sacrifice, and heaven itself doesn't even know the things you and I know. So, what are you worried about?"

Because we were discussing a very serious topic, because her tears were pouring out even more dramatically than before, and because her sudden sorrow had stanched my ardor, our passion dissipated like smoke. I gazed at her with endless regret. Ashamed, she said, "Aijun, this is all my fault." I turned off the radio and replied, "It's OK. Now that we have this radio, we can do that thing whenever we want." As I was saying this, she got dressed, folded the blanket, and straightened the sheets. Then she turned over the tear-soaked pillowcase and placed it back on the pillow. Finally, she opened the window, so that the early spring light could pour in, bathing the room in bright light as though it were a revolutionary's heart.

By this point it was already noon, and there were golden specks of dust flying around in the sunrays shining into our room. In the sunlight, the portrait of Chairman Mao and the image from the model opera *The Red Lantern* that were hanging on the wall appeared dazzling and indistinct. Looking out the window, we could see the evergreens in the guesthouse courtyard, and in this early spring period their needles were either tender green or black. These trees had all been carefully trimmed such that they were low and square. When I looked more carefully, I noticed that they had been planted in the shape of the Chinese character for "loyalty." I said to Hongmei, "Look, Secretary Guan asked me to consider accepting a position in the county seat, and I think that after becoming county head or Party secretary, the first thing I'll do will be to plant a garden at every intersection in the county seat, and in each garden I'll arrange pine trees and cypresses in the shape of the character for 'loyalty.'" Hongmei straightened up the bed and walked over and looked out at that green character. She remarked that the character for "loyalty" was too monotonous, and asked why they couldn't have arranged the trees to form the phrases "Three Loyalties" and "Four Boundlessnesses." I asked how many trees that would require and how large of a garden? Hongmei reflected for a moment, then smiled and rested her hands on my shoulder. She said, "Not only will we pursue revolution and develop our understanding of agriculture, we will also master forestry, water conservancy, and rural animal husbandry. In mastering forestry, you should find a hillside and plant trees so that they spell out the phrase 'Long Live Chairman Mao.' That way, the phrase will be legible to people located dozens of *li* away and even to those flying overhead in airplanes. As a result, we'll become famous throughout the nation, and people will come from Beijing and make a documentary about this incident, which will then be screened around the country."

Intrigued by this idea, I turned and grasped Hongmei's face with both hands. I saw that there were wrinkles around her eyes, which pierced my heart like needles. She noticed my sudden change of expression and asked, in an anxious and aggrieved tone, "Do I look old?" I replied, "People may age, but heaven never will. If heaven could experience emotion, however, it too would age." She said, "Will you still like me when I'm old?" I said, "We are a revolutionary couple, and when we are together there will be revolution, regardless of our age or beauty. As long as the revolution hasn't yet concluded, the love we feel for each other will persist." I don't know whether or not she was satisfied with this reply, but I do know that she didn't respond. Instead, she silently sat back down on the edge of the bed. In order to reassure her, I pulled over a chair and sat down beside her. Grasping her hand in mine, I said, "Do you want to be director of the women's federation, or deputy county head? Being deputy county head definitely sounds better, but you would have to follow the orders of the county head. Being director of the women's federation might not sound quite as good, but you would be in complete control of the federation."

She let me grasp her hand, like a warm and soft bird sleeping in its nest. She gazed thirstily at my face and my mouth, even as the corners of her own mouth continued to twitch. "I know you want to be appointed county Party committee secretary and that you don't want to be county head. The Chinese Communist Party directs the core power of our national enterprise. The Party directs everything, even the army. Therefore, if you want to be Party secretary, guess what I want to be? I want to be deputy county head *and* director of the women's federation. After we are properly married, I hope the day will come when you'll be assigned to the district, and you will have me be county head or Party secretary."

I said, "How could that be?"

She said, "Why couldn't it?"

I said, "Would Secretary Guan agree to this?"

She said, "Not only should we have Secretary Guan serve as a matchmaker when we get married, we should also invite him to be our children's godfather."

I released her hand and said, "Are you like an imposter trying to imitate the great hegemon-king Xiang Yu?"

She laughed. "Do you think that wouldn't be possible?" She wiped her hand—which I had squeezed so hard that it was soaked in sweat—on the bed. Then her eyes became even brighter, and she gazed at me as though looking at her younger brother. She said, "From when I was young, I knew that the Red Liberation Army soldiers in the county cadre's sanatorium were fond of adopting godsons and goddaughters. If you and I get married, and Secretary Guan serves as the matchmaker, we will have a special relationship with him. With this special relationship, we'll be able to periodically visit him in his home, and furthermore, we'll be able to let Hongsheng, Honghua, and Tao'er call Secretary Guan 'Grandfather' and call his wife 'Grandmother.' We could ask where Secretary Guan's family is from, and if they are from the south, then whenever we visit we could take them some chili peppers and pickled vegetables, but we would make sure not to take them anything valuable. If they are from the north, then we could take them some rice or red dates. Our children would sweetly address them as 'Grandmother' and 'Grandfather,' so how could they not recognize them as their godchildren? After Secretary Guan recognizes our children as his godchildren, how could he not permit us to work together? How could he not let me be appointed both deputy county head *and* director of the women's federation? And even if he appoints you as county head and not Party secretary, why wouldn't you be able to be reappointed whenever you wanted to serve as Party secretary?" (My soul and my flesh, my revolutionary lover and wife!)

Hongmei's comments left me speechless, as though a student had stepped in for a teacher and solved an age-old riddle. Infatuated, I stared at her mouth, her face, her hair, and her shoulders, and after a while I suddenly grasped both of her hands, as though grasping a couple of birds that had just flown away. I said, "I believe Secretary Guan is a northerner. If he is from the northeast, whenever we visit we should take him yam jelly and cold noodles. If he's from Shandong, we should take him chives and fried pancakes. If he's from Shaanxi, we should take him rice and sorghum. And if he's from Shanxi, we should take him some aged vinegar."

During that time before lunch, we sat in our room in the guesthouse, planning out our revolutionary work, our careers and our futures, our marriage and our family, our relationship and our friendship. We had already decided to wait patiently until the announcement of our appointments and our marriage, whereupon we would use a "double happiness" marriage scroll outside our door to add a bright smile to our brilliant lives, so our revolutionary ship could set off at full sail toward a destination where the brilliant sun shines down on people who are ascending to heaven at high speed. It would be best if we (or I) left the county seat and proceeded to the district seat between the age of thirty-three and thirty-five, to be appointed district-level deputy commissioner or mayor of the city of Jiudu.

At that moment, at that instant, the director of the guesthouse came to invite us to come eat.

The food was, of course, of the highest quality, given that the guesthouse was treating us as though I were already the newly appointed county head. All sorts of exquisite dishes were arranged on the table in front of us—including rice and vegetables, broiled fish, stewed chicken, ribs, salted duck, and meatball soup. In the end, however, the only person who came to join us was Director Liu from the prefectural Party committee's organizational bureau. It had originally been agreed that the county's political leaders would all attend, and Secretary Guan would introduce us to them, in the style of a piece of "internal information," so that we could familiarize ourselves as quickly as possible with each department's leaders and their responsibilities. In the end, however, Secretary Guan didn't come, and neither did the county's political leaders. Instead, the only people present in the county committee guesthouse dining hall—with its four tables overflowing with food—were Director Liu, Hongmei, and myself. In retrospect, it occurred to me that the earthquake of our revolutionary enterprise had already begun to develop, and the previously firm ground on which we stood had already begun to sway. However, at the time, we were blinded by our own success, and our vision of the revolution's brilliant future obscured the enormous tragedy that had already begun to unfold.

We came down from the second floor of the guesthouse and proceeded to the large dining room on the eastern side of the guesthouse. When I saw Director Liu, I warmly shook his hand, in the appropriate manner of a newly appointed county head. Hongmei said, "Hello, Director," in a crisp and precise voice, like the red cherries that at that time had just ripened. However, as Director Liu was shaking my hand, he merely touched my fingertips, and in responding to Hongmei, he merely glanced in her direction.

I looked at the large dining room with its four tables overflowing with food and wine, and asked, "Has Secretary Guan not arrived yet?"

Director Liu sat down at one of the tables and replied, "He's not coming."

I experienced a jolt of surprise, and said, "Then . . . what about the county's other political leaders . . ."

Director Liu picked up his bowl and chopsticks.

"Let's eat first. We can discuss things afterward."

I began to feel as though a cold wind were blowing, and the ground were shaking beneath my feet. I looked at Hongmei, and saw that she had begun to turn pale. She clearly also felt that Director Liu's actions and attitude were odd and inauspicious. Given that we had both passed through the cauldron of revolutionary struggle, and that in the course of pursuing revolution we had observed all sorts of trials and hardships, we knew very well that sometimes the revolution can bring success at one moment and failure at the next. We also knew that simply because the revolution was succeeding, that didn't mean that the struggle had concluded. As long as class differences persist, class struggle will never conclude. The struggles between the proletariat and the bourgeoisie—the class struggle between various different political factions and the power struggle and ideological occupation between the proletariat and the bourgeoisie—are long-standing and circuitous, and sometimes may even change abruptly and become unusually intense. When I saw that Director Liu had already begun eating, I gave Hongmei a look, whereupon we each sat down across from him and began to eat as well.

The steam from the food on the four tables circulated through the well-lit dining hall. The newborn flies and those that had been roused from their hibernation were brazenly eating, drinking, and enjoying themselves at those other three tables, producing a gray humming sound like the flute melody in the model opera *Raid on the White Tiger Regiment*. The sunlight was blazing, and it shifted from the table to our faces and bodies, and it felt as though our bodies had been wrapped in an oil-soaked cloth. The director of the guesthouse was waiting outside the dining hall door, unaware of what was happening. Director Liu ate half a bowl of rice but kept tapping his chopsticks against the side of a bowl of fried meat with chili. Hongmei and I both had bowls of rice, but we only held the bowls in front of us without eating from them. When we served ourselves

318

from the serving plates, we took only vegetables and didn't dare help ourselves to any fish or ribs, stewed chicken or salted duck. Time coagulated at the end of our chopsticks like pig lard. The sound of Director Liu chewing his food resembled dusty tiles falling onto the table. Hongmei kept looking at me, dark clouds hanging like a wet black cloth over her face.

I held out the rice bowl and said, "Director Liu, what happened?"

Director Liu looked at me and said, "I should be asking *you* what happened. I should be asking you."

I put my rice bowl on the table and said, "We are both comrades and Party members. We are committed to the revolution, to Chairman Mao, and to the Communist Party. Whatever happened, please tell us directly."

Director Liu gazed at me with a befuddled look.

Hongmei also put down her rice bowl and said, "Director Liu, you are about the same age as our parents and belong to an earlier generation of revolutionaries. Needless to say, you are our political superior. If it's necessary to criticize anyone, then of course, you should criticize us. But if you don't say anything, then in the event that we might have done something wrong, we won't be able to change even if we want to."

Director Liu finally put down his bowl, then went over and closed the door to the dining hall and returned to his seat. He wiped his mouth, spit out a grain of rice that had gotten stuck between his teeth, and said, "Little Gao, little Xia." With a face resembling a stone slab, he continued: "This counts as my formally addressing you and as the Party formally addressing you. You are a couple of revolutionary successors with limitless potential. When Secretary Guan saw your dossiers, he immediately decided he needed to nurture you. And it should be noted that Secretary Guan is someone who will be eventually promoted to a provincial-level position, and who frequently interacts with Party Central Committee officials. However, you haven't lived up to Secretary Guan's expectations or the expectations placed on you by the Party organization when it educated and nurtured you. As for what exactly happened, I myself don't know. However, you made Secretary Guan so angry that his face turned green and he threw down the telephone. The two of you must certainly know very well what it was you did. You simply need to look and see whether or not your loyalty to the organization, to the Party, and to Chairman Mao is genuine. If you confess now, perhaps there'll still be time to make amends, but if you don't, then the question of whether you might be promoted to county head or director of the women's federation will be the least of your worries, because it is likely that all of your political ambitions will be finished." At this point, Director Liu paused and looked out of the dining hall, then he looked back at us, closed his mouth for a while, and after waiting for a couple of passersby to walk away, he added, in a half-inspiring and half-intimidating manner, "You know even better than I how serious revolution is and how complicated and ruthless class struggle is. But in class struggle, you absolutely mustn't try to be too clever and you mustn't crush your own foot with the stone you're trying to carry. You mustn't transfer yourself from the revolutionary camp to the anti-revolutionary camp."

After saying this, Director Liu picked up his bowl and resumed eating. Acting as though he had just finished doing what he needed to do, he contentedly brought a chicken leg up to his mouth.

We knew something momentous had taken place, and it must have occurred not long after we saw Secretary Guan—perhaps while we were doing that thing in the guesthouse and making plans for the future. We suspected that it must have involved our underground tunnel and Cheng Qingdong's death. I looked at Hongmei, whose face was as white as a sheet. Her hands were resting on the edge of the table and were trembling violently, as though someone were holding her wrists and shaking them. I was also alarmed but knew that I was a man and furthermore was the former deputy town mayor, the newly appointed county head, a revolutionary youth, a politician of rare quality, and a soldier who had made it through countless political battlefields. The expression with which Hongmei looked at me was one of a child who has fallen into a river gazing up at her father standing on the bank. I couldn't let her feel that I was not up to the task of being her husband and a revolutionary or of being a soldier or a politician. She was my flesh and soul, my spirit and my companion, so naturally I couldn't disappoint her. Therefore, I cleared my throat and gestured for her to remain calm. Even if we found ourselves in prison, we had to have the determination and fortitude, the courage and guts to sit it out.

I shifted my gaze from Hongmei's face to Director Liu's greasy hands and said, "Director Liu, Chairman Mao observed that everything we say and do must be pertinent and well grounded, because only in this way will people be sincerely convinced."

Director Liu stopped gnawing on his chicken leg and stared at me coldly. "Little Gao, I'm telling you the truth. I'm not the one you've angered, but it's Secretary Guan from the prefectural Party committee. Moreover, you two are the only ones who know what you did to anger him. After you finish eating, why don't you return to your rooms and reflect on this, while I go report to Secretary Guan and ask for additional instructions. Perhaps he'll then be willing to speak to you directly about this matter."

Hongmei and I left the dining hall.

4. The Special Detention Chamber

While it took nearly a month for Wang Zhenhai and Zhao Qing to be imprisoned, less than a day elapsed from when Hongmei and I began anticipating being appointed to our new positions to when we found ourselves in the police station's special detention chamber.

After lunch, Director Liu came to where Hongmei and I were staying and said only three things, whereupon he took us to the police station to be subjected to a special interrogation.

He said, "First, given that this afternoon Secretary Guan will go to the provincial seat to attend an urgent meeting, he has decided not to see you again. Second, as to the seriousness of your actions, the two of you must know this better than anyone. When he has time, Secretary Guan wants to come and talk to you himself, and he hopes you won't refuse to recognize your errors and crash headfirst into the iron wall of the proletarian dictatorship. Third, Secretary Guan says that if he doesn't have time to come himself, he will send someone he trusts implicitly to speak to you, and he hopes you will not hide or evade anything. If you answer everything honestly, Secretary Guan will forgive you."

Director Liu then left the room where I was staying. It should be noted that Director Liu was a good comrade, and when he reached the doorway he turned and said sympathetically, "You are both still young, so don't try to cover things up. Just say everything that needs to be said. Given that this month someone was appointed to an official position despite having killed more than a dozen people in the name of the revolution, what is there for you to be afraid of?"

After Director Liu left, four burly uniformed men entered our room and, without saying a word, proceeded to search us from head to toe—even searching Hongmei's hair and behind her ears. Then they handcuffed us and led us away. At that instant, the corners of Hongmei's eyes began to tear up, but she bit her lip to prevent herself from crying. Before Director Liu arrived, Hongmei and I had already reached an agreement. I said, "Hongmei, do you have any regrets?" She replied, "As long as you still love me, I don't regret anything." I said, "I do have regrets—I regret I didn't have a chance to formally marry you," whereupon she burst into tears. She lay on me and cried, and said, "Aijun, for me your love is enough; for me this is worth it. Having what you just said, I know it was definitely worth it to have pursued the revolution with you." We agreed that no matter what happened, we wouldn't permit ourselves to cry.

We agreed that we wouldn't allow anyone to treat us—a pair of revolutionaries—as if we were merely made of mud, straw, or paper.

> *Heads may roll and blood may flow*
> *but revolutionary consciousness can never be lost*
> *Don't worry that we are wearing chains and shackles*
> *and that our hands and feet are locked up*
> *because they will never be able to tie down our lofty ideals and aspirations*
> *Hatoyama used torture to obtain the code*
> *my bones are broken and my flesh is flayed, but my will is as strong as steel*
> *we'll proceed to the execution ground with elevated spirits and with our heads*
>   *lifted high*
> *we see—*
> *the red flag of revolution fluttering in the wind*
> *the beacon of struggle has set the fields ablaze*
> *but as we are waiting, the storm passes and a hundred flowers bloom*
> *a new village, resembling Chaoyang, illuminates the mortal world*
> *at that point, throughout China, red flags are everywhere*
> *when we think of us, we become more confident and more determined to fight*
> *my contribution to the Party, and her contribution to the People,*
>   *have been miniscule*
> *but what concerns us most is revolutionary sentiment, comradely love,*
>   *and whether our reputation will persist for centuries*
> *and will be passed down from generation to generation.*

We were placed in handcuffs and blindfolded, just like real prisoners, then we rode in a car for about two hours. When our blindfolds were finally removed, we saw that we had arrived in a special detention chamber inside a prison. This chamber consisted of three rooms and was about the size of the Party committee conference room in Chenggang. The only difference was that the conference room had several windows, which were all large and bright, while this detention chamber had only a single window that was only half as large as a Mao badge. This window was positioned much higher than a person's head, so even if you were to stand on tiptoes you would reach only the lower edge. Over the window there were steel bars as thick as a finger and as densely woven as a thornbush, and at most you could insert only a fist in the space between them. In sum, the detention chamber originally seemed to have been a granary, built in preparation for the nation's future anti-imperialist and anti-revisionist struggle.

What was most distinctive was not that this chamber resembled a granary but rather that—apart from the various corners where spotlights were mounted—the room's floor, ceiling, and walls were completely covered with a dense patchwork of quotations from Marx, Engels, Lenin, Stalin, and Chairman Mao (more than eighty percent were from Chairman Mao)—including quotations printed in red, yellow, and green characters and written in a combination of imitation Song dynasty script, new Wei dynasty script, new Liu script, and a facsimile of the lively and vigorous characters that Chairman Mao used for his poetry. After our blindfolds were removed (prior to which we hadn't realized that we had been locked in a chamber), Hongmei and I were both at a loss. We were suffocated by the room's fiery-red atmosphere. In the center of the ceiling was an enormous reddish-yellow star with five points, from each of which there hung a large lightbulb. Around the lightbulbs were portraits of Marx, Engels, Lenin, Stalin, and Mao, and surrounding these portraits was an array of these luminaries' slogans and quotations, stretching from one end of the ceiling to the other. Meanwhile, each of the room's four walls was covered in five identical rows of quotations written in yellow characters against a red backdrop, all of which were exactly the same size but with different content. The quotations extended from floor to ceiling, and between those five rows of quotations not even half a brick of the wall was visible. Finally, facing the door, there was a pair of one-meter-tall stools with seats a little smaller than a sheet of notebook paper, while the rest of the room was filled with Chairman Mao busts facing different directions. The person who removed our handcuffs and blindfolds was a young soldier wearing a collar insignia and a cap badge. Holding the handcuffs in his left hand and the blindfolds in his right, he gave us an odd look, then nudged the stools with his foot until they were about a meter apart. Next, and without any hint of class affection, he ordered, "Stand on these, and call us when you're ready to confess!"

After a brief hesitation, Hongmei and I stepped onto those stools and then stood as though planted there, a meter above the ground. It was then that we noticed that in the center of each stool, there were three upward-pointing nails that protruded through the seat by more than two centimeters. As a result, we could only stand or squat on the stools, but we couldn't sit down. I remembered the statement that we wanted to carry out revolutionary humanism, and I wanted to say a few words to that soldier, but I watched as he stooped over and walked away. Before leaving, however, he took an enormous Chairman Mao poster, applied glue to the back, and then pasted it to the ground between our two stools. Next he proceeded to take the Mao busts and place them in the path leading from the stools to the door. He moved dexterously, and as he did so, he kept mumbling to himself, as though reciting a magic formula. By the time he reached the door, he had left four continuous rows of busts that completely blocked the way out.

It was only at that moment that I realized we were trapped inside this room, which was actually a prison. We had never heard of this kind of detention chamber and had never imagined that there might be something like it in this revolutionary world. With a cold, clattering sound, the soldier shut the steel-rimmed wooden door, whereupon the room immediately became dark and silent. We found ourselves completely cut off from the outside world, and although we were now in a revolutionary environment, it was nevertheless a different revolution and a different environment from any we had ever experienced. Hongmei stood on the west-side stool and I stood on the east-side one, and between us there was the enormous Mao poster. In the light of the setting sun shining in through the window, I saw that Hongmei's face looked calmer now, as though she finally understood everything. She even appeared somewhat heroic. I don't know whether, when she was riding sitting in that car (perhaps it was a jeep), her tears had trickled out when the car shook, or whether she had maintained her poise, like Li Yuhe being led to the execution ground. As the setting sun shone down on the western mountains, the final rays of light crawled through the observation window into that room full of red slogans and bright images. We could hear the rhythmic footsteps of the sentry stationed outside, and through that small window we could see someone repeatedly peer into the room (they must have erected some sort of platform beneath the window outside). Every time someone peered in, the room instantly grew dark. Therefore, every time the room grew dark, we instantly knew we were being observed. I glanced at the slogans and quotations that were posted around the detention room, and saw they were more or less the same ones I had used during our Chenggang revolution, which virtually everyone knew by heart. *The core force leading our cause is the Chinese Communist Party, and the theoretical basis guiding our thought is Marxism-Leninism . . . Class struggle is easily solved . . . The route is the headrope of a fishnet, and when it is pulled, its mesh will open . . .* and *Study, study, and study some more; advance, advance, and advance some more.* However, in the most conspicuous location, at the center of the room, the quotations were more complex, with profound and far-reaching implications and bountiful resonances that were both thought-provoking and terrifying. In the center of the wall in front of us was the phrase *Leniency for those who confess, severity for those who resist.* Meanwhile, on the wall in front of me there appeared a passage that read:

Who are the People? In China, at this historical juncture, the People includes workers, peasants, the urban petite bourgeoisie, and the national bourgeoisie. Under the direction of the working class and the Communist Party, these classes will unite and establish their own nation, elect their own government, and exercise a dictatorial rule over those imperial running dogs—which is to say, the landlord class and the bureaucratic bourgeoisie, together with the Kuomintang reactionaries who represent those classes, and their accomplices. We want to oppress these people, and permit them only to be well behaved and not run amok.

On the wall behind me, where Hongmei was looking, there was a passage that read: *To sum up our experience and concentrate it into one point, it is: the People's democratic dictatorship under the leadership of the working class (through the Communist Party) and based upon the alliance of workers and peasants. This dictatorship must unite as one with the international revolutionary forces. This is our formula, our principal experience, our main program.* Under the window were two famous phrases that resembled explosives. On the left side of the window there was the phrase *Fight, fail, fight again, fail again, fight again . . . until their victory; that is the logic of the People, and they will never go against this logic.* On the right side there was the phrase *In class struggle, some classes triumph, others are eliminated. Such is history; such is the history of civilization for millennia.* Meanwhile, on the ceiling was Marx's wise and prophetic declaration about a dictatorship of the proletariat, which served as a beacon to guide socialism: *Between capitalist and communist society lies the period of the revolutionary transformation of the one into the other. Corresponding to this is a political transition period in which the state can be nothing but the revolutionary dictatorship of the proletariat.* On the floor was a passage from the great work in which Lenin extended Marx's revolutionary theory of class struggle: *The dictatorship of the proletariat is fierce war. The proletariat has been victorious in one country, but it is still weak internationally . . . Never before in history has there been a struggle like the one of which we are now witnesses . . . The People have had no way of acquiring experience in wars of this kind. We ourselves must create this experience.*

327

It's possible that, in the daily life of revolution, we don't necessarily appreciate the power and magnificence of these sorts of quotations and slogans, but in this special detention chamber, after reading these quotations and slogans, I felt as though there were an enormous undercurrent rumbling beneath my feet. It was as if the Yellow River or the Yangtze were buried ten or fifty meters beneath me, as though a mudflow were struggling beneath the stools on which Hongmei and I were standing, or as though magma from a live volcano were in the process of forcing its way up through the earth's crust. I could feel the earth shaking and the stool's legs trembling, as though we might fall off at any moment.

After reading those slogans and quotations, I saw that Hongmei had turned around on her stool and was silently reading them as well. Her face was ashen, though in the light of the setting sun her pallor had a dull shade of red. We were positioned a meter apart from one another, and on the floor between us was the enormous Chairman Mao poster, separating us like snow-capped mountains and vast fields of grass. It was as if we were separated by a glass wall or a glass mountain, such that we could see one another but were unable to hold hands, and although we could speak, we couldn't let our spittle fall to the floor. We assumed that the reason they had locked us inside this special detention chamber was because we were already a pair of dyed-in-the-wool revolutionaries and were only a day or so away from being promoted to county head and member of the standing committee. We assumed that the fact that they hadn't sent us to a real prison was a gesture of humanism and comradely love, in light of our revolutionary efforts. We assumed that after we had endured this sort of revolutionary test they would escort us back and celebrate us.

I said, "Hongmei, are you OK?"

She nodded and said, "My legs are trembling."

I said, "Then you should squat down for a while, but you must make sure that you don't touch the ground."

She said, "Yes, I know."

Then the shadow in front of the window moved, and we saw a long and thin face peering in. Parallel to the man's long and thin face, there was a bayonet strapped to the man's shoulder. Hongmei and I looked at him, and seeing that he wasn't stopping us from speaking or squatting, we once again felt the warmth of revolutionary humanism. We squatted down, grasping the edges of our stool seats (which appeared to be made from willow wood), and I said, "The quotations on the walls around us have remolded our ideology, and the Chairman Mao busts on the floor have prevented us from fleeing. If we were to touch the ground we would be committing a political mistake, which would make us doubly guilty." Hongmei looked at the Mao busts on the floor in front of her, and a smile flickered across her face. She looked as though she were about to say something, but didn't.

I added, "As long as there is revolutionary friendship and our hearts are united, then if there is anything you feel you shouldn't say, just give me a glance, and I'll understand."

She said, "Will they make us squat here all night?"

I said, "I don't know."

She said, "If they make us squat here all night, we'll surely fall to the ground and step on the Chairman Mao poster."

I said, "Then we'll have done exactly what they want, and our guilt will be doubled."

At that moment, as the setting sun's final rays lingered outside the window, and darkness began to fall, the detention chamber was suddenly lit up. All the room's lights were turned on. There were five spotlights on the ceiling, and each wall had two more. These thirteen spotlights had two-hundred- or five-hundred-watt bulbs, and their parabolic reflectors were all oriented toward us. We felt as though our bodies were on fire and our eyes were in agony, poked with red-hot needles. We frantically rubbed our eyes, and by the time we had had a chance to adjust to that blinding light, the tiny window had already been shut tightly. We heard the footsteps of the sentry stepping down from his post, together with the creaking sound of the wooden steps under his feet. It was as if, after we had been thrown into the revolutionary furnace, everyone had simply departed, and would return to retrieve us only after we had been melted into an anti-revolutionary residue, at which point they would stomp on us and drive us to our deaths—and in this way they would forever reduce us to the status of despicable dogshit.

We used our intuition to discern all this.

We anticipated their intentions and objectives. The Mao poster on the floor beneath us was perfectly spotless, and if we stepped down we would inevitably leave a footprint. In fact, even if we first removed our shoes, our bare feet would still leave a mark. There were also the Chairman Mao busts that were arranged in an array of four streams leading to the door. When the lights came on, I saw that several of them had simple Chinese characters written on the side, including the characters 工, 十, 五, and 三, together with punctuation marks such as : and 、. I realized that the location and orientation of these busts must follow some sort of secret code. Hongmei and I observed the layout carefully and saw that it wouldn't be sufficient to merely move two or three of the busts—if we wanted to get down off the stools and stand on the ground, we'd have to move at least five or six busts out of the way, and furthermore, every time we took a step forward, we'd have to return the busts to their original positions. At this point, the situation would become even more difficult, because we'd have to remember not only the precise position but also the orientation of each bust. No two busts were oriented in the same direction, and furthermore, they were not necessarily oriented along the four cardinal directions, but rather they might be oriented between east and northeast, or between southwest and southeast, or southeast and southwest. As a result, the busts positioned in the four streams resembled a revolutionary eight-diagram configuration, and if you

330

entered it without knowing the secret path, you would surely never be able to re-create it again.

Hongmei and I gazed silently at one another. Fortunately, it was not yet the height of summer and not terribly hot. After dusk (at least I *think* it was after dusk), we didn't hear the rumbling sound of the factory in the city or the whistle of the trains that pass through the suburbs every night transporting coal. (Oh, that unforgettable rail line through the suburbs!) We could faintly discern the scent of fields, which entered through the window and door like strands of silk. We smelled what resembled the odor of a brick kiln combined with the scent of grassy fields (or perhaps it was the scent of grassy fields combined with the odor of a brick kiln). Although I couldn't see my own face, I could tell that my heart was as cold and gray as a wet blue cloth, and I could see that Hongmei's face had begun to turn pale, as though she were once again beginning to panic. Time came to resemble viscous mud that overflowed into this big, cavernous room full of revolutionary echoes. We continued squatting on the seats of those willow-wood stools, each of which had only enough room for us to stand on. We alternated between peering down at our feet, looking at the images of Chairman Mao below us (that old fellow still had his kindly smile), and gazing at each other. We desperately wanted to come up with an encouraging word to raise the other's spirits. (Substance is primary and spirit is secondary, but at certain times and under specific circumstances, substance must yield to spirit and spirit must replace substance as primary, becoming a leader and commander and chief—this is the worldview of materialist dialectics and of historical materialism.) We very much wanted to find something we could say to raise our will to struggle. I reflected for a long time and finally came up with something.

I said, "Hongmei, are you hungry?"

She shook her head.

I said, "Had we known that things would turn out this way, we should have eaten some of that food at lunch."

331

She smiled but didn't reply.

I said, "How do you think Secretary Guan found out about us?"

She stared, thought for a moment, then said quietly, "Perhaps while we were in that room waiting to see him, someone . . ."

I immediately said, "That's not possible. The curtains were drawn so tightly there wasn't a single opening."

She said, "Then . . . maybe someone reported us?"

I said, "Perhaps."

She said, "Who could it have been? Not even heaven or earth knew about us . . ."

I said, "Only your father-in-law, Cheng Tianmin. After Wang Zhenhai was seized, Cheng Tianmin realized that after our revolution succeeded, you and I would be rapidly promoted. Do you think he would have been happy to see us promoted? Could he have been concerned about the fate of his son? Could he have been secretly observing our activities?" I glanced out the window and noted that it was so quiet, it was as if you could hear the wind blowing in your ear. She said, "He saw us this morning when we left town." I replied, "Maybe, after he saw us leave, he returned home, went into your room, and discovered the opening into the tunnel beneath your bureau. After discovering that opening, he would have realized everything. Then he would have followed us to the city and would have reported us right after we spoke to Secretary Guan."

Half-convinced, Hongmei looked at me. Her legs had begun to go numb from squatting for so long, so she carefully stood up and stretched. As she did so, the stool shook a bit, so she immediately squatted down again and grasped the edge of the stool with both hands. At this point her face suddenly broke out into a cold sweat, and she turned even more pale than before—becoming as white as a sheet of paper. (Could one use this paper to draw a new, beautiful picture?) I said, "You have to be careful." She replied steadily, "Aren't your legs numb?" I said, "Yes, they are." She said, "But my room was

332

locked. How could he have gotten in?" I said, "Cheng Tianmin is a wily old fox. Maybe he had made a copy of your key?"

She stared at me. "Even if he had made a copy of the room key, there's no way he could have made a copy of the bureau key, because I had the only one."

I asked, "Are you positive you locked your bureau when you left?"

She said, "Yes." But then she reflected further, looked down at the light red short-sleeve shirt she was wearing, and suddenly became uncertain as to whether or not she had in fact locked it.

She added, as though speaking to herself, "As I was leaving, I opened the bureau to change my shirt, but did I lock it afterward?"

I said, "Think carefully."

She said, "I suppose it's possible I didn't."

I said, "It's definitely possible you didn't. I saw you leave it unlocked on several occasions."

She didn't say anything else. It was as if, upon realizing she might not have locked the bureau after all, her face came to assume a dirty expression of remorse, as if earth from the fields and dust from the ripe grain were covering her bright face. She gazed at me silently for a while, then bowed her head.

I said, "A single ant hole can cause the collapse of a thousand *li* of dikes."

She looked up, with tears streaming down her face. It was clear she felt an acute sense of shame and regret and could barely restrain herself from bashing her brains out in order to express her guilt and repentance. Under the bright lights, her face appeared snowy white and deep blue, and the tears dripping down onto her pink top looked like black ink drops. "If I did in fact forget to lock it, would you hate me?" Her bright eyes looked as though she were begging for forgiveness—as though there were an array of peeled wheat stalks positioned between our faces. Her voice trembled and a pair of teardrops fell onto the stool seat beneath her, where they fractured into countless droplets that splattered onto the Chairman Mao poster like grains of sand falling onto a sheet of paper. I said, "Hongmei, you mustn't cry. You mustn't let your teardrops fall onto the Chairman Mao poster."

By this point she couldn't be troubled about this and instead continued to let her tears fall onto the stool seat, from which they then splattered onto the poster. She insistently asked, "If it turns out that I really did bury your political life, would you hate me?"

I also started to believe that it was her failure to lock the bureau that had led to the current tragedy, yet there was no way I could possibly hate her for this. She was my soul and my flesh, my revolutionary companion and the driver of my revolutionary passion. I told her, "Hongmei, I don't hate you at all. Nor do I have any regrets. I just hate myself, and regret that I didn't take the opportunity to formally marry you when I could." She stared at me with tears streaming down her face, as though trying to determine how much of what I was saying was true.

I continued, "If I had been able to marry you, then even if we were executed, the villagers would still have to bury us together."

The teardrops in her eyes suddenly grew to the point that they were as large as beans. Glittering, they hung from her eyelids— looking as though they were about to roll down, but she somehow managed to keep them in place. I smelled the sharp salty scent of her tears. She was extremely moved by what I had said, and I was overcome by those two teardrops, by the anguished gaze with which she looked at me, and by the pale hue of her complexion. From the depths of my heart, I resolved that if it was really true that it had been her failure to lock the bureau that had led to our being sent to this special detention chamber in this special prison, then not only would I forgive and absolve her with the magnanimity of a politician and a revolutionary, I would love and treasure her even more than before. I would love our revolutionary affection and treasure our comradely love. I wanted our revolutionary passion to become a model for posterity—an exemplary model that people would continually praise. I very much wanted to say something grandiose in order to express my steadfast friendship, but a deep agony rose up in my heart, preventing me from uttering a single word. Instead, all I was able to do was bite my lower lip and stare at her face, which appeared even more delicate because of its pallor, and at her eyes, which appeared even more captivating because they were filled with tears. We stared at one another for what seemed like an eternity, maintaining a profound silence. Our eyes were moist and heavy, while our hearts were pure and noble. We heard shards of time illuminated by the lamp whiz by us, and we heard the urgent pounding of our hearts, like dewdrops falling from tree leaves and grass blades onto the ground below. We smelled the bricks' sulfuric odor seeping in through the cracks in the door and the corners of the roof—a damp, warm smell that infiltrated our nostrils and throats. We wanted to open our mouths and swallow it. We gazed silently at one another, until even this became exhausting. Finally, Hongmei lifted her hand and wiped away her tears, then she lowered her head and said with a smile, "Aijun, do you know what I most want to do right now?"

I shook my head.

She wiped away her smile and said very seriously, "What I wish most of all is that I could take off my clothes in front of you one final time. I want to stand there naked and dance crazily, like we did that time in the tomb. Then I want to lie down in front of you and do whatever you want me to do, and let you do to me whatever you want."

I didn't find this remark at all unexpected. Instead, it was as though this was precisely what I most wanted to hear. I was moved by her confession. I'm not sure whether what I said at that point was something I had been planning for a long time or whether it was something I came up with on the spur of the moment in order to validate her heartfelt confession. I stared at her face and at a strand of black hair that lay across her ear. With a rare pleasure and happiness rippling across my heart, I asked, "Is this true?"

She seemed surprised and confused by my question, and replied, "You don't believe me?"

"I do believe you," I said. "But do you know what I want most right now? Right now, I suddenly have a desire to take some explosives and, like the Communist hero Dong Cunrui, blow up Cheng Temple, so that we can then stand naked where the temple used to be and, fearing neither heaven nor earth, crazily do that thing."

She asked, "How did you come up with that?"

I replied, "I don't know. I just suddenly had the idea."

She said, "Blowing up Cheng Temple is not our revolutionary objective."

I said, "But ever since I was little, whenever I saw the Cheng clan gathered there to worship their ancestors, I always imagined how one day I would demolish the temple and memorial arch."

She shook her legs, which had gone numb, then carefully stood up and squatted down again. Looking carefully at my face, she asked, "Why would we crazily do that thing in Cheng Temple?"

I replied, "To do that thing in Cheng Temple would be so much more pleasurable than slapping the temple in the face or kicking it in the groin."

She said, "Do you think they'll ever release us?"

I said, "I don't know."

She said, "If we're able to get out of here, I'll do whatever you want!"

At this point we heard footsteps outside. A soldier climbed a wooden ladder, pushed open the window, and peered inside. Then he climbed back down again, and it was unclear where he went after that. From his comings and goings, however, we realized that it was already dark outside and that it must be long past dinnertime. We suddenly felt very hungry. Our calves ached, and our feet were numb. I desperately wanted to call out to that person who had come to check on us—so that we could ask him to bring us some food or at least bring us a bowl of water. However, by this point his footsteps had already faded into the distance. We decided that the next time someone looked in on us, we would ask him for food and water. As it turned out, however, that night no one else looked in on us.

I had underestimated the revolutionary punishment to which we were subjected in that detention chamber. With hunger descending and our mouths dry from talking, after we finally managed to make it through the night, alternating between squatting and standing on those stools, we finally experienced the true cruelty of our torture.

Fatigue assailed us from all directions. Piercing sunlight assaulted our eyes like needles driving into our eyeballs. The glowing nails poking up through the seat of the stool were like fangs or claws. We were unable to sit; our legs grew weak when we tried to stand, and when we squatted our legs became numb. I have no idea how we managed to make it through the night—squatting and standing, standing and squatting. When we truly couldn't stay awake any longer, we squatted down and dozed while grasping the edges of our stool. But we knew we absolutely couldn't get down. We understood that it would be an incredible mistake if we were to step on the Chairman Mao poster, move one of the Chairman Mao busts, or touch any character in any of the Chairman Mao quotations. For even if we didn't utter a word about our original crime, the act of touching one of these Mao icons would constitute a far greater crime. We were people who had emerged from the revolutionary storm. We were true revolutionaries and therefore could certainly appreciate the consequences of getting down from the stools. We were intelligent, wise, and talented, and definitely wouldn't permit ourselves to be sent to the guillotine.

In the latter half of the night, when everything was completely still, we could just barely make out a mechanical sound from a factory and the rumbling of two trains traveling down the tracks. From

337

those sounds, we determined that we were located at least thirty or fifty *li* from the county seat. The cool night air seeped into the detention chamber. The heat of the spotlights made us feel irresistibly drowsy, and on several occasions we dozed off and almost fell off our stools. Moreover, when we fell asleep and sat down onto the stool seat, the nails would poke us in the butt. Once, Hongmei was poked by a nail, whereupon she screamed so loudly that dust was shaken down from the ceiling, but after she woke up, fatigue continued to weigh down her eyelids. She said, "Aijun, I'm afraid we won't survive this torture." I asked, "Are you unable to stay awake any longer?" She replied, "Sooner or later, we'll both fall off these stools and immediately become active anti-revolutionaries." I said, "Even when it feels as though you can't endure anymore, there'll inevitably be a turn for the better, and victory will be within our grasp." She said, "My feet are numb, my legs are rubbery, and my eyelids are sore. I'm afraid I won't be able to hold out much longer." I said, "You can hold the edge of the stool and shut your eyes. That way, you can nap while listening to me count. When you hear me get to ten, you can open your eyes, and if you can't rouse yourself, I'll wake you up." She therefore grasped the edge of the stool and closed her eyes, as I began to count out loud while watching her carefully. When I saw her head begin to tilt, I quickly called out to her. We continued in this way, with one of us napping while the other watched and counted to ten, whereupon the person who was counting would wake the other person up.

Relying on our fortitude and our wisdom, we somehow managed to make it through that endless night.

When the sun came up, and that young soldier, holding the toothbrush and cup he had just used to brush his teeth, opened the door, he placed his toothbrush and cup on the floor inside the doorway, then randomly pushed aside those four streams of Mao busts, opening up a path through them. In the process, he revealed a couple of Chinese characters or graphic elements written in chalk on the ground. He came to a stop in front of our stools and stared down at the Chairman Mao poster between us. Using the sunlight shining in through the door, he checked to see whether or not the poster had any footprints or handprints. After confirming that neither of us had stepped on it, he turned his attention to the Mao busts positioned around the stools. He spent at least ten minutes inspecting the area around the stools, and when he finally confirmed that we had indeed remained on the stools the entire night, he looked up at us in surprise.

I said, "We really didn't get down."

He said, "You are the first ones who have managed to stay on the stools for an entire night."

I said, "We are starving and parched. You must let us eat something, even if it is just a sip of soup."

He said, "There is something to eat and drink, but I'm afraid that if I give you anything, then I'll be the one who'll have to stand on those stools."

I said, "You can't refuse this most basic humanitarian request."

He said, "Confess! Once you do, you'll be able to get down from these stools. Otherwise, not only will you be forced to confess, your crimes will be doubled, and you'll be labeled an acting counterrevolutionary."

I inquired, "What do you want us to say?"

He stared at me coldly and said, "You're asking *me*? You know perfectly well what crimes you committed, and if you're not willing to confess, then you can simply stay on those stools and let your crimes to be doubled." Upon saying this, he again started to back out of the room, and as he did so he returned each of the Mao busts to its original position. At times, he appeared to forget where a particular bust should go, and then he would turn it over and look at the base and at the Chinese character or graph on the ground and then would move a different bust to its place. Hongmei and I were completely engrossed by his actions. We couldn't hear what he was muttering, but we could see his mouth repeatedly opening and closing. We watched as he revealed the characters and graphs beneath two of the streams of busts leading up to us. Under the first stream, there were the graphs 五、山、委、辶、月, and under the second there were the graphs, 人、氵、水、扌、云. In order to quickly engrave these ten graphs in our memory, we fashioned their corresponding characters into a phrase: 五山委走月，人水水手云, which literally means, "Five mountain committee walks moon, person water water hands cloud." After the young soldier left the detention chamber, I repeated those two phrases to myself, then turned to Hongmei and said, "Do you remember what graphs appeared under those busts?"

She replied, "I remember seven or eight of them. The front four are *five*, *mountain*, *committee*, and something else, and the rear four are *person*, *water, water*, and *hand*."

I asked her, "Do you know what that means?"

She replied, "If I knew, then we would be able to get down from these stools."

I began to ask myself, *What is the relationship between these ten graphs and Chairman Mao? And how does each graph indicate the correct orientation of the corresponding Mao bust?* We knew that every graph accomodated a different bust, but what was the relationship between the graphs themselves? We were absorbed in this game for a long time, trying to use this exercise to forget our hunger, thirst, and exhaustion, and also to endure the endless wait. We speculated that the graphs with a greater number of strokes might correspond to the taller busts, but we noticed that the bust placed over the 委 graph was in fact a half-body bust that was only as large as a fist. Then we speculated that maybe the graphs with fewer strokes corresponded to the larger busts, but then we noticed that a full-body Mao statue was sitting on a 云 graph that had only four stokes, while an average-size bust was sitting on a 人 graph that had only two strokes. We speculated that only the busts positioned on full characters were oriented toward the east, northeast, or southeast, but then we noticed a bust positioned on a graph that was also oriented toward the east. We speculated that all the busts positioned on graphs might be oriented toward the west, or toward the northwest or southwest, but then noticed that the bust positioned on the graph 氵 (meaning "water") was oriented due east. We speculated that the characters and graphs might combine to form a sentence, an aphorism, or a line from a poem, but for the life of us we couldn't figure out what "five mountain committee walks moon" or "person water water hands cloud" could possibly mean, though we did recognize that the "moon" at the end of the first line appeared to parallel the "cloud" at the end of the second line. We scoured our memories for all the poems we knew, reviewing the pitifully small number of old poems with the words "moon" and "cloud" that we could recite from memory, but none of them could be linked to the lines "Five mountain committee walks moon, person water water hands cloud." We knew all of Chairman Mao's poems by heart, but his poetry was always concerned with themes of humanity and heroism, and you definitely couldn't find one that rhapsodized about moons and clouds and the like. Therefore, we eventually found ourselves in a dead end. It was as though we had walked into a dark room and found the door locked behind us or as though we had entered a gully and found ourselves facing a sheer cliff. Accordingly, we had no choice but to turn around and go back.

"It seems we couldn't figure out the meaning of those graphs even if our lives depended on it." Upon saying this, Hongmei looked away from those four streams of Mao busts.

At this point I noticed that, once again, a sentry was walking back and forth in front of the window, which was now open. I saw the sunlight shining in through the window, like light from a spotlight. After a moment, I began to feel a faint warmth circulating through the room. Hongmei was standing there massaging her knees and calves, after which she began pounding the soles and heels of her feet. We had already been standing and squatting on those stools for an entire night and the better part of a day—at least fifteen hours in all—and if Secretary Guan didn't send someone to talk to us soon, we'd have to remain on those stools for another day and night. It seemed certain that the task of making it through that next day and night, through a combination of standing and squatting, would become our most hated enemy. Needless to say, in the end, we would be defeated generals in this battle. However, we couldn't permit ourselves to say anything without first having a formal discussion—even if it were to take the form of an interrogation. We couldn't sell ourselves out before achieving our objective. We had to talk to Party secretary Guan from the prefectural Party committee. After all, we were Red successors who had been recognized by Secretary Guan, and therefore, perhaps, in recognition of our revolutionary feats and achievements, Secretary Guan could erase our crimes with a mark of his pen. At the very least, Secretary Guan was a high official, and therefore might be able to be lenient toward us. When Director Liu left us, didn't he say, "If someone who has killed more than a dozen people can still become an official, then what is so extraordinary about what the two of you have done?" If you want revolution, then you must sacrifice, and death will become something common. Secretary Guan must surely understand this revolutionary law and revolutionary logic. We surely just had to wait for him to arrive, or at the very least wait for him to send someone to see us. Meanwhile, at the present moment, the most pressing thing was that we had to find some way of passing the time while remaining on those twelve-by-twenty-centimeter stool seats, and we somehow had to find a way to forget our hunger and thirst, our sore backs and weak legs, and our aching tendons and numb feet. At the same time, we absolutely couldn't fall off the stools and thus step on the Chairman Mao poster.

Hongmei said, "Aijun, will someone come to arraign us today?"

I replied, "Irrespective of whether or not we are arraigned today, we absolutely mustn't fall off these stools."

Hongmei said, "Aijun, I'm afraid I won't be able to make it to nightfall. I'm afraid I'll fall off the stool and step on the Chairman Mao poster. My feet and ankles are already so swollen they feel like leavened dough."

I told Hongmei to roll up her pants legs, and sure enough her ankles were bright and shiny and as thick as her calves. She asked, "What should we do? Will we die here on these stools?" I said I would tell her a story, but she replied that she didn't want to listen. I said that there was someone who was very loyal to Chairman Mao, very loyal to the Party, and whose thought was even more enlightened than ours. When that person heard that tens of thousands of students could see Chairman Mao at Tiananmen Square, he asked himself why shouldn't he go as well? Therefore, he proceeded to sell all of his pigs and goats, as well as his household's grain and lumber, and then used the money to go to Beijing. He traveled by car and by train, and when he reached mountain regions that couldn't be traversed by vehicle, he instead proceeded on foot. He traveled from spring into summer and from summer into fall—until he finally reached the vast square in front of the gate tower in Beijing's Tiananmen Square. Can you guess what he said while standing there?

Hongmei simply looked at me.

I repeated, "Can you guess what he said?"

Hongmei said, "Did he shout, 'Long Live Chairman Mao'?"

I said, "No, he didn't."

Hongmei said, "Did he shout, 'Long Live the Communist Party'?"

I said, "No, that's not right either."

Hongmei said, "In the center of Tiananmen Square, there is the Monument to the People's Heroes. He must have gazed at that monument and composed a poem, such as:

After you become free, you mustn't forget the Communist
   Party,
And after you are liberated, you mustn't forget Chairman
   Mao.
When you drink water, you mustn't forget who dug the well,
and when you are happy you mustn't forget to plant a red flag.

Or something like that."

I said, "No, that's even less right."

Hongmei asked, "Then what did he say?"

I replied, "Guess again."

Hongmei said, "I really have no idea."

I said, "He walked around the square, and then he stood in the middle and exclaimed, 'Heavens, this is really huge! I can't even calculate how many *mu* it is. It doesn't have any trees and is immaculately clean. Why doesn't Chairman Mao issue a directive that all the country's grain be brought here to dry in the sun?'"

When I said this, Hongmei laughed. She laughed so hard she almost fell over, and had to hold the edge of her stool with both hands to steady herself. The sentry stationed outside heard her and peered in, tapping the window. But after he did so, Hongmei forgot about her swollen ankles and the fact that she hadn't slept all night. She even forgot that we were in a detention chamber inside a prison. Instead, she said, "Aijun, tell me another one." So, I proceeded to tell her three revolutionary jokes in a row. Afterward, she still wanted more, but I was completely out of stories. (I discovered I was a revolutionary, but not a revolutionary storyteller or comedian.) Therefore, we proceeded to engage in a game of exchanging poems. She would begin by offering a line and I would supply the next.

She said, "*My family lives in Anyuan at the head of the Ping River, and for three generations we have relied on coal mining to raise our horses and oxen.*"

344

I said, "*When I bow my head and think of the old society, I can't restrain my tears from flowing.*"

She exclaimed, "Good! *The moon shines on our path to battle, and the wind is refreshing. The air forces launch a surprise attack against Shajiabang.*"

I said, "*We sing as we march, the moon is dark and the winds are strong, but they are not able to suppress our happy heart, our strong will, or our fighting spirit.*"

She said, "That's merely average—it sounds like it was borrowed from some opera lyrics. Now, pay attention. I'll say a few words, and you must say a few words in response. They have to rhyme, match in both sound and sense, and they must be original."

I said, "OK."

She said, "*At the cock's crow, the land brightens.*"

I thought for a moment, then replied, "*With the cries of the oriole, praising the moon.*"

She thought for a moment, then said, "*On the broken bridge beyond the post station.*"

I thought for a moment, then said, "*Lonely flowers bloom brilliantly.*"

She thought for a moment, then said, "*The Red Army doesn't fear the travails of a Long March.*"

I laughed and said, "*Holding light ten thousand crags and torrents.*"

She said, "Don't laugh. Whoever laughs first loses. *Five Ridges' meandering peaks are but rippling waves.*"

I said, "*Mountains and hills like balls of mud.*"

She said, "That isn't a line of verse, but rather a mere jingle. *Warmth from Jinsha waters crashing onto cliffs.* Now you have to respond with a matching line from a seven-character regulated verse."

I pondered for a moment but didn't immediately respond.

She said, "Think carefully. Didn't you say that when you were in the army, you published poems in the *Liberation Army Daily*?"

I still didn't say anything.

She repeated, "*Warmth from Jinsha waters crashing onto cliffs.* You've been thinking for a long time."

Finally I said, "What did you just say? Was it *Five Ridges' meandering peaks are but rippling waves?*"

She said, "The previous line was *Five Ridges' meandering peaks are but rippling waves.* The current one is *Warmth from Jinsha waters crashing onto cliffs.*"

I suddenly had a flash of inspiration and heard a cracking sound inside my skull, as though a mountain were splitting in half. I suddenly grasped the connection between the two strings of graphs, 五、山、委、辶、月 and 人、氵、水、扌、云, on the one hand, and the two lines of verse, *Five Ridges' meandering peaks are but rippling waves* and *Warmth from Jinsha waters crashing onto cliffs*, on the other. As a result, I was able to figure out the corresponding pattern of the Mao busts on the floor. I suddenly grasped the golden key that would permit us to open the revolutionary eight-diagram configuration in front of us. It was in that instant that I realized that 五、山、委、辶、月 corresponded to the first five characters of the line *Five Ridges' meandering peaks are but rippling waves* (五岭逶迤腾), and that 人、氵、水、扌、云 corresponded to the first five characters of the line *Warmth from Jinsha waters crashing onto cliffs* (金沙水拍云). I turned to those four streams of Mao busts, and Hongmei said, "So you're unable to offer a response line to *Warmth from Jinsha waters crashing onto cliffs*, isn't that right?" I raised and lowered my hand, indicating for her to be silent and to squat down and examine that array of Mao busts, as I was doing. She realized I had figured out how to find a path through the busts, so she fixed her gaze on that array of snowman-like figures. I counted up the busts, and found that there were fifty-six in all, which corresponded exactly to the number of characters in a seven-character regulated verse poem. Meanwhile, each of the four rows had fourteen busts, which happened to be the number of characters in a single couplet. That is to say, the fourteen busts in the first row must correspond to the first two lines of Chairman Mao's poem "The Long March": *The Red Army doesn't fear the travails of a Long March / holding light ten thousand crags and torrents*. Similarly, the fourteen busts on the second row corresponded to the lines *Five Ridges' meandering peaks are but rippling waves / The magnificence of Wumeng Mountain is but balls of mud*. The third row of busts presumably corresponded to the poem's fifth and sixth lines, while the fourth row would correspond to the seventh and eighth lines. In order to confirm this hypothesis, I noticed a 又 graph partially visible beneath the seventh bust in the first row, and sure enough the seventh character in the first line of the poem, 难, has a 又 graph on the left-hand side. Similarly, a 口 graph was partially visible beneath the second bust in the fourth row, and sure enough the second character in the seventh line of the poem, 喜, contains a 口 graph on the bottom.

After verifying that the arrangement of the four rows of Mao busts followed that of the watermarks of the fifty-six characters in Chairman Mao's "The Long March," I figured out the correspondence between the orientation of each of the busts and the pronunciation of the corresponding character in the poem. In particular, I determined that characters pronounced with an even first tone corresponded to busts oriented toward the east, characters pronounced with a rising second tone corresponded to busts oriented toward the west, characters pronounced with a dipping third tone corresponded to busts oriented toward the south, and characters pronounced with a falling fourth tone corresponded to busts oriented toward the north. Next, I quietly recited the line *The Red Army doesn't fear the travails of a Long March*, and noted that the seven characters that made up the line were pronounced with a second tone, first tone, second tone, fourth tone, third tone, first tone, and second tone, respectively, indicating whether the corresponding Mao busts should be oriented toward the west, east, west, north, south, east, and west. Then I looked at the busts in the first row and saw that they were indeed oriented in this matter. I quietly recited the line *The three armies march on, each face glowing*, noting that the tones of each character were pronounced first tone, first tone, fourth tone, fourth tone, fourth tone, first tone, and second tone, respectively. I speculated that this indicated that the last seven busts should be oriented toward the east, east, north, north, north, east, and west, respectively, and when I checked to confirm, I saw that they were indeed oriented accordingly.

I had successfully cracked the revolutionary eight-diagram code!

Everything now was self-evident. I had once again proved that I was not only a revolutionary genius and a political genius, I was also a genius in military strategy, even a revolutionary seer. When I quietly explained this to Hongmei, she counted up the Mao busts on the ground, and considered the relationship between the graphs 五、山、委、辶、月 and the characters 五岭逶迤腾 from the first line of Mao's "The Long March." Then, after observing the orientations of several of the busts in the third and fourth rows, her eyes lit up—as though she were someone on death row who had just received an amnesty, someone dying of thirst who suddenly saw a rushing river, or someone buried underground for eight days who suddenly saw the morning sun. The light in the room had long since been turned off, and mixed in with the sunlight coming in through the window was the sound of cars driving back and forth. The sentry stationed in front of the door kept peeking in through the window, but it was unclear what he was looking at or what he was thinking. Last night the sulfurous odor from the brick kiln had disappeared, and now the only thing we could smell was the sun-baked odor from the fields and the humidity in the room. We were energized by our great discovery and stared at each other for a long while without saying a word. I saw that the bright red excitement on her face showed no sign of diminishing, and furthermore, this was an excitement I normally only observed when we were doing that thing—and even then, only when she was about to climax. Her bright red charm and grace, together with this great discovery, combined to heat up my frozen blood to the point that it seemed about to boil. It made it such that my hunger and thirst for her began to surge through my body like the Yellow River, with flowers bursting into bloom. I looked at the Mao quotations, slogans, and posters that were hung throughout the room, and felt as though those passages and posters were blocking my veins like dikes or gates. I remembered how the first time we saw each other, on the railroad tracks outside of town, she had a relaxed beauty and impetuousness. I remembered our crazy encounter in the tomb and the warmth and casualness of our countless rendezvous in the tunnel over the course of two years. In that instant, I resolved to escape from this prison—to escape with her. Even if it were only in order to go out into the fields, strip naked, and crazily do that thing one final time. Even if it were to do that thing just once more, I simply had to escape from this place.

At the thought of escaping, my palms became sweaty and my face felt as though it were being singed by fire. The sentry stationed outside the room peered in again, but when he saw we were still squatting there, he returned to his original position. I glanced at the window and then at the door. Then, I faced Hongmei and drew the characters for the word "escape" in the air. I had to write the characters five times in a row before Hongmei finally understood, but once she did she didn't appear surprised, and instead she simply stared at me with pursed lips, after which she similarly wrote the characters for "OK" in the air.

I nodded vigorously.

With pursed lips, she considered for a while, then nodded back to me even more vigorously.

(My flesh and soul, my spirit and marrow!) With Hongmei's nod, a great, adventurous, bizarre, unprecedented, and history-making plan was born.

349

Chapter 12

A Triumphant Return

1. With Frustrated Ambitions, We Vow to Never Give Up
We finally succeeded in escaping the detention chamber, and the prison too, through the "Long March" secret passage. The prison was located in a granary. We subsequently learned that during that period, there were as many political prisoners as horses and oxen, as a result of which all the prisons filled up, and the county had to look elsewhere for ideas on how to expand its prison capacity. Consequently, the county decided to transform a grain warehouse into a specialized prison for political detainees, and created this special detention chamber. On that day, we still hadn't eaten, and they still hadn't permitted us to drink any water (there wasn't a single grain of humanism to be found in inside this entire granary). We were cheered by our success in cracking the "Long March" code and energized by our plan to escape. With pounding hearts and valor surging like great rivers, we escaped from the eight-diagram configuration. When the sentry got down from his post to go eat, we squatted silently, without moving a muscle. We waited for the sentry to finish his dinner and connect the electricity in our detention chamber, which would turn on all the spotlights. The sentry shouted to us, "When you're ready to confess, let me know!" Then he got down from his sentry post.

We found ourselves caught within the enemy's strategic encirclement. We simply had to escape from this encirclement, and until we accomplished this objective there was nothing else to discuss. So we took action.

I climbed down from my stool and stood in front of the Mao busts, then picked up the first four busts and confirmed that beneath them were the characters and graphs 红、乌、金、更. Next, I helped Hongmei down from her stool, and we quickly hugged and kissed. We pushed aside all those different-size and differently oriented busts, and after walking through the path we had created, we made sure to reposition the busts according to the "Long March" code. In this way, we were able to make it to the door in no time.

We never expected we would be able to escape so easily, nor that the detention chamber's steel-plated door would be unlocked and fastened only with a latch. It turned out that the door to the so-called special detention chamber was still the same old warehouse door, and it even still had "WAREHOUSE 208" inscribed on the side. We didn't have time to look around or listen to the hubbub in the room across from us, where several soldiers were playing cards. After Hongmei used her long, slender fingers to unfasten the latch, we stepped out. The sentry stationed outside the main gate was in the process of asking another sentry to bring him a glass of water, but the other sentry told him to get his own water, since the platoon leader and company leader were both inside playing cards. Then the first sentry, still carrying his rifle, headed toward the room to the west of the iron gate (the moment that the enemy is paralyzed is when we can attack and secure victory). I quickly pulled Hongmei, who by this point was trembling from head to toe, out of the detention chamber and proceeded to relatch the door. We then snuck along the base of the wall until we reached the outer gate, then proceeded to crawl out though the fifteen-centimeter-high opening under the iron door.

This was the middle of the month in the lunar calendar, and the moon was extraordinarily beautiful. As soon as we crawled under the prison's iron gate and stood up, we felt the watery moonlight pouring onto our faces and bodies. Our eyes were so moist, it felt as though they were infected and stinging from medicine. We began to quickly back away, and the grass under our feet and the trees around us became a blur as we passed. Once we were certain the sentry could no longer hear our footsteps, we turned around and began sprinting toward a nearby hill, our bodies becoming covered in sweat, breathing heavily.

> (*The journey is urgent*
> *We whip our horse to urge it forward*
> *The moon and stars shine down on the ground*
> *Tomorrow the sun will be bright*
> *But tonight the night is dark and windy.*
>
> *We are surrounded by enemies*
> *Every bush and tree resembles a soldier*
> *The wind blows and cranes call out*
> *Heads may roll and blood may flow*
> *But we have no fear.*)

When we were halfway up the mountain, Hongmei simply couldn't go on, so we stopped to rest. We saw we were in the middle of a forest of scholar trees, and the trees' sharp, sweet smell assailed us from all directions. Bug-eaten leaves were fluttering in the moonlight, and when they fell to the ground they made a faint crackling and twittering sound. Through the canopy, we could see the full moon, as white as snow and as round as a dinner plate, and so bright that we could clearly make out the mountains, trees, and rivers, and see villagers, rabbits, and goats moving in the distance. It was extraordinarily quiet under the trees, so we could hear the rabbits, goats, and people. We could hear the crickets in the trees and insects fighting, as though the entire world was filled with their cries. We knew we were already safe. We glanced down at the prison located at the base of the mountain, and without taking the time to examine our entire surroundings, we looked at the route we had just taken up the mountain and saw that the crescent-shaped path following the banks of the dry river bed was unchanged from before. Seeing that there wasn't a trace of human presence on that path, we sighed and relaxed. We exchanged a celebratory look and fell into each other's arms. We hugged and began madly kissing and ravenously devouring each other. When my lips touched hers, I almost couldn't resist biting off her beautiful lower lip. As I was caressing her head, neck, and chest, she bit my shoulder through my shirt, which felt both unbearably painful yet also incomparably pleasurable. I truly wanted for her to bite off a piece of my flesh and consume it. It was as if we had escaped from the prison precisely in order to come to this forest, and as if we had come here precisely in order to caress each other. The ground was covered in ankle-high grass, together with dry branches and the remains of the previous year's fallen leaves. These leaves and branches had already fallen silent, having been buried by the early summer greenery, but because of our arrival they once again began to breathe and chatter. They began to enjoy a new youth and a new life, a new happiness and a new meaning. A well-known foreigner (whose name I can't recall at the moment) once made a great and wise observation, that the most precious thing is when someone, in their final moments, is able to look back at their life with no regrets. At that moment we were enacting this principle. I pressed Hongmei beneath me (or maybe it was that Hongmei climbed under me). The insects grew silent as they watched us, listened to us, and smelled us. They even came up to caress us. Feeling her desire, I brought my hands up under her clothes until they reached her breasts—those breasts, which seemed both familiar and mysterious, were now trembling and covered in warm sweat, as if they were anxious to escape from my grasp and enter my body through my hands. The moonlight shining down on our heads was cool and peaceful, and at that moment we forgot that we were no more than two *li* away from the prison. We forgot everything we had thought and said before leaving the prison, even the direction, path, and objective of our escape. We forgot that we were not merely revolutionaries and political figures but also brilliant strategists and seers. We forgot about the future and about fate, as well as the complicated nature of revolution and the tasks and objectives that were hanging over our heads. We forgot about the landlords, wealthy peasants, anti-revolutionaries, bad elements, and rightists within China, and about the imperialists, revisionists, and anti-revolutionaries outside of China. We forgot about the topography and geology of the nearby terrain, and we forgot about our enemies. We forgot about everything and were heedless of everything. Just moments after our escape from prison—right there under the moon, next to the prison, in the mountain forest—we did that great, glorious, and correct thing. Just three days earlier, we had taken advantage of the period when Tao'er was in school to get naked in Hongmei's house. Now, however, we felt as though it had already been more than three months since we had last done that thing. It was as if we hadn't seen each other for more than three years, and we immediately needed to do that thing. We didn't need revolutionary music, nor did we need to first strip naked and admire each other's bodies, and much less did I need for her to spank and pinch me, like a stepmother beating her child. Without unfastening our buttons and without even a word, we fell into each other's embrace and proceeded to passionately do that thing.

We did it in as short an amount of time as possible—shorter than half the length of a chopstick or the amount of time it takes a drop of water to fall down from the eaves of a house. After we finished, still without saying a word, we quickly straightened up, whereupon I impulsively grasped her hand, and we quickly headed along a shadowy path up the mountain. As we were doing that thing, we did not experience that soul-flying ecstasy that we had felt in the past, but nor did we experience the abrupt and sudden feeling of

354

regret and resentment. We felt as though it was precisely in order to do that thing that we had escaped from prison, and otherwise it would have been impossible for us to attain peace of mind and calmly consider revolution and fate, our circumstances and lives. After we finished doing that thing, we were finally able to calm down, as though we were able to drink water after feeling parched or able to rest after feeling exhausted. It was like a rainstorm after a prolonged drought, like a meal after enduring acute hunger, or like stepping into a cool, shady forest after enduring excruciating heat. Afterward, although we proceeded quickly up the mountain, we didn't feel the slightest sense of trepidation or fear. It was as though even if someone were to seize us and take us back, we wouldn't feel much regret.

We had already done that thing, we had already scaled the mountain.

On the mountaintop, everything was peaceful and covered in translucent moonlight. We emerged from the trees and stood on a stone-covered plateau. We sighed, then looked down the mountainside, and only then did we notice that there was a cluster of illuminated houses next to the prison. In the moonlight, those red-tile-roofed houses appeared brown, as though they were but piles of bricks nestled at the base of the mountain. Behind the houses, a faintly visible row of barbed wire along the top of the courtyard walls resembled a frame swaying back and forth. In the rearmost corner of that frame was a row of brick kilns protruding from the ground. It appeared that the first two kilns were in the process of being extinguished, and we could vaguely make out several figures— all convicts, of course—carrying buckets of water to the kilns. The plumes of milky-white smoke emerging from the tops of the kilns became dark green in the moonlight and then quickly dissolved. A couple of *li* beyond the kilns, a village was sleeping peacefully, as though someone had casually placed it in the middle of this forest. We were fortunate that we hadn't been thrown in with those convicts and forced to work the kilns. We were, after all, revolutionaries.

We were revolutionaries who had successfully brought revolution to rural China and had transformed Chenggang from a backwater feudal village into a new, red revolutionary base. Our revolutionary experience had been disseminated to the entire county or district more than a dozen times, and provincial-level officials had added handwritten "editorial notes" to our experiential documents. Chenggang is, after all, a revolutionary pearl and a beacon of China's northern countryside, and we are a rare pair of rural revolutionary geniuses. They shouldn't treat us as ordinary criminals and force us to work the kilns. Perhaps one day they might rejoice that they didn't treat us fascistically while we were in prison, and regret that they refused to bring us food and water. We had almost been promoted to the positions of county head and director of the women's federation, and if I had indeed become county head, I could have determined who would be sent to this prison. At that point, the strength of the dictatorship of the proletariat would have been under my command, but in the end, under a bizarre set of circumstances, we ended up entering that same prison ourselves. Does the fact that we were sent to the prison mean that I'll never have a chance to become county head? Or that Hongmei will never be able to assume the lead position at the women's federation?

Current affairs are inherently unpredictable, and it is impossible to foresee the future. In the long river of China's revolutionary history, how many of our predecessors had been sent to prison? Isn't their greatness *precisely because* they spent time in prison? Li Dazhao, Qu Qiubai, together with General Ye Ting (the doors through which people walk in may be closed, though the holes through which dogs crawl out are often open)—their personal histories appeared even brighter and more glorious precisely because they had been sent to prison. It was because they had gone from the revolution to prison, and then from prison back to the revolution, that they were subsequently able to become military and national leaders and serve as exemplary revolutionary models for their successors. Without the experience of being sent to prison during the revolutionary flood, would they have had the positions that they enjoy today?

We weren't upset that we had had to spend an entire day and night in prison, nor were we angry at having had to endure observation, hunger, and thirst in that special detention chamber saturated with revolutionary brilliance. Perhaps this episode might obtain new meaning during our future struggles to compensate for whatever losses it had brought. Surely our situation would improve soon, when Secretary Guan would announce our appointments to county head and director of the women's federation. After our new appointments, would those people in the prison still dare to refuse us food and water? Would they still dare to arrange an eight-diagram configuration in the path leading to the doorway based on the poem "The Long March"? As the moon moved from the northern to the southern sky, the mountainside's stillness gradually swallowed up everything, reducing the distant wilderness to a dark mass. It became impossible to discern where exactly the irrigated fields ended or the knee-deep grassland began. We could vaguely make out wheat or grass swaying in the breeze, like the rising and falling seascape I had seen while in the army. At that point I was still grasping Hongmei's hand. Her face was as gray as rain or fog, and her fingers were icy cold. In the end, she was, after all, a female comrade and a revolutionary who suffered from a vulnerability of worrying about gains and losses. I thought that—as a man, as her political leader and her war companion, as a revolutionary with high ambitions, as her exemplary sweetheart and her revolutionary helmsman, and as a political figure with a broad vision—I should support Hongmei and make her realize that having been in prison was not a big deal and that having escaped from there was also nothing to be frightened about. I should convince her that this was just a joke that the revolution was playing on us, and in the end it was all merely a misunderstanding. I should try to convince her that it was as if, in the history of the revolution, the Party had committed a "leftist" or a rightist opportunistic error, but without this "leftist" or rightist opportunist error, would the Party have ended up as great and mature as it is today?

Similarly, if we didn't commit any errors and didn't take any wrong turns in our revolutionary careers, if the revolution never played a joke on us, and we never had any misunderstandings, could we ever become strong and mature? Could we ever accumulate a multitude of diverse revolutionary experiences? Could we, after being exhausted from performing our revolutionary duties, still make the thousands of people attending the meeting we convened burst into tears? Could we make them acknowledge that we are excellent politicians and leaders in rural revolutionary work? I had to console my Xia Hongmei; I had to educate and encourage her. She is my soul and my flesh, my body and my heart, my marrow and my spirit. I grasped her hand even more tightly, gripping her fingers and kneading them in my palms. I said, "What are you thinking?"

She said, "Nothing."

I said, "Have you ever seen the ocean?"

She said, "No."

I said, "Someday, I'll take you to Qingdao to see the ocean, and I'll take you to Beijing to see Tiananmen Square."

She gazed at my face and said, "Will that day ever come to pass?"

I looked her in the eye and said, "How could it not?"

She said, "Aijun, why did we run away? If we are caught, won't our punishment be doubled?"

I said, "Do you resent me on account of the fact that, when we just did that thing, it was too quick?"

She took her hand out of mine and said, "Did we escape from prison merely in order to do that thing?"

I said, "Of course not. We also need to return home and destroy Cheng Temple and the memorial arch, in order to complete the long-cherished revolutionary wish of our youth. You need to return home and confirm whether or not anyone discovered the tunnel opening.

Yes, this is how we deal with our mistakes and fight for leniency, and thereby give ourselves the opportunity to make a new contribution to the revolution. If the tunnel opening is still as tightly sealed as before, then Secretary Guan must have imprisoned us for other reasons, and we can use other methods and attitudes to deal with them."

Hongmei became anxious. She looked up at the sky to determine our location, then said, "Even if that is true, then why didn't we go directly? Why did we stop here to do that thing? What are we going to do if we are unable to make it back before the sun comes up?"

I said, "First, let me figure out where we are. Do you know whether we are east or west of the county seat? Do you know whether we should head north or south to return to Chenggang?" When I said this, her look of confusion and anxiety faded, whereupon I gazed out over the tops of the trees and saw that in the night sky, about ten or twenty *li* away, there was a faint light shining down on the earth, and halos periodically appearing in the sky. I said, "Does the county seat have any machinery plants or car repair plants?" Hongmei said, "Yes, and it also has a farm machinery factory, but all of these factories have stopped production." I said, "If there are people pursuing revolution, there will be people promoting production, but the more factories are closed down, the more people will engage in nighttime skirmishes. This is an immutable law of revolution and struggle. Needless to say, the county seat must be over there." Then I touched a tree to determine which was the smooth side facing the shade and which was the rough side facing the sun, and from this I was able to determine that we were directly north of the county seat and south of the prison. Chenggang, meanwhile, was also located between the prison and the county seat but slightly to the north. In this way, the prison, the county seat, and Chenggang formed an acute triangle, with Chenggang and the prison positioned at either end of the shortest leg of triangle. The geometry I learned in middle school was still imprinted in my brain, and I hadn't forgotten it while serving in the army. At that point we were on a mountaintop next to the prison, and were on the side closer to home. We could definitely make it to Chenggang and back that night, meaning that by dawn we could be back on our stools in the prison's detention chamber without anyone realizing we had left.

Cutting through brambles and thistles to escape from the enemy's
    prison,
and longing for Chenggang as we gaze into the distance.
This further stimulates our fighting spirit,
as the Party has entrusted us with limitless hope.
Relatives and comrades offer sincere words and earnest wishes
and repeatedly exhort us to push our limits.
A warm heart warms a person's chest.
We must remember to be both bold and cautious.
We must excel by relying on our bravery and resourcefulness.
With every word, the Party guarantees victory.
Mao Zedong Thought will shine forever,
brave, resourceful, and decisive.
We see the road, yet it is as if we were blind.
Despite the countless barriers on Tiger Mountain,
and despite the fact that the road at the base of the mountain seems
    endless.
In carrying out revolution and maintaining our lofty ideals, we will
    have the morning sun in our hearts.
In traversing an immense forest and crossing a snow-covered
    plain, it is necessary to maintain a noble spirit and boundless
    enthusiasm,
expressing one's passion and ideals when facing a mountain chain,
welcoming the spring to change the world,
welcoming the dawn to illuminate the cosmos,
welcoming the nuptial chamber's flowers and candles to reflect life,
welcoming new prospects and new developments,

and writing history in warm blood.
If our aspirations are unrealized, we vow never to stop
and instead will wait for the day when we can celebrate together
and watch as red banners are unfurled around the world.

I said, "Hongmei, let's head northeast."

She asked, "Are you sure this is the right direction?"

I replied, "Yes, I'm sure."

I took her hand and proceeded northeast along a moonlit path, leaving the prison, the forest, and the county seat behind us.

Without straying from our intended route, we crossed over a mountain ridge, then continued along the moonlit path to the road to Chenggang. When we reached the main road, we hailed down a tractor hauling coal and rode it for more than ten *li*. We explained to the driver that we were a married couple who worked in a factory in the county seat, but because my mother-in-law had fallen ill, we had been forced to hurry home without even eating dinner first. The driver was in his forties and was very moved by our story. Not only did he invite us to ride his tractor, he even invited us to eat his rations. He said, "In this day and age, it wouldn't be unusual for someone to travel more than ten *li* through the night to see his own mother, but for a son-in-law to leave home without even eating and travel through the night to see his mother-in-law is, indeed, quite rare. The two of you should help yourselves to my food."

Class feeling and brotherly love are very moving; sisterly love and class feeling can also be heartrending. We offered the driver our heartfelt thanks as we ate the three steamed buns that he had in his pouch. (One day, when I am appointed county head, I'll definitely make sure that this driver is appointed to serve as director or deputy director of a machinery factory. I committed his name to memory: his name was Liu Hongli, and he was a member of the Liulin production brigade of the Kunei commune; he had a primary-school education and was a poor peasant.) Because we were able to hitch a ride for more than ten *li*, we managed to make it back to Chenggang in good time. By this point it was the middle of the night, and Hongmei and I stood in front of the Cheng Brothers memorial arch, gazing out at the sleeping town. We saw the trees and electrical poles lining Front Cheng Street and the dung pits and piles of manure in front of each house. We saw the old millstone in the middle of the street, as well as the second production team's oxen and haystacks. The moonlight was as clear as water and was equally distributed to each house in the village, to every centimeter of ground, and to every object. The field behind us was full of the sharp, sweet smell of ripe wheat, which wafted over and made us feel a vast sense of sorrow for our revolutionary setbacks. We knew we couldn't stay here for very long, since we had to be back in the prison before dawn so that we could return to our stools in the detention chamber without anyone noticing. We hoped that if we could make it back early enough, the sentry might be asleep, or perhaps the predawn chill might have made him return to his room, thereby permitting us to crawl back in under the iron door unseen. The revolution has not yet succeeded, and comrades therefore need to continue to struggle. For us, this little time was like finding a handful of wheat when facing an interminable famine, and if we didn't seize our chance immediately, the consequences would be unthinkable. Hongmei and I stood beneath the memorial arch for a few seconds—just a few seconds—whereupon I proceeded to pee on one of the arch's support columns, and Hongmei went over and squatted down and peed on the other column. When she returned, we separated.

She said, "Where should I go to find you?"

I said, "You should be careful when you arrive at your house. If Tao'er and her aunt are there, you mustn't disturb them (when Hongmei initially left home, she had entrusted Tao'er to the girl's aunt). And when you get back, just go to the base of the Cheng Temple courtyard wall. If you don't see me, then clap three times."

She said, "Aren't you going home to see your mother and children?"

I said, "There isn't time. At most you should peek at Tao'er through the window, but you absolutely mustn't wake her up. Also, remember to bring me some matches." Hongmei then walked toward that tall tile-roofed house on Front Cheng Street.

2. Bombarding the Headquarters

From the memorial arch, I turned into Center Cheng Street and then proceeded straight to the production brigade office. My revolutionary footsteps startled some dogs, who barked a few times, after which everything fell silent again. The village streets were completely empty, and you could even hear the moonlight as it swept over the village streets. I went to the entranceway of the production brigade office and opened both the production brigade's main door and the door to the warehouse next to one of the production brigade's bathrooms. This warehouse had two hundred kilos of explosives and detonators, which the county used for irrigation projects and for digging ditches and canals. I took thirty half-kilo packets of gunpowder wrapped in oilpaper, together with three detonators, two blasting fuses, and a new pair of scissors. Then I relatched the warehouse door and the main door to the production brigade office and strode up to Cheng Temple. (The revolutionary cause has no choice but to use violence to expand its base, liberate China, and emancipate the entire human race.) The musky smell of gunpowder seeped into my nostrils, filling me with revolutionary fighting spirit. My heart was pounding, and my palms were drenched in sweat. In order to calm myself down, I wanted to sing the line *Through the forest and over the snowy plain, I maintain an enthusiastic spirit*, from *Taking Tiger Mountain by Strategy*, or Zhao Yonggang's verse from *Fighting in the Plains*:

For the past few days, the Japanese invaders and I have been circling
  around the plains
and upon being transferred to the stronghold, I felt like a fish enter-
  ing the sea
The Japanese, Wang Jingwei, and Chiang Kai-shek colluded and
  were wildly arrogant
The villagers were traumatized by fires and flooding
I could hear my family sleeping peacefully inside
I yearned to see them but was afraid I might wake up my aunt
at that instant, the People's safety and well-being were of my great-
  est concern
to the point that I was unaware of the thunderclouds passing over
  the star-filled sky.

As I was recalling this verse, I felt as though it had been composed just for me, and if I slightly modified the lyrics they would express perfectly what was on my mind:

For the past several days, my enemies and I have been circling around
  the mountain range
I transferred to Chenggang, like a fish entering the sea
The insidious enemy is still wildly arrogant
Causing me to suffer trauma and false charges
I heard my relatives in the village sleeping soundly
I yearned to see them—I yearned to see them but was afraid I might
  wake up my mother and son
at that instant, the People's safety and well-being were of my great-
  est concern
but all I saw was the moon-filled sky over my head.

As I headed to Cheng Temple, I wanted to sing out loud but didn't dare to, so instead I thought about how I would alter the lyrics of the song. When I began thinking about these lyrics, however, my mind kept going in different directions, and when I finally came up with the line *I transferred to Chenggang, like a fish entering the sea*, my pounding heart came to a halt on the words I wanted to change, and my turbulent emotions slowly began to calm down. It came as a surprise that these lines could calm down even someone whose jacket was stuffed with explosives, and I was therefore grateful to the literary warriors who penned them. I wanted to salute them, and I thought how wonderful it would be if only they could see how calmly I was carrying the explosives to the temple, and how excellent it would be if they could watch with their own eyes as I demolished Cheng Temple. That would surely be such a moving, spectacular climax to the play.

The process of planting explosives, installing detonators, and connecting the fuses was all very simple for an exemplary military engineer like myself. I was able to complete all of these tasks in under an hour. I installed explosives and detonators in the rear wall of Cheng Temple, and in the corners of all the other walls. I inserted a double-packet of gunpowder in each corner, then placed single packets at several points along each courtyard wall. Then I stuffed the remaining explosives and detonators into my shirt and climbed from a scholar tree over onto the inner courtyard wall and back down a cypress tree. I proceeded toward the Spring Breeze Arbor and Standing Snow Pavilion in the temple's front courtyard and installed explosives under the pillars there. Several minutes later, I headed to the center courtyard's Taoist Hall, and placed explosives below the front pillars and under the rear walls of the Gentle Wind and Sweet Rain Room and the Scorching Sun and Autumn Frost Room. As I was placing explosives under the pillars of the temple's main audience hall, a mouse ran out from under one of the walls and stepped on one of the detonators I had left there. My heart began pounding like a grenade, and sweat poured down my face. Upon determining that this was a false alarm, I nonetheless placed an explosive in the mouse hole as well. At this point, it was extremely quiet in the temple. The white moonlight was fluttering back and forth, the shadows of the trees were dancing in the breeze, and everything felt mysterious. In Cheng Temple, I placed a total of twenty-eight explosives in twenty-two different locations, and as I was putting the last few explosives and detonators back in my pocket, it occurred to me that Hongmei should have returned by now. By that point she had been gone for longer than it takes a fuse wire to burn, and if she didn't return soon it might undermine our plan. Carefully opening the doors to the center courtyard and the front courtyard, I walked out and saw her standing in the shadow of the temple.

I asked, "Why didn't you clap when you got back?"

"I heard you moving around inside," she replied, "so I decided to stand guard for you out here."

"What is the current situation?"

She bowed her head. In the moonlight, her face appeared deathly white.

"The situation remains as it was."

After saying this, she paused, then looked up at me, as if looking at someone who could make her cry her heart out and make her confess and beg for forgiveness. Softly, she said, "Aijun, the situation is just as you predicted. Tao'er is with her aunt, and when I returned home I first went to my room, and although the door was locked the window swung open when I pushed it. Startled, I reached in and unlocked the door, then entered. When I turned on the light, I saw that it looked as if someone had moved the blanket on the bed, and the pillows seemed to be out of place. The door to the bureau was open, and although all of my clothing was still there, the quilt that had been lying over the opening to the tunnel had been moved. I always made sure that the peony blossom on the quilt was oriented toward the bureau door, but this time it was oriented away from it."

Hongmei's tears once again began to pour out, and remorse was draped across her face like a gray cloth. Her regretful tears splashed loudly onto the floor. By this point, the moon had already descended to the southern end of the sky, and the stars had begun to fade. In one of the village's streets an old ox was lowing and chewing its cud. At that moment, seeing Hongmei's tear-soaked face, I could barely restrain myself from slapping and biting her. This was not only because she had inadvertently revealed our secret, but more importantly, it was because in only two or three days—or perhaps even in just a single day—they would have announced my appointment as county head and her appointment as director of the women's federation. But now all of our efforts had been for nothing. It was as if we had sweated blood to build a giant levee, only to have it collapse due to ant holes or mouse burrows. The current situation would not only make it impossible for me to be appointed county head and for Hongmei to be appointed director of the women's federation, but she and I would remain peasants, despite having devoted ourselves to the revolution for so many years! Our residency permits were still assigned to the village of Chenggang in the Balou Mountains. Upon my realizing that we were still peasants, my hands began to tremble, and a sharp, bitter odor mixed with the dark smell of brown sugar began to emanate from them. I knew that this odor was from the residual gunpowder stuck to my hands. When I smelled it, I belatedly realized that my hands were clenched into fists, and sweat mixed with gunpowder was seeping out through my fingers. I wiped my hands on my pants, then patted the detonators and packets of gunpowder I had left in my pockets. I looked up at the sky, where the morning star was already visible overhead, and there was also the red star that was always visible over the Balou Mountains in late summer. Distant and bright, it generated a gentle and beautiful light, like a lamp wrapped in blue silk cloth. Whenever this red star appeared, it indicated that the night was already more than half over. Hongmei wiped away her tears and pulled back the hair that had fallen over her ears and forehead, and sighed: "Aijun, if only I had sealed off the tunnel opening, like you did."

I replied, "Did you check under the quilt, to see whether anyone had moved the wooden planks at the base of the bureau?"

She said, "I did, but I couldn't remember how they had been arranged before."

I said, "Did you check to see whether Cheng Tianmin's prints were on the table or windowsill?"

She stared in surprise. "No, should I go back and check?"

I said, "It doesn't matter. He's a crafty old scoundrel, and he probably wiped away any prints before leaving."

She said, "Does that mean it was all for nothing that you and I participated in the revolution?"

Her question struck me like a wooden board. It stuck in my throat. I stared at her face and saw that she no longer seemed as grief-stricken as before, and instead showed a look of remorse that our pursuit of revolution had failed due to her carelessness. This expression made her face appear as milky white as the moon in the night sky. Her face dissolved into the moonlight, and if it hadn't been for her pink shirt and black hair, she might have become pure beautiful moonlight herself. The revolution didn't permit revolutionaries to simultaneously look forward and backward, nor did it permit its participants to become discouraged by setbacks. A valuable asset of the revolution lies in its ability to let people learn from their mistakes, which is why struggle and battle are the best medicine. I said, "I obviously cannot let our future plans, or the revolution itself, be ruined like this. Why do I want to demolish Cheng Temple and the memorial arch? This is not only my childhood ideal and long-cherished wish, it is also a key step in my efforts to carry out the revolution. It is my final gift to the revolution. Yes, it looks like your father-in-law sent us to prison and ruined our future appointments as county head and director of the women's federation. Do you think it would be sufficient for us to merely blow up Cheng Temple? Wouldn't that be going too easy on him?"

She said, "So, what do you propose we do?"

I said, "If others don't bother me, I won't bother them. However, if they do attack me, I'll definitely attack them. Do unto others as you'd have them do unto you. Didn't Cheng Tianmin report us as adulterers? Didn't he recommend that we be hacked to pieces? Well, it's true, we are adulterers, so let them try to come hack us to pieces. Let's place the final two packets of explosives under the memorial arch columns. We can then go back and enter through Cheng Temple's rear courtyard and do that thing right in front of Cheng Tianmin. Let's make him watch our adultery with his own eyes. Let's make him watch how I, Gao Aijun, love you, Xia Hongmei, and how you, Xia Hongmei, love me, Gao Aijun. Let's make him understand that we are not just a couple of revolutionaries, we are a revolutionary couple—a couple who will love each other until death parts us. Let's show him the true power and true love of two revolutionaries and make him appreciate how thoroughly we have committed ourselves. We'll make him understand that we are a couple of crazed revolutionaries. Let's make him regret he ever reported us. Let's make him regret it to his grave!"

Even as the first half of my statement was coming out as planned, the second half was already forcing itself though my clenched teeth, driven by sheer fury. I had assumed Hongmei wouldn't approve of my plan, given that she wasn't a through-and-through revolutionary like me, and furthermore, when we did that thing, she would be facing her own father-in-law—Cheng Qingdong's father. However, upon hearing my suggestion she didn't immediately express any opposition and instead merely gazed at me, as though trying to determine from my expression whether what I was proposing was a well-conceived plan or simply a blind expression of anger. After staring at my moonlit face for a few seconds, she said something that only the most extraordinary woman in the world could possibly say: "Aijun, given that we have already reached this point, we have no choice but to continue forward—for the sake of the revolution and for the sake of the struggle."

In this way, an earth-shattering plan was conceived and put into action. (In fact, we had to move quickly to implement *all* of our plans, for we might not have any other opportunity.) This is how things stood, with the revolutionaries wanting to be giants in action and not just in speech. For the revolution and for the struggle, we resolved to use our last weapon and do that earth-shaking thing right in front of Cheng Tianmin, after which we would demolish Cheng Temple and the memorial arch.

We quickly planted the remaining explosives under the arch.

We strode triumphantly out of the temple. I went first and Hongmei followed behind me, holding the remaining half roll of fuse wire. As we walked through the door of Cheng Temple, the severity and solemnity of the revolutionary struggle immediately enveloped us. We felt a sense of nervousness immediately preceding the arrival of this, our greatest moment. At the realization that we had seized victory from the jaws of defeat, our blood became like a gushing river, and our hearts began pounding like war drums. The dark and thick shadow of the cypress tree in the front courtyard resembled an enormous corpse. Hongmei closed the door behind me. The court-yard was full of a white, rotting odor that made me feel very anxious. When I remembered we were revolutionaries, however, my anxiety was transformed into energy and excitement, which simultaneously calmed and aroused me. We entered the middle courtyard, where the grape trellis enveloped us like a tent. Like white lime powder, moonlight streamed into the courtyard at the four corners, where there were openings in the vines. I saw the explosives I had placed under the Taoist Hall, and noticed that one end was visible. The fuse snaked along the base of the wall like a rope. I had carefully calcu-lated the length of those fuses and had planted the explosives so that they would proceed from the center courtyard to the front courtyard, and then from the inside of the temple to the outside, continuing on to the outer periphery of the rear courtyard's main hall, and finally reaching the base of the memorial arch's two columns. After all of these had exploded, and after the fuses of all thirty packets of gunpowder had been lit, there would still be almost a half meter of fuse left—and in the time it took for that remaining half meter of fuse to burn, Hongmei and I would be able to climb to the mountaintop, and from there watch the magnificent scene of an endless string of explosions. The only problem was that one detonator hadn't been placed deeply enough, so I wanted to go and bury it. After Hongmei closed the door to the center courtyard, and as we were heading toward the Taoist Hall, the door to the rear courtyard opened with a clatter.

"Who is it?"

Cheng Tianmin emerged wearing white undershorts and an unbuttoned white silk undershirt (it seems that before the founding of New China, landlords and rich peasants all wore this sort of silk). He stood in the doorway, and when he saw Hongmei, he quickly moved to button his shirt. He asked with alarm, "Is that you, Hongmei? Why are you here? And who is that with you?"

Hongmei stood frozen beneath the grape trellis, not daring to utter a word. Needless to say, we had to take action immediately, because if we waited for Cheng Tianmin to cry out and summon the other villagers, our success would once again turn to failure. I saw Hongmei turn around to look at me, whereupon I began walking toward Cheng Tianmin—Chenggang's decrepit former mayor and our enemy.

"This isn't your daughter-in-law, Xia Hongmei," I said coldly. "She is an exemplary revolutionary worker. She is a peasant revolutionary, politician, and leader. She is also my wife and dearest friend. Through thick and thin, she has been my comrade and my trusty battle companion." As I said this, I walked up to Cheng Tianmin. His face was hidden in the shadows from where the courtyard doorway blocked the moonlight. As a result, I couldn't see whether there was any change in his expression, and all I could see were his hands, which had been rushing to fasten his shirt buttons but were now frozen in place. At that moment, I leapt forward like an arrow and seized him in the crook of my arm. With my left hand I covered his mouth, muffling his cry.

To my surprise, I discovered that he was as light as a bundle of kindling. I hadn't expected that the techniques I had learned while in the army would come back so easily to my hands, legs, and feet. I felt as though I were grasping a bundle of cotton, and as I was pushing Cheng Tianmin toward the doorway of the rear courtyard's east lecture hall, Hongmei was still standing, stunned, under the center courtyard's grape trellis, the half roll of fuse wire at her feet.

I said, "Hongmei, quick, hand me the wire."

She continued standing there, motionless.

I shouted, "The struggle has reached a point of life and death. Why are you still staring into space?"

Roused by my shouts, Hongmei bent over and picked up the roll of wire, ran over and handed it to me, then immediately rushed to the west side of the Qixian Great Hall. In the blink of an eye, she retrieved a chair and a pillowcase from a room in the rear courtyard's west lecture hall and ran back. She placed the chair in the center of the rear courtyard, then handed me the pillowcase. She said, "Use this," then she retraced her steps to the same room in the west lecture hall. I had no idea what she planned to do. As I accepted the pillowcase, I smelled its dark odor of hair oil and realized that the room in the west lecture hall must be Cheng Tianmin's bedroom. I watched as she ran back into that room. Light from a lamp inside the room shone out through a window, creating a perfect square, as though the courtyard were a white wooden board.

I snapped my gaze back and quickly stuffed the pillowcase into Cheng Tianmin's mouth, then tied his hands to the back of the chair. I proceeded as smoothly and naturally as a mother nursing her child. Cheng Tianmin was over sixty, and although his mind was still functioning, his body was already feeble. At this age, he should have been taking care of himself, but instead he was determined to attack us and send us to prison. We therefore had no choice. Things had been determined by Cheng Tianmin's ideology and his class position. Consciousness is a product that develops from the material world until it reaches a certain level. It is a necessary result of the social struggle that has come before it. Cheng Tianmin's brain was an unteachable and unchangeable bourgeois headquarters that had been formed during his long-term engagement in social activities. This headquarters was now declaring war on us, envisioning a victory it had never anticipated. However, we wouldn't passively await our fate; instead, we had to make sure that Cheng Tianmin encountered failure and regret. I tied his hands, his torso, and his ankles to the chair.

The Cheng Brothers' prized student, the reactionary Song dynasty philosopher Zhu Xi, was the one who first developed and peddled the Cheng Brothers' putrid teachings. He wrote countless books and said countless things, but now everyone has forgotten all about them. However, there is one phrase we could never forget: *Do unto others as you would have them do unto you.* This is how we were taught, and this is also how we behaved. This is all that we could do. While the nature of a revolutionary dictatorship and an anti-revolutionary dictatorship are mutually opposed, the former nevertheless may still learn from the latter. This learning process is very tense, but if revolutionary people are unable to understand the anti-revolutionary class-based ruling method, they won't be able to hold onto power, and instead their power will be overturned by reactionary elements. These reactionary elements will first reestablish themselves in rural China, whereupon the revolutionaries will suffer disaster—this is a lesson that has been proven by historical experience. Today, in the rear courtyard of Cheng Temple, we will once again begin implementing this kind of learning. I don't know why, but when I was tying up Cheng Tianmin, he didn't move, resist, or struggle, though some sounds could still be heard from behind the pillowcase wedged in his throat. Perhaps he always knew this day would come. Perhaps at his age he knew that the more he resisted, the worse the result would be. Resist . . . be defeated . . . resist again . . . be defeated again. He knew he would be unable to escape the logic of this rule. He was someone who had been singing behind the scenes of the revolution his entire life. He may be good at conspiracy and intrigue, but once you ask him to fight us face-to-face, he'll find himself at a loss. This is the predicament in which many members of the landlord and feudal classes find themselves, and it is the condition that allows us to subjugate and destroy them. Cheng Tianmin was sitting in that chair with his hands bound but was neither struggling nor resisting. Instead, he was staring at me as though it were he who had tied me up and not the other way around. He was looking at me as though he were watching a performance, and his thin, sallow face appeared preternaturally calm in the moonlight. His eyes were neither warm nor fiery and revealed no hint of struggle or anger. Instead, they were wide open, and the whites of his eyes were unusually visible. The wrinkles in his forehead appeared particularly deep, and his neck was stretched long. What other changes were there in him? Oh, his white silk shirt had gotten tangled up in the fuse wire I had used to tie up his wrists, so it resembled an old dishrag. Also, one of his shoes had fallen off in the doorway to the third courtyard, and he resembled a revolutionary captive sitting there with one bare foot.

Cheng Tianmin, you never expected that this day would ever come, did you? You never expected that the revolution, in the end, would bring a dictatorship crashing down on your own head, did you? You never expected that we would use your own methods against you, did you? If others don't harass us, we won't harass them, but if others insist on harassing us, we will definitely harass them in return. I will harass you, attack you, and overthrow you even more aggressively than you would do to us. This is the law of struggle. This is the method of revolutionary struggle. This is the means of revolution. The enemies who took up arms have been killed, while those who didn't still survive and at some time may attack us even more mercilessly than before. We therefore have no choice and no alternative. Former mayor Cheng Tianmin, Uncle Cheng—you will sit there and watch as Hongmei and I do that thing in front of you! I want you to watch as your daughter-in-law and I produce clouds and rain right in front of your eyes! That way, you'll forever regret ever having gone to the county seat to report our adultery to Secretary Guan!

But why didn't Hongmei emerge from the west lecture hall?

I headed toward the west lecture hall, and when I entered that medium-size room, I saw that Hongmei was in the process of cutting up the blue mattress on Cheng Tianmin's bed. I asked what she was doing, and she replied, "Look!" She pointed to the half-open mattress and explained, "I originally came to get the bed, but when I pulled back the mattress, I noticed that it felt like there were manuscripts inside. So I sliced it open, and hidden inside this mattress I found all the works by Zhu Xi and the Cheng Brothers that had originally been stored in the manuscript depository upstairs." I smelled a warm, musty odor, as though someone had just cut up damp straw in the middle of winter. As I looked in the direction from which the odor was coming, I saw that Hongmei had already moved the bed next to the window, and inside the mattress was a pile of thread-bound books, each volume wrapped in plastic in order to prevent it from being damaged by sweat and humidity.

I lifted up the mattress and dumped out the books, as though dumping grain out of a cloth sack. Each of these long, narrow volumes was a lithograph copy of a book by the Cheng Brothers or Zhu Xi, printed in traditional characters to be read vertically, with blue cloth covers. The volumes that clattered onto the bed and the floor included copies of the Cheng Brothers' *Posthumous Works*, *Additional Works*, and *Collected Works*, as well as their commentaries on the *Book of Changes*. The volumes lay in a pile under the yellow light, as though they hadn't yet woken up. Some had fallen out of their plastic bags and had curled-up pages, as though they were blinking their hazy eyelids. Others remained in their bags, as though still in bed. They didn't realize that their owner had been tied up in the courtyard, and they didn't know that today, soon, they would die a natural death. I took all those books out of their plastic bags and discovered that in addition to the volumes mentioned above, there were also *Commentaries on the Classics* and *Pure Words*, as well as Cheng Yi's essays "Memorial to the Renzong Emperor," "A Letter of Resignation Submitted to the Faculty of the Xijing Imperial College," "Treatise on How Yanzi Is Able to Learn So Well," "A Letter to the Prime Minister on Behalf of My Father," and so forth. As for Cheng Hao, the elder brother, there were his essays "Memorial to the Palace Master," "In Response to a Letter from Zhang Hengqu," "Inscription for Yan Leting," and so forth. Some of those works consisted of a single volume, while others were multivolume sets, but every work remained absolutely pristine and bore no trace of having ever been opened. From the time I was small, I had heard that Cheng Tianmin could recite many of his ancestors' works by heart, and that when he was serving as the town's schoolmaster, before the founding of New China, he would spend all his time reading *The Cheng Brothers' Complete Works*. But if these volumes were completely untouched, then what had he been reading? I looked around and was surprised to note that Cheng Tianmin's room was as messy as any ordinary residence. Apart from the table and bed on this side of the room, behind me was a long narrow table with a bamboo water bottle, two rice bowls, and several pairs of chopsticks. Under the table there were pots and bowls, and next to them was a wooden crate. I opened the crate and found only clothing and bedding. I opened a drawer and saw writing brushes, fountain pens, and a bottle of blue ink, together with an old inkstone. I opened another drawer and found several copies of Chairman Mao's books, all neatly arranged, wrapped in red paper covers emblazoned with *Mao Zedong's Selected Works* in Liu Gongquan–style calligraphy. On top of that set of *Mao Zedong's Selected Works*, there were plastic-covered pocket editions of *Chairman Mao's Quotations, Chairman Mao's Poetry*, several Mao badges, and other items. This arrangement was no different from what you would expect to find in any other Chenggang household, the only difference being that some people might place Chairman Mao's books at the head of the bed, others might put them on the windowsill, and others might keep them on the table.

I closed the drawer.

After closing the drawer, I immediately opened it again. I felt that these copies of *Mao Zedong's Selected Works* were a little too long, and there was something odd about them. I opened one of them, and a column of traditional, small-block characters written in red ink suddenly erupted into my line of sight:

The path of the gentleman relies on sincerity, benevolence, and love.

I looked again at the other texts and saw that they were written in this same style of classical Chinese as that earlier volume. I immediately turned over the book's cover, and inside I found a second cover that read: *The Cheng Brothers' Complete Works.* I took those volumes titled *Mao Zedong's Selected Works* that were actually *The Cheng Brothers' Complete Works* and handed them to Hongmei, then shook the pillow at the head of the bed again. As I expected, several bundles of paper written in calligraphic brushstrokes fell out. This paper was horizontal double-line stationery, at the top of which appeared the words "Serve the People," but below consisted of Cheng Tianmin's writings from the past decade. Fuck his ancestors! I haven't yet written a book, yet he already has! Fuck his ancestors! If I can't destroy him, then who *can* I destroy? I picked up the first couple of pages of that bundle of stationery, and read several lines:

A New Understanding of Cheng Neo-Confucianism

1. The political implications of Cheng Neo-Confucianism in Song dynasty China
2. The political implications of Cheng-Zhu Neo-Confucianism in the dynasties following the Song dynasty

377

3. What should be the uses of Cheng Neo-Confucianism's new society?
4. What has been the influence of Cheng Neo-Confucianism in the Balou Mountains?

(Melody, Lotus Falls; backstage singing, with bamboo clappers.)

> *Heavens, heavens! My heavens, my heavens! Birds long to enter the earth, and mice long to ascend to heaven. Grass longs to become a rainbow and a tree that produces grain, while ants want to cross the sea and pose as heroes. Originally, a hen's former home was a phoenix nest, and those suffering from famine as well as those who have sufficient food need to establish a state and make a court.*

(A pale, thin man is pulled forward by several others, and made to kneel at the front of the stage.)

A (with surprise): *Quick, look, what is this?*

B (astonished): *Heavens! . . . This is a written record in anticipation of our future comeback!*

(Silence descends, and everyone stares at the old man, who is now standing, trembling, at the front of the stage.)

A (steps toward the front of the stage): *We have been liberated, New China has been founded, and the armed enemies have been driven out. However, as for the unarmed enemies, the hidden enemies (he looks at the old man), they haven't halted their dream of toppling the socialist fatherland, nor have they arrested their scheme to usurp the proletarian state. Although the trees are still, the wind has not diminished . . .*

C (takes the record of a future comeback, and sighs): *Had it not been for this record of a future comeback, how could I ever have believed that Old Wang, this seemingly honest peasant, is actually a special agent left behind by Chiang Kai-shek for the purpose of counterattacking the mainland?*

B (glares angrily at Old Wang, who is kneeling at the front of the stage, then pounds his knee with his fist): *Ha! . . . It was only yesterday that Old Wang said he had no more grain at home, and I myself delivered a sack of returned grain to his house.*

A: *That's fine—this way, you'll be even more able to wipe your eyes and see more clearly the face of the class enemy.* (He turns to face the others.) *Comrades, fellow villagers, now that this record of our future comeback has fallen into our hands, what do you think we should do with Old Wang?*

B (furiously): *Seize and flay him!*

C (grinding his teeth in anger and waving his hands): *Rip out his tendons!*

(Old Wang is so terrified his face is covered in sweat.)

D (with clenched jaw): *Chop off his head and display it on the village gate!*

E: *Douse him with gasoline and light him on fire!*

F: *Mount him on a torture rack!*

(In response to everyone's excitement and surprise, Old Wang's expression continually changes, until finally he falls unconscious on the stage.)

A (calls for a halt): *Now, now, we can't let ourselves be driven by our emotions. We have our democracy, and we have our laws. We have our dictatorship . . . Now, release Old Wang!*

(Everyone releases the trembling Old Wang. Applause.)

We dragged Cheng Tianmin's bed out to the center of the temple and placed it in front of him. Perhaps he didn't realize what we were going to do, didn't realize to what point the revolution had developed. He sat on the chair and watched as we went in and out of his room, his face completely expressionless—like a wooden board covered in dust that has been left under a bed for many years. The moon had never been as bright as it was that night, and we could even make out the various colors of the grass growing between the bricks in the temple floor. Occasionally a cloud, as white as silk, would float in front of the distant moon. The village remained as peaceful as before—without any footsteps, barking dogs, or crowing roosters. Periodically the crow in the front courtyard would caw, the sound of its cries falling from its nest, then fading away, eliciting responses from sleep-talking sparrows under the eaves of the third courtyard's Qixian Great Hall.

When we brought out the bed, we left behind the bedding and mattress and didn't even use Cheng Tianmin's sheets. Instead, we unrolled the bamboo mat that he had on his bed. Hongmei asked whether or not we should place a mattress on top. In response, I asked, didn't she think it would be dirty? She replied that Cheng Tianmin's younger sister had washed the mattress a few days earlier, when she returned to her mother's house. I replied that, even after it had been washed, the mattress had still been used by a class enemy. Hongmei replied that we couldn't use only the bamboo mat.

I said, "What if we pad the bed with the Cheng Brothers' books and Cheng Tianmin's own manuscript?"

Hongmei said, "That would work—let's send these Cheng clan bibles straight to hell."

We proceeded to place the Cheng Brothers' writings and several volumes of Zhu Xi's annotations on the bed's bamboo mat, as though they were piles of straw. As we were laying down those piles of volumes, Cheng Tianmin's eyes grew wide, and a thick, white gurgling sound began to emerge from his throat, as though at last he was trying to ask us what we were doing. Finally, when we brought out Cheng Tianmin's manuscript, the so-called *New Understanding of Cheng Neo-Confucianism*, ripped and crumpled it up, and placed it on the bed—it was only then that he seemed to realize what we were doing and began violently shaking his head and even moaning. When, in the moonlight, he was able to see that it was, in fact, his own manuscript that we were ripping up, he tried to stand up by placing the tips of his toes on the ground and lifting up the chair he was tied to. When the chair fell back to the ground, it made a loud clank, so that the courtyard's moonlight and starlight and the shadows from the buildings and the trees all began to tremble.

"Cheng Tianmin!" I hollered at him. "Don't you dare try to move! Did you think that, by writing this sort of old-style book, you'd be able to alter the heavens? Did you think you'd be able to overthrow the socialist regime and the dictatorship of the proletariat?" While saying this, I continued tossing his ripped-up manuscript onto the bed, page by page, shred by shred, as if it were a blizzard of snowflakes falling to the ground.

Sure enough, Cheng Tianmin eventually stopped moving, and even the gurgling sound in his throat faded away. It was as if it was only after being jostled a bit that he remembered that he had been tied to a chair by the dictatorship of the proletariat, and it was only then that he realized that he was facing not only a pair of young, strong, and vigorous revolutionaries but also, more importantly, a whole camp of powerful revolutionaries—while he represented decadent, feudal capitalism.

We finished padding the bed with *The Cheng Brothers' Complete Works*. We ripped up the *New Understanding of Cheng Neo-Confucianism* manuscript and tossed the pieces into the air. The temple courtyard became filled with glittering stars, with fucking Cheng Neo-Confucianism floating in the air and a layer of snow on the ground. The bed of love became even more sacred. Cheng Tianmin, I want you to open your eyes wide and watch as Hongmei and I engage in conjugal bliss in front of you. We aren't afraid that you'll react violently or fiercely, nor are we frightened that you'll report us as adulterers or claim we aren't proper revolutionaries. Real revolution or fake revolution—history will decide. *Windy rain has sent spring away, and flying snow has welcomed it back. After the mountains are again covered in blooming flowers, she will be sitting there, laughing.*

Once the bed was padded, Hongmei took a step toward it, then looked at me—as though waiting for a command from me that would turn on all the world's lights. The moon was already in the southwestern part of the sky, and we seemed to have spent more time preparing the bed than we had anticipated. The shadow from the center courtyard wall was now longer and thicker than before, and it was only at this point that I had a chance to take a proper look at the rear library. The Qixian Great Hall was just as I remembered it from my youth—big and tall, with flying buttresses and hanging eaves, and in the moonlight it appeared more mysterious and majestic than ever. But on either side of this enclosure, which was more than two *mu* in size, there were two parallel sets of lecture halls. It is said that, back in the old days, this is where the Cheng Brothers' students came to attend classes and do their work, and later this was where descendants of the Cheng School gathered to drink tea and discuss the Tao. After the founding of New China, these lecture halls were no longer of any use, apart from being filled with emptiness and the dust of history, and therefore it was here that followers of the Cheng Brothers would gather to conduct observations and research, discuss the past and present, and indulge in endless talk. This was where, with their red mouths and white teeth, they set about confusing the masses and making preparations for restoring feudal dynastic rule. Currently, this whole place—including the Qixian Great Hall and the four lecture halls; the yellow tiles, aeolian bells, and the dragon and phoenix carvings on the roof; together with the grass and vegetation in the courtyard and the brick-laid ground beneath the bed—knew that it was fated to die a natural death, because the revolution wouldn't permit such things to continue hiding out, enjoying a leisurely and carefree life while waiting for an opportunity to counterattack. The place remained silent—even the wind chimes hanging from the four upturned corners of the main audience hall.

It seemed that Cheng Tianmin still didn't fully understand why we had brought out his bed, nor why we had padded it with pages from *The Cheng Brothers' Complete Works* and from his own manuscript. Even if he were facing death, he still wouldn't have been able to really believe that Hongmei and I were about to do that thing right in front of him—the same way that capitalists, even as they were about to disappear from this world, still couldn't believe that socialism could have the power to set a prairie ablaze with a single spark. The truth has this sort of unbelievable power, and the more you attack it, the more your attacks empower it. The source of truth's power lies precisely in the people, events, and things that attack it. Cheng Tianmin would never understand this, because he is one who attacks truth. He has never understood politics, society, or humanity. A thick, moldy smell was rising up from the bed in front of Cheng Tianmin, since the bamboo mat had not been washed for years. As the smell was spreading, Hongmei's nose jerked up. Gazing at the moon and stars in the sky, she said, "Aijun, put down a sheet." I also looked up at the sky and said, "There's no need. We're going to carry out a revolution, so we should let these decayed things be directly targeted and destroyed by our attack."

"It's getting late." She looked at me hesitantly, then glanced down at Cheng Tianmin. As if begging me, she added, "You should get undressed first."

I knew that at this point her feminine modesty was presenting itself. She had apparently forgotten that we were engaged in a struggle and that our every word and action was made in response to the enemy's attacks—everything was undertaken for the sake of the revolution's smooth deployment and to ensure revolutionary achievements.

I began to unfasten my buttons.

I said, "Are you also going to strip?"

She began removing her clothes, fumbling about as though she were harvesting wheat.

As we were stripping, Cheng Tianmin finally realized what we were about to do. As he rocked his body back and forth, such that his chair began banging on the floor, I finished removing my clothes and hung them on the end of the bed. Hongmei stood naked next to the end of the bed that was farthest from Cheng Tianmin, and with her bare foot she stepped on a page from the *New Understanding of Cheng Neo-Confucianism* manuscript that had fallen to the floor. Although she had endured a hellish assault in prison, her body was nevertheless as bright and translucent as ever, and her skin still as soft and white as the moon overhead. After her whiteness, her softness, and her nakedness caused a strange, coarse, delayed but prolonged cry to erupt from Cheng Tianmin's throat, he abruptly fell silent again, and his chair stopped moving. It was as if, after issuing a curse, he was able to begin to calm down again and swallow his fury. Even as he was calming down, however, his face remained green, and the veins in his neck continued throbbing. As he stared at Hongmei, his eyes opened so wide it looked as if his eyeballs were about to fall out.

His fury, it seemed, had reached its apex.

I shouldered a bag full of bullets and bravely went to the front. I stepped over hand grenades, and wanted to exterminate that Nationalist bandit gang. I pulled my bayonet out of its sheath as it gleamed in the light. However . . . however, just at that moment, just as Hongmei was removing her final items of clothing, I discovered that despite being filled with revolutionary passion and desire for revenge, my body seemed to have no drive or energy to do that thing. I knew that my embarrassing hang-up had returned. That damned thing was now hanging between my thighs like a soundly sleeping bird. I noticed this just as I was about to remove my underwear, and realized that I had been thinking too much about revolution and Cheng Temple and not enough about Hongmei.

Hongmei noticed that my hands were hanging motionless next to my hips, and she immediately realized what had happened. A look of dismay and embarrassment flashed across her face as she sat down on the edge of the bed, with her back to her father-in-law. (My soul and my flesh, my spirit and my marrow!) She sat on the edge of the bed, then abruptly stood up again and proceeded to pull down my underwear and then, like a lightning bolt, slap my member twice.

384

Those slaps were bright and clear—like snowy chunks of ice flying toward the temple from all directions, sounding like shattered glass striking the moonlight or a wooden club striking the walls. I cried out in surprise and took a step backward, and before I realized what was happening, Hongmei lunged toward me and, half-squatting and half-kneeling, repeatedly slapped and tugged at my member. She hit and tugged, pinched and gouged, while cursing, "I want you to report us! I want you to report us! You reported us as adulterous anti-revolutionaries, yet you are the true anti-revolutionary! The true vicious and sinister executioner! The conspirator who can kill without blinking an eye!" At that moment, a fiery pain and a boiling bulge appeared between my legs. My member became engorged like leavened dough, as all the blood in my body surged screaming in that direction.

In that moment of agony, my member grew hard.

I immediately embraced Hongmei on the bed.

As I was embracing her, Hongmei continued mumbling, "I told you to report us! I told you to report us! You yourself are a counterrevolutionary, yet you reported *us* as counterrevolutionaries!"

The divinely stimulating moment had finally arrived.

The moonlight was still, the stars were flickering, the trees stood tall, the great hall bowed its head, the wind chimes fell quiet, the cypresses bent over, the grapes stared intently, the courtyard walls puffed out their chests, the roof tiles stretched out their arms, the shadows stopped moving, the village grew quiet, the mountains stopped breathing, the oxen stretched out their necks, the birds opened their eyes wide, mosquitoes halted in midflight, and the air itself stopped moving. As I was about to enter Hongmei, her body began trembling like it used to, and under her breath she emitted a fiery-red scream. It was as if this was the first time in her life she was doing this. I knew her scream was partially an irrepressible expression of pleasure, and partially it was also for her father-in-law's benefit.

Her fiery-red scream energized me and, oblivious to everything around me, I proceeded to do that thing. I didn't look at Cheng Tianmin. I once again heard him muttering and grinding his teeth, and I noticed the thumping sound of the chair legs against the brick floor as he attempted to turn away from us. But what was particularly energizing was not the sounds that Cheng Tianmin made but the woofing sound of the bed as I thrust up and down. This was the heartrending wailing of the pages and papers that were plastered beneath my and Hongmei's bodies. A milky-white pungent odor filled the air, bright drops of sweat flew in all directions, and the purplish-red smell of flesh enveloped us. The noise flew up and down, the moonlight was blue and white, and the stars were red and green. I stopped thinking about Cheng Temple and Cheng Tianmin and instead focused only on hardness and revolution. I thought about happiness and ecstasy. I thought about naked Hongmei and about how long I'd be able to maintain this hardness. When I started wondering how long I'd be able to maintain this hardness, I immediately began to fear the mountain would collapse and the earth would give way. At this moment, when I saw that the shadow of the wall projected from behind me was still in its original position, and that the edge of the bed's shadow was still positioned along the same line on the brick floor, I knew that my hardness would last only as long as half of an incense stick, or the time it took to inhale and exhale a lungful of cigarette smoke. In fact, I was afraid I wouldn't last even that long, and after ejaculating would collapse again. After all, in prison I had had to squat for an entire night and day, and it was only in the first half of that night that I had finally been able to eat half a dry bun. And that same night, Hongmei and I had already had to walk more than ten *li*. My entire body began to tense up, my throat became dry, my skin became covered in sweat, and I was afraid I couldn't hold out any longer. I knew that if I collapsed now, not only would it mean that I wouldn't finish doing that thing with Hongmei, it would also mean I would leave the revolution incomplete, running out of food and ammunition after initiating a counterattack—like stepping aside to let the enemy escape just after routing them.

I was afraid that after ejaculating I would immediately collapse. Yet I couldn't resist the seductive lure of ejaculation.

I began thrusting even more frantically.

Beneath me, Hongmei clearly felt something more intense. We were connected by heart and soul, and although technically we were not husband and wife, in reality we were even more than that. She knew me like the palm of her hand, and when she felt my movements begin to fade, she suddenly stopped screaming and instead grasped my shoulders with both hands and shouted, "Aijun, listen! You must listen!"

I shuddered in surprise. "What?"

She said, "I think I hear someone singing."

I again began to move.

She pounded my back with her fist. "Listen again! I think I hear the sound of 'Revolutionary Guards Raise Their Weapons' coming from the mountaintop."

I listened more carefully.

It seemed as though I could, in fact, hear a faint trace of music in the sound drifting down the mountain, and it seemed as though in that music I could hear the lyrics:

> Osmanthus fragrance in the ninth month
> Military songs all around
> The poor fighting for emancipation
> Workers and soldiers lifting their weapons.

Hongmei asked, "Do you hear it?" I nodded. Hongmei said, "Listen more carefully. The sound is getting louder, it's flowing like water." I leaned my hands on her breasts and lifted my ears into the air. But this time I didn't hear the sound of "Revolutionary Guards Raise Their Weapons" drifting down from the top of the Balou Mountains; rather now it was the faint sound of "March toward a New Victory" coming from the south. The source of that song seemed to be very far from us, perhaps 108,000 *li* away, and furthermore the loudspeakers playing the song didn't seem to have a good connection, and consequently the sound would start and stop intermittently. I wanted to continue listening, but the song suddenly changed to "Liuyang River," and now it was much louder. There was a woman with a voice like water flowing from a mountain spring, and it seemed as if she were singing while standing on the banks of the river to the south of Chenggang. It was as if the musical instruments—a *xianzi* fiddle and a *shengxiao* flute— were set up on that willow-covered embankment on the riverbank. Ordinarily, I liked the song "Liuyang River," and every time I heard it I would immediately think of a beautiful village girl walking down a path with a sickle and a bamboo basket, singing as she cut the grass, and finally, when her basket was full, and she was hot, she would strip and bathe naked in the river, splashing her fair skin with water. She sings, asking how many twists and turns there are along the Liuyang River? How many dozens of *li* is it to Xiangjiang River? What counties are located next to it? What kind of hero do we need to achieve liberation? At this point, that scene with the village girl once again appeared in my mind's eye. The girl was only seventeen or eighteen years old, and even after stripping naked and singing the first verse, she continued laughing and beckoning for me to come and join her. I had no choice but to go over to her, so I stepped into the water while keeping my gaze riveted on her nubile body. When I approached her, I reached out and very carefully caressed her purple, goose-bumped nipples, while at the same time joining her in song. What I sang was:

> Liuyang River passes through nine turns,
> after fifty li it reaches the Balou Mountains,
> at the base of the mountains there is the town of Chenggang,
> where there is a Gao Aijun,
> who leads the people to emancipation.

When the girl heard me, she leaned her head on my shoulder, caressed my chest, and sang an adaptation of the third verse of "Liuyang River":

> *Liuyang River passes through nine turns,*
> *After fifty li it reaches Chenggang,*
> *the river continues rushing forward,*
> *but it can't compete with the kindness*
> *with which Gao Aijun treats the People.*

I was utterly moved by her song and conquered by her smooth, tender, and fair body. In her singing I could hear the sound of running water following the summer and autumn heat, together with the tender green smell and milky fragrance of budding vegetation in early spring. She was young and didn't have a single wrinkle on her entire body. The tiny white hairs over her upper lip were covered in a soft glow—as though there were some steam suspended there, and it might condense into a water droplet and fall off at the slightest touch. And she also appeared mature, and when she sang or laughed her face became covered in autumn splendor. She had ample breasts and hips, a thin waist, and long legs, and when she stood in the water, she resembled a willow or poplar tree. Apart from these enchanting parts of her appearance, the most extraordinary aspect of her was the way in which she worshiped me, her loyalty to me and flattery of me. I kissed her hair, her lips, and the bridge of her nose, and I nibbled the tip of her tongue.

Hongmei said, "Aijun, what is the melody that the accordion is playing so vigorously?" I replied, "Don't you recognize it? That's 'The Guerilla March.'" Hongmei said, "Can you tell what the *erhu* fiddle over there is playing?" I replied, "Isn't that the melody from *Tunnel Warfare*, from when the Japanese devils enter the village?" Hongmei said, "And how about that one, coming from the southeast?" When I climbed onto her and angled my ear in that direction, I heard an *erhu* fiddle and a *shengxiao* flute, as well as a piano and a Western-style flute, playing a piece that combined local and foreign sounds, Chinese and Western elements. At times the piece sounded like a small creek, and at others it resembled a roaring river; at times it was as high as the mountains and the clouds, and at others it surged forth as fiercely as a flood. I asked, "What is this melody?" Hongmei replied, "It's a revolutionary march," and I said, "I've never heard this one." She said, "Your sweat is dripping onto me." I said, "What time is it? How is it that we haven't heard the cocks crow yet?" She said, "Tonight, after we do that thing, we might as well just die in bed." I said, "I feel like I'm about to collapse," to which she replied, "Why don't you lie beneath me for a while, so you can rest?"

I lay down beneath her, so that she was now liberated on top of me. When I lay down, I felt my sweat soaking the pages from *The Cheng Brothers' Complete Works* and Cheng Tianmin's *New Understanding of Cheng Neo-Confucianism* manuscript. Under my back, those pages resembled soggy tree leaves, as the stench of ink and the scent of Hongmei's body assaulted my nostrils. The moonlight was dim, and there were fewer stars overhead than before, and in the temple, the smell of predawn dew was growing stronger. We forgot about time, forgot about our surroundings, forgot about revolution and the world and even about our enemies and our struggle. We didn't hear cocks starting to crow and dogs starting to bark in the villages; we didn't notice that half the stars had faded and that the moonlight was now dimmer and moister. We didn't wonder whether Cheng Tianmin had been watching us this whole time, or whether he had instead ground his teeth and turned away. Was he still cursing us under his breath? Was the chair to which we had tied him still clattering about?

Songs flew through the air, and love covered the earth. The mattress squeaked, and the manuscript pages were soaked as if in mud. Hongmei lay on me. She sat on me. I entered her from the front. I entered her from the rear. I placed her feet so they were facing the sky, then stood in front of the bed. I had her lie facedown on the bed, with her butt in the air, then I stood behind her. I had her lie sideways, while I lay next to her. I had her bend her knee and place one leg beneath the other. Hongmei had me sit on the edge of the bed so that she could straddle my member. She had me lie supine on the edge of the bed while she stood at the base of the bed. She used her hands, she used her mouth, she used a combination of her hands, her mouth, and her body to pleasure me, and also had me use my hands, mouth, and body to pleasure her. We were indefatigable and insatiable. We racked our brains to come up with new positions, taking inspiration from around the world. We were like pigs and dogs; we were like chickens and phoenixes. We were as gentle as willow catkins and as crazy as wild beasts. Life is like water flowing east, and we saw death as a return to revolution. We were in fact pigs and dogs. But we weren't chickens, and how could we compare to phoenixes? We were more like a pair of donkeys, oxen, horses, or mules. Wolves are kinder, lions are more bashful, tigers are gentler, and jackals are softer than we were. We were completely naked and completely tireless. We had just begun and would never stop. Nudity is the best weapon for struggle, and so there was no need to cover up or be coy. For the sake of revolution, we could even let the enemy dump a toilet bowl over our head. Revolution is love, because both revolution and love originate from the same deep well. Women are lovely because of the revolution, and men are heroic because of the revolution. There is no weapon more powerful than nudity, and there is no revolution more glorious than a naked revolution. Pursue revolution and face the dark night; go to battle and greet the dawn. If you say we are pigs, then we are pigs; if you say we are dogs, then we are dogs. If you call us livestock, we'll just laugh at you, and if you say that we're not even worth being called livestock, we'll nod in agreement. No one is more broad-minded than a revolutionary, and there is nothing stronger than the will of a revolutionary. We pursued revolution and went to battle. Life goes on, and the battle persists. We hoisted standards on our shoulders and followed in the footsteps of heroes, as the perpetual revolution continued to advance. We bravely went to battle and never left the battlefield. We looked around, and saw storms everywhere. The prairie was ablaze, and workers and peasants were armed. We swore to bury all the world's reactionaries, and what illuminated us were the eternal rays of the red sun. The Big Dipper was visible in the sky, the bright moonlight shone on the ground; in the still night of the Balou Mountains, everyone was fast asleep; Chenggang sighed, and the memorial arch stared straight ahead; the explosives had already been planted; Cheng Temple was restless; when would dawn arrive?

As I gazed at Xia Hongmei, my passion surged, and I remembered my revolutionary sentiment and comradely love. Beyond the clouds, I could hear the sound of military songs, and in the night sky I could see revolutionary flags fluttering in the wind. The Balou Mountains were brilliantly illuminated, and the road was broad and majestic, as a love song opens a new chapter for humanity. Hongmei's pretty face and beautiful body made my pulse race, but more importantly, we cherished the same ideals and followed the same path, and we were both willing to lay down our lives for the sake of revolution. Time passed, and the moonlight gradually faded; the morning dew was falling and the dawn's rays rising. It seemed as though a song was returning from afar, and all we could hear was our heavy breathing.

Exhausted, we were down to our last gasp; depleted, we dashed forward a hundred meters to greet the dawn. Our bodies were soaked in sweat, as if we had just taken a bath, and even though our bones were weak and our muscles were sore, our final climax couldn't be stopped. Greeting the tide, panting crazily, standing at the front of the tide, with my chest toward the sun, I exerted all my strength. After all sorts of twists and turns, Hongmei was left injured or nearly dead. Looking up at the sky, she screamed in ecstasy, and when I heard this sound, my own attack call grew even louder. I originally thought I would gush out a second earlier, but Hongmei said that it would be best to come together. I replied that this time was most intoxicating and extraordinary, and that after this I would be happy to accept death. She said, we've done this thousands of times, but this is the first time we've had this kind of simultaneous climax, as though our bodies are entering the mist and our hearts are entering the clouds; we feel both drunk and divine, as our souls rise to heaven and our spirits spread in all directions. After making love tonight, the sweetness of life will be forever embedded in my heart, and this single encounter will supercede the hundreds of others that preceded it, just as these few seconds of extraordinary beauty appear to have lasted longer than centuries of ordinary life. After a night of clouds and mist, rain, dew, and fog, tomorrow morning we'll return to prison, and with a smile we'll face our warden. Even if we are sent to the execution ground, I'll still be grateful to the revolution for the opportunities it has provided. Love is as strong as a tree, and revolution produces fat, like affection produces fruit. Love is an eye, and revolution is a fishnet, and only by pulling the headrope can you open the mesh. Love grants our revolution endless strength, and makes our will stronger. Revolution makes us genuine and sincere, and our love will outlast the heavens and the earth. There is no spear, nor is there a shield; and if there is no headrope, what is the point of talking about opening the mesh? The moon derives its brightness from the sun, so what would be the point of the sun if there were no moon? The glory of the revolution will illuminate thousands of generations and will shine in all directions. After cleaning up the mess and getting out of bed, we notice that the temple is now incredibly still and shrouded in mist. As the moonlight shifts, the tree shadows shudder, and the dew dripping resonates throughout the newly awakened world, as the light begins to appear in the eastern horizon . . .

Ah . . .

Ah . . .

Aiya aiya aiya aiya . . .

Finally, finally, the final moment is like a rope tied around my hands and feet. Finally, finally, the final moment is like a bayonet that impales my heart.

Finally . . .

Finally . . .

Finally I turned and looked at Cheng Tianmin, and saw that he was still tied to the chair and the pillowcase was still stuffed in his mouth. But now the chair was turned with its back to us. This way, Cheng Tianmin could avoid seeing us. Eventually, however, he turned around and stared at the bed. His neck was as rigid as a green bamboo pole; his mouth was slightly open, even as his jaw remained firmly clenched. His eyes were opened wide and were staring so intently, without blinking, that two drops of dark blood had seeped out and pooled on either side of his nose, like ears of wheat hanging from a flagstaff.

Finally . . .

Finally . . .

Finally, we walked out of the temple courtyard, hand in hand. At that point—when most of the people in the Chenggang production brigade were still asleep, and those who had worked were still lazing about in bed—we lit all the detonation fuses.

An instant later, there was a deafening explosion, followed by a string of loud booms. Afterward, there was the sound of shattered bricks and tiles falling to the ground like rain. These sounds could be heard up to ten *li* away, and after they finally faded, Chenggang was engulfed in the sulfurous smell of explosives. The town fell silent, as though it wasn't merely Cheng Temple and the memorial arch that had been demolished but rather the entire world that had disappeared.

The revolution had already advanced to a new level. The revolution was now standing on the shore and gazing out to sea, where it could see the mast of a ship; it was a nearly mature fetus inside its mother's belly; it was standing on a mountain peak looking in the direction of the rising sun that was about to illuminate the entire land. The sun came up, appearing red and bloody, as though it too had been detonated by the explosives. By this point it was no longer possible for us to make it back to the prison before dawn. Moreover, after we returned, we planned to reveal everything to the Party and not keep anything a secret. We were determined to act like an honest couple of respectable, pure, moral individuals who had freed themselves from vulgar tastes. We were determined to act like a couple who would be useful to the People. So, why did we need to rush back?

Hand in hand, like a couple of newlyweds, we slowly walked through the beautiful dawn light, heading back to that prison on the outskirts of town.

Chapter 13

Coda

1. Coda (I)

We returned to the prison.

By the time we got back, it was already midday.

Shortly after noon, Secretary Guan sent someone to subject us to a round-the-clock interrogation, then quickly left the county seat. The reason he didn't speak to us was because the Central Committee of the Chinese Communist Party sent an urgent telegram to all the nation's cadres at the county level or above, reporting that the Chinese-Soviet border situation had become critical and that the enemy was deploying troops to our side of Zhenbao Island. Day and night, our leaders were sending aircraft, tanks, and artillery; they were deploying millions of tireless troops in anticipation of unifying the army and the nation; they were constantly defending against invasion; they were bringing together the nation's troops to build a great wall; and they were shattering the ambitions of Soviet revisionism. Apart from needing to attend a coordination meeting regarding civil air defense construction and a mobilization meeting for militia training, Secretary Guan also had to oversee numerous issues relating to the sending of local troops to relieve a garrison stationed at the border. Given that he needed to attend to these matters of national security, he naturally had no time to come speak to us in person, so instead he sent his trusted colleague, Director Zhao, from the district security office. He engaged us in a conversation that was as long as the distance from the Balou Mountains to Hainan Island.

We spoke for an entire day and an entire night.

Hongmei and I (but mainly it was me) reported to him for an entire day and night.

By the time we were finished, our mouths were dry and our lips were numb. We were utterly exhausted and wanted nothing more than to collapse and sleep for three days straight, or even for weeks. Throughout it all, Director Zhao remained as still as a clay sculpture, staring straight ahead as though watching an extraordinary play, listening to a heartrending song, or reading a heroic poem. At this point, light from a new day entered through the window of that detention chamber and fell on my face, my mouth, and my eyebrows.

A red sun rose in the east. We revolutionary youth didn't fear heaven or earth, and instead all we feared was that you might elevate everything to a level of ideological abstraction. As long as you don't elevate things, we'll still be able to hoist the red flag; we'll be able to sow the fields of Dazhai and brandish arms on Hutou Mountain. The revolution will continue moving forward, and the battle will continue to rage; for every square centimeter of land there will be a heart, and all of our hearts will be entrusted to the Party; we must hold our position without yielding, and attack without fear of death. If you insist on abstracting things, then the moon may rise but we won't be able to see the light, the stars in the sky will remain dark, and the sunrise in the eastern sky will be obscured by rain. Revolutionary love becomes bullshit; revolutionary enthusiasm becomes a pool of excrement; revolutionary spirit becomes evil qi; revolutionary blood becomes night soil; revolutionary drive becomes feces; and revolutionary awakening nothing more than intestines. It must be said that the revolution is following an anti-revolutionary path: its red fingernails have come to resemble a bad example, its straw sandals have become straw ash, its pants have become a disguise, its jacket is locked away in a chest, its cap has become a manure basket, its scarf has become shackles, and its face is oriented toward the west. The revolution is on its knees, the revolution has its back to the Party, the revolution's red heart is making tears flow, the revolution can't straighten its neck, the revolution's head has become a target, and dark blood trickles out of its heart. Heaven and earth, revolutionaries are holding guns up to the heads of other revolutionaries. They're not afraid of blood, and they're not afraid of work. All they fear is that no one will be carrying the red flag of revolution. Heads may roll and blood may flow, but we definitely must let the sun rise in the east and shine bright. When the clouds part at dawn, the sun will be there, and after sunset, over the western mountains the moon will appear. If we look up, we'll see the Big Dipper, and when we wake up, the east will be bright. We sacrifice without fear, as long as we can exchange it for the ability of people to live happily for thousands of years.

After our report concluded, Hongmei was in tears, and Director Zhao sat to one side silently reflecting. By the time we had finished speaking, I was distraught. Director Zhao reflected for a while, then said, "Hey, keep going."

"I've finished."

"You've told me everything?"

"Yes, everything."

"What time was it when you returned after blowing up Cheng Temple and the memorial arch?"

"It was already noon. Everyone was already scouring the area looking for us."

"What was your motivation in voluntarily returning to prison?"

"Revolutionaries are open and honest, generous and magnanimous. There is no need for them to pursue intrigue, resort to tricks, or go into hiding."

"Did you know that Cheng Tianmin died?"

"Rain falls from the sky and flows across the earth. That is the good ending that he deserved."

"Cheng Temple was destroyed to the point that not even a piece of tile remains, and Cheng Tianmin was buried beneath the rubble. Did you know that not even a shred of his flesh was to be found?"

"We didn't know, we didn't know. But so what?"

"Now that you do know, what is your response?"

"It's very fitting that he was buried under Cheng Temple's shattered bricks and tiles. That leaves behind revolutionary soil that will be good for sowing and transplanting seedlings."

"Gao Aijun, is there anything else you'd like to say?"

"No, I've already told you everything. I put my entire red heart on display for the Party."

"Think carefully. Are you sure there isn't anything else you want to say?"

"If I think of anything, I'll let you know. I wouldn't hide anything from the Party."

"And you, Xia Hongmei?"

"Aijun has already said everything I wanted to say. He has spoken for me, and his thoughts are the same as mine."

"Do you have any regrets about what you've done? Do you feel any sense of shame?"

"I've devoted my heart and soul to the revolution, and I love the Party with all my heart. My affection for Aijun is a revolutionary affection, and my love for Aijun is a revolutionary love. I don't regret the blood we've shed or the sacrifices we've made, nor am I heartbroken about the heads we've severed."

"Then . . . why is it that you can't stop crying?"

"I am crying because the revolutionary wave has crashed into the revolutionary skiff, and the revolutionary ax has smashed the revolutionary gun. When the enemies made us bleed, we smiled, so why should we be upset when revolutionaries send us to prison?

The happiest thing in the world would be to die by an enemy's gun, and the most sorrowful thing would be if one's own parents were to develop murderous tendencies toward their own children."

"OK, then, this conversation will conclude here. The two of you have been honest and have been loyal to the Party. You haven't concealed anything. I will give Secretary Guan a faithful report and recommend that he be lenient. I will endeavor to give you another opportunity to prove yourselves and to devote yourselves to the revolution."

"Thank you, Director Zhao. We will remember your affection, the Party's love, and the endless concern that the higher-level organization has expressed on our behalf. If, one day, we are able to dive back into the revolutionary current, we will cherish and treasure that opportunity even more. We are willing to die for our principles and to pursue revolution, and we are willing to let ourselves to be smashed to pieces in order to establish a new chapter."

"Then I'll go back, but before I leave I want to ask you one final question—which is also one of the key issues Secretary Guan sent me to discuss with you. I hope that you will answer me truthfully and fully."

"Director Zhao, please ask us whatever you want. We'll tell you everything we know. We are willing to put our heart and soul on display for the organization to see, and let Secretary Guan assess them."

"OK, then, I'll ask you: When Director Liu from the organizational bureau invited you to the county seat, wasn't there a period of time when the two of you were left alone in Secretary Guan's office?"

I said, "Yes, there was."

Director Zhao asked, "Wasn't it about thirty minutes?"

Hongmei said, "Yes, it was about half an hour."

Director Zhao asked, "During that half hour, what did you do? Did you see a photograph on Secretary Guan's desk? A photograph of a middle-aged female comrade dressed in a military uniform?"

I said, "Yes, we did."

Director Zhao stared at me and asked, "Where is that photograph now? Did you take it?"

I looked at Hongmei.

Hongmei said, "No, he didn't take it. Neither of us took it. He looked at the photograph, then handed it to me, and just as I was looking at it, Secretary Guan happened to walk in. The photograph had the sentence 'My beloved wife' written on it, and I was savoring that phrase. So, when Secretary Guan walked in, I became flustered and dropped the photograph."

Director Zhao asked, "Where did you drop it?"

Hongmei said, "It must have fallen between the couch's seat cushions."

Director Zhao said, "Think carefully. Are you sure it fell between the seat cushions?"

Hongmei reflected for a moment, then said, "Yes, it must have."

Director Zhao stood up and seemed to be about to leave.

"Do you know who the women in the photograph was?"

Hongmei and I shook our heads.

Director Zhao said, "You really don't know?"

I said, "I really don't."

Hongmei added, "She looked very familiar, but I couldn't place her."

Director Zhao said, "Given that we've already reached this point, I might as well tell you the truth. The woman in the photograph was our great leader Chairman Mao's wife and comrade-in-arms, Comrade Jiang Qing, but the phrase on the photograph was written by Secretary Guan. If we can find that photograph, your revolution will be preserved. But if we can't find it, and if some day it were to fall into someone else's hands, not only would Secretary Guan lose his position, he might even lose his life. If Secretary Guan loses his position and his life, do you think that the two of you can be permitted to live? At that point there would be no need to think any more about revolution."

With this, Director Zhao left. With lightning speed, he rushed off to look for the photograph.

We advanced further and further. We wanted revolution and longed for the struggle. The revolution is a ship, and we are its helmsmen; the revolution is a wheel, and we are its axle. The revolution is a harvest, and we are the soil. The revolution is the soil, and we are the golden harvest. The revolution is a battlefield, and we are warheads. The revolution is a tall mountain, and we are a mountainside performance. The revolution is flowing water, and we are water games. The revolution is a field, and we are horses and cattle. The revolution is the Gobi Desert, and we are an oasis. The revolution is an ocean, and we are a wave. Just as fish cannot survive without water, if we leave the revolution we will become reduced to rust. Just as horses cannot leave the fields, we cannot leave the revolution without losing our lives. Just as spring cannot exist without the sun, we cannot leave the rain and dew of the revolution. Revolution cannot proceed without flags and banners, and we are the banner bearers. Progress cannot be made without bugles, and we are the buglers. The train cannot advance without wheels, and we are its stainless steel axles. A ship cannot navigate without beacons, and we are a towering lighthouse. We long to pursue revolution. We want to raise the revolutionary banner and let the call to advance resonate over the enemies' hilltops. Life will not rest, the battle won't cease, running water will not stagnate, and rolling wheels won't rust.

2. Coda (II)

Photograph, photograph, photograph . . .

Photograph photograph photograph . . .

Photograph photograph photograph . . .

Photograph photograph photograph . . .

Oh, photograph! Photograph, I'll fuck your ancestors!

3. Coda (III)

We were honest and direct. We were revolutionary and noble. But they weren't at all magnanimous toward us. We originally assumed that, since we were a pair of revolutionary geniuses who had made an extraordinary contribution to the rural revolution, they would therefore release us in the name of the revolution and permit us to return to the revolutionary crucible. Instead, they threw us into a real prison. (Comrades who are afflicted with acute revolutionary illness cannot see the revolution's subjectivity, and instead focus on the potental power of anti-revolutionaries. The result will be a path of adventurism that will injure others, ourselves, and the revolution.) This is a lesson we learned through blood—a blood lesson. I was confined to a prison cell that was so small that apart from a bunk and a toilet, there was barely room for an ant. The room had thick brick walls and iron bars. At mealtimes food was passed in through an opening in the door, and if we needed anything we had to shout out through that same iron door. I spent eight months in that cell, or perhaps it was a year and eight months. I almost forgot the day, and even the season, when I was initially imprisoned, and I almost forgot Hongmei's expression and appearance when we were separated. Apart from the tormented time I spent reading Chairman Mao's collected works and the model operas stored at the head of my bed, in order to reform my thought, I spent the remainder of my time lying in bed and providing sustenance for lice and fleas. In the end, I almost forgot about heaven and earth, Soviet revisionism and American imperialism. I didn't know what month or year it was; I didn't know about the rapid change in the revolutionary situation, and I forgot how high the floodwaters of the revolution had reached. I realize that by the time waves hit the beach, they have already lost their power. The world was turned upside down, and the sun began to rise in the west. Every morning and evening you don't look up at the sky, and every evening and morning you don't look down at the earth. Instead, day after day, you just look forward to the possibility that someone might come to arraign you. You don't look forward to the earth or sky, or to the possibility that there might be some news from Hongmei.

I didn't have any news from Hongmei.

Every night, however, I was with Hongmei in my dreams.

Suddenly, one day, they began interrogating me nonstop. By this point they had already posted the announcements of my and Hongmei's scheduled execution along all of Chenggang's streets and alleys. Our names and photographs even appeared over the well platform on Front Cheng Street and the millstone on Center Cheng Street, with red Xs over our names. Behind the village were the ruins of Cheng Temple, where the original columns of the Qixian Great Hall and the manuscript depository building were still standing. Flyers announcing my and Hongmei's scheduled execution were posted on the columns and fluttered in the wind. Cheng Qinglin told me about this when he came to see me, and after he left they began to subject me to a nonstop interrogation.

They made me recount my story over and over, beginning with my transition from the army to Chenggang; from the first day of the rural revolution to the day I demolished Cheng Temple; from the deaths of Cheng Guizhi and Cheng Qingdong, to Cheng Tianqing's insanity and Cheng Tianmin's fate of being buried alive under the demolished temple. For the sake of those comrades sitting in the interrogation room listening to my stories, I maintained my loyalty to and faith in the organization. I didn't conceal anything, nor did I exaggerate anything. They said Hongmei and I were the most honest prisoners they had ever encountered (unfortunately, they didn't call us revolutionaries). They said that our accounts of our crimes (which is to say, our revolutionary activities) were identical, and the only discrepancy involved our discussions of our sexual relationship, in that Hongmei apparently used euphemistic language, while I was more direct (revolutionary affection, comradely love, the extraordinary splendor of a prairie set ablaze by a single spark, telling the

Party frankly, not concealing a single thing, the revolution will mend holes as large as the sky, and we'll correct errors as large as the earth, the revolutionary cauldron can smelt things that seem impossible to smelt, and revolutionary sentiment can embrace all kinds of love).

However, they still executed us.

On that day—an early spring day following a long winter—the entire world was brimming with the tender smell of budding vegetation. The execution site was on the banks of Thirteen Li River, two *li* from Chenggang. At that location, the riverbank was wide, the flowing water could be heard clearly, and there were large red and white egg-shaped stones everywhere. There were countless slogans everywhere, such as *Bring down the Gang of Four, the People must be liberated* and *Viciously criticize Gao Aijun's and Xia Hongmei's anti-revolutionary and adulterous murder, and stomp on their perpetually stained corpses.* (The desolate autumn wind has returned and has changed the world.) On the embankment, on the willows, the stones, and the columns supporting the stage that had been erected for the public trial—those hyperexcited slogans were like autumn leaves, and the black ink of those words was like summer rain. The trial stage was a meter and a half high and had been erected on the embankment. People had gathered beneath the stage, their heads resembling goat droppings covering a mountainside. People filled every road leading to this site like pigs, horses, or oxen that had been released from their enclosures. On the stage there was a solemn and respectful atmsophere, but below it was a giant hubbub. The crowds gathered included members of Chenggang's dozen or so production brigades, who had all come to watch the public hearing, and also outsiders who had come from all over for the spectacle. When the official used a megaphone to order me to be transported from a tent truck to the trial stage, I saw the people who had gathered below the stage were frothing like a river or ocean, as they shouted to one another, spittle flying in all directions. Their slogans collided in mid-air, as the tide ebbed and flowed, while on the ground voices jostled.

Those shouting slogans raised their fists, such that the arena came to resemble a forest of arms, and the chattering of those who had come to watch the excitement sounded like a wild animal caught in a torrential rainstorm. The people in front craned their necks to look up at the stage, while the ones in back stomped their feet and cursed the people in front of them. One person stepped on another person's foot, making him croak like a frog, while someone else bumped into another person's head, making him howl like a wolf. Feeling distressed and agitated, I searched the crowd for my mother; my son, Hongsheng; and my daughter, Honghua; and Hongmei's daughter, Tao'er, but in the seething mass I couldn't find even a single person I recognized. The sun was blazing, and my mother and children were like blades of grass hidden in a vast field.

> *The sky is vast and the earth is boundless*
> *when the wind blows and the grass moves, I see sheep grazing*
> *the earth is boundless and the sky is vast*
> *my family, where are you now?*
> *I look forward to the stars and to the moon*
> *I only look forward to the sun rising over the mountains*
> *I look forward to being able to see my family in the crowd assembled*
>   *below the stage*
> *I only look forward to seeing Hongsheng grow big and strong*
> *I only look forward to seeing Honghua able to bloom in winter*
> *Like Hongmei, I only look forward to the possibility that after the revo-*
>   *lution, each new generation will supercede those that preceded it*
> *I only hope that they'll accept the revolutionary guns*
> *and carry the red banners on their shoulders*
> *and proceed with the Party into the storm, without looking back*
> *through rain and waves, their will won't flag*
> *if we are going to do something, we should do this sort of thing*
> *and if we are going to be someone, we should be this sort of person*
> *my children, you are neither young nor old*

why can't you help your father out?
for example, your father is shouldering a load that weighs over a thou-
    sand jin
while your own load weighs only about eight hundred
the scene on the stage was solemn and dignified
while below the stage there were vast crowds
the thunderous sound of slogans rose and fell
and the sound of talking flowed forward like a storm
people bump into each other in a bloody state of military emergency
fists pound each other as the noise of battle creates an urgent situation
I see that across the land the four seas are rising and waters are surging
I watch as around the world the five continents are shaking and
    storms are raging
suddenly the wind and waves grew still
and the voices fell silent . . .

I didn't know what had happened, I simply saw a loudspeaker's piercing cries streaking across my muddled brain. The crowd standing below the stage fell silent, and I saw that under the loudspeakers' cries, Hongmei—who, like me, was also tied up—was escorted from a truck and made to kneel down on the stage.

This was the first time I had seen Hongmei (my soul and my flesh, my spirit and my marrow!) since the interrogation after we had blown up Cheng Temple. She was still wearing that same pink, small-collared shirt and the same low-heeled shoes with the square toes. The moment she knelt down, our gazes collided. I saw that she was much thinner now, though her face was much more delicate and beautiful than before. When she saw me, her pale face began to turn light red. At that moment, I very much wanted to ask her where they had been holding her this past half year, and what they had been doing to her in prison every day. However, the moment our gazes met, and before her tears had time to appear, two armed police soldiers placed themselves between us, and like a wall they blocked our vision of one another, while also cutting off my train of thought.

I had originally assumed we would have to kneel down together for half a day, like in a revolutionary struggle session, and therefore was surprised to discover that this so-called public trial merely had us kneel for about ten minutes while a judge who had been sent from the county court declared, "Let the public trial begin!" Another judge then read a quote from Chairman Mao, followed by our sentence, after which the public trial came to a close.

The judge announced that we were counterrevolutionary adulterous murderers, and as punishment for our multiple crimes we were sentenced to death, and the sentence would be implemented immediately.

The judge who sentenced us to death had a low and sonorous voice that sounded majestic, and when he read the words "implemented immediately," it was as if these were bullets being shot at our bodies. As he was reading those words, I thought I was going to collapse on stage, but to my surprise, after those words were broadcast over the loudspeaker, my body initially trembled and my heart lurched, but then I suddenly felt very calm, like a hero who has just forded a river. I remembered Li Yuhe's spirited appearance before he was executed.

The prison guards howl like wolves as I step forward . . . (appear on stage, "strike a pose") . . . *out of my cell.*

(Two Japanese military police push their way forward, as Li Yuhe stands there, majestic and unyielding. "Two horizontal steps" becomes "a single step," then stop; "turn on one leg," "lean on one leg to strike a pose." Fearlessly he proceeds forward and pushes back the two Japanese military police.)

(Li Yuhe touches his wounded chest and rubs his knee. Scorning his shackles and chains, he displays his noble spirit.)

(Back flip followed by forward flip.) *Don't look at me, wearing these iron shackles / you can bind my arms and legs / but you can't bind my lofty aspirations!* / (Sings *yuan ban* tune) / *That villain Hatoyama used every torture imaginable to get the secret code / My bones are broken, my flesh is flayed / But my will is as firm as steel. / Walking boldly to the execution ground, I look afar; / The red flag of revolution is raised on high, / The flames of resistance spread far and wide. / Japanese bandits, let's see how much longer you can rage! / Once the storm has passed* (changes to *man sanyan* tune) *flowers will bloom, / New China will shine like the morning sun, / red banners will fly all over the country. / This thought heightens my confidence / And my resolve is strengthened.* (Changes back to *yuan ban* tune) *I have done very little for the Party / as the indomitable soldiers bravely march forward . . .*

Hongmei was struck by the bullets of the words "implemented immediately." She had still been kneeling at the feet of the military police, but after hearing that the order would be *implemented immediately*, I saw her fall like a toppled tree or a collapsed mountain, after which she lay immobile on the stage. It was as if it was only then that she realized that she was going to be executed. Standing on the other side of those military police, I shouted, "Hongmei, everyone dies in the end. While we are still alive, we should live like people, and when we die, we should die like people."

Through the uproar, Hongmei heard my shouts. She raised her head and looked at me, and when she saw that I was standing in front of the stage, with my chest out and my head held straight, heroic and high-spirited, she appeared enlivened and attempted to stand up. At this moment, the loudspeakers once again began playing music and revolutionary melodies (like a timely rain).

In addition to the loudspeakers positioned at each corner of the trial stage, the loudspeaker on the vehicle that had brought us over also started up, as did the village and town loudspeakers. In the blink of an eye, all the loudspeakers in every village and town nearby began playing simultaneously, as though struck by a highly infectious disease. The loudspeakers on the public trial stage were playing "Victory Relies Entirely on the Direction of the Party"; the ones on the escort vehicle were playing "Advancing while Holding High the Banner of the Dictatorship of the Proletariat"; the ones in Chenggang were playing "Singing about National Unity"; the ones to the south of town were playing "A Brand New Sun and Moon Shine Down on the Rivers and Mountains," from the Peking Opera *Red Brigade of Woman*; and the ones on the banks of Thirteen Li River were playing "Fighting for the Liberation of Humanity" from the movie *Song of the Dragon River*. Also, coming down from the sky was "A Surprise Air Attack on Shajiabang"; from the west there was "Let the Red Banners of Revolution Be Planted Everywhere"; and from the north there were the heroic and brave calls of "An Eye for an Eye, and a Tooth for a Tooth." Music fell like snowflakes, lyrics gurgled forth like ropes and cables, and songs spilled forth like waves churned up by a storm. The public trial stage became completely soaked in music, and the commune members standing below the stage were blanketed by snow-like music. Thirteen Li River was flooded with songs, and Chenggang was completely inundated. Everyone, for some reason, began to shout, but it was unclear whether they were celebrating, or were cursing because the event was going to be so short. Some were complaining that it had not been worth it for them to have come ten, twenty *li* or more, just for *this*! Hongmei and I were completely surrounded by and soaked in music. I saw that someone had taken the shoe on which he was sitting and thrown it into the air; and I saw a large crowd of people surging toward the riverbank (where we were going to be executed). Someone who looked like Cheng Tianqing was getting trampled by the crowd, whereupon he suddenly lifted his fist and began hitting people. I saw that Hongmei, hearing that spring shower of music, had managed to stand up without any help, and that the pallor that had covered her face had begun to melt away, replaced by a blush of excitement. As the music grew louder, lyrics fell to her feet like ripe fruit, and the excitement on her face was replaced by a deep-red agitation. She turned and looked at me through the gap between the soldiers' shoulders, her gaze as bright as a torch. I knew that her blood, like mine, was surging through her body, and that her forehead was feverish with agitation and fear.

I took a step toward her.

She took a step toward me.

We suddenly rushed past the soldiers standing between us and began frantically kissing. Because we were both still tied up, we weren't able to embrace or caress each other. Instead, she pressed her chest against mine, and I pressed my shoulders against hers. We looked up at the sky over the stage, her lips squeezing mine were cold as fire, while my tongue grabbing hers was hot as ice. Revolutionary passion can melt a thousand layers of snow, and comradely love can melt ten thousand meters of ice. The sun comes up in the east and shines down on the four seas, as countless sunflowers bloom in its direction. Seedlings sprout under the spring rain, and they'll never change color until the end of time. My heart, my flesh, my soul, my love . . .

Heaven, oh heaven, oh heaven! Earth, oh earth, oh earth! At this moment, amid the madly broadcasting red music and revolutionary songs, the people standing below the stage suddenly grew silent. The people jostling their way to the other bank also suddenly turned around and fixed their gaze on the scene unfolding on the stage, staring intently at me and Hongmei. They stared at our affection, at our love, and at our revolutionary lips and tongues. The armed soldiers on stage stared blankly. After announcing the sentence, the judge appeared to be in a trance as he left the stage. The crowds standing beneath the stage continued staring intently. Even the specks of dust floating in the air came to a standstill. Meanwhile, the stones on the riverbank kept hopping up and down to try to see us kissing. The fish and crabs in the river happily leapt out of the water. My tongue played with Hongmei's, while her wet lips engaged mine in battle. My shoulders pressed into hers like floodwaters against a levy, while her breasts pushed against my chest like a house bearing down on its support columns. Our affection shone brilliantly, and our love sparkled brightly . . .

And just at that moment, just for that instant, there was a stillness that lasted perhaps a minute, perhaps a night, a day, or perhaps for centuries—or perhaps it was just a few seconds—and then revolutionaries pulled the trigger against other revolutionaries.

They executed us not in the sandpit they had dug on the other riverbank but right there on the stage, before the echoes of the sentencing pronouncement had even faded. However, as our sacrificial blood was falling, Hongmei and I remained tightly stuck together, our lips interlocked, until finally the bloody smell smothered us.

Death is a common occurrence. Some deaths are as weighty as Mount Tai, others are as light as a feather. The revolution has not yet succeeded. Comrades, you must continue to struggle.

4. Coda (IV)

Many, many days later, Hongmei and I were permitted to return to the Balou Mountains from that "tender land." We noticed that people everywhere were reading a novel called *Hard Like Water*, while illiterate people were relating stories about us. When we reached the riverbank west of Chenggang, where we had been executed, we discovered that the stage was no longer there, but the spot where our bloody bodies had fallen was now green and flourishing. In a patch of green vegetation, a group of boys and girls were cutting grass and watching their cattle graze, as they playfully explored each other's private parts. Afterward, the children proceeded to strip naked and engaged in couple games like adults. An old woman with a hunched back and gray hair called out to them from the village, telling them to come home to eat. Therefore, the children had no choice but to hurriedly get up, put their clothes back on, grab their baskets, and herd the cattle back to the village.

Hongmei and I had no choice but to return to the tender land.

The revolution has not yet succeeded, and comrades must continue to struggle.

Goodbye, revolution!

Farewell!

Translator's Note

There is nothing in the world that is softer and weaker than water,
and yet for attacking things that are hard and strong there
is nothing that can take precedence over it.

—Dao De Jing

Opening with the enigmatic statement "The Way that can be wayed
is not the true Way, and the name that can be named is not the true
name," the sixth century BCE Taoist classic the *Dao De Jing* is famous
for its embrace of conceptual inversions and apparent paradoxes.
One of the best-known examples of these paradoxes is the text's
observation that although water has no shape or form of its own, it is
nevertheless able to overpower even the hardest substances. The title
of Yan Lianke's *Hard Like Water* riffs on this observation while giving
it an erotic twist. In the novel, hardness is exemplified by the male
protagonist Gao Aijun, a soldier-turned-revolutionary whose given
name literally means "loves the army" and who throughout the novel
brings the revolution to his small Henan town of Chenggang. Gao
Aijun's revolutionary ardor is matched by his erotic passion, and his
extramarital affair with Xia Hongmei, daughter-in-law of the town's
former mayor, is the major driving force of the novel. But even as
Aijun's libido is held up as an exemplar of his revolutionary fervor,

he repeatedly finds himself attacked by bouts of impotence—with his erection, when most needed, becoming "like water."

In exploring the libidinal investments that drive both revolutionary engagement and sexual desire, *Hard Like Water*, first published in China in 2001, builds on a literary subgenre known as "revolution plus love," which was popular in China in the late 1920s and 1930s. Like Yan Lianke's later novella *Serve the People!* (which unlike this work was eventually banned in China), *Hard Like Water* approaches the erotics of revolutionary activism by turning not to the early decades of the Chinese Communist Party (as with the "revolution plus love" genre) but rather to the tumultuous Cultural Revolution period (1966–76), during which strident calls for adherence to Maoist doctrine and revolutionary change led to widespread suffering and societal disruption. Many canonical works from this period bristle with sexual energy just below the surface, and there is anecdotal evidence that, with millions of school- and college-age Red Guards leaving their families and traveling the country to carry out revolution during the initial years of the Cultural Revolution, this was also a period of considerable sexual experimentation. One of the quirks of *Hard Like Water*, moreover, building on its premise that revolutionary fervor mirrors romantic passion, is that Aijun and Hongmei find in revolutionary and propagandistic works a particularly potent aphrodisiac.

More generally, the Cultural Revolution period was a study in contrasts. On one hand, the Cultural Revolution demanded a highly doctrinaire adherence to Maoist orthodoxy; on the other hand, it was also stridently iconoclastic, encouraging the totalistic destruction of the so-called Four Olds (old customs, old culture, old habits, and old ideas). In the novel, the most visible manifestation of these Four Olds is Chenggang's memorial to the Song dynasty Confucian philosophers Cheng Yi and Cheng Hao (known as the Cheng Brothers and both originally from Henan province). A paradoxical characteristic of this era is that although the Mao regime explicitly tried to strengthen the nuclear familiar structure (particularly through abolition of concubinage, prostitution, and so forth), one of the side effects of the Cultural Revolution was a systemic undermining of these same family structures, as individuals were frequently encouraged to betray their own relatives, and accused rightists would often deliberately distance themselves from their families so as to protect them. In *Hard Like Water*, these iconoclastic tendencies ultimately intersect in the topos of the town's Cheng Temple, which contains a shrine to the "feudal-era" Cheng Brothers.

Hard Like Water's racy allusion to the *Dao De Jing*, meanwhile, is just the beginning of the work's intertextuality. In addition to quotations from theoretical works by Marx, Engels, Lenin, Stalin, and Mao, the novel also references many of Mao's essays, poems, and aphorisms, as well a variety of Mao-era songs, plays, and slogans. These allusions often subtly distort the language—and even the meaning—of the original text, while being seamlessly incorporated into the novel's own narrative (where their appearance is usually not signaled by means of quotation marks, italics, indentation, and so forth). Although Chinese readers would instantly recognize many of these allusions, even in their distorted form, for the benefit of English-language readers I have placed some of the citations in italics when they first appear in the text. As the work progresses and readers hopefully become more attuned to Yan's habit of interweaving intertextual references into his narrative, I gradually drop the italics, offering a reading experience that more closely replicates that of the original.

In order to give a taste of how these allusions work in the original text, I will briefly discuss the work's opening paragraph, which includes references to a 1947 film, a Mao Zedong speech from 1957, and a 1960s opera. The novel begins with Gao Aijun offering a series of first-person reflections immediately prior to what he anticipates will be his own execution. Roughly halfway through the opening paragraph, however, there appear a couple of lines alluding to *someone else's* execution: *Prior to the execution, I drank a bowl of wine, and did not feel a trace of resentment. Hatoyama prepared a banquet for me, with ten thousand cups.* The lines in question are adapted (with slight modifications) from the Peking Opera *The Red Lantern* (1965), which was one of eighteen socialist-realist works hand-selected by Mao Zedong's wife, Jiang Qing, for general dissemination during the Cultural Revolution, and which came to be known collectively as revolutionary "model operas." This particular Peking Opera version of *The Red Lantern* was based on a 1963 movie and a 1958 novel, which in turn was based on a true story about Communist secret agents working in a rail station in northern China during the Second Sino-Japanese War. The lines cited in the opening paragraph of Yan's novel are adapted from a passage near the end of the opera, in which the protagonist, a railway worker named Li Yuhe who has been secretly working for the underground Chinese Communist Party, is about to be executed by the Japanese military police. Hatoyama, the Japanese police chief, has been trying to force Li Yuhe to divulge a secret code he was assigned to convey to the Communists, but Li Yuhe steadfastly refuses to betray his cause. Although at this point Yan Lianke's readers don't have any indication why Aijun himself has been sentenced to death, the allusion to Li Yuhe's execution suggests that Aijun similarly sees himself as a Communist hero who has been unjustly condemned.

A few sentences later, *Hard Like Water* alludes to the epic film *The Spring River Flows East*. Centered around a fractured Shanghai family during and immediately after the Second Sino-Japanese War, the film was initially released in two parts in 1947 and 1948, becoming one of the most popular works of the period. The film was rereleased in 1956 during the Hundred Flower Movement and embraced by viewers who saw it as a welcome change of pace from the more doctrinaire worker-peasant fare that by then had become ubiquitous in China. *The Spring River Flows East* borrows its title from a line from a poem by Li Yu, the last ruler of the Southern Tang, which was composed shortly after his kingdom had been conquered by the Song dynasty. The final line of the poem could be rendered as:

> How much sorrow can one man bear?
> As much as the spring river flowing east.

In both Li Yu's poem and the 1940s film, the eastward flow of the river functions as a symbol of historical inevitability (due to China's geography, all of its largest rivers flow in a generally eastward direction). In his own citation of the line in question, however, Yan Lianke inverts the direction of the river's flow, and adds another allusion that similarly pivots on questions of cardinal directions: *The spring river water flows west, as the east and west winds engage in fierce battle.* The latter reference is to a well-known line from a speech Mao Zedong gave in Moscow in 1957, in which he announced:

> *It is my opinion that the international situation has now reached a new turning point. There are two winds in the world today, the east wind and the west wind. There is a Chinese saying, 'Either the East wind prevails over the West wind, or the West wind prevails over the East wind.' It is characteristic of the situation today, I believe, that the east wind is prevailing over the west wind. That is to say, the forces of socialism are overwhelmingly superior to forces of imperialism.*

The Chinese saying that Mao alludes to here, "Either the East wind prevails over the West wind, or the West wind prevails over the East wind," comes from the classic Qing dynasty novel *Dream of the Red Chamber*, which is a favorite text of Yan Lianke. In this novel the phrase is spoken by the work's female protagonist Lin Daiyu to describe the vicious power struggles that perennially rage within her socially elite extended clan. Yan Lianke, meanwhile, implicitly builds on Mao's allusion to Cold War tensions but reverses Mao's insistence that socialism necessarily has the upper hand. Instead, Yan reverts back to a version of the original *Dream of the Red Chamber* formulation, in which the two winds are imagined as being in perpetual battle—suggesting perhaps that the historical inevitability implied by the Li Yu line has not yet been set in stone, or perhaps that continual struggle is itself that which is inevitable.

These sorts of subtle political and cultural allusions recur throughout *Hard Like Water*. Sometimes they appear in passing, and other times they are developed in a more sustained fashion. For instance, the novel features numerous casual references to famous Mao aphorisms such as "revolution is not a dinner party," as well as slightly more obscure ones, such as "the only thing the world fears is [the Communist Party's] conscientiousness" (which the novel ironically inverts to read: "the only thing the Communist Party fears is conscientiousness"). At the same time, the novel also features a more extended engagement with texts such as the model operas *The Red Lantern* and *Taking Tiger Mountain by Strategy*—including several passages that reimagine key scenes from these two works in the form of an opera script (complete with stage directions, music cues, and so forth).

Like *The Red Lantern*, *Taking Tiger Mountain by Strategy* (1958) was a modern Peking Opera that was based on an earlier movie and novel that, in turn, drew on a real-life incident involving a People's Liberation Army soldier (named Yang Zirong in the opera). During the Chinese Civil War, Yang successfully infiltrates a pro-KMT (Kuomintang, i.e., Nationalist) bandit camp led by a "bandit chief" named Zuo Shandiao (a.k.a. "the Vulture"). In the novel, allusions to *Taking Tiger Mountain by Strategy* are offered as a commentary on Aijun's own attempt, at one point, to sneak behind "enemy lines," even as the novel explicitly cites the opera as one of the works that Aijun and Hongmei use to ignite their sexual passion.

Hard Like Water does not explicitly reflect on the work's own intertextual practice, and in this translation I have similarly refrained from adding supplementary annotations or explanations (beyond this brief discussion). All the parenthetical remarks that appear in the translation are reproduced as they appear in the original novel, and have not been added for this English edition. Regardless of how familiar or unfamiliar readers may be with the precise textual history of the novel's various citations and allusions, they will appreciate the work's engaging story line, its innovative narrative structure, and its dark and often humorous commentary on the potential perversities of revolutionary practice and erotic obsession.

—Carlos Rojas

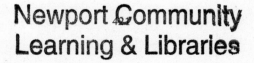